W9-BFZ-921

A Good Man

a novel

Judith Henry Wall

Simon & Schuster Paperbacks
new york   london
toronto   sydney

SIMON & SCHUSTER PAPERBACKS
Rockefeller Center
1230 Avenue of the Americas
New York, NY 10020

First Simon & Schuster paperback edition 2005

SIMON & SCHUSTER PAPERBACKS and colophon
are registered trademarks of Simon & Schuster, Inc.

For information about special discounts for bulk purchases,
please contact Simon & Schuster Special Sales:
1-800-456-6798 or business@simonandschuster.com.

Designed by Jeanette Olender

Manufactured in the United States of America

1   3   5   7   9   10   8   6   4   2

Library of Congress Cataloging-in-Publication Data
Wall, Judith Henry.
A good man : a novel / Judith Henry Wall.— 1st Simon & Schuster pbk. ed.
p.   cm.
1. Female friendship—Fiction. 2. First loves—Fiction.
3. Betrayal—Fiction. 4. Secrecy—Fiction. I. Title.
PS3573.A42556G66 2005
813'.54—dc22   2004061783

ISBN 0-684-87388-5

To Philippa Brophy

for two decades as my agent and friend

Acknowledgments

Special thanks go to Daranna and Michael Bradley for sharing their home and city with me.

I am indebted to JoAnna Wall and Joan Atterbury for their suggestions and encouragement.

And I am especially grateful to my editor Amanda Murray for her wisdom and guidance.

$\mathcal{C}$hapter one

Rhonda recognized him as soon as he strolled into the waiting area for Gate 27—the guy from the Houston airport.

Every bit as handsome as she remembered, the man looked her way, lifted his eyebrows in recognition, and smiled.

Rhonda was surprised that he remembered her.

She had been returning to Dallas after a particularly contentious meeting with a client's husband and his lawyer. When the flight was delayed while thunderstorms passed overhead, she and the good-looking man had been among a group of passengers who migrated to a nearby concourse bar to watch the end of a Mavericks game. She was aware of him standing next to her and glanced at his reflection in the mirror over the bar. He was still in his thirties, she decided. She was older than he was by at least five or six years. Maybe more. She resisted the urge to smooth her hair, to take out her compact and check her makeup.

Which was silly. He wasn't going to notice her. And what would she do if he did?

Nothing, of course. It was just nice to be admired once in a while. To know that all that jogging and Retin-A were paying off.

He did make eye contact with her in the mirror, however, and leaned close to ask if she was a Mavericks fan. If she lived in Dallas. Then he touched her elbow and said, "I love your perfume."

She thanked him. Then they cheered together for the game-winning, at-the-buzzer basket. That was all. Their flight was announced, and it was time to board. Their seats were half an aircraft apart. The seat-belt sign was illuminated throughout the short flight. There was no sign of him when she got off the plane. Shouldering her carry-on bag, she headed up the concourse.

But she had thought about him that night, in bed with her husband. She thought about a stranger while she and Dennis made love and got really turned on—so much so, she had to restrain herself. She had only been away for two nights. Missing Dennis would not be a justification for what she was feeling. It was pretty pathetic, a woman getting aroused just because an attractive younger guy complimented her on her perfume. She didn't usually wear perfume during the business day, but she had freshened up at the hotel before checking out and added just a touch to her wrist, with Dennis in mind. She knew he was planning to pick her up at the airport and take her out to dinner.

If Dennis had noticed her perfume, he didn't say. But he had said she looked wonderful.

Her sexual craving continued long after Dennis had kissed her good night and settled into sleep. Her friend Holly would tell her that she hadn't been getting enough sex lately and advise her to buy naughty lingerie at Victoria's Secret to wake up the sleeping tiger in old Dennis.

But actually, she and Dennis had a good sex life. They both knew what the other liked and needed. Yet she had been more excited than she had been in years and unwilling to reach for her sleeping husband, unwilling to slip her hand between his legs and say she wanted more. It had been years since they had gone for a second round. She wasn't even sure Dennis could manage one. He would wonder what had gotten into her.

That had been over two months ago—the week before she learned about the death of her high school sweetheart.

Now, here was that same man again, apparently booked on the same flight she was taking to New York. Rhonda nodded in his direction, acknowledging his smile, and busied herself fishing for her ticket in her purse, hoping he did not notice the embarrassed flush she could feel enveloping her neck and cheeks. My God, the thoughts she had allowed herself to have about the guy!

She took a seat in the waiting area and, out of the corner of her eye, watched him talking to the gate agent, who was young, pretty, and all smiles. At one point, he touched the woman's hand and pointed in Rhonda's direction. The gate agent looked over at Rhonda then shook her finger at the man and laughed. It occurred to Rhonda that he might be trying to change his seat assignment. To sit next to her. Then she discarded the notion.

But just in case, she headed for the ladies' room to check her makeup. Staring at her face in the mirror, she couldn't decide if she should be pleased at the prospect of spending more than three hours with the man or annoyed that he would be so presumptuous.

She boarded before he did, stored her carry-on in the overhead bin, and took her seat in the first-class compartment. Almost immediately, he was taking the seat beside her.

"This isn't just a coincidence, is it?" she asked.

"Actually not," he admitted with a sheepish grin. "I work for the airlines, and fortunately this seat was open. I've found that long flights pass much faster if I have a beautiful woman to talk to."

Rhonda took a minute to consider the compliment. "So you're in the habit of rearranging seat assignments?" she asked with a wry smile.

She was glad she had a fresh manicure and a great new haircut. Glad she was wearing a smart pantsuit. Glad she was wearing that same perfume. Glad she had used her cache of frequent-flyer miles to treat herself to first class, a decision that would allow her to change her return flight without penalty, just in case she decided to cut short her trip.

"Why don't you withhold judgment until we have a chance to

get acquainted," he suggested. His grin changed into a full-fledged smile. He had wonderful teeth. A great smile.

He was almost *too* good-looking, she decided. A vain man, obviously, who kept his body professional tanned. Even the skin behind his ears was tan. And with his broad shoulders and impressive thighs, he had that bulked-up look that came from pumping iron on a regular basis. His sleek blond hair was trimmed to perfection, his nails professionally manicured. His sport coat was expensive, his jeans starched and creased. The whole encounter would give her something to talk about when she got to New York, she decided as she leaned back in her comfortable seat and relaxed.

A smiling flight attendant appeared to ask if they wanted a preflight drink. Her seatmate ordered an imported beer, Rhonda a Bloody Mary. Then Rhonda pondered what to do next. Ordinarily she opened a magazine or book so she wouldn't have to enter into small talk with whoever was sitting next to her.

She reached in her purse for her reading glasses.

"How about those Mavericks?" he asked, demonstrating that he remembered their previous encounter.

"It's been a good year," she said. "Of course, I was hoping for a better outcome in the playoffs."

"Do you go to the games?"

"Sometimes. My husband and I have season tickets, and we make as many of the games as we can." The mention of her husband made her feel immediately better. Virtuous even. So much so, she kept going. "He used to play basketball in high school, as did our sons."

She was ready to explain that her twin sons were now college freshmen, that they had been named second-team all-Dallas guards their senior year in high school and been offered scholarships by two small state colleges but decided to forgo basketball and go to the University of Texas instead. She was saved from prattling, however, by the arrival of their beverages.

Rhonda took a sip of her Bloody Mary and told herself to calm down and shut up.

Then the man leaned quite close. "I still like your perfume," he said. "In fact, I stopped by the perfume counter at Neiman's to try and figure out what it was. Thought I might get some for my wife. What's it called?"

Rhonda couldn't decide if he was being forward or offering a quid pro quo mention of his wife. "Intimate," she answered, keeping her tone a careful neutral.

"Good name," he said and reached for her left hand. She watched with fascination as he lifted her wrist to his nose and inhaled deeply. Then he carefully returned her hand to her lap.

"Oh, my," Rhonda said. "Well, aren't you something!"

He laughed and lifted his glass to her. "And so are you, I suspect."

Suddenly she decided she didn't want a pair of schoolmarmish reading glasses parked on her nose and slid the glasses case into the magazine pocket on the seat in front of her.

His name was Michael. They didn't exchange last names, which Rhonda found reassuring. She could relax and enjoy the flight. She took another sip of her Bloody Mary, already knowing she was going to have a second.

He asked her if she was going to New York on business.

"No, I'm meeting a couple of old high school friends for a reunion of sorts," she explained.

Michael said that he was representing his company at a meeting of airline executives.

When their elbows touched on the broad armrest, she didn't move hers. What harm could elbow touching do? She had no intention of starting an extramarital relationship with this man or any other. She was happily married to a very fine man whom she loved very much.

Minus her reading glasses, she thumbed through the in-flight magazine during takeoff, able to read only the titles of stories and stare at pictures. As soon as the seat belt light went off, the flight attendant took their orders for a second drink.

After they had been served, she asked to see his Rolex. "I've been thinking about getting one for my husband," she said, which was true. Dennis would be celebrating his fiftieth birthday in November.

She drew Michael's wrist closer for a better look. Of course, without her reading glasses, the face of the watch close up was a blur. When she let go of his wrist, Michael's hand brushed against her breasts. Just lightly. It could have been accidental. But then he put his lips close to her ear. "I meant it when I said you were beautiful," he said. Rhonda realized the young flight attendant was looking at her with envy.

"Is your wife beautiful?" Rhonda asked pointedly.

"She is drop-dead gorgeous," Michael said. "What does your husband look like?"

"He's tall, dark, and handsome," she said. Which wasn't true. Dennis was of medium height and his blond hair was turning gray. He was more genial-looking than handsome. But of course, her conversation with this man had nothing to do with truth. It was just a form of in-flight entertainment.

When their meals arrived, Michael ordered another beer to go with his Mexican dinner. Rhonda had selected crab cakes as her entrée and said yes to a glass of Chablis. The food was rather good, but she was too distracted to eat much. Apparently Michael was, too, as he engaged her in a hypothetical discussion about why a younger man might wish to get involved with an older woman. Such a relationship was uncomplicated, he explained. No one expected marriage. Maybe they were both already married. A mature, married woman could be trusted when it came to birth control. Such a relationship was just about a man and a woman enjoying each other's company and having great sex.

She started to tell him that this hypothetical man was just the sort of unfaithful husband she crucified in the courtroom. But she didn't want him to know that she was an attorney just in case he decided to search the Dallas yellow pages for an attorney whose first name was Rhonda. Instead, she asked what happened when the spouses of this hypothetical man and woman found out about their indiscretion.

"If they're smart, that's not going to happen," he said. "And in a way, they are doing their spouses a favor. Good sex breeds good sex, you know."

"No, I didn't know that," Rhonda said, suddenly tired of the game.

She excused herself and walked very carefully to the restroom, acutely aware that she had had too much to drink. Once in the restroom, she realized she had forgotten to bring her purse. Her nose was shiny and her lipstick gone. She blotted her nose with a tissue and fluffed her hair a bit. Back in her seat, she told Michael that she needed to close her eyes for a while.

She wanted to drift off for a few minutes in order to clear her head, but random thoughts kept popping into her mind. Had she remembered to sign her time sheet at the law office? Had she packed a bathrobe? Just on the verge of dozing, she realized she hadn't reminded Dennis to leave a check for the cleaning woman. If she weren't sitting next to a hunk named Michael, she would use the air-to-ground phone to call her husband. Except the real reason she felt the need to call Dennis was because she was feeling guilty about the whole flirtatious episode. Michael was not a worthy man, and her husband was.

She and Dennis had never flirted much. They simply met, started going out together, and had sex when they could find the time. He was in the third year of a very demanding five-year thoracic surgery residency at the Southwestern Medical Center in Dallas; she was finishing her first year at the Southern Methodist

University law school. The following year, when the sex led to pregnancy, they got married—not the greatest romance the world had ever known. She had been surprised that the marriage endured.

She dozed off for a time, waking when the plane began its descent. She pulled out her compact and emitted a frustrated sigh as she attempted to fluff her hair back into shape.

"You look lovely," Michael said.

Her first thought was to argue with him. *She did not look lovely. She looked like a reasonably youthful, reasonably attractive woman who would soon celebrate her forty-third birthday.* But she decided to accept the compliment for whatever it was worth. "Thanks," she said. "I'm just feeling a bit nervous."

"Has it been a long time since you've seen your friends?"

"Actually, I saw them both two months ago. But that was the first time I had seen one of them since our freshman year in college. I'm meeting them in New York because I didn't have the guts to say that I didn't want to."

"How long are you staying?"

"Several days," she said, deliberately keeping her answer vague.

"I'd very much like to see you while you're here." He took one of her hands in both of his.

"I don't think that would be a good idea," she said, gently pulling her hand away.

"How about giving me your cell phone number?" he asked. "That would be safe enough, wouldn't it?"

God, he was handsome. And sexy. *Very* sexy.

"This entire encounter has been good for my ego," she acknowledged, "but I am not interested in turning it into a relationship."

"A faithful wife," he commented. "Your husband is a fortunate man."

"Oh, I'm not so sure about that."

She stared out the window as the plane landed and began its long taxi to the gate. Holly and Gina Kay had departed from the Waco airport on an earlier flight. Unless their flight had been delayed, they would be waiting for her outside of the baggage claim area.

Whatever had possessed her to say yes to this trip? She didn't have the time to spare.

And she had never forgiven Gina Kay.

❦

Rhonda's suitcase was one of the first down the chute. She wrestled it from the conveyor belt, attached her carry-on to it, and pulled them behind her as she headed toward the exit.

And there were Holly and Gina Kay, with their suitcases already collected, smiling and waving. They were standing next to a man in an ill-fitting blue jacket and a billed cap. He was holding a sign with ROBERTSON printed on it.

Rhonda started in their direction, when suddenly Michael was at her side, his hand on her arm. "You left this," he said, holding out her glasses case. "My name is Michael Forester," he said. "I put the name and telephone number of my hotel inside. I want you to call me."

"But . . . ," Rhonda began.

"I know," he interrupted. "You love your husband and need to spend all your time with two friends from high school. But I bet you can get away for an hour or so." He put his hand on her arm. "I would *really* like to see you again."

❦

On the ride into Manhattan, Holly asked Rhonda about Michael. "A friend of yours? God, what a hunk! A *young* hunk."

"No, not a friend," Rhonda said, feeling a flush taking over her neck. "He sat next to me on the airplane."

She thought of the glasses case in her purse, which had his New York phone number inside. Michael *Forester's* New York phone number. He had taken a next step by telling her his last name.

Did women really get so needy for a romp in the hay that they fucked strange men they met on airplanes?

But she had been attracted to him, no denying that, she thought, remembering the contours of his face, his knowing smile, his powerful body. Now she was in turmoil, and Holly was looking at her, an odd, questioning look on her face.

Okay, Rhonda told herself. *Let's get a grip here.* At the first opportunity, she was going to tear up the piece of paper tucked inside her glasses case.

If she hadn't come on this stupid trip, she would not have met that man and would not now be facing this crisis of conscience. She either needed to turn around and go back home or try to remember what her expectations had been when she agreed to this trip.

As late as yesterday evening, she had considered backing out. She imagined calling Holly and making her voice scratchy and hoarse as she explained how rotten she was feeling.

Of course, Rhonda had felt a need to make a pilgrimage of sorts to New York since the terrorist attack on the World Trade Center. She loved the city and had spent one glorious summer there studying family law at New York University. She had enjoyed her time in New York so much that she'd considered transferring, but she had a scholarship at SMU and was on track for Law Review and other accolades. But oh, how she would have loved it. New York was so full of life and endless variety, just walking to class had been a thrill. Not like the small Texas town where she had gone to high school, or like Dallas, where she now lived. There was no variety in small Texas towns, and the state's cities lacked the density that made New York the city that it was. In Dallas, one spent mind-numbing hours each day in a car. In New York, those hours were spent on sidewalks or subways, immersed in a swirling stream of life. In New York, as a fair-skinned, brown-haired, hazel-eyed WASP with a Texas drawl, she had felt almost exotic. Certainly not the norm. Which was fun. Sometimes she had even played up the drawl, peppering her speech with flirty *y'alls* and *sure 'noughs.*

She didn't talk like that anymore. It didn't play well in court-rooms.

The only trip she had taken to New York in the intervening years was the mandatory take-the-kids-to-visit-the-UN and see the sights. She'd found the trip almost painful and realized that she should have taken the risk, even if it meant taking out student loans, and stayed in New York to finish her law degree. If she had done that, she probably could have gone home to Texas and the rest of her life without this feeling that maybe she had missed something important. As it was, she got pregnant the first week back and ended up marrying Dennis.

Why *had* she agreed to this trip to New York, Rhonda pon-dered. Certainly not because of some silly promise she and Holly and Gina Kay had made at their senior prom.

When it came right down to it, she needed something from Gina Kay. An apology maybe. Certainly an explanation.

Probably, she never should have gone to Terry's funeral.

Chapter two

It had been early on a Sunday afternoon when Holly called with the news about Terry's death.

"You sitting down, honey?" Holly's voice asked, her tone somber.

"Is something wrong?" Rhonda demanded. She was not sitting down. Rhonda usually paced during phone calls. She had already carried the portable phone to the long hallway that divided the first floor of her home from front to back.

"Terry's dead," Holly said softly.

Rhonda took several steps, then dropped down on the bottom step of the staircase. "Say that again," she said.

Holly blew her nose before answering. "Terry was plowing a field, and the tractor tipped over on him. He'd tipped over on the same slope once before but had been able to jump clear, but this time he wasn't so lucky. He died before they could free him. Gina Kay and their son were with him at the end."

Terry dead? Rhonda closed her eyes to digest the news. "When?" she asked.

"Early this morning. When he didn't come in for breakfast, they went to look for him. Gina Kay asked me to let you know. I would have anyway, but I thought you should know that she specifically asked that you be informed." Holly paused, then asked, "Are you okay, honey?"

"Sure, I'm okay," Rhonda said. "Terry was a long time ago." She rose from the step and started walking again, more slowly this time, but even so, she stumbled on the edge of the carpet runner. "I haven't seen Terry since . . ." she said, but her voice trailed off.

"Probably since the night of your eighteenth birthday party," Holly suggested, "when you broke up with him."

Not even Holly knew the details of that night, Rhonda thought as she wandered back into the kitchen, where she had been making coffee when Holly called. Even now, all these years later, thinking about it was difficult for Rhonda. It had been a night of fear and craziness, the worst of her life. It had not been the last time she saw Terry, however. But Holly didn't know that.

"Hey, Rhonda, are you still there?" Holly asked.

"Yes," Rhonda said, trying to collect her thoughts. *Coffee.* She needed a mug for her coffee.

"Gina Kay asked that you come to the funeral," Holly continued. "She thinks you need to be there. She said that you loved him, too, once upon a time."

"Yes, that's true," Rhonda said, reaching into the cupboard for a mug, "but it didn't stop Gina Kay from marrying him."

"That was a long time ago," Holly said, "and you and Terry probably never would have gotten married anyway."

"You don't know that," Rhonda said, taking a sip of the coffee, then carrying the mug with her as she resumed her pacing.

"What about his funeral?"

"I really can't, Holly. I have a full schedule all week and several cases I'm getting ready for trial. You know that I need to plan for days off."

"You mean that if you'd known in advance that Terry was going to die, you could have penciled him in? What if it was me? You'd come to my funeral, wouldn't you, even if you had a full schedule?"

Rhonda paused while a wave of irritation swept through her body. "Don't say such a stupid thing."

"Hey, I don't drive tractors, but I could have a car wreck or slip on a banana peel. You'd come cry for me and comfort my family, wouldn't you?"

"Of course, I would. But that's not the same. You and I have stayed friends all these years. Actually, you are my best friend." The acknowledgment surprised Rhonda. *Was it true?* Holly was just good old Holly. Someone she had known forever. Someone who predated every other friend she had in her present life. They knew each other's families and knew each other's history—the good and the bad. They had stayed friends mostly because Holly had been diligent about keeping in touch. She initiated the majority of the phone calls and emails and stayed with Rhonda whenever she came to Dallas. And their families got together for UT football games and had taken some vacations together over the years. Of course, Rhonda realized that Holly and her family had also gotten together with Gina Kay and Terry and their kids from time to time, which was irritating and made Rhonda consider ending her own family's involvement with Holly's clan. But Dennis especially seemed to appreciate their time with them, which allowed him to get completely away from the world of medicine and indulge himself with sports talk and fishing with Holly's husband, Sandy. Yet it had been years since Rhonda had bothered to evaluate Holly's position in her life. Not since she finally accepted the fact that Holly also planned to maintain her friendship with Gina Kay. Holly was caught in the middle, walking a tightrope back and forth between Rhonda and Gina Kay, abiding by an unspoken agreement never to reveal any confidences they had shared with her.

"*Best friend*," Holly repeated with a low whistle. "Gee, thanks, honey. That's how I feel about you. And Gina Kay. Remember how we used to link little fingers and say 'BFF'?"

"Yeah," Rhonda acknowledged. "Best Friends Forever." An image of the three of them, riding bareback along Simmons Creek, came to mind. And of them lying on a blanket in Rhonda's backyard, staring up at the nighttime sky—*moon bathing,* they called it. They had been best friends, but the forever part turned out to be a pipe dream.

"I didn't know you still felt that way about me," Holly said. "Sometimes I wonder if you think I'm a pest."

"And sometimes I wonder why you bother with me at all?" Rhonda admitted. "I'm always so busy. So preoccupied."

"True. But hey, what are best friends for? And sometimes you are funny and nice, especially with a few drinks under your belt. Come to Terry's funeral. Gina Kay doesn't keep hard liquor in the house, but I'm sure she'll have wine for us after the funeral crowd has left. And we can go see my mother."

"I can't, Holly," Rhonda said as she stared out the kitchen window at her wooded backyard. A pair of binoculars and Peterson's *Field Guide to Western Birds* rested on the windowsill. She and Dennis had elected trees over a swimming pool when they bought the house and had stood firm on their decision over the years in spite of their sons' constant carping that other kids had pools and it wasn't fair for them to be pool-less. If she had married Terry, she wouldn't be living in this house, and she wouldn't have the same children, the same life. "I have a major trial coming up," she added, "and Jason and Scott are coming home next weekend for their birthday. But honestly, Holly, I wouldn't go to Terry's funeral even if I weren't so busy. What's the point? Terry is ancient history. I haven't thought about him in years."

"Are you sure about that now? Not in *years*? I think about him a lot. I think about all of us and how we were. I think I remember every damned thing about those times. *Every* party. *Every* wiener roast out by the lake. *Every* football game. Life was so intense back then. We lived in an ordinary little town, but nothing about my life seemed ordinary. Every day was an adventure to dress up for and make sure my hair was fixed just right and my lipstick went with my sweater. I remember having a pimple on my chin the night of our senior prom and how beautiful the gym looked with all those decorations. And that fountain. I thought Mr. Kingston was going to stroke out when the three of us hiked up our dresses and went wading. The front of Gina Kay's dress got so wet you could see her nipples right through it. And I imagine that in the wee small hours of the morning after the after-party, you and Terry drove off someplace and promised to love each other forever and ever."

"All right. All right," Rhonda said, not bothering to conceal the irritation in her voice. "Your point is made. I still think about Terry. *Sometimes*. He was my first boyfriend and my only boyfriend until I went to college, but that doesn't mean I have to go to his funeral. I didn't go your father's funeral, which was a very difficult decision for me. But I hadn't been to Lamberton since my folks moved away, and I decided I needed to keep it that way. I still need to keep it that way."

"After all these years, you're still spooked, aren't you?"

Rhonda squeezed her eyes shut and took a deep breath. There was no point in getting angry, she told herself. "Good-bye, Holly. Thank you for calling."

"I am not giving up," Holly warned. "You think about this real hard, Rhonda Catherine Hayes Chadwick. I'm heading over to Lamberton as soon as I can get things organized here on the home front. I'll call tomorrow and let you know when the funeral will be."

"I am sure you will. Thanks for calling. You have a good heart, Holly, and I love you for it."

Rhonda pressed the disconnect button on the phone and continued staring out the window, surrounded by her silent dwelling, which was more a house and less a home with her sons gone.

Dennis had decided to drive up to Lake Texhoma for the afternoon and take the boat out. He liked to do that on Sunday afternoons. He usually did it alone now. Even when the boys came home for the weekend, they were too busy with their friends to have time for sailing with their dad.

Dennis had asked her to go with him. "It's been more than a year since I've had my first mate on board," he'd pointed out. "I wouldn't have bought the boat if I'd known I'd be sailing solo."

But she had protested that it was too chilly and she needed to work. That work was waiting for her now. Consequential work that must get done.

Terry was dead, though. Could she concentrate after learning that someone she knew had died? Someone who once had been very important to her?

She refilled her coffee mug and carried it to the small room across from the kitchen she used as a home office. Once a maid's room back in the days when live-in help was the norm for families who lived in this stately Dallas neighborhood, the room suited Rhonda perfectly. Its out-of-the-way location meant she could close the door on the clutter. And cluttered it was. Computers were supposed to create a paperless environment, but they had done just the opposite. Her office at the law firm had to be kept reasonably tidy, but she didn't bother with tidiness here. Stacks of paper covered her desk, and file folders were piled on the shelves of the two mismatched bookcases, each folder representing some- one in trouble—a divorcing someone or a client involved in a child-custody suit. And sometimes an adoption, but mostly she dealt with grim stuff. Sometimes she wondered why in the hell she had chosen family law. But someone had to help people with failed marriages get their lives untangled. And she liked to think that the stability in her own marriage helped her be objective. She didn't hate all men, just the ones who wanted to screw their wives out of an equitable divorce settlement.

She sat down, switched on the computer, and stared at the

screen, waiting for the icons to appear. But when they did, she didn't reach for the mouse. She felt numb. And disconnected. She had planned to spend a couple of hours researching child-custody case law on the LexisNexis legal website. A client's former wife was now married to a self-proclaimed evangelist who conducted tent revivals for a living. Her client's children lived in a motor home going from town to town and were being homeschooled by their stepfather with the Bible as their only textbook. On the surface, the case seemed cut and dried. Her client was a high school basketball coach and social studies teacher. The student body at the school where he taught had twice voted him Teacher of the Year. Obviously he was more suited to be the custodial parent. But his ex-wife accused him of being a godless man incapable of raising Christian children. And Rhonda's client acknowledged that he had no use for organized religion and didn't want his children raised by a Bible thumper.

Anything involving religious issues got so ticklish. No one was ever unbiased. No one wanted to make concessions to another way of thinking.

Well, the task wasn't going to get any easier by putting it off, Rhonda told herself and reached for the mouse. But her hand began to shake. Which made her angry. God, how neurotic.

She shook the offending hand furiously. "Stop it," she demanded. "Just stop it."

When the phone rang, she jumped. And cursed.

Caller ID showed her parents' phone number. Her mother, most likely. She started to let it ring.

But what if there was an emergency?

Rhonda took a deep breath and picked up the receiver. "Hi. How are things?"

"Fine," her mother's voice said. "Your dad is golfing. I'm going to head for the library. Who were you talking to?"

"Holly," Rhonda said, relaxing a bit, taking comfort in the sound of her mother's voice.

"How is that dear girl?"

"Fine, I guess. She called to tell me that Terry Robertson had died. A tractor accident early this morning."

"How terrible! I am so sorry. Are you going to his funeral?"

"No," Rhonda said, reaching for her coffee mug. Its contents had already grown tepid, but she took a sip anyway. "Gina Kay told Holly that she wanted me to come, but I see no reason to."

"Perhaps. But his death must make you feel sad, though. You spent more than five years of your life being his girlfriend. Funerals are about closure, you know. They help people draw a line and move on."

"I moved on years ago, Mom. I don't want to see Gina Kay, and I certainly don't want to see a dead Terry." Then Rhonda paused, remembering Terry. Dazzling Terry, whose smile could make her heart turn over. "Though it might have been nice to see the living Terry one more time," she admitted. "I have thought about that from time to time. We never said good-bye. And there was never any explanation as to why he up and married Gina Kay. He knew how that would hurt me. He must have truly hated me to have done that."

"Oh, I don't imagine he hated you, honey. Terry probably came to realize that you weren't cut out to be a rancher's wife."

"Little towns have lawyers, too," Rhonda said, putting down her cup and using her free hand to type in her password on the LexisNexis site. Her hand was fine now. No shaking.

"Rhonda, you can't possibly have regrets about not spending your life on a cattle ranch."

"No regrets," she said. "Just a bout of nostalgia. Whatever I felt for Terry back then was real, but it ended badly. I tried to tell Holly that I hadn't thought about him in years, but she called me on that one. Do you ever think about the boy you didn't marry? And don't tell me there was only Daddy. I read all those pledges of undying love written on the inside front cover of your high school yearbook. And some of his letters were tucked between the pages. Jeremy was his name."

"Well, can a mother have no secrets! Yes, Jeremy Stockton. I loved him until I met your father."

"At that dance," Rhonda said, recalling the familiar tale. The officers' daughters at Fort Sill, Oklahoma, had been invited to a dance honoring West Point cadets who were on a tour of major stateside military installations. It had been love at first sight. There actually was a picture of them taken together that night, her mother wearing a white strapless dress with a full skirt, her father in summer dress whites. They looked like a prince and princess in a fairy tale. They wrote to each other for the rest of the summer, and Rhonda's grandparents allowed their daughter to fly to West Point for a carefully chaperoned visit during a home football game weekend. Poor Jeremy had been left in the dust. The following year, her parents had a military wedding at West Point. There was a picture of that, too, of the triumphant bride and groom passing under crossed sabers in front of the West Point Chapel. After their honeymoon, her father had headed for combat duty in Korea.

"Is Jeremy Stockton still alive?" Rhonda asked.

"As far as I know. He's a retired federal judge, living in Oklahoma City last I heard."

"Would you go to his funeral if he died?"

"Probably not," her mother acknowledged. "Maybe if I were younger I might have considered going, but there is a world of difference between a woman my age and a woman your age."

"How's that?"

"I've been married for fifty-six years. It's been a long time since I've thought about another man. And there's no question about how my marriage will end. One of us will bury the other. But you and Dennis have reached those restless middle years when everything is a bit foggy."

Rhonda started to bristle, to say that she and Dennis weren't restless, that they were the same as always. But she let it pass. "Were you and Daddy ever restless?" she asked instead, even though she wasn't sure she actually wanted to hear the answer.

"I sure was, but I don't think I want to go down that road with my daughter. Now, the reason I called is the boys' birthday. Your dad and I have decided to fly in for the weekend, if that's okay."

"Jason and Scott will be pleased," Rhonda said. "They were hoping you would come. Me, too."

"And I guess Terry's funeral will have been held by then—in case you do decide to go."

"I am not going, Mom. I haven't seen or talked to Terry or Gina Kay in years—in almost twenty-five of them."

"But you can't just ignore the fact that he's dead. Why don't you just pick up the phone and call Gina Kay? Talk to her, and then see how you feel about going to the funeral."

Rhonda cringed at the thought. *No way.*

Then she realized there were tears rolling down her cheeks. "Oh, Mom, I don't have the courage."

"Sure you do. You and Gina Kay and Holly were like sisters. You used to finish one another's sentences. Three peas in a pod. Remember how much you cared for Gina Kay back then and give her a call. *Right now.* The minute you hang up the phone. It's the right thing to do."

"Maybe," Rhonda hedged, not planning to do any such thing. But as soon as she said good-bye, she did as her mother had suggested, dialing 1411 and asking for the Terry Robertson residence in Lamberton. Her hand started shaking again when she tried to write down the number, so she agreed to the additional charge and let the operator place the call.

A woman with a Hispanic accent answered, "Robertson Ranch."

Rhonda cleared her throat. "May I speak with Mrs. Robertson?"

"Who is calling, please?" the woman asked politely.

"Just tell her it's Rhonda."

And suddenly there was Gina Kay's still familiar voice. "Rhonda? Oh, my God! It is really you?"

"Holly called. I am so sorry about Terry," Rhonda said, choking up, the words coming with difficulty.

"Oh, Rhonda, I would know your voice anywhere. Did she tell you that I want you to come to the funeral?"

"Yes, but I can't. I would feel so strange."

"It feels strange to me, too. It's so hard to comprehend that he's really gone. But that's not what you mean, is it? It would feel strange for you because of the way it all ended." Gina Kay paused. When she began speaking again, her voice sounded different. More distant. "You do whatever feels right to you. I'll understand. But I would like you here . . . for old time's sake."

Rhonda closed her eyes. Another image of three young girls came to her mind. This time they were in Holly's bedroom fixing one another's hair. There would have been music on the stereo. Linda Ronstadt. Fleetwood Mac. Helen Reddy. James Taylor. Stevie Wonder. Such great music. Such great times. She still listened to the music but had avoided thinking of those times. It had ended too painfully. Even now, just thinking about it made the pain come back. She touched it, right there in the middle of her chest. Just a small, withered kernel now, but once that pain had filled her up.

"I know things ended badly for us," Gina Kay said, "but maybe it's time we talk about what happened."

"After all these years, maybe the reason why no longer matters," Rhonda said.

"Or maybe it does," Gina Kay pointed out. "Please, Rhonda. I want you and Holly to come to the house after the funeral and stay after everyone else has gone. You can spend the night. I want the three of us to be together again."

This time when Rhonda hung up the phone she began to sniffle. And then to cry out loud. To weep.

She went back to the hall and wept while she paced. The elderly beagle came to sit by the stairs and watch her. After a time, she sat on the bottom step and hugged the dog's neck. "Oh, God, Mildred, Terry's dead. The most beautiful boy who ever lived is dead."

She had loved him more than anything and knew deep in her young heart that no love in her entire lifetime could ever be as sweet, with endless kisses in the moonlight and promises of forever. She had meant those promises with all her heart.

If she hadn't been the very best student in the entire high school, she might have said to hell with college degrees and a significant career. Not that she was all that smart. She just paid attention in class and always read the assignments. It wasn't like she was cut out to be a mathematician or scientist. It would have been no great loss to humanity if she had forgone college altogether and married Terry and had babies with him. That's what her body had felt like it was waiting for—Terry's love and babies to fill it up. She had ached to tell him that. Ached to promise forever and ever, not as words whispered in the heat of passion but as words spoken out loud in the light of day. She imagined the relief that would have appeared on Terry's beautiful face when she told him that she loved him enough to give up her college plans. But she kept putting off saying those words. What she really wanted was to convince him to wait a few years before they got married.

She had told her mother that she would have liked to see Terry one more time. For years, she had thought about that. She wanted to have him smile at her and tell her that he still thought about her from time to time.

Sometimes her fantasies went further than that.

But she hadn't had a Terry fantasy in a long time. Mostly she fantasized about winning cases and being considered a brilliant attorney.

She faced the computer, but after entering the LexisNexis site, her mind refused to focus. She had not wanted to hear that her parents had passed through a restless time in their marriage. She had never seen it, never felt it. Her parents loved each other completely and were each other's best friend. They kissed and held hands. They were both avid readers with one of them often waiting impatiently for the other to finish a book so they could discuss it. Current events also provided endless rounds of conversation for them; reading the Sunday *New York Times* was a ritual. Maybe her parents made it through those restless years because they had more than love and babies to share.

Rhonda had realized that might not be the case for her and Terry. Mingled with her overpowering love for him was fear. She was afraid that life with him would not be glorious. Afraid that he would not settle down and be a good husband and father. Afraid they didn't have as much going for them as her parents did and would someday have regrets.

If she and Terry had gotten married, she would now be a widow. Or perhaps he would have taken more care plowing that slope if he had been married to her. Perhaps he would have been thinking of the nice breakfast she would cook for him and looking forward to her welcoming smile when he walked in the kitchen door. She imagined a table with a red and white cloth, cinnamon rolls baking in the oven, a hot griddle ready for sausage and eggs, the smell of brewing coffee.

"Stop it!" Rhonda told herself, making Mildred jump. She knelt and kissed the top of the dog's silky head by way of apology. "Come on, girl. To hell with LexisNexis. Let's go cook a super deluxe dinner for your daddy."

Should she tell Dennis that her high school boyfriend had died? *Oh, by the way, Holly called to tell me that Terry Robertson was dead. He was the boy I went with in high school. A tractor accident. I called his wife. She wants me to come to the funeral.*

Then Dennis would ask her if she was planning to go. If in spite of her busy schedule and upcoming trials, in spite of her never having time to go out on the boat with him, she would drive all the way to Lamberton, a town she hadn't bothered to visit in all the years since she started college, to attend this guy's funeral?

She toyed with the idea of being less than truthful. She could say she was going to visit Holly and just not mention that the two of them drove to Lamberton. Except Holly was going to Lamberton this afternoon to be with Gina Kay in her time of need. Just as she would come to Dallas if anything ever happened to Dennis.

Chapter three

Holly sat by the kitchen phone for a time, mulling over her conversation with Rhonda and deciding on a game plan for the rest of the afternoon. Before she could pack a suitcase and make a grocery run to assure that her family wouldn't starve in her absence, she had to deal with Amber Bernard's wedding gown.

Normally she didn't darken the door of her workshop on Sunday. She worked damned hard the other six days of the week, and while she didn't mind cooking Sunday dinner if there was going to be anyone around to eat it, she liked to spend the rest of the afternoon catching up on her reading or taking a nap.

This Sunday afternoon, however, Terry was dead, and she should already be on her way to Lamberton. But Amber Bernard couldn't get her wedding gown zipped.

Amber had been scheduled to have her bridal portrait taken yesterday but discovered her gown was too small; at the final fitting only two weeks before it had fit like a glove. Amber's wedding was scheduled for Saturday evening. Her father was a state senator, and her mother's family came from old money. The wedding was going to be the social event of the year in San Antonio, with the ceremony to be performed by a bishop, and the governor and his wife and numerous other dignitaries among the guests. Amber and her mother had driven to Waco yesterday afternoon, arriving at Holly's door unannounced and hysterical.

Holly suspected the bride would be a mother by Thanksgiving. Before she could abandon ship and head for Lamberton, she would have to figure out some way to make the waistline of Amber's wedding gown two inches bigger.

Holly picked up a pencil and began making sketches of possible ways to deal with the problem, but her mind was still on the telephone conversation with Rhonda. Why couldn't Rhonda have just shed a tear or two in Terry's memory instead of claiming she never thought about him? Which was bullshit, of course. Terry hadn't been just another boyfriend. Rhonda had been madly in love with him and he with her. Neither one of them so much as looked at another person. And for the most part, they'd been good for each other. He softened Rhonda's competitive need to be the very best at every endeavor she undertook, and she kept him from flunking out of school. Toward the end, though, Terry had been frantic. He feared that if Rhonda went off to college, she was never coming back to Lamberton and never going to marry him.

Holly let out a sigh. *Terry gone.* It was hard to comprehend. The first of their graduating class to die. The twenty-fifth reunion of their class was this summer. She would need to plan some sort of memorial for him.

And she would have to write an obituary for the next newsletter, of which she seemed to be the editor for life, along with the position of reunion organizer. *Good old Holly*. The class workhorse.

An *obituary*. That would be tough. How could she possibly capture the essence of Terry in a few short paragraphs? Terry with the flashing dark eyes and devil-may-care grin.

He had been the most popular boy in their class, hands down. But no one ever seemed to be jealous of him. Maybe that was because he wasn't the best athlete and certainly wasn't the best student. And even though his father was wealthy and Terry always drove around in a late-model pickup, his mother was dead and his daddy was a mean old cuss, so wealth was forgiven. In spite of the fact that Terry had a wild streak and was the one who introduced the guys to booze and drag racing—or maybe in part because of it—every boy wanted him for a friend, and every girl was at least a little bit in love with him.

Holly seldom ever looked at her college yearbooks, but the ones from high school were well worn. She meant what she'd told Rhonda. She thought about those years a lot. But then Lamberton continued to be an important part of her life. Her mother still lived in the same house in which Holly had grown up. And lots of the kids she had grown up with still lived in the town, including Gina Kay. Holly had stayed friends with both Gina Kay and Rhonda, which put her in an odd position. Holly had never told Rhonda that she was godmother to Gina Kay's son, Mitch, and she had never told Gina Kay that she was godmother to Rhonda's twin sons.

Mitch had seen his father die. Gina Kay said she thought he was going to kill himself trying to get that tractor off his daddy. Tears welled up once again in Holly's eyes at the thought.

She reached for the phone and dialed Sandy's cell phone, but he didn't answer. He was attending a coaches clinic in College Station on the Texas A&M campus and probably had it switched off. She left him a message, telling him that Terry Robertson had been killed in a tractor accident and she was going to Lamberton as soon as she got things organized at home.

Holly put forth another sigh and rose from the chair. She had to figure out what to do with that wedding dress and leave instructions for her two employees, Marilyn and Lil. Then she needed to pack.

She crossed her backyard to the building she had erected six years ago to house her flourishing business. She made more money now than her husband did coaching high school football, a situation that had not been the very best thing that ever happened to their marriage. But with one child in college and two more on the way, Sandy begrudgingly admitted that having a second income came in handy.

The now-too-small wedding dress hung in the fitting area. Holly washed her hands then carefully took down the dress and turned it inside out. Not only would the bodice have to be removed from the voluminous skirt and train, but the side seams would have to be carefully picked open, stitch by stitch, with great care taken not to damage the heavy satin. A gusset of the same fabric would then have to be inserted and camouflaged by carefully appliquéing cutouts of the same Venetian lace overlay used on the front of the bodice. Then the pleats on the skirt and train would have to be reworked to fit the expanded bodice.

Holly drew sketches and scribbled notes for Marilyn and Lil detailing how they should alter Amber's gown. They were to call her in Lamberton if they didn't understand. And could they please plan on working next weekend? The alterations on Amber's gown were going to put them behind on Melody Marshall's gown.

Amber Bernard was not the first of her brides who had turned up pregnant, and she wouldn't be the last, Holly thought as she hung up the dress and turned out the lights. Perhaps she should start making wedding dresses with two-inch seams, just in case they needed to be let out.

Some of the pregnant brides warned Holly up front. Others got caught by surprise or were hoping they wouldn't start showing until after the wedding. Or that the pregnancy would just go away. Holly always felt sorry for them. What was supposed to be the most glorious time in their lives had turned into a difficult situation with upset parents and unkind whispers. Of course, Holly considered weddings somewhat overrated. Why was a woman's wedding the one day in her life that she got to dress up like a princess? Life as a married woman had nothing to do with princesshood. Except Holly still got teary-eyed whenever a bride walked down the aisle.

Holly had spent the last two decades creating princess gowns for bride after bride. God, how many hundreds over the years.

And bridesmaid dresses. Flower girl dresses. Mother-of-the-bride dresses. An occasional mother-of-the-groom dress. And she created pageant dresses. At least she never had a pregnant beauty pageant contestant. Those girls were pretty focused on maintaining body measurements.

Holly was looking for a third seamstress to work with Marilyn and Lil. As her fame had spread throughout the state and beyond —thanks to word of mouth and numerous newspaper articles and television interviews—more and more girls and their mothers made the trek to Waco. Which was satisfying, of course, but Holly was weary of brides and beauty queens and their hovering mothers. At least the brides didn't all have perfectly proportioned bodies. How in the world had a chunky girl like her ended up making gowns for beauty queens?

Of course, it all started with Gina Kay. Their junior year, the three of them took money Gina Kay had saved from her carhop salary to search for a prom dress, first in Temple and then in Waco. But the only dresses they could find in Gina Kay's price range were made of sleazy material and had crooked hems. Rhonda suggested they look for fabric instead. "Holly can make you a dress that you won't be ashamed to be seen in," she told Gina Kay.

Holly protested. Her mother taught home economics at Lamberton High School, and Holly had been making her own clothes since she was in grade school, but she had never made an evening gown.

At a fabric store, they found emerald green satin the exact color of Gina Kay's eyes—not rayon satin but one hundred percent silk. It was rich and heavy and took every cent of Gina Kay's hard-earned money. Holly and Rhonda dug into their own purses to pay for the pattern and notions, money that Gina Kay had paid back out of her next paycheck. They found a Vogue pattern for a fitted sheath with spaghetti straps that Holly thought she could manage. But the thought of cutting into that expensive fabric made her stomach hurt. What if she ruined it?

But with her mother looking over her shoulder, Holly made a dress that was completely lined, had an invisible zipper, and fit Gina Kay to perfection. Gina Kay looked at herself in the mirror and burst into tears. "How can I ever thank you?" she asked.

Gina Kay probably would have been named prom queen even if she'd been wearing a dress from Sears, but when she was interviewed for the local newspaper, Gina Kay gave all the credit to Holly. Gina Kay was wearing the same green satin evening gown the following week when she was crowned the state sweetheart of the Future Farmers of America. And with the addition of a cotton lace overskirt, Gina Kay was wearing the same gown when she was selected as the Texas Maid of Cotton, entitling her to a custom-made, all-cotton wardrobe to wear when she competed in the national pageant, which she did not win. But the following fall, Gina Kay won the national Miss American Teenager pageant in New York City wearing an evening gown Holly had designed and made.

Holly went on to major in fashion design at the University of Texas and had hoped for a big-time career as a fashion designer in New York or California. Or the real dream was designing clothes for the movies, like Edith Head, who had designed Grace Kelly's clothes in *Rear Window* and Paul Newman's and Robert Redford's in *The Sting*. If Holly ever did become a famous Hollywood designer, she wanted to be known for sleek sophistication. She would never think of designing a dress with a poof or a ruffle or appliquéd lace. But then Sandy came along, and she never went to Hollywood. Never designed for the stars.

George "Sandy" Warner came to UT on a football scholarship but ruined his left knee during his sophomore year and was left with a limp that had lessened over the years but was still with him. Sandy was a big teddy bear of a man who didn't seem to mind that Holly was overweight and didn't assume she would be an easy lay because of it. With his dream of a career in the professional ranks dashed, Sandy decided on a coaching career. When he started hinting about marriage, Holly did some real soul searching. She and Rhonda and Gina Kay had promised themselves that the one thing they were never going to be was ordinary. By then, Gina Kay was a married woman with a baby on her hip, but Rhonda was still on track. Rhonda was a shoo-in for outstanding senior woman at UT and planned to go to law school.

Holly knew she had talent and believed that she might have a chance at a career in fashion design and probably owed it to herself to find out. Rhonda was adamant that Holly had to at least try and would regret it for the rest of her life if she did not.

It wasn't so much her love for Sandy that kept her from at least trying. It was her love for a baby named Mitch. The birth of Gina Kay's first child had as much impact on Holly as it did on Gina Kay herself. Holly adored Mitch. Every tiny thing about him was so perfect. And he was so silly. So cute. An endless source of fascination for her. Baby Mitch made primordial yearnings swell her breasts and tug at her womb. Intellectually, of course, Holly knew that adorable babies grew into children who were frequently bratty and teenagers who were often obnoxious and finally into adults who had lives of their own. But what she *knew* occupied her head. What she *felt* came from lower down.

What if Sandy Warner was the only man in the entire world who would ever want to marry her and make babies with her?

How did one decide about the rest of one's life?

For lack of a crystal ball, Holly made a pact with herself. If Sandy didn't make a big deal out of proposing to her, she would say no. If he made his proposal memorable and romantic, she would say yes.

When he told her he had a special surprise for her birthday,

Holly hoped it was nothing more than a nice dinner at a good restaurant and a proposal afterward. She practiced saying "no" outright. She also rehearsed a counterproposal. Sandy could come with her to California. She knew he had his sights set on coaching high school football in the state of Texas, but why should a man assume that a wife would always put his career first? And besides, a counterproposal seemed kinder than an out-and-out "no."

He blindfolded her. And when he took the blindfold off, there in the middle of a field on the outskirts of Austin was a fully inflated hot-air balloon—a beautiful blue balloon decorated with fluffy white clouds. That was the day she realized how seriously she suffered from acrophobia. With the sides of the gondola only waist high, she clung to the ropes with both hands. She could hardly bear to look over the side at the field that had "MARRY ME HOLLY" mowed across it. Once that sickening task was accomplished, she concentrated on the distant horizon. Even if she hadn't been feeling like she was going to puke, it wasn't very romantic with the balloon pilot standing toe-to-toe with them in the cramped quarters. She could only make out a word or two here and there of Sandy's rehearsed speech over the sound of the roaring propane burner that was supplying hot air to keep them aloft, but Sandy was no thespian, so maybe it was just as well.

The ring was too small, so he had to put it on her little finger. And Holly could manage only a very tiny sip of the celebratory champagne. But Sandy did get an *E* for effort, she supposed, or maybe she just said yes so the flight would end and she could get back on terra firma.

With the ring at the jeweler's being sized, Holly put off telling Rhonda that she was engaged. Rhonda was taking women's studies classes and using such terms as "self-actualization," "reproductive freedom," and "fifty percent parenting."

Finally, about a week after the balloon flight, Holly confessed.

She was changing her major from fashion design to vocational home economics. She was going to be a home economics teacher like her mother and marry Sandy Warner.

For a long time, Rhonda said nothing, and Holly began to sob.

Rhonda climbed down from the upper berth and crawled into bed with Holly. "Are you happy?" Rhonda asked.

"Not really, but I don't have the courage to pass on Sandy. He's a good person and doesn't mind my pudgy body, and what if he's the last train out of the station?"

Rhonda began a monologue of how females are born with such contradictory forces buried within their souls. "We can't decide if we want to take care of ourselves or be taken care of, but in the end neither one happens. We take care of others and not ourselves. If we belly up and opt for wifehood and motherhood, we always wonder about what we gave up. The one thing we are not going to do is become our mothers, which is exactly what we do in the end."

"Then you forgive me?" Holly said.

"Not exactly, but I guess I understand. All of history is against you. Against *us*. We are doomed to dissatisfaction no matter what we do."

Holly began to plan her wedding. Always before, she thought that, if she ever got married, Rhonda and Gina Kay would be her attendants, but since Gina Kay was now married to Terry and the two of them were no longer a part of each other's lives, Holly was faced with a dilemma. Rhonda solved it for her by claiming that she had promised to be in her cousin's wedding in Kansas. Or maybe Rhonda just didn't want to witness an end to dreams.

Best friends. Rhonda had actually said that. Holly had been touched. Finally an acknowledgment after years of putting up with the uptight, distant woman Rhonda had become. Maybe news of Terry's death had cracked that all but impenetrable facade she had erected around herself. Rhonda even sent out nauseating

Christmas letters detailing the perfection of her life that were absolute nonsense. She had an okay marriage, and her kids had never been arrested. "If she irritates you so, why don't you give up on her?" Sandy would ask. *Why indeed?* Holly would wonder. It wasn't as though she had no other friends.

She thought of the round they used to sing at Girl Scout meetings—about new friends being silver and old ones gold. But sometimes all that old gold weighed her down. Sometimes she felt like telling Rhonda to go screw herself.

When Gina Kay called to tell her what had happened to Terry, she'd asked if Holly could please come be with her.

"I need you," Gina Kay had said. Maybe Rhonda needed her, too, but just didn't know it.

Gina Kay thought it was time to get the three of them back together. "I've been thinking a lot about it in recent weeks," she said. "Now that Terry is gone, I want it more than ever."

"Don't get your hopes up," Holly had told her. "I seriously doubt if Rhonda is going to show up at Terry's funeral."

Holly headed back to the house, making a mental list of all the things she needed to do before she headed for Lamberton. In the kitchen, she picked up the phone and tried to reach Sandy again but to no avail.

She wondered whatever happened to the picture of her and Sandy standing in front of the sky blue balloon.

Her kids loved the story of how their parents got engaged.

Chapter four

With the LexisNexis website waiting on her computer screen, Rhonda spent the entire afternoon in the kitchen. Fortunately, there were some chicken breasts in the freezer, and after considerable time browsing through cookbooks when she really should have been working, she decided on a recipe for chicken tetrazzini. Tomorrow was going to be an impossible day if she didn't put in at least a few hours getting organized for a deposition she had scheduled, but she didn't have the heart for dealing with failed marriages and their aftermath on this particular Sunday afternoon.

With the first pie she'd made in years baking in the oven and the chicken tetrazzini waiting for its turn, she considered going for a run—just a short one so she could get back in time to take the pie from the oven. She started up the stairs to put on her shorts and running shoes, but when she reached the second floor, instead of crossing the landing to her bedroom, she headed down the hall to the enclosed staircase that led to the third-floor attic.

The attic was completely floored and full of light from four dormer windows. When she and Dennis bought the house, Rhonda thought that she eventually would finish out the space for some use other than as a repository for all those possessions for which she had no further use but couldn't bring herself to discard. However, there had never been a legitimate need for more living space in an already spacious home.

Her high school yearbooks were boxed with other paraphernalia from her Lamberton years. Rhonda selected the yearbook from her senior year and dragged an old rocking chair over to the nearest window, which she opened to the sound of birds chirping in the backyard trees and distant traffic on Central Expressway. She sat there for a time in a puddle of sunlight, the yearbook resting on her lap as she tried to decide if she really wanted to open it and look at those young faces from so long ago, if she wanted to go back to that time and place when for years she had deliberately avoided the journey.

❦

The Lamberton that Rhonda remembered was a sleepy little town with a remarkable old stone courthouse and a handsome stone bridge over the Lampasas River. Her father had been stationed at Fort Hood when it became time for him to retire from military service, and he convinced his wife to give Lamberton and country living a try. Real estate was affordable there, and he could own some land and a pickup truck for the first time in his life. Colonel Frank Hayes planned to fill his retirement with gardening, tinkering, and raising registered quarter horses. And Cathy Hayes planned to take up canning and quilting but worried that she would miss the social side of military life and the instant bonding with other wives and their families that it facilitated. At the time, Rhonda was only twelve and her two brothers were married and pursuing military careers of their own. It took a few years for Cathy and Frank to acknowledge that they weren't truly suited for country living and would probably be happier living in a bustling retirement community with a golf course. They decided, however, to wait until Rhonda had graduated from high school before they moved away from Lamberton, knowing they would have to drag her kicking and screaming away from the friends she had made there.

Holly and Gina Kay befriended Rhonda the week after the moving van delivered the eclectic collection of household goods accumulated by the Hayes family during their various postings, both stateside and abroad. Out of boredom, Rhonda was riding her bicycle to a highway service station and grocery store, where she planned to buy a candy bar and ride back home—the same routine she had followed yesterday and the day before. But that day was different. Holly and Gina Kay were coming from the opposite direction, having already made their daily ride to the store. They peddled right by Rhonda, but almost at once she heard a voice calling out, "Hey, new girl." She stopped and turned around.

The two girls had hopped off their bikes and were walking them in her direction. One of the girls was tall with a mass of curly strawberry blond hair, vividly green eyes, and developing breasts quite apparent under her T-shirt. The other girl was short and a bit chubby and had straight brown hair, big brown eyes, and an as yet undeveloped chest. The tall girl was pretty—so pretty that Rhonda wanted to stare.

A pickup truck drove by, and the two girls waved at the driver. Then the shorter girl introduced herself. "I'm Holly Burgess. And this is Gina Kay Matthews. You want to come over to my house and make some cookies?"

The three girls spent every day together for the rest of the summer. They baked cookies and paddled around in the aboveground swimming pool that Holly's father, who was the shop teacher at the high school, had installed in their backyard the summer before. They listened to music on Rhonda's stereo, singing along with Sonny and Cher, Donna Fargo, Olivia Newton John. At Gina Kay's house, they ate potato chips and watched soap operas with her mother, who talked to the characters on the screen as though they were right there in the room, warning them that so-and-so was lying or planning to steal their true love or kill them dead. Mama Matthews, which was what everyone called Gina Kay's mother, was the fattest woman Rhonda had ever seen in the flesh. Mama Matthews passed her days on the tattered sofa in the living room, with her skinny husband and beautiful daughter running the household and taking care of her needs. Mr. Matthews eked out a meager living driving a school bus, working as a handyman, and selling whatever hay and alfalfa he was able to grow on his unirrigated land.

The Matthewses were the first poor people Rhonda had ever known. At first her mother and father were unsure about their daughter spending so much time at the Matthews home, a prefabricated dwelling that had been installed on the site decades before, was in sad need of paint, and had rusting truck bodies in the backyard. But like everyone else, Rhonda's parents fell under the spell of Gina Kay's beauty. And her sweetness. Anyone who had raised a child that beautiful and dear must be doing something right.

There was never any question about her parents approving of Holly. On first meeting, Holly had marched right up to them, shook hands, and told them they had a lovely home and must be marvelous parents since Rhonda had the best manners of anyone she had ever met in her entire life. Holly became Frank and Cathy Hayes's source of information about life in Lamberton. She told them who was the best mechanic, where to find the best chicken-fried steak, where to get their hair cut, and which doctor still made house calls. And she helped them select a church, explaining which ministers were tightlipped and which were known to enjoy a beer and a game of cards every now and then.

When school started, the three girls would save seats for one another on the school bus that, with Gina Kay's father at the wheel, took them to the brand-new junior high school on the north side of town. Holly took Rhonda in hand, seeing that she joined the Pep Club, Future Homemakers of America, and the school choir. Rhonda went with Gina Kay and Holly to sock hops and hayrides and was able to make other friends. But she knew that Gina Kay and Holly would always be her *best* friends.

Because of them, Rhonda loved school, thought Lamberton was the best place to live in the whole wide world, and was deliriously happy.

Rhonda had seen Terry around town before school started and, thanks to Holly, already knew his history. He was acknowledged by all to be the cutest boy in their grade and a tragic figure in spite of the fact that his daddy owned the largest cattle ranch in the county. When Terry was barely five years old, his mother, with Terry's baby sister in her arms, had fallen down the stairs and died instantly of a broken neck, with the baby dying shortly thereafter. Mr. Robertson had never remarried. Some people thought Mr. Robertson, who was known to drink a great deal and sometimes beat Terry with a belt, might have pushed his wife down the stairs because he thought she had been stepping out on him. Holly had to explain to Rhonda what was meant by "stepping out."

"My mother says that Marie Robertson was not that sort at all," Holly added, "and that some people have nothing better to do with their time than make up dirt about the dead."

Terry would sometimes nod at Rhonda when they passed in the hall between classes. Then one day he called out her name.

Rhonda became so flustered that she couldn't remember which class she had next.

Terry Robertson actually knew her name!

Even though she told herself that he was just being friendly and that he also called out the names of other girls he passed in the hall, she washed her hair that night and wore her favorite shirt and sweater to school the next day.

Terry said her name again. And Rhonda said his.

For weeks that was all there was—a saying of names—during which time Rhonda spent a great deal of time analyzing the appeal of Terry. He was borderline skinny, but he had Farrah Fawcett teeth, dark wavy hair, large dark eyes surrounded by thick lashes, and there was something about his lower lip that Rhonda found particularly appealing. In fact, his whole mouth was appealing. It was quite the nicest mouth she had ever seen, especially when he smiled. And he smiled a lot and walked with a bit of a swagger and was easily the most popular boy in their grade even though he didn't make good grades and wasn't a particularly good athlete.

The only class Rhonda had with Terry was English. Holly had advised Rhonda that the kids in her classes would like her better if she didn't raise her hand every single time the teacher asked a question and suggested she limit her hand raising to every third question. Which was difficult. Rhonda's right hand had this way of automatically shooting into the air almost before the teacher had completed a question. But in English class, she was aware that Terry *never* raised his hand and raised her own less and less; of course, the teacher often called on her when no hands were in the air, and Rhonda would answer the question. One day the teacher wrote a simple sentence on the board and asked Terry to identify the subject and predicate. He guessed and got it wrong. Rhonda was mortified for him, so much so that it made her stomach hurt and gave her courage. After class she asked him if he would like her to teach him about subjects and predicates.

He shrugged and said, "Sure."

That night after dinner he came to her house. Rhonda was ready for the lesson. She had written numerous nouns and active verbs on index cards and asked Terry to make two-word sentences with them. Then she asked him which of the two words was the name of something and which told what that something was doing.

A couple nights later, she taught him about compound subjects and compound predicates.

According to Holly, Terry and Gina Kay had liked each other in the sixth grade. And since he was the best-looking boy in their grade, he deserved the most beautiful girl, who was, in spite of the fact that she wore hand-me-down clothes, Gina Kay Matthews.

Holly thought it was appropriate that these two beautiful people—the motherless boy with a mean father and the dirt poor girl
who took care of her obese mother—rise above the burdens that
life had thrust on them and find true love. At least in theory,
Rhonda agreed. And even though Terry was beginning to find his
way into her daydreams, she tried to hold back from harboring
any realistic expectations that she would someday be his girlfriend. She would remind herself how pretty Gina Kay was. What
boy in his right mind wouldn't want to have a girl that pretty for a
girlfriend!

But on Valentine's Day, there was a valentine from Terry in the
mailbox that stood at the end of the Hayes driveway. He had written her name with a pencil that needed sharpening and spelled it
"Ronda," but she forgave that small error and could not have felt
more honored if England's Prince Charles had hand-delivered a
valentine to her mailbox.

It wasn't just a dinky little valentine that came a dozen to a box.
It had real lace around a satin-covered heart that had "To the Girl
of My Dreams" written across it in glittery letters. The card was
signed "Terry Lee Robertson," even though there was no other
boy named Terry in the entire junior high school.

Did Terry Lee Robertson really dream about her? The thought
of him in his bed thinking about her while she was in her bed
thinking about him made Rhonda feel as though she were made
of air and at any moment was going to float right up to the ceiling.

Rhonda put the valentine back in its envelope and hid it under
her jacket before carrying the rest of the mail into the house. She
didn't want her parents to know about it, and she already knew
she would not be showing it to Holly and Gina Kay. Not only was
it a private matter, she didn't want anyone to know that Terry had
misspelled her name and signed a valentine with a pencil. Her
mother, especially, was a stickler for such things, which Rhonda
assumed came from having been an army officer's wife and having

to do everything by the book. Besides, she had to figure out the significance of the valentine. Maybe Terry had given out lots of fancy valentines. Maybe there was one waiting in Gina Kay's mailbox right now.

The next morning, with her heart fluttering around in her chest like a bird with a broken wing, she thanked Terry for the valentine. He was standing by his locker. There were lots of kids milling around in the hallway, but no one close enough to hear what she said.

"I'm glad you like it," he said, pushing a stray lock of hair back from his forehead and staring down at the notebook in his hand. Then he looked at her with his beautiful dark eyes and said with a sheepish little smile, "I like you."

Rhonda was stunned. In the seventh grade, "like" was a very important word. She wanted to say that she liked him, too, but didn't have the courage. She watched as he fell in with two other boys. The three of them began punching one another good-naturedly as they walked down the hall.

Pairing off came gradually. Terry would usually manage to sit by her during assemblies or at the movies. At parties, he danced more with her than other girls. And he would ride his bike or Appaloosa mare over to her house in the evening. Sometimes they would sit at the dining room table while she helped him with his math assignment or a book report even though she was fairly certain that he had read only a chapter or two of the book. Afterward they would sit on the front porch and talk about school and what music they liked to listen to and which movie stars they liked the best. Once in a while her daddy would come out on the porch, and he and Terry would talk horses and sports. She heard her daddy tell her mother that Terry seemed like a nice enough boy but it was a good thing his father was rich because he would never amount to a hill of beans on his own. It made Rhonda angry that her father would say such a thing. After all, Terry didn't have a mother to make him do his homework and encourage him to read books, and his father had a drinking problem, so of course Terry struggled in school. All he needed was encouragement. He was sweet and handsome and Rhonda wanted for him to kiss her with that wonderful mouth, for him to be the first and only boy ever to kiss her in her entire life. That was what she thought about when she hugged her pillow in the night.

Holly, on the other hand, daydreamed about a different boy almost daily. She just wanted a boyfriend, and any of a number of boys would do. All the boys seemed to like Holly, but none of them asked her out, and Holly was reluctantly forced to acknowledge that the "baby fat" her mother promised would disappear on its own when she started her periods wasn't showing any signs of melting away. As a result and with the help of her mother, who as a home economics teacher knew all about nutrition and caloric requirements, Holly began her very first diet. She lost twenty pounds in three months and, with her mother's help, made herself a new wardrobe to fit her slimmer body. The problem was, her body did not stay slim. At home her mother monitored every bite she put in her mouth, but away from home, Holly was on her own, and the weight gradually returned.

Gina Kay went out with several boys and was determined not to go steady, which was counter to the culture in a small town like Lamberton, where teenagers tended to pair off early and often married their high school sweethearts. But both of Gina Kay's older sisters had to get married and had two kids by the time they were eighteen, and Gina Kay insisted that she was not going to go down that road.

Gina Kay's mother firmly believed that God had made her youngest daughter beautiful so she could marry a rich man and be able to look after her parents in their old age. God certainly realized that Gina Kay's sisters weren't going to do that, Mama

Matthews pointed out. If Gina Kay went to college, she would find someone with prospects, and the only way she could attend college was to use the scholarship money that she would receive as a winner of beauty pageants. Mama Matthews loved for Gina Kay to be invited to dinner at Rhonda's house, where the evening meal was served in the dining room with the television turned off, the table properly set, dessert served on a clean plate with a clean fork, and conversation always polite. Gina Kay needed manners to go with her beauty. No one was going to put a crown on a girl who would be an embarrassment to the pageant organization. Beauty queens didn't chew with their mouths open or fiddle with their hair. Beauty queens didn't say "ain't" or giggle. And Gina Kay needed to pay attention in school not just so she would not have to settle for some little backwater college, but so she could impress the judges during interviews and give eloquent answers during the question portion of the competition. Mama Matthews told Rhonda and Holly that if they wanted Gina Kay to be able to go off to college with them when the time came, they were going to have to help her get ready for her career as a beauty pageant contestant.

"Is that what you really want to do?" Rhonda once asked Gina Kay.

"Sure," she said, "if it will help me not end up like my sisters. If I don't find a rich man to marry, I'll still have a college education and can earn a lot more money than I would waiting tables or carhopping."

"But what if it doesn't work out?" Rhonda asked. "What if you don't win a scholarship?"

"Then I guess I'll have to work my way through beauty college," Gina Kay had said.

In the eighth grade, Terry spelled Rhonda's name correctly on the valentine he gave her, but it was still written in pencil. By then, their classmates all regarded them as a couple, and she felt secure enough to ask him why he hadn't given that seventh-grade valentine to Gina Kay. He explained that his dad told him a long time ago that he'd better hook up with a smart woman, and Rhonda was the smartest girl he'd ever known.

Rhonda thought long and hard about his answer. How could she be insulted because he admired her intelligence? And she certainly hadn't wanted him to lie and say she was the most beautiful girl he'd ever known. She was pretty enough, but not like Gina Kay, not so people wanted to turn and stare.

A few days later, Terry amended his answer. "I gave you the valentine because I was thinking about you a lot and knew I wanted you to be the first girl I ever kissed." Rhonda always wondered if Holly had coached him, but nevertheless, she was extremely thankful for whatever forces had made him gravitate toward her. At school sometimes she would turn down a corridor and catch a glimpse of him among the milling students. And he would grin at her with his beautiful mouth and wonderful dark eyes with their thick black lashes, and her heart would quite literally skip a beat and her knees would go weak. Being Terry's girlfriend was more important to Rhonda than making straight As, than pleasing her parents, than being popular at school, more important than anything else in the whole world. It defined her. That was who she was—*Terry Robertson's girlfriend.*

As early as the ninth grade Rhonda's parents began to remind her with annoying regularity that they expected her to go to college. What they didn't have to say out loud was that Terry was never going to college. And it wasn't just because his grades were poor. He was the sole heir to the Robertson Ranch; his future was assured with or without a college education.

Rhonda's parents believed that a college education was the most important gift they could give their daughter, much more important than inherited wealth. During her sophomore year, they started taking Rhonda on weekend trips to visit college campuses. She never explained the nature of these visits to Terry. He thought her family just liked to visit museums and look at old buildings. The trips he took with his father revolved around rodeos and cattle auctions.

Terry lived alone with his father in a large stone house kept by a Mexican woman named Antonia, who lived in a small house that Mr. Robertson had built for her in back of the big house. Rumor had it that Antonia frequently drank whiskey with Mr. Robertson and sometimes slept in his upstairs bedroom. When she came to town to do the shopping, men did not tip their hats to her, and women looked the other way.

Rhonda had never been inside the ranch house, but she had seen the graves of Terry's mother and sister in the family plot, which was surrounded by a rusting iron fence covered with masses of climbing roses. She thought of the big lonely house and the whiskey-drinking father and the sad little cemetery out back when she held Terry in her arms. If ever there was a boy who needed loving, it was Terry, and she could not bear the thought of any other female supplying that need.

But on each college campus she visited, she could imagine herself being there and taking part in campus life—hurrying off to class and meetings and parties and soaking up knowledge and making her parents proud as she won accolade after accolade on her way to medical school or law school or graduate studies abroad. College brought so many options, so many possibilities.

But for now, she was living a wonderful life. She woke up excited about every day with the outfit for that day carefully laid out on a chair and her shoes freshly polished. She loved Terry and her two best girlfriends. She loved the football games and parties. She loved studying for tests and making As. She loved her teachers, and they heaped praise on her. For now, her life was perfect.

Absolutely perfect.

Except that Terry was starting to drink. Beer mostly, but whiskey, too. Like his father. Sometimes Rhonda could smell it on his breath. And she heard things at school about boys drinking until they passed out. And drag racing with a bottle of whiskey in their hands. Even though Terry swore that he wasn't one of those boys, she knew that he was.

Chapter five

The sound of a distant siren aroused Rhonda from her reverie. She glanced at her watch, then set aside the still unopened yearbook and went downstairs to check on the pie baking in the oven.

The house was beginning to fill with the wonderful spicy aroma of cinnamon and apples. Rhonda hoped she had some cheddar cheese to serve with the pie, which needed about ten more minutes in the oven. In the meantime, she set the table and selected a bottle of wine to chill.

The pie was baked to perfection, Rhonda noted with pride as she set it on a rack to cool. "Nothing says loving like something from the oven," she told Mildred, who thumped her tail on the floor in reply. "Of course, that's a lie," Rhonda added and tried to think how she would amend the slogan. *Nothing says loving like staying married for twenty years?* Or perhaps, *Nothing says loving like going sailing with one's husband on a Sunday afternoon?* Her husband probably would have preferred her presence on their sailboat this afternoon to a freshly baked pie. No, not *probably*. Rhonda was certain that he would have. Dennis had purchased the thirty-five-foot sloop *Texhoma Belle* two years ago with thoughts of their post-child-rearing years in mind.

So how was she going to explain all this cooking if she had been too busy to go sailing? She would either have to say that the online server was on the blink or that she had bought ready-for-the-oven food and take no credit for the home-cooked meal.

"Shit!" she said out loud. Was there any such thing as an honest marriage, or was it just her own that seemed to run on falsehoods and half-truths? And omissions? Omissions most of all. She would never tell Dennis that she went searching for her high school yearbook just so she could to gaze once again on the face of a boy she had once loved to obsession.

Except that she was *not* going to do that, she decided as she put the chicken tetrazzini in the oven. She would go back up to the attic, close the window, and put the damned yearbook back in the box *without* looking inside. Then she was going to wash her hair and put on some makeup. And she would greet her husband with a smile and a kiss.

The rays of sunlight cut across the attic more sharply now, illuminating millions of gently stirring dust motes, and the air coming through the open window had taken on a definite chill. Rhonda closed the window and picked up the yearbook. Such a thin little thing. There had been fewer than four hundred students in the entire high school. Back then, only a handful aspired to attend college. According to Holly, almost half of the kids in their graduating class still lived in the town, many married to the person they had dated in high school. She had come very close to that life herself, Rhonda acknowledged.

During her junior year, her parents began pressuring her to make a decision about college. They wanted her to go out of state, but she finally settled on the University of Texas in Austin just to get them off her back. Terry begrudgingly approved of her decision. If she had to go to college, Austin was best. It was only a two-and-a-half-hour drive from Lamberton, which meant she could come home on weekends. When Rhonda reminded him that she didn't have a car, Terry said he would drive over and get her.

Coming home on weekends didn't dovetail with Rhonda's desire to be a busy college coed. She wanted to pledge a sorority, join clubs, go to football games and parties, and be tapped for honor societies. She wanted the whole package.

She also did not want to lose Terry.

What she wanted was to put him on hold for four years, and *then* they could get married. Unless she went to graduate school.

Earlier on the phone, Holly said she remembered everything about their high school years. Even with the yearbook closed, Rhonda could almost feel the memories it could evoke stirring around between the covers, waiting for her to let them out.

Rhonda glanced at her watch then seated herself in the rocking chair. Just a few minutes, she promised herself, and with a sigh, she let the book fall open on her lap.

And with just two flips of the pages, there he was—Terry Lee Robertson, senior class president. Dressed in his letter jacket, jeans, and cowboy boots, he was looking over his shoulder as he opened the front door of the high school. She touched his smiling face and felt, after all those years, such an ache in her heart. It had been more than a high school romance. When he told her he would rather die than lose her, she believed him. A part of her felt the same way about him. She had been living two lives; she was the girl who wanted to be with Terry always and the girl who wanted other possibilities, so she had engaged in a game of Russian roulette that almost ended both of their futures.

She turned to a full-page picture of Gina Kay taken the night she had been named Miss American Teenager. She was standing at the end of the runway, a crown on her golden hair, eyes glistening with tears of joy, smiling and waving. The same picture had occupied almost the entire front page of the *Lamberton Weekly News* and appeared in color on the front page of the *Dallas Morning News*. The inscription under the picture said that year's edition was dedicated to Gina Kay Matthews "for bringing honor to our school and town."

She had been truly beautiful, Rhonda had to acknowledge. The face of an angel, her father used to say. And indeed, there was something almost otherworldly about such flawless skin, perfectly formed features, eyes the color of emeralds, and hair like spun gold that actually shimmered when the sunlight found it. But Gina Kay had not been angelic. Rhonda stared at her picture, trying to see some indication of the depravity that lurked beneath all that beauty.

Rhonda almost didn't recognize her own senior picture. Her face was so smooth and impossibly young. Her wavy brown hair had been shoulder-length then; now she wore it in a shorter, easier-to-care-for style. Most of her classmates' faces she recalled. But not all. Not like Holly, who would certainly know every face, every name, where each one now lived, and how many children he or she had. Holly had stayed connected to the town and organized a class reunion every five years that Rhonda never attended.

Rhonda thumbed through the pages, looking at pictures of the various clubs and athletic teams, of sporting events, assemblies, theatrical productions, the Homecoming and Christmas dances. The prom always came too late to make the yearbook, but for the juniors and seniors, it was the most anticipated event of the school year.

Rhonda searched for a picture of her favorite teacher, Miss Alma Thornton, the art teacher who had served as adviser to the prom committee for as long as anyone could remember. For decades, Miss Thornton had been proposing that her all-time favorite movie, *Three Coins in the Fountain*, be selected as the theme for the prom, but until their senior year, no prom committee would ever go along with her proposal.

Rhonda remembered when they were juniors and it was their year to put on the prom, Miss Thornton showed the prom committee a video of the decidedly dated, 1950-ish film as part of her annual pitch. At first, Rhonda found the movie rather silly, with Frank Sinatra crooning a sappy song about which one would the fountain bless and the plot totally predictable. But Rome was beautiful, and her heart had soared at the end as the three American women's wishes were fulfilled. The ingenue won the heart of an Italian prince, the dying writer finally realized his faithful secretary was worthy of his love, and the career girl captured the heart of her charming Italian coworker.

Later, over Cokes at the Shack, the three best friends decided that they would go to Rome someday and throw coins in that very fountain—the Trevi. Maybe one of them would find a real live prince to fall in love with.

"But whether or not we ever make it to Rome," Holly had reminded them, "the one thing in our lives that we're not going to be is *ordinary*. That means we absolutely can*not* stay in Lamberton, Texas, and collect casserole recipes."

Holly was been looking pointedly at Rhonda when she said those words. Rhonda was the one who might waiver. Gina Kay and Holly were committed. No small towns in *their* future. But Rhonda was in love with Terry, and Terry wasn't going anywhere.

Rhonda, Gina Kay, and Holly had voted for the *Three Coins* theme, but *Star Wars* won out, and the gym was turned into outer space, with planets and space ships hanging from the rafters and a moonscape of fake rocks.

The summer between their junior and senior years, Rhonda and Holly accompanied Gina Kay as she traveled about the state competing in seven different pageants. Sometimes Holly's mom would go along as chaperone, other times it was Rhonda's, but it was Holly and Rhonda who served as Gina Kay's backstage mothers. Holly had added two other gowns to Gina Kay's wardrobe—a slinky black sheath with a thigh-high split and a strapless red gown that flared at the knees. And Rhonda became quite proficient at putting Gina Kay's hair into a regal upsweep for the evening gown competition. Gina Kay's singing voice was sweet but far from spectacular. Holly and Rhonda had convinced her to change her talent from singing "The Impossible Dream" to presenting a dramatic reading, and at Miss Thornton's suggestion, they chose a selection from *Our Town*. With Holly and Rhonda as her drama coaches, Gina Kay practiced the selection over and over again until each word, inflection, and gesture became ingrained as Gina Kay endeavored to became the ghost of Emily watching her young husband weep beside her grave. In June, Gina Kay won the Miss American Teenager–Texas title, which meant she would be going to New York in August to compete for the national Miss American Teenager title.

At the time, beauty pageants, especially on the East and West Coasts, were being picketed by feminists who believed the message of the pageants was that a woman's worth came from how close she came to the 34-24-34 ideal. The demonstrators were the same women who decried shaved legs, makeup, bras, and high-heeled shoes. While Rhonda had a hard time identifying with these strident, angry women, she suspected they were exactly right about beauty pageants. But how else was Gina Kay going to get to college? And by then, the three of them going to college together was a shared dream.

Rhonda remembered how she and Holly watched the national telecast of the pageant in the Matthewses' living room. They held hands while the names of finalists were read and whooped and yelled when the master of ceremonies called out, "Miss American Teenager–Texas, Gina Kay Matthews."

When it came time for Gina Kay to answer the all-important question, Rhonda held her breath and directed a fervent entreaty to Gina Kay. *Just be yourself, honey. Just be yourself.*

The question was: "Who is the most important person in your life?"

Gina Kay didn't hesitate. "Why, my mother," she said, her voice full of relief. "My daddy is mighty important, too, but he would expect me to put Mama first. He puts her first, too. My mama and daddy can't be here tonight because Mama is disabled, and Daddy needs to be there to look after her. But she is the center of our universe. Her love is our well, and I know she is watching me now and feels so proud. But Mama, I want you to know how proud I am of you. Whatever I am is because of you."

Holly squeezed Rhonda's hand. "Bingo!" she whispered.

Mama Matthews clung to her husband's hand and sobbed.

Rhonda hadn't even felt nervous at the end when it was just Gina Kay and Miss Oregon standing there, holding hands, waiting to hear the name of the first runner-up announced, which was Miss Oregon, of course. How could anyone have voted against Gina Kay? Miss Oregon was presented with a bouquet of roses and hurried off the stage while the smiling master of ceremonies announced that Gina Kay Matthews of Lamberton, Texas, was the nation's new Miss American Teenager.

Rhonda and Holly wept for joy as they watched *their* Gina Kay being crowned and taking her victory walk down the runway. She stopped at the end and blew kisses. Rhonda knew those kisses were aimed right for this shabby little room where her family and two best friends were watching.

Mama Matthews cried for the rest of the evening as people came by to congratulate her and Mr. Matthews. Holly and Rhonda's parents came, as did neighbors, the town mayor, the editor of the *Lamberton Weekly News,* and the principal and Miss Thornton and several other teachers from the high school. Mama Matthews thanked the Lord over and over again that she had lived to see her dream come true. Her daughter was a national beauty queen with enough scholarship money to pay for her college education.

Practically the whole town turned out for a parade in Gina Kay's honor featuring the Lamberton High School marching band, the Round-Up Club with Rhonda's father carrying the American flag atop his favorite mare, the town's two fire trucks with sirens blaring, six police cars with sirens blaring, a flat-bed truck carrying the residents of the local nursing home sitting in lawn chairs and waving little American flags, an armored truck from the town's National Guard unit, and floats from several high school clubs. Then with everyone clapping and cheering, Gina Kay came down the street riding in a brand-new white Cadillac convertible supplied for the occasion by the General Motors dealership in Temple. At Gina Kay's request, Holly and Rhonda rode with her. A banner across Main Street announced that Lamberton was the home of Miss American Teenager Gina Kay Matthews. The next day, a goodly number of the town's citizens trekked down to Austin to hear the governor proclaim Gina Kay Matthews Day in the State of Texas. Rhonda's father made movies for Mama Matthews of both the parade and the governor honoring Gina Kay.

Gina Kay had a fancy new wardrobe, not just cotton garments this time, thanks to the Miss American Teenager folks, who throughout the following year flew her all over the country for special appearances. She crowned winners at Miss American Teenager state pageants, cut ribbons to open new shopping malls and car dealerships, and appeared at high school assemblies, where she told students to stay in school and never to let a friend drive a motor vehicle after drinking alcoholic beverages. Gina Kay's teachers didn't even require her to make up her missed schoolwork. She had, after all, put Lamberton, Texas, on the map. Gina Kay Matthews was their town's most famous resident.

Their senior year was to be Miss Thornton's last at Lamberton High School before she retired and went to live with her sister on Galveston Island. Everyone knew that Miss Thornton had lived and studied in Rome as a young woman, but after the Christmas break, a rumor began circulating throughout the school that she had once been in love with an Italian painter and had planned to return to Rome after the war to marry him, but the young man had been killed fighting with the resistance. So, in spite of the popularity of *Saturday Night Fever,* that year's prom committee finally decided to let Miss Thornton have her way. *Three Coins in the Fountain* would be the theme of this year's prom. Even without the help of pictures, Rhonda recalled the night as though it were yesterday.

It was late April. Spring was in the air. She really hadn't needed the little black velvet wrap, but it looked wonderfully glamorous with her very grown-up dress. Last year's prom dress had had a scooped neckline. This year, her mother had not protested when she selected an electric blue strapless number. Rhonda wondered what had happened to all those snapshots and movies her father had taken of her in that dress, some with the velvet wrap and some with Terry, who was handsome beyond belief in his rented tuxedo. Were the pictures still stashed away in a box someplace or had they been culled during her parents' move from Lamberton? After all, by then Terry had fallen from grace.

Rhonda and Terry's relationship had become ever more intense that last year. As the prom drew near, he kept telling her it was going to be the night they went all the way. After years of doing everything else but actual intercourse, he was wearing her down. She was having a hard time concentrating on her schoolwork. She was a shoo-in for valedictorian no matter what her grades were for the final grading period, but she didn't want to ruin her perfect four-year record at the top of the honor roll. Yet her mind would wander so. She couldn't go two minutes, it seemed, without being distracted by thoughts of what would or would not happen after the prom. She wanted it, too. *Going all the way.* God, how she wanted it. She thought of all the reasons why a girl should not go all the way. *An unwanted pregnancy. Damaged goods. Sin. Loss of her boyfriend's respect. Loss of her own self-respect. Taking the meaning out of her wedding night.* But after five years of holding back, maybe Terry had a right. Maybe he would calm down about her going to college if they started having sex.

The junior class, under Miss Thornton's guidance, had done a spectacular job decorating the gym. A canopy of blue crepe-paper streamers completely covered the ceiling, and canvas backdrops painted with famous Roman landmarks—the Colosseum, the Forum, the Pantheon, and Saint Peter's Cathedral—stood in each corner of the room. In the center of the room was the fountain. The pool part of the fountain was an extra-large horse tank covered with a pool liner on loan from the aboveground pool company in Temple. The recirculating fountain was on loan from a landscaping company in Belton. Miss Thornton had even overseen the re-creation of scaled-down but impressive papier-mâché replicas of Neptune and his two horses to reign over the creation, and she had made an ornate sign that proclaimed the fountain to be "The Texas Trevi." Encircling the entire creation was artificial grass on loan from the local funeral home and dozens of potted flowers and ferns supplied by the local greenhouse.

Everyone came supplied with coins. Terry had his pockets full of quarters and even a few silver dollars. Rhonda knew what he was wishing for every time he threw one in. *Going all the way. Going all the way.* She felt wired. Her skin was on fire. Was she or wasn't she? Every look from Terry was questioning. Every touch.

The band played the "Three Coins in the Fountain" song for the last dance. When the lights came on, Gina Kay insisted that the three Best Friends Forever hike up their dresses and go wading in the fountain. She gave them each a penny she had personally placed on the railroad track. The smashed coins symbolized great change, she explained, and they must use them to wish that someday they would go to Rome together and toss coins in the real Trevi. After making their wish, they hugged and laughed and even got a bit teary-eyed. The moment seemed both silly and sad. Real life was just around the corner. Probably the three of them would never go to Rome, but they would always remember this moment.

After changing from their prom-night finery, Rhonda and Terry went to an after-party being held at the American Legion Hut. They had danced in a dark corner of the room, his crotch rubbing against her belly. And just as Holly remembered, she and Terry left the party early. After sneaking out a side door, they drove along one of the narrow trails that crisscrossed the Robertson Ranch to a gently sloping hill overlooking the river. On the crest of the hill a huge live oak tree grew, its spreading branches dipping almost to the ground, forming a cloistered space underneath.

Terry spread a blanket on the ground, and she lay with him, allowing him to take off her clothes and look at her body in the moonlight. The only thing she had ever denied him was going all the way. But tonight there was bourbon in her belly and an unbearable fever between her legs. And she had just finished her period. He could not make her pregnant.

She didn't so much as consent to the act as simply allow him to slide between her legs. And immediately, it was as though an electric shock went through her. Maybe she didn't want to do this after all.

"Now you belong to me," Terry said triumphantly and just held her for a time. They were two conjoined people who promised to belong to each other for eternity. What else could all this mean if not forever?

Then he began to move, and her body moved with him as a feeling like no other took possession of her body and carried her outside of herself. It was both wondrous and terrifying.

Even as her rapture waned, however, the emotion that came over her was unbearable sadness. There would never be another first time. She would not be a virgin on their wedding night.

The following night, before they drove out to the ranch, she insisted that Terry stop at the bus station and get a package of condoms from the dispenser in the men's room. "It probably isn't necessary tonight," she admitted, "but we do need to be really careful."

"Tomorrow night, I will," he promised her and turned in the opposite direction.

"Terry Robertson, you either turn this truck around or you can stop right this minute and let me out," Rhonda said. "You've got to use one of those things every single time we make love or else I won't let you!"

Terry begrudgingly did as she said. And promised that in the future he would keep a package on hand.

But a dozen nights later, Terry told her that he was wearing a condom when he was not.

She hadn't realized what had happened until she sat up and felt the wetness of his semen seeping out of her. He was still stretched out on the blanket, and she pounced on him, beating his chest with her fists.

"Goddamn you, Terry, you promised me! You *promised* me! I never would have let you go all the way if I thought you were going to pull a stunt like that. I hate you! I hate you with all my heart and never want to see you again as long I live. *Never! Never! Never!*"

She pulled on her clothes and marched down the dirt road. When he pulled up beside her, she got in the pickup but kept as much space between them as she could manage. Already she was afraid. And began to cry.

Terry stopped the truck and reached for her. "No," she screamed. "Don't you touch me. I want to go home right now."

Maybe if she took a long very hot bath she could wash away his sperm before they had a chance to go very far. Or maybe she could sneak into her parents' bathroom and get the douche bag from behind the towels on the top shelf of the linen closet.

"What if I'm pregnant?" she wailed.

"That's what I had in mind," Terry admitted, his voice grim. "If you're pregnant you won't be going off to college next fall."

Rhonda put her forehead on her knees. She felt sick. And so scared that she wanted to die.

The following two weeks were endless while Rhonda waited to see if her period came, to see if she was going to be faced with either a backstreet abortion or breaking her parents' hearts. When she refused to talk to Terry at school or on the phone, he pried the screen off her bedroom window in the middle of the night. Suddenly, there he was in her bed, pushing himself into her body. "I want you pregnant," he whispered in her ear, then dug his teeth hard into her shoulder. Rhonda knew that one scream would put an end to things. Her parents would come. Terry would be banished from her life.

But she did not scream. She didn't want them to know what she had done.

Her period began the day before graduation. She got down on her knees in the bathroom and thanked God, who probably expected her also to promise that she would never have sex again until she got married. Lying on the cool tile of the bathroom floor, she wept with relief. Then she washed her face and went to her room. She curled up on her bed for a time to savor the feel of not being pregnant. Of having her life back.

Then she stood in front of her dresser mirror to practice her valedictory speech, which was about the future and following one's dreams. "Dreams are the touchstones of our characters," she said, quoting Thoreau. She paused and looked at herself in the mirror, at the girl with no character who had come so close to letting her dreams slip away.

Her parents were among the sponsors of the all-night graduation party held at the pavilion in the city park. There was dancing, and the swimming pool remained open all night. Breakfast was served at dawn. On the way home, her parents told her that they had decided she was going to spend the summer with her aunt Betsy in Hutchinson, Kansas. They wanted her to have some time away from Terry before she started college. By then, a for-sale sign already stood in the front of their house, and her parents had purchased a lot in a retirement community in Arizona.

Rhonda cried and begged. She couldn't possibly leave her friends. She told her parents that she would hate them forever if they did that to her. But a small voice at some corner of her consciousness wondered if starting over wouldn't be a good thing.

Later, when Rhonda came out of the bathroom, her mother was sitting on the bed. "Are you having sex with Terry?" she asked.

Rhonda swore that she was not. She acted hurt that her parents didn't trust her. Of course, she was not going to jeopardize her future by getting pregnant. There was no reason for them to send her away.

Rhonda felt dirty. Not so much because of the sex but because she had lied to her mother. Her parents relented. Rhonda went with them to visit Aunt Betsy, but she didn't have to stay.

The next time she and Terry were together, she opened the foil package and put a condom on Terry's penis herself. He let her do that but extracted punishment for the deed in the form of pain. He dug his fingers into her throat just hard enough to let her know that he was in charge. The next day, she had to conceal the bruises with makeup.

She knew about drugs and addiction. Terry was a drug.

That summer she and Terry had sex every night. Even when it was her period, they had sex. Even when she didn't want to, they had sex. Sometimes she wished she had spent the summer with her aunt. But mostly she was in a constant state of lust.

Again, just as Holly remembered, it had indeed been the night of Rhonda's eighteenth birthday that she told Terry she didn't want to go steady anymore, which was probably the most courageous thing she had ever done in her life.

She had not been pleased when she unwrapped her birthday present from Terry. It was a friendship ring. By putting it on her finger, she would be saying that she and Terry were engaged to be engaged.

Of course everyone at her birthday party was waiting for her to do just that. She hesitated but felt Terry's gaze.

What else could she do but slip the ring on her finger?

It was beautiful—a pearl with two small diamonds—but too big for her. She started to put it back in the box, but Terry insisted she wear it. He would get it sized tomorrow.

When the party ended, she and Terry went for a ride in the black Chevy convertible his father had given him for a graduation present. He had a pint of whiskey in the glove compartment along with the package of condoms. Once they were outside the city limits, he reached for the whiskey and took a long swig. Normally Rhonda refused to ride with him when he'd been drinking, but it was just a deserted country road. And he wasn't driving fast at all.

When he offered her the bottle, she took a couple of small sips and almost immediately felt the warmth radiating through her body.

It was a beautiful moonlit night. She stared down at the ring on her finger. The pearl looked luminous in the moonlight.

The ring felt strange, heavy almost, like it didn't belong there.

"I love you, Terry," she said. "I love you more than anyone or anything in the whole wide world. And someday, I really do want to be your wife, but I need a few more years for being young and finishing my education before we settle down. You've always known that's what I wanted. It's not like I've been trying to hide it from you."

When he didn't say anything, she kept talking, promising that she would see him as often as she could manage in the fall but not every weekend like he wanted. She was going to be busy with her studies and she hoped to pledge a sorority and there would be meetings and social events. And while she might go out with another boy once in while, she would *never* get involved.

She reached over and touched his arm. "I swear on the lives of my parents that I will never have sex with any other boy, but I do want to enjoy college, Terry. I don't want to always be worrying about making you mad at me."

He responded by slamming his foot down hard on the accelerator. Rhonda watched in horror as the needle on the speedometer crept farther and farther to the right. Terry had always driven too fast, but nothing like this. They were going a hundred miles an hour on a dirt road with sharp curves and narrow bridges. She was too frightened to scream. He knew that she didn't want his ring.

She knew that he intended to kill them both.

She unfastened her seat belt and scooted close to him. "I love you, Terry," she said into his ear. "Only you."

He put his arm around her shoulders just as she knew he would, so they'd be touching each other when they died, which gave her the opportunity to reach forward and turn the key in the ignition. Before he realized what was happening, she had thrown the keys from the open car.

With a sharp turn of the steering wheel, Terry left the road, careened across a ditch, crashed through a fence, and aimed the car at a huge live oak tree. Rhonda grabbed the steering wheel and fought him for control. With all her might, she fought him. Suddenly the car spun around and hit the tree broadside, on the driver's side, with a horrible crunching sound.

And then there was silence. Deafening silence.

Terry was slumped over the wheel. Rhonda didn't know if he was stunned or dead. All she thought and felt and tasted was fear.

She scrambled from the car and ran. For her life, she ran. From a farmhouse, she called her father who came to take her home. "Terry and I had a fight" was all she said. But she smelled of her own urine.

In her bed, Rhonda vowed that she would never again allow herself to love anyone as intensely as she had loved Terry. That kind of love was a disease that ate away your heart and mind and robbed you of self.

She had almost died. She wondered if Terry had survived, but mostly she felt her own mortality as she trembled in her bed, the face of death no longer an abstraction. She curled her body tightly in an attempt to control the trembling. And wept. She stuffed a corner of the pillow in her mouth to keep from moaning out loud. Finally, she cried herself into a fitful sleep.

In the night, she thought she heard a scratching at the window screen. But Terry wasn't there. The rest of the night, she listened for him. Was he dead?

She imagined herself weeping at his funeral. Then he would be a memory, and she would be free.

If he weren't dead, would he come for her?

Maybe he was outside now setting fire to the house. Maybe he would crawl through her window and shoot her in the head with his hunting rifle, then put the barrel in his mouth. His brains would splatter all over her bedroom wall like President Kennedy's had all over that convertible and his wife's pink suit.

The next morning, no one called her to say that Terry had been found dead in his car. When she brushed her teeth, she realized that the friendship ring was no longer on her finger.

That afternoon, her mother took her to Waco for one last shopping trip before sorority rush week. Her mother asked if she wanted to drive, but Rhonda declined. Her mother kept giving her sidelong glances as she drove. All day, Rhonda wondered if Terry had tried to call. If he would try to see her before she left tomorrow. And if he did, what would she say? Would they have sex? How should she act? Maybe she should call him and tell him they could run off and get married.

But he had almost killed her. Almost killed them both. She had never known such fear.

That night, she and her mother finished packing. Her daddy loaded the station wagon with her trunk, desk lamp, stereo, bulletin board. Holly and Gina Kay came by, insisting that she had to cruise Main Street with them one last time before they turned into sophisticated college girls. "Just for a little while," Rhonda insisted. "I've still got things to do." No one at the drive-in said a word about Terry. Or a wreck.

After she was finally in bed, she thought of creeping down the hall to the kitchen and picking up the phone. She also composed a letter to Terry in her head.

But she did not call him or write to him. He should be the one to make amends. And when he did, she would make a deal with him. After two years of college, she would marry him and finish her degree by driving back and forth to Baylor in Waco or Mary Hardin-Baylor in Belton even though they were Baptist schools and she had been raised a Methodist.

With her mind made up, she finally fell into an exhausted sleep.

Once in Austin, Rhonda immediately had gotten caught up in college life. She and Holly pledged the same sorority. Gina Kay didn't go through rush. She would be working four evenings a week at a pizza parlor and had neither the time nor the money for a sorority. The three of them had drawn straws to see which two would room together, and Holly had been the odd man out, but she lived in the same freshman dormitory as Rhonda and Gina Kay. Life was incredibly full and exciting. Except through it all Rhonda kept waiting for Terry to call. Every time she entered the dorm, she would check the messages in her box for one that said Terry had called and was driving over to see her. She was waiting for him to tell her he was sorry and promise that he would never frighten her again. She would close her eyes and imagine him telling her that he loved her more than anything. Then they would make love. She missed the sex. Missed it a lot. In her bed at night, with Gina Kay sleeping across the room, her body would burn with desire.

She was certain that eventually Terry would come to her. He would have to. No two people could have experienced what they had and simply go their separate ways. She and Terry were a part of each other. Their souls were mingled. That was how she calmed herself, by reminding herself that they belonged to each other, that neither one of them could possibly love another person as much as they loved each other.

She wondered at times if there had not been that fearful last night, would she have simply kissed him good-bye and trotted off to the fun of college life, only giving him a thought every now and then? But he had almost loved her to death. No one would ever again love her that intensely.

Finally, she did write him a letter that said not much of anything. But when she put it in the mailbox, her heart soared. A letter would break the ice.

Then Rhonda made an appointment with an Austin physician. She told him she was getting married in two weeks and needed a prescription for birth control pills.

Chapter six

The phone rang just as Holly was heading out the door.

"I got your message," her husband's voice said. "I am so sorry about Terry."

"Me, too. I'm still in shock. Where are you?"

"Just leaving College Station. How's Gina Kay holding up?"

"She's very sad, of course, but she'll get through it. Gina Kay is probably the strongest person on the planet."

"Yeah, she's quite a gal," Sandy acknowledged. "You want me to come with you?"

"No, I'm all packed up and need to be on my way. I won't be able to calm down until I get there. Just hold down the home front and bring the kids to the funeral. I've got food in the refrigerator, and Joey and Melissa's schedules are written down by the phone. And your mother's birthday is Wednesday. Don't forget to call her."

"Did we send her a present?"

"Yes, *we* sent her a present. A yellow bathrobe."

"I've missed you, honey. After four days with the guys, I was looking forward to an evening with you."

"I've missed you, too," Holly said, which wasn't exactly true. She always looked forward to little vacations from the routine of married life and wondered if Sandy did, too. But maybe not. "Save those good thoughts until next weekend," she told him.

"I love you, babe."

"I love you, too, honey. You're a good guy, and I don't tell you that often enough. The kids and I are lucky to have you." Which basically was true, Holly thought as she hung up the phone. Sandy was easygoing and a good family man. A good coach, too, both in the win column and in character building. He was respected, even beloved, by players and parents alike. Of course, with the high school football games and their children's various athletic endeavors, family life pretty much revolved around sports, which was for the most part wholesome and fun. Holly loved it all but also had these feelings that something was missing. Touchdowns, baskets, and home runs were exciting but not all that fulfilling long term. And with a business and family to manage, every minute of her life was scheduled. Sandy still referred to her business as "sewing," as in, "Did you get much sewing done today?" It would be nice, once in a while, if he acknowledged that what she did was important and said he was proud of her success. It would be nice, once in a while, to attend an event other than athletic.

Holly put the last of her things in the car and went back inside to say good-bye to Joey and Melissa. And found herself mediating one last fight.

"I was here first," Melissa was insisting, her jaw set, hands on her hips. "Make him go watch the television in the kitchen."

"Whoever heard of watching a basketball game on a ten-inch screen?" Joey whined.

"Joey watches in the kitchen until half time then you switch places," Holly told them. "I'm leaving now. Your father should be home by dinner. No going anyplace without checking with him first. His cell phone is on."

She gave each of them a hug, relishing the clean, young smell of their skin and hair. Ten-year-old Melissa clung for a minute. *Her baby.* Melissa was plump, and it broke Holly's heart. "I'm sad about Terry," Melissa said. Joey put his hand on his mother's arm, to show that he, too, was sad. Joey was thirteen and had been put on this earth to irritate his sister.

"Why don't you each write a note to Gina Kay," Holly suggested. "It just has to be two sentences. Say that you are sad and will miss him. If you want to add a third sentence, tell her one of your favorite memories of Terry, like horseback riding or fishing. I'll call you to discuss what you should wear to the funeral. And please try not to kill each other in my absence."

She breathed a sigh of relief as she backed down the drive. A few hours alone in a car sounded so peaceful. Except the reason for her trip was a tragic one. *Terry was dead.*

It was almost predictable that Terry would die tragically, Holly supposed. Lord knows he'd crashed enough vehicles over the years. And then there was the accident when his daughter Ann Marie was a baby. What a nightmare that was!

Holly recalled a conversation she'd once had with Terry. They were walking along the beach at Padre Island, their children racing in and out of the surf. Gina Kay and Sandy were building a fire behind a sand dune for later, for roasting wieners and marshmallows. Terry gestured toward the endless expanse of ocean and told her that sometimes when he swam out there, he felt like there was something he desperately needed to see just over the horizon, even if it meant swimming so far out that he would never get back. "That might be a good way to go," he said. "Probably better than flying through a windshield." Then he grabbed her hand and pulled her into the surf, throwing serious conversation to the wind. They had splashed like two children, their own children racing over to join in the fray. That was how she wanted to remember Terry, Holly decided. Windblown, wet, laughing. His skin was weathered from a life spent out of doors, his dark hair beginning to gray. But he was still her standard for male beauty. And he was her friend.

She and Terry had been friends all their lives. After his mother died, he had started hiking the miles from his house to hers— before they were even old enough to go to school. Almost daily, he came. If he didn't come to her house, he went to watch television with Mama Matthews. Finally, Holly's mother stopped calling Mr. Robertson to tell him where his son was. She and Terry and Gina Kay played together for years, until Terry was old enough to help his father at the ranch. And even then, he often showed up at her house for Sunday dinner.

Holly had remained Terry's good friend. And now he was dead. A cold dead body at the funeral home. Soon to be buried in that little cemetery behind the ranch house beside his mother and baby sister.

Holly shuddered at such thoughts and fished in her purse for Kleenex. Then she pulled out her cell phone and called Gina Kay.

"I'm on my way," she announced. "I didn't ask earlier. How is Mr. Robertson holding up?"

"Ward is very sad, of course, but he admitted that he was surprised Terry lived as long as he did," Gina Kay said. Then she paused before adding, "Rhonda called."

"Oh my gosh! She actually called you?"

"Yes. She's coming to the funeral."

"You sure that's what you really want?" Holly asked.

"How can anyone ever be sure about anything? But I've always wanted at least to try and make things right with her. Then maybe I can stop thinking about it. And I have thought about her a lot over the years." Gina Kay hesitated before adding, "The funeral director is coming by in a little while. I need to decide what I want Terry to wear. He almost never wore a suit. Do you think it would be terrible if I picked out a pair of well-worn jeans and a faded plaid shirt?"

"Not at all. Have you cried yet?" Holly asked.

"Some. Mostly because I feel so bad for the children. Maybe I should let them pick out the clothes they want him to wear. Holly?"

"What?"

"Do you think I'm an awful person?"

"No."

"Thank you. Drive carefully, okay?"

By the time Holly reached the drive to the Robertson Ranch, it was dusk. The wrought-iron gate was standing open in anticipation of her arrival. She wound her way between the now stately box elders that Gina Kay had had planted shortly after she and Terry married. She rounded the last curve of the half-mile drive, and the ranch house came into view.

The stone house looked particularly impressive silhouetted against the western sky with its vividly pink and orange sunset. When Holly was a girl, the house had a barren look to it, with no trees or shrubbery, no broad front porch, no handsome iron fences to keep livestock away from the house, no welcoming circle drive, no flower beds and handsome fountain. But over the years, Gina Kay had changed all that. The house had been built with oil and cattle money, but most of the wells had been pumped out years ago, and cattle were less profitable than before. But apparently Gina Kay was a good manager, and money never seemed to be a problem. The entire spread, including the outbuildings, fences, and well-tended lawn, had a look of prosperity. A fleet of late-model vehicles was parked out front, including Gina Kay's Mercedes SUV.

Gina Kay was waiting on the porch, wearing white slacks and a green blouse, as slim and elegant as always. No longer a dewy-fresh beauty queen but still lovely. Holly's eyes filled with tears as they embraced. "I'm so sorry," she said.

"I know. Me, too. But maybe he is finally at peace." Then Gina Kay hugged Holly again. "I feel like I can breathe now that you're here."

Dennis arrived home about six. Rhonda had changed into slacks and a sweater. She'd shampooed her hair. Her makeup was fresh. Dinner was almost ready.

"Home cooking? But I thought you had so much work to do," Dennis said, puzzlement in his voice.

Rhonda explained that she was too distracted to work after Holly called to tell her that the husband of a high school friend had been killed. "I felt the need to practice a little husband appreciation and found myself in the kitchen cooking and wishing I'd spent the afternoon at the lake with you."

"So whatever it was that you *absolutely* had to do this afternoon must not have been that pressing after all," he said in a challenging tone as he sat at the bar and helped himself to a handful of nuts.

"You're mad at me," she said.

"No, Rhonda," he said in a weary voice. "I am not mad, just disappointed."

"Maybe we can go next weekend," she offered.

"I'm on call next weekend. And I don't want you to go sailing if you feel that it's something you have to do."

She knew she needed to walk around the bar and put her arms around his neck and reassure him that she loved sailing with him, which she did, but it was increasingly hard for her to spare the time.

"I'm sorry," she said from her side of the bar. "I promise that I'll organize my time better in the future. And we do need to plan a trip for just the two of us to some lovely place without cell phones. Soon." But even as she said the words, she thought of her appointment book at the office. She probably didn't have a completely free week until well into next year.

"I baked an old-fashioned, made-from-scratch apple pie, and there's a really nice Chablis chilling," she said.

"No wine for me. I may have to head for the hospital after dinner. One of my patients is going bad."

"I thought Frank was on call," Rhonda protested.

"His brother-in-law had a heart attack. He and Sally are on their way to Shreveport."

The phone call from the hospital came halfway through dinner.

"Don't wait up for me. This may take a while," Dennis said. "Maybe I can have a piece of that pie for breakfast," he added. Then he kissed her and told her that he loved her.

Rhonda felt relieved. The storm cloud had blown over—as it usually did. Dennis tended to avoid conflict. Which was probably one of the reasons he was so well liked by his students, colleagues, and patients. But he wanted to retire from the medical school faculty and give up his practice in order to fill his days with birdwatching and painting and leave awesome responsibility to others. Just a few more years, he would say, after they had finished educating their sons. He wanted to have the sailboat hauled to the Gulf and build a retirement home on a sand dune. The Gulf Coast was a mecca for bird-watchers. Rhonda did not encourage such talk.

When she finished in the kitchen she went to look at the painting Dennis had done of a roadrunner that hung over the mantel in the family room. She didn't know a great deal about birds, but she did have an eye for art. And the painting was good. Her husband had a plan and wanted her to buy into it. Which maybe she would someday. But not in the foreseeable future.

She went to her under-the-stairs office for a time to organize her thoughts for the next day's deposition. Then she went upstairs for a long bath and to look through her closet for funeral attire.

She watched the ten o'clock news then curled up in bed with a book, but memories of Terry bombarded her mind. She decided to take a sleeping pill.

Before the pill had time to take effect, Dennis was there gently kissing her cheek.

She pretended to be groggier than she really was, hoping he would not expect more than perfunctory sex.

"You're home already," she said.

"We lost the boy," he said.

"Oh, honey, I'm so sorry," she said sitting up.

"The motorcycle had been a birthday present from his parents. Their lives will never be the same."

The light from the bedside lamp highlighted every line on his careworn face. "You okay?" she asked, smoothing the lines with her fingertips.

"No," he said, closing his eyes. "It was one of those cases where you wonder if perhaps you'd tried a different tack the outcome might have been different."

"Oh, Dennis, honey, don't do that to yourself. All you can do is what you believe is best at the time."

"I suppose," he said, kicking off his shoes and leaning against the headboard. "I'm glad our boys are coming home next weekend."

"Me, too," Rhonda said. "Our *nineteen*-year-old sons."

"Yeah. They're good kids. I miss having them around."

"I do, too. Hey, I forgot to tell you. My parents are coming for the weekend."

"That's good," he said. "I wish my parents were still alive. I think they would be proud of the way the boys turned out."

"No doubt about it. I've always been so sorry Scott and Jason never really got to know their other grandparents. You still miss your folks, don't you?"

"Yeah. They both died too young. I hope I have a few years in the rocking chair before I die."

Rhonda smiled. "Somehow I can't see you spending much time in a rocking chair."

"I rocked the boys when they were babies."

"Yes, you did. That old rocking chair is still up in the attic. I saved it for when we have grandkids."

"I wish I had rocked them more," he said, kissing her forehead. Then her fingertips. "Would you hold me, please? I need to be with my wife."

Chapter seven

As she drove down Lamberton's Main Street, Rhonda felt as though she had entered a time warp, even though some of the storefronts were boarded up and others had different names from her high school days and one of the stone pillars on the river bridge had crumbled. But the town had changed very little in the last quarter century. Just a bit shabbier. Or maybe it had been shabby then, and she just hadn't noticed.

She was early, and the parking lot at the Methodist church was just beginning to fill. Rhonda pulled down the visor to check her face in the mirror. How much had *she* changed? Would anyone recognize her? Holly claimed that classmates asked about her at the reunions.

"And what do you tell them about me?" Rhonda had once asked.

"I tell them you are a successful attorney, married to a chest surgeon, and have twin sons," Holly responded. "As for why you don't come to the reunions, I think they assume you have gotten too uppity for that."

"But that's not true," Rhonda said.

"Isn't it? What would you have me tell them?"

Rhonda had no response.

Now here she was. The uppity classmate who never came to reunions had shown up for the funeral of her old boyfriend—the boyfriend Gina Kay had stolen away from her.

She wasn't quite sure *why* she had come. Maybe, as her mother had suggested, she needed the sense of finality that Terry's funeral would bring. She could come to terms with his death and know that never again would she wonder if she would ever see him again. In life, he had been a distracting specter that flitted around the edges of her marriage. Perhaps in death she could put him to rest.

A man with slicked-down hair and a dark suit and tie handed her a program as she entered the vestibule and asked her to sign her name on the lined pages of a guest book. She hesitated, then picked up the pen and wrote "Rhonda Hayes Chadwick."

She sat in the far corner of the back pew. Only a few other mourners were scattered about the church. The closed casket covered with a floral blanket of yellow roses was already in place at the front of the church. Masses of floral displays filled the front of the church and spilled over into the side aisles, and a large photograph of Terry in his high school football uniform rested on an easel beside the casket. He was on one knee, holding a helmet under his arm, his hair damp and tousled, a cocky grin on his face.

An avalanche of thoughts assaulted Rhonda. Memories, good and bad. Her love for him had been genuine and not just the stirrings of an adolescent heart. And she had *made* love with him many times. She wondered if he had made love to other women besides her and Gina Kay. But what an inappropriate thought to be having. She shouldn't be thinking of sex. Except that sex had consumed her that last summer with Terry. Maybe without sex they could have conducted themselves more sanely. Maybe they could have parted friends. And perhaps they would have parted eventually. Her mother had pointed that out after he married Gina Kay.

She had started seeing Terry again. In secret. She didn't tell Holly and Gina Kay. Or her parents. Her parents had been so relieved when she broke up with him, and she dreaded telling them that she and Terry were back together again. And she didn't want the girls at the sorority house to know she was going with a boy who had no plans for college. Of course, Terry did have a rich father. That had to count for something. And he was incredibly good-looking. No other boy in the world had more beautiful eyes. Or a more irresistible smile. Except Terry didn't smile anymore. He resented the secrecy, and he accused Rhonda of playing games with him. He wanted a public acknowledgment that they were a couple, that they planned to get married. That was what she wanted, too, she insisted, as soon as the time was right. She wanted to break the news to her parents gradually. She owed them that much.

Terry would drive to Austin, and they would make love in one of the dingy motels on the edge of town, which seemed indecent somehow. She missed the night sky overhead, but it was such a relief to have him in her arms again. They did not speak of the night he almost killed them both. She still thought about it, though. A lot. And she suspected that Terry thought about it, too. He both frightened and thrilled her with his intensity.

Then suddenly, on a Friday afternoon, Gina Kay packed up and went home, claiming that she had mono. She married Terry that same evening, in the front room of her parents' house.

Fearful of how the news would affect Rhonda, her parents had driven to Austin on Sunday afternoon to tell her in person. They had heard the news at church. Apparently it was all over town.

She closed her eyes and took herself back to that dormitory sitting room. Her mother had tried to soothe, explaining that they suspected she had taken up with Terry again but were hopeful that college would make her realize that he wasn't the boy for her. If she married Terry, it never would have lasted. She would have grown restless and longed for a different life. And maybe that was so, Rhonda acknowledged as she stared at the casket holding Terry's dead body, but as it was, the relationship never had a chance to play itself out.

It had taken strength borne of pride to prepare for finals and complete her first semester. Even though their new home in Arizona was not yet completed, her parents advanced the date of their move so Rhonda would not have to spend her Christmas break in Lamberton. They cooked Christmas dinner on hot plates because the stove had not yet been installed, but the meal was eaten in the dining room on china plates with the good silver and a centerpiece of fresh flowers. Rhonda had calmed herself by concentrating on the two things she knew with certainty: her parents loved her very much, and she would never again set foot in Lamberton.

Rhonda turned her attention to the program she had been handed on entering the sanctuary. She recognized the names of several pallbearers, including Willie Clyde Washington, who had played high school football with Terry then gone on to a remarkable collegiate and professional football career. For a time, Gina Kay would have been the most famous person ever born and raised in Lamberton, but Willie Clyde's fame would surely have eclipsed hers.

Many of the male mourners wore cowboy boots and western-cut clothing. Rhonda had forgotten about that. Her father had even worn cowboy boots and a Stetson while they lived here. She recognized many people she'd known in high school and nodded to some who looked her way. A few of the women came to give the prodigal daughter a hug. Which was nice. With her presence acknowledged, she could relax a bit. Some of her high school friends had changed dramatically, others were simply older versions of themselves.

When Holly arrived with her family, she looked around until she spotted Rhonda, then motioned for her to come forward and join them, but Rhonda shook her head.

Terry's family filed in from a side door. Rhonda caught a glimpse of Gina Kay's reddish gold hair and slender form. Even as a grieving widow, she carried herself well. She always had, Rhonda recalled. While all those other beauty contestants had had years of ballet to give them poise, Gina Kay's had come naturally. She was born one step above trailer park trash but carried herself like a queen.

Pushing old Mr. Robertson in a wheelchair was a tall, dark-haired young man who looked so much like a young Terry Robertson that Rhonda had to gasp. *Terry's son.* There was a daughter, too. And a third, much younger child; Rhonda couldn't remember if that child was a boy or a girl.

The minister preached a standard funeral sermon to which Rhonda was too preoccupied to listen. After a long prayer, he introduced Terry's son, Mitchell, who took the minister's place in the pulpit.

The young man stood quietly for a moment, looking around at those who had come to mourn his father's passing.

"I realize that each of us here knew a different Terry Robertson," he began. "Some of you knew him as a rancher. Some of you shared his concern for the future of our town. Some of you played hooky with him when you were young and poker with him later on. Some of you were his fishing and hunting buddies. Mr. Hobson there gave him every haircut he had in his entire life. Juan Gomez shod his horses for as long as I can remember. I see most of the people who ever worked for him sitting out there, and I do think that all of you knew him, above all, as a fair man."

Mitchell Robertson paused at this point and seemed to be composing himself for what was to follow. "But I want to tell you about the Terry Robertson I knew," he continued. "In my earliest memory of my father, I am sitting in front of him on a horse. He loved horses. He loved all animals, even the cattle he had to load up and take to the slaughterhouse. He didn't like feedlots and raised only free-roaming range cattle because he thought they deserved that before we make steaks out of them.

"My daddy only whipped me twice in my whole life. Once was when I threw a cat off the barn roof to see if it would land on its feet. It didn't. The other time was when I sassed my mother. After he whipped me, he told me that I was to honor my mother above all others, that I should get down on my knees every night and thank the Lord that I had such a fine woman to raise me and love me all her life. He told me that again last Sunday morning while he was dying under that tractor." The young man paused and nodded at his mother.

Rhonda put her hand to her mouth to hold back the conflicting emotions that she was feeling. Terry's last thoughts were of Gina Kay.

Terry's son gripped the sides of the pulpit as he continued. "Those of you who knew my father well know he had his own set of demons that he fought all his life and that brought him great sadness. But I know that some of you are here today because he bailed you out of jail or helped with your mortgage payments. Maybe he loaned you the money you needed to fix your tractor or dig a new well after the old one went dry. Often he 'forgot' to collect those loans. He had a good heart, and that's what I'd like for all of you to remember about him, and forgive him for the rest. I know that in his way he loved you all. I never heard my father say a mean thing about any man, woman, or child on this earth, and I stand before you proud to be the son of Terry Robertson."

With that, Mitchell Robertson drew himself up to his full height for a second as though to demonstrate his pride. Then he said, "My family and I thank you for being here today and helping us honor my father's life and memory. We invite all of you to lunch at the ranch after the burial."

Rhonda was impressed by the young man's poise. And by his words. Her chest swelled with the need to sob, but she held it back. Any tears on her part would be unseemly.

Terry's demons. Was she to blame for some of them? But he had married Gina Kay, she reminded herself, when only days before he had made love to her and promised to love her always.

After the eulogy, the funeral director stepped forward to open the casket. And a church full of people watched as Terry's family had their last moments with his mortal remains. Rhonda had no intention of watching but couldn't force herself to look away. Gina Kay bent over the casket to offer her husband a final kiss. His adult children, too. Mitch helped his grandfather rise from his wheelchair, and he, too, kissed his dead son. Then a little girl of seven or eight came forward and took Gina Kay's hand. Gina Kay whispered in her ear, and the child touched the casket, then leaned forward and kissed it. The older two children had their father's dark hair, but this child's hair was reddish gold, like Gina Kay's.

Then row by row the mourners were given an opportunity to view the body. *I won't look,* Rhonda told herself when it was the last row's turn to come forward. *I won't look.*

But she did. Instead of averting her eyes and passing on by as she had planned, she found herself wanting to linger, to study the countenance of the man who had once been the most important person in her life. His face was lined and leathery, his features coarser, not the smooth young face of the boy she remembered. His dark hair was peppered with gray. The hands folded across his chest were work worn and speckled with brown spots. Yet she could see in him still the boy of her youth, the boy she once had loved more than anything. She did not want to kiss his lifeless lips, but she would have liked to touch his hand.

She didn't do that, of course. But since she was the last in line, she whispered, "Good-bye, Terry." And in her mind, she told him that she never stopped thinking about him and that she blamed Gina Kay more than she did him for what had happened.

❦

Holly and her family were waiting for her in front of the church. "You doin' okay?" Holly asked, her voice full of concern.

"Of course," Rhonda responded and gave everyone a hug. Carter was every inch a college man, with a navy blazer, striped tie, and tan slacks. Joey looked uncomfortable in a starched shirt and tie. Melissa was wearing a loose-fitting print dress. With her shining brown hair and big brown eyes, she looked much like her mother had that long ago day when Holly and Gina Kay befriended the new girl in town. Rhonda had never seen Sandy in a suit before; he looked quite handsome. He blushed when she told him so.

At the burial, the minister offered a few additional words, some scripture, and a prayer. The little girl held Gina Kay's hand throughout the brief service, which concluded with Willie Clyde Washington singing "Amazing Grace" a cappella in a hauntingly beautiful voice that blended with the sound of rustling leaves before it drifted heavenward. Rhonda recalled him singing the same hymn at their high school graduation.

Rhonda remembered being fascinated with the tiny cemetery that occupied a knoll a hundred yards or so behind the ranch house. The leaning iron fence stood erect now and had been given a fresh coat of black paint. The climbing rose bush was gone, a tidy boxwood hedge in its place. She remembered who was buried under each tombstone—Terry's mother, his baby sister, his grandparents and great-grandparents, an uncle who died in childhood.

From the knoll, there was a commanding view of the surrounding countryside, all part of the Robertson domain. And Rhonda could see the back of the house with its broad veranda and a large swimming pool that occupied a side yard. A vast, sloping lawn separated the main house from the outbuildings, which included the small house where the Mexican housekeeper had once lived and another house nestled among a grove of live oak trees. On the back side of the hill were a bunkhouse, horse barn, silo, water tower, a huge open shed that housed tractors and other farm implements, and other smaller buildings. And there were trees everywhere, and not just the usual mesquite, blackjack oak, and live oak that Rhonda remembered, but magnolia, post oak, sycamore, silver maple, willow, elm, birch, pecan, and some she didn't recognize. An oasis of trees. Gina Kay's doing, Rhonda supposed.

When the burial service was over, Terry's son pushed his grandfather's wheelchair toward the little house under the oak trees, and Gina Kay and her daughters led the way back to the house.

Shortly Gina Kay and her two adult children had stationed themselves in the entry hall, ready to greet their guests and receive their condolences. Rhonda held back, not wanting any onlookers when her turn came with Gina Kay. When the moment arrived, Gina Kay opened her arms, and Rhonda hesitated, then stepped into her embrace. What else could she do? "Thank you for coming," Gina Kay said. "It means a great deal to me."

Rhonda wanted to tell Gina Kay not to read too much into her being there, that she wasn't really sure why she had come. But she didn't say that, of course. Instead she said, "It seemed like the right thing to do."

Gina Kay introduced Rhonda to her two older children, who greeted her with curiosity on their faces and politely responded to her questions. Kelly was a student at UT in Austin. Mitch had graduated from Texas A&M and was an economist with the state Department of Agriculture.

The little fair-haired child slipped in between the adults and took her mother's hand. "And this is my daughter, Ann Marie," Gina Kay said.

Ann Marie shook Rhonda's hand. "Did you know my daddy?" she asked.

"Yes, a long time ago when we were in high school. You have his beautiful dark eyes."

"And my mother's hair," Ann Marie added.

The inside of the house was full of light and handsomely decorated, when before it had been dark and unwelcoming. On the spacious veranda, an incredible array of food—casseroles, cakes, and pies brought by friends and neighbors, as well as catered fare—was being served by a small army of uniformed waitstaff. More than food, Rhonda wanted something alcoholic to drink, but only iced tea and soft drinks were being offered.

She sought out Holly. "I could use a drink," she admitted.

"I'm sure we'll have wine after everyone has gone," Holly said. "You are staying, aren't you?"

"For a while."

"Gina Kay is counting on us spending the night."

"I need to get back," Rhonda said as she glanced toward the entry hall, where Gina Kay and her children still stood, accepting condolences, handshakes, and hugs. Little Ann Marie was pulling on her mother's hand, and Gina Kay leaned down and whispered something in her ear then kissed her cheek.

"Come on," Holly said, pulling on Rhonda's arm. "Let's get my family on the road, then get something to eat and circulate. There are people who remember you well and would like to say hello."

With Holly's help, Rhonda was able to put names with the faces of people who stepped forward to shake her hand, some to offer a hug and exchange a few words. *It had been so long. She was looking good. Wasn't it sad about poor Terry?* Some of them recited special memories they had of her. Rhonda found herself relaxing a bit, actually enjoying herself, realizing what a snob she had turned into. She had assumed the people who stayed behind in Lamberton would be country bumpkins. But they weren't, any more than Holly's parents had been. And even the most countrified among them were good, kindly folks. Of course, it was a bit uncomfortable when people asked if she'd kept in touch with Gina Kay and Terry. Her answer became pat. "Only through Holly," she would say.

Finally, with Gina Kay and her adult children once again standing in the entry hall to thank people for coming, the crowd began to thin. Holly gave Rhonda a tour of the house, explaining how Gina Kay over the years had enlarged and renovated the original house and made it her own while still keeping the massive stone fireplaces and some of the original family furniture, including the ornately carved armoires and the stately dining room pieces. Upstairs, they paused in what was obviously Ann Marie's bedroom, with unicorns on the wallpaper and shelves full of dolls and teddy bears.

"Such a darling little girl," Rhonda said. "I'd almost forgotten they had a third child."

"I was surprised when Ann Marie came along," Holly admitted. "She's been a real comfort to Gina Kay. Mitch and Kelly were closer to their father."

Holly went back downstairs while Rhonda used the bathroom. When she came out, she saw Ann Marie sitting on the top step, watching the people below. Rhonda sat down beside her and saw that tears were rolling down the child's face.

She put an arm around the little girl's shoulders. "I know you must be very sad," she said.

Ann Marie nodded. "I don't want my daddy to be dead."

"I bet he loved you very, very much."

She nodded again. "He called me 'Sunshine,'" she said in a small voice.

Tears filled Rhonda's eyes. *Terry's little Sunshine.* She kissed the top of the child's head. "You will carry your father's love with you all your life. Whenever you are sad or lonely, you think of him and remember that you were his sunshine girl."

"Have you ever been to my house before?" Ann Marie asked. "I don't remember you."

"I came here a long, long time ago, way before you were born."

"Why haven't you come back?"

"I live in Dallas," Rhonda said. "And my parents don't live in Lamberton anymore. The town is no longer a part of my life."

"Did you like my daddy?" Ann Marie asked.

"Yes, I liked him a lot," she said, and leaned her cheek against the top of the girl's head and closed her eyes to relish the sheer poignant pleasure of the moment. *Terry's child.* How nice it would have been to have a little girl, she thought, a little girl just like this one. When she opened her eyes, she realized that Gina Kay was looking up at them.

Feeling oddly guilty Rhonda hastily withdrew her arm from Ann Marie's shoulders. "Shall we go back downstairs?" she asked.

It was early evening when the caterers had finally packed up and left. Mitch and Kelly excused themselves and left to spend the evening with friends. After giving the housekeeper instructions about Ann Marie's dinner, Gina Kay drove Rhonda and Holly to the Burgess house for a visit with Holly's mother, who was recuperating from a heart attack. Rhonda was stunned at how much Mrs. Burgess had changed. She was at least a decade younger than her own mother but looked older and was so thin and feeble.

"You can't imagine how happy it makes me to see you three girls together again," Mrs. Burgess said clinging to Rhonda's hand. Rhonda promised to come back. And she would do that, she promised herself as they drove back to the ranch. She regretted not having come to Mr. Burgess's funeral. Or paying a condolence call. The Burgesses were good people who had been like a backup set of parents to her, but she had been so afraid of running into Gina Kay and Terry, she stayed away from Lamberton. The only times she had seen Holly's parents in all these years were two occasions when her visit to Holly's house in Waco had coincided with theirs.

As they left, Gina Kay asked Rhonda if she wanted to drive by her old house.

Rhonda shook her head. "I'm sure it looks quite different

now, and I'd rather remember it the way it was when we lived there."

It was dark when the three women settled onto comfortable chaises on the veranda, which was now warmed by two glowing terra-cotta *chimeneas*. Gina Kay opened a bottle of really fine Merlot. A pair of handsome Appaloosas came to watch them over the back fence and offer an occasional soft whinny. Ann Marie snuggled with her mother for a while until the housekeeper came to take her to bed. Rhonda watched as the child hugged her mother's neck. "Can I sleep in your bed?" she asked.

"You bet," Gina Kay said and reached out for one more kiss. "But leave some room for me. Only two or three dolls, please."

Ann Marie told Holly good night and gave her a hug. Then she hugged Rhonda. "You're a nice lady," she said and danced off at the housekeeper's side.

"She's adorable," Rhonda said.

Gina Kay smiled. "She is the light of my life."

"She told me that Terry called her 'Sunshine.' "

Gina Kay nodded and took a sip of wine.

When the housekeeper brought them a tray arranged with a variety of cheeses and fruit, Gina Kay thanked the woman warmly and told her to go home. They could take care of themselves for the rest of the evening.

Rhonda had promised herself that she would leave after only one glass of wine, but it was so peaceful here after the stress of the day.

She leaned her head against the back of the chaise staring up at the star-studded heavens. She had forgotten how spectacular the night sky was out here, away from city lights. And she had forgotten the smell of newly cut hay and the night sounds of the countryside, including the distant lowing of cattle and the calling of the night birds. All this could have been hers, she found herself thinking.

But she had a beautiful home of her own in an exclusive Dallas neighborhood, Rhonda reminded herself. She and Dennis enjoyed a different sort of life, one that included a busy social calendar and the symphony, theatrical productions, art exhibitions. Her sons were doing well at UT. And more and more, her very name struck fear into the hearts of divorce-seeking husbands.

As she sipped her wine, Rhonda listened while Holly and Gina Kay took a trip down memory lane, reminiscing about football games and hayrides, about what the three of them had once meant to one another.

When Gina Kay brought up the senior prom and the trip to Rome they never took, Rhonda felt a sense of unease. That was the night she first made love with Terry, but of course, Gina Kay and Holly didn't know that. Rhonda asked if Miss Thornton was still alive.

"She's in her nineties now," Gina Kay said, "and still lives in Galveston with her sister. I called her after the accident and told her you were coming to the funeral. She asked about you and said to give you her best. She actually giggled when she recalled the three of us standing in the fountain with our dresses hiked up. She said we were her favorite students ever."

Gina Kay paused to refill Holly and Rhonda's glasses. Rhonda started to protest that it was time for her to start back to Dallas. She had planned to bake a cake for her sons' birthday when she got home this evening. But she had the feeling that Gina Kay had something more important to talk about than reminisce about the senior prom. After all, she had indicated during their phone call that it was time to "*talk about what happened.*"

Gina Kay put down the wine bottle, but instead of returning to her own chaise, she sat on the foot of Holly's. "Please don't laugh," she said, addressing them both, "but I have been invited to take part in the upcoming national Miss American Teenager pageant in New York City to commemorate the twenty-fifth anniversary of 'my reign.' At first I didn't give a thought to going, but I got to thinking about all those good times we had on the pageant trail. Then, when you called, Rhonda, and said you would come to Terry's funeral, I decided I would at least bring it up."

Gina Kay paused, running her finger around the lip of her wineglass before continuing. "I'd like for the three of us to go . . . to make up for our never having taken that trip to Rome. Terry wasn't much for travel. His world was here on the ranch," she said with a wave of her hand to indicate the sea of land around them. "Unless family vacations were short and close to home, I was the one who took the kids to Yellowstone and Washington, D.C., and Disneyland. And I traveled alone sometimes to beaches and mountaintops, but I don't want to return to New York alone. The more I thought about it, the more I knew that I wanted you two to go with me. You were the ones who helped me prepare for that pageant twenty-five years ago. You tried out dozens of hairdos on me and made me rehearse that dramatic reading over and over again. If fact, I can still recite every word, should you ever care to hear it. It seems only fitting that you two should go with me to mark the anniversary of that time and our very special friendship."

Rhonda was shocked when Gina Kay leaned forward and took her hand. "I always knew that if anything ever happened to Terry, I wanted to try and make us friends again. I know how terrible it must have been for you when Terry and I got married, how confusing and painful that must have been. Come to New York with me and I will explain what happened back then."

"Is that a bribe?" Rhonda asked, pulling her hand away.

"Yes, I guess it is," Gina Kay admitted.

Rhonda wanted to tell her not to get her hopes up. She was not here to renew their friendship, just to pay her respects, but Holly began to hum "Three Coins in the Fountain." Gina Kay joined her and supplied some of the words. Rhonda also joined in. *Why not?* she thought. She remembered a few phrases but mostly hummed along. For just a moment she allowed herself to go back to the time when they were still friends. It had been the most intense friendship of her lifetime. Nothing in the years since even began to equal it, not even her continuing friendship with Holly.

At the end of the song, the three of them even harmonized on, "Make it mine. Make it mine. Make it mine."

"You know, I always hated those words," Rhonda admitted. "What selfish little bitches those women were, each one hoping she got the fountain's blessing and not the other two."

"Here, here," Holly agreed, lifting her glass. "Down with selfish little bitches."

"I'll drink to that," Gina Kay said with a hopeful smile.

The three of them downed their glasses, and Holly reached for the bottle and poured another round. "And here's to the gown that I, the finest designer of pageant gowns in the entire state of Texas, shall create for your New York appearance," Holly said, lifting her glass once again.

"Oh, would you?" Gina Kay said, clutching a hand to her breast.

"I'll design you a gown that will make the little teenybopper contestants drool," Holly promised. "I'm working on a gown for the Texas contestant, who looks a bit like a teenage Brigitte Bardot."

"My gown can't be too sexy," Gina Kay warned.

"Your gown will be regal," Holly said, having a bit of trouble with the "r" in regal.

Suddenly Rhonda realized that Gina Kay and Holly assumed this trip was actually going to take place. Well, they were welcome to go, but she certainly was not.

But why dash the spirit of the evening? There was plenty of time to back out later. Rhonda stood, planning to announce that she needed to leave, but carefully headed for the bathroom instead. She needed to sober up a bit before she drove back to Dallas. Already she knew that she would have to bake the birthday cake in the morning. Early. Before she left for the office. Of course, she also needed to pick up the food she had ordered, stop by the liquor store. And the florist. She always had fresh flowers when her mother came.

When she returned from the bathroom, Gina Kay herded them into the kitchen. They decided against leftover funeral food, and Gina Kay prepared omelets. The wine had loosened Rhonda's tongue, and she found herself recalling the day the three of them first met. "I heard someone calling, 'Hey, new girl,' and my life was never the same." By then, Holly had found another bottle of wine in Gina Kay's pantry and was searching for the corkscrew.

As Rhonda allowed Holly to pour her another glass, she realized she would be spending the night. "I have to be on the road by dawn," she warned and tried to calculate how long it was going to take her to bake that cake and what time she could get to the office. Not until afternoon. And she would have to leave early in time to pick her parents up at the airport. Briefly she considered buying a cake, but she'd never missed baking a cake for her sons' birthday. It was Scott's year to choose what kind, and he had requested a fresh coconut.

She considered the possibility that she wouldn't make it into the office at all. She didn't have a court date or a deposition scheduled. And it wasn't like she was going to get fired. After all, she was a partner.

$\mathcal{C}$hapter eight

Rhonda waited outside of security for that first glimpse of her parents coming up the airport concourse—a moment she always relished. Cathy and Frank Hayes were a handsome couple still, full of life and health.

When she spotted them, she waved. They smiled and waved back.

Her mother's smile seemed a bit lopsided.

In baggage claim, it took two or three surreptitious glances for Rhonda to diagnose the problem with her mother's face. The right corner of her mouth did not quite match the left. It drooped a bit. And the corner of her right eye.

Rhonda looked in her father's direction, but he would not meet her gaze. Cathy put her hand on her daughter's arm. "It was just a tiny stroke," she explained matter-of-factly. "I'm almost back to normal. It was a blessing really, a warning signal. Now I'm on medication, absolutely dedicated about going to my aerobics class three times a week, and walking two miles on the days I don't do aerobics. And your dad and I still swim in the evening. I'm going to be so fit you probably won't even recognize me."

Rhonda felt as though she had been socked in the stomach. "You had a stroke and didn't tell me," she said incredulously. She turned to her father. "My God, Daddy, why didn't you let me know?"

"Your mother didn't want me to," he explained, not quite meeting his daughter's challenging gaze. "We called your brothers, but she said that you would feel like you needed to fly over and hover.

And she didn't want that. She said you were too busy with important trials coming up, and her condition wasn't serious."

"And we were already planning to come for the boys' birthday," Cathy added, linking arms with her daughter as they headed for the baggage claim area.

"When did it happen?" Rhonda demanded.

"Last week," Cathy said. "My speech was kind of mushy when I woke up Thursday morning, and my right side was a bit weak. Your darling father took me straight to the emergency room, where they gave me an injection of some wonderful drug that needs to be given in the first few hours after symptoms appear. And by the next day, I was pretty much back to normal, except for my face, and every morning when I look in the mirror, it seems a little closer to normal. I called you on Sunday, thinking that I would let you know what had happened, but you had just talked to Holly and were preoccupied with news of Terry Robertson's death."

A wave of nausea hit Rhonda as she internalized the knowledge that her mother had had a brush with mortality. She thought of Holly's mother, who had had a "close call" and was now an invalid, and of Holly's father, who had died of a heart attack.

And irrationally, she thought of the fresh coconut layer cake waiting in her kitchen for her mother's oohs and aahs.

On her way back from Lamberton early this morning, Rhonda had called her office to tell her secretary that she would not be in until early afternoon and that any "must take" calls could be forwarded to her cell phone. She did not, however, explain why she was not coming in.

As soon as Rhonda had the cake layers baked and on a rack to cool, she went to pick up the food she had ordered for that evening and run her other errands. After she had put the food away and set the dinner table, she searched through the cupboards for the candy thermometer and double boiler she needed to cook the white-mountain frosting. Once the cake was iced and covered with freshly grated coconut, she calculated that—with the shopping, grating, mixing, baking, searching, cooking the frosting, and assembling the finished product—she had spent a total of four hours making the cake. If she'd been practicing law for those hours, she would have earned hundreds of dollars but would not have felt the satisfaction she now was experiencing as she admired the cake, which looked like something from the cover of a cookbook. She had been amused at how foolishly proud she felt and how much she looked forward to her mother's accolades.

All her life, she had relied on her mother's praise and support. Good grades on her report cards had achieved significance only when she showed them to her mother, as had a spotlessly clean bedroom, shined shoes, or a chore well done.

Now, as a grown woman in her forties, Rhonda enjoyed telling her mother about her legal successes. And by Cathy Hayes's own admission, she lived vicariously through her daughter's accomplishments. *Her* daughter had done it all. Rhonda had been a brilliant student, successfully juggled the demands of motherhood and career, and was now on track to be president of the state bar association. Probably one of the primary reasons Rhonda had not caved in and married Terry Robertson the summer after they graduated from high school was because she needed to live up to her mother's pride and expectations.

But now her mother's stroke forced her to acknowledge that at some indefinite point in the future, perhaps sooner that she might have thought, her mother's life would end. Then who would care about her successes? Part of her dream of someday becoming president of the state bar association was having her parents there to see her sworn in, to see pride radiating from her mother's face.

Dennis wanted her to be happy and fulfilled but probably

didn't care if she found those things through practicing law or digging in the garden or eating bonbons in bed with a book. Her sons probably would have preferred that she had been more like her own mother—always there, always attentive, always putting her children first, so much so that she hadn't wanted to bother her only daughter when she had a stroke lest it interrupt her busy life.

Her mother was dutifully impressed with the birthday cake—and with the new rug in the dining room and the new arrangement of plants on the sunporch. "You could have been an interior decorator if you hadn't gone to law school," Cathy insisted. Then, instead of asking how she could help with dinner, she went upstairs to rest a bit before the boys arrived.

Rhonda installed her father on a stool in the kitchen and gave him his usual scotch and water before barraging him with questions. Yes, he answered, they now had a blood pressure cuff and knew how to use it. Yes, he went with Cathy on those two-mile walks. And yes, she had seen a specialist at the university health center in Phoenix. She was in good hands.

"What about you?" Rhonda demanded, scrutinizing her father. He was tanned and trim. No spare tire. But his shoulders were more rounded than they used to be, and the lines in his face etched more deeply. "You're having annual physicals, aren't you? You aren't covering up something I should know?"

Her father smiled. "Except for the arthritis, I'm fine, honey. Daily exercise and stretching along with doses of aspirin help with the aches and pains. But the fact is your mother and daddy are getting on. Every issue of the West Point alumni magazine, I see death notices for my classmates. Your mother and I have pre-paid our funerals, and our wills are in order. We even signed on as organ donors, although I don't know what use they'd have for our very used body parts."

Rhonda abruptly changed the subject. What did he think about home schooling? In response to his puzzled frown, she launched into an explanation of how the home-schooling issue affected one of her child-custody cases.

After Dennis had arrived home and changed into his jeans, the two men, with Mildred at their heels, went out in the backyard to fire up the grill. For a time, Rhonda watched them out the window over the sink, wondering what they were discussing as they monitored the coals, her father still nursing his scotch, Dennis holding a beer. Her mother's stroke probably. Dennis would be reassuring but truthful, just as he would be when she asked him the same questions later.

Rhonda got the shish kebabs out of the refrigerator that she'd bought preassembled at the Whole Foods Market on Greenville, where she had also purchased the salad, French bread, relish tray, and ready-for-the-oven squash casserole. What she wouldn't have given for such a market when the boys were growing up. And with that thought, she heard a horn sound in the driveway.

They were home! Scott and Jason were home.

Rhonda went racing out the door to greet her sons, to relish the sight of them and the feel of their embrace. Jason even lifted her off her feet and spun her around. So tall and strong they were, and once she had carried them in her arms.

Over dinner, Scott and Jason entertained their parents and grandparents with stories of college life—fraternity parties, coed football games, water fights on the frat house lawn. Scott told them about his eccentric English professor who wore a dusty frock coat to class and sometimes took off his sandals and picked at his toes while he gave his lectures, which were sometimes delivered in verse.

When Cathy asked if either of them had a girlfriend, Jason blushed. Her name was Sarah, he said. They'd only had three dates, he hastened to explain, but she was pretty and quite intelligent. "I really like her," he admitted with such earnestness and hope that Rhonda had to look away. She wanted to tell him not to fall in love. Not yet. There was plenty of time for that. But she feared he already had. Which meant he could have his heart broken. The days when she could protect her sons from harm's way were long past. And the days they would spend under her roof were numbered. She had counted on them being home this summer, but they had taken jobs as wranglers on a dude ranch in Colorado. She had wanted to protest that they knew nothing about horses but knew it would do no good. They were old enough to make their own decisions about summer employment.

After dinner, when Rhonda suggested her mother sit on the kitchen stool while she did the dishes, Cathy didn't protest. And she declined a nightcap, asking instead for a cup of hot tea, explaining that liquor didn't mix well with her medications. "Tell me about Terry's funeral," she said from her perch. "Did you see Gina Kay? Is she still beautiful? Are you glad you went?"

"Yes, I saw Gina Kay. Holly and I ended up staying over at the ranch until this morning. I left at dawn before anyone was up. You wouldn't believe what Gina Kay has done to that house. And yes, she is still beautiful. She asked about you and Daddy."

Rhonda paused, unsure how much more she wanted to say about her return to Lamberton.

"Are you glad you went?" her mother asked again.

"I'm not sure," Rhonda admitted. "I wasn't as uncomfortable as I thought I would be, but I think Gina Kay read too much into my being there. This coming June is the twenty-fifth anniversary of Gina Kay's being named Miss American Teenager, and she has been invited to New York to appear at the pageant. She wants Holly and me to go with her."

"My goodness, after all these years," Cathy said with genuine surprise. "What do you suppose motivated her to do that?"

"She says that she never would have won the title without Holly's and my help. I guess the trip is supposed to be sort of a belated thank-you. We're to book our own plane tickets, and she will pay for the rest."

"Are you going?"

"Probably not."

"But if you do decide to go, what would be *your* motivation?"

Rhonda busied herself putting the last of the dishes into the dishwasher. "Gina Kay said that if we came with her, she would explain what happened back then . . . you know, how come she and Terry ended up married."

"You've never forgiven her, have you?" Cathy asked. "And you've never quite forgiven Holly for staying friends with Gina Kay."

"I suppose I'm guilty on both counts," Rhonda admitted. "I've continued to cling to Holly because she's the only person, other than my dear mother, I can pick up the phone and call just for a chat with no agenda. It makes me feel normal to have a woman friend like that. As for Gina Kay, back then I thought I would die from the pain she caused me. And in all the years since, I've never had a friendship like the one I had with Gina Kay and Holly. But even after all this time, I find myself wondering how long she and Terry had been screwing around on me. For it was an act against me, you know. There is no getting around that. And I did love Terry Lee Robertson. I loved him a lot."

"I know you did, honey, but it was so long ago, and you were all so young," Cathy said. "Children still. I would have thought you had put all that to rest years ago."

Cathy took a sip of tea before continuing. "Dennis is such a fine man," she told her daughter. "Maybe it's time you deal with the ghosts of the past and give Dennis a chance. He's reaching a crossroads, Rhonda, and is ready to create a different life for himself. And if you're not willing to be the woman at his side, I suspect he'll find someone else."

She wanted to argue with her mother, to point out that she and Dennis had a good solid marriage, but she said nothing.

Would Dennis do that? Give up on her and find someone else?

Rhonda looked out the window. At Dennis, her husband of almost two decades. He and her father were tossing a baseball around with Scott and Jason.

Her twin sons were far from identical. Scott was blond, fair-skinned, and husky like his father. Jason resembled Rhonda's father—tall and lanky with dark hair and an olive complexion. But they were equally beautiful in her eyes, and she loved them completely. In fact, she sometimes worried that the bountiful love she felt for them had squeezed out poor Dennis. But then, when she first met Dennis, she might as well have been wearing a suit of armor. She had entered into sexual relationships with numerous men after Terry, but love was something else altogether. Whenever any man started talking about love, she backed away. Either Dennis had been perceptive enough to figure that out or, like her, was simply interested in having an available sex partner. The demands of his residency training were horrendous. Only occasionally did they actually go out. And when they did, they avoided any discussion of the future. Mostly they screwed. Usually he would call and simply say "My place or yours?" She knew what he meant. Often he had to return to the hospital afterward, leaving her alone in a bed with the sheets damp from sweat and semen. When she got back from her summer in New York, she decided not to go back on birth control pills and had an IUD inserted instead. Apparently it hadn't stayed put. There was no sign of it when the doctor informed her she was two months pregnant.

At first she agreed when Dennis offered to arrange for an abortion, but when they arrived at the clinic she started shaking. She was shaking so that she couldn't hold the pen when it came time to sign her name on the consent form. She looked at Dennis and shook her head back and forth. The look on his face was one of relief.

At that moment Rhonda felt her heart begin to melt. She did care for him. And was grateful to him. *So very grateful*. They drove to the courthouse and got a marriage license.

They got married the next day with courthouse clerks serving as witnesses. Afterward Dennis had to race off to the hospital for his next shift. She spent her wedding night alone. Throwing up. It had been a difficult pregnancy. A difficult beginning for a marriage. She liked Dennis and respected him, but she didn't love him. And she fully realized that he did not love her. He was a decent man who had done the decent thing. She had no expectation of their marriage lasting.

Somehow, she had managed to get herself through her final year of law school. As early as her fifth month of pregnancy, her fellow law students and faculty members would regard her with alarm, asking if she was all right, worrying that delivery was imminent. People were continually telling her that she looked like she was having twins. She didn't even bother to tell them that she was. Conversation took too much energy. She needed all her energy for her studies. Her water broke in the middle of her last final. The amniotic fluid splashed down the risers of the tiered classroom like a small waterfall. The proctor wanted to call an ambulance, but she waved him away and finished the exam. The labor pains started the minute she handed it in. She drove herself to the hospital.

The pain was hideous, beyond anything she ever could have imagined. But when she was finally able to hold her two tiny babies for the first time, she felt the memory of that pain floating away. They were so perfect and so beautiful. She felt love wash through her body and swell her heart to the point that she thought it was going to burst.

She thought fleetingly about writing a note to Terry and Gina Kay to let them know that she was the mother of twin boys and that her life was going well, but she never did. There would have been an implied forgiveness in such an act, and she could never forgive them.

It was her babies, however, who allowed her finally to put Terry on the back shelf of a remote, dark closet. Of course, motherhood also had been exhausting and overwhelming, but at its heart was absolute adoration. Dennis also adored their sons, but so much of the time he was off saving lives. Even after he completed his residency and established his practice, she had been the hands-on parent. She never had evolved a clear image of what she expected out of life and always had vague feelings of missing the mark, of failing. Maybe if she had been named a partner at the law firm earlier in her career or been madly in love with her husband, she might have felt differently.

Or maybe not.

She and Dennis had stayed married, she supposed, because neither one of them fell in love with someone else. One night when Dennis had had too many martinis, he told her that he believed that true love would one day smite them like a lightning bolt from heaven. He was waiting for that day to come, and they could begin anew.

Rhonda had allowed Dennis to believe that when the boys left home, they would spend more time with each other, that it would be a time of renewal in their marriage. But she didn't know how to go about renewing a marriage. And as it turned out, it was not a bad marriage. It had served them both well. Perhaps it was best to leave well enough alone.

She told her mother that as she scoured the kitchen sink. Neither she nor Dennis was unhappy, she explained. She probably did need to reassure him about the future, though, and help him figure out how they would conduct their marriage after he retired.

Scott and Jason came inside to say good night to their mother and grandmother before they headed out to spend the rest of the evening with friends. Dennis and Frank followed them inside, and the six of them finalized plans to drive up to Lake Texhoma the next afternoon. As a special treat for her parents, they were going to sail across the lake and have a picnic on the Oklahoma side with friends from their army days who now operated a marina on the lake.

After her parents had said good night and headed up the stairs, Rhonda and Dennis carried a nightcap out to the backyard with Mildred at their heels. With the night sounds all around her, Rhonda settled onto a chaise and stared up at the moon. Then she asked Dennis for reassurance that her mother was going to be all right, that she would live on for years and years.

"She could," he said, "but remember, Rhonda, that your brothers were half grown by the time you came along. Your parents are getting on in years. They could live for a decade or more, but anything from now on is a gift."

"Wow, what a day!" Rhonda said, her tone sarcastic. "Finding out that my mother had a stroke and Jason is serious about a girl."

"I would hardly put your mother's health scare and our son falling in love in the same category," he said.

"Jason is too young to fall in love," she said flatly.

"Hadn't you fallen in love by the time you were his age?" he asked.

Rhonda's skin prickled with wariness. "Young love is vastly overrated," she said. "Give me a good, sexy man pushing fifty any day of the week."

Then she patted the foot of the chaise. Dennis sat there, and she wrapped her arms around him from behind and kissed his neck. He was still firm and strong. Not an ounce of fat. A sexy man still. Her kisses became nibbles. And she reached between his legs. "Mmmm, what have we here? An interested member of the party? Maybe we should go inside."

"You won't be inhibited by your parents in the next room?" he asked.

She rubbed her breasts against his back. And felt his erection grow firmer in her hand. "Why don't we go upstairs and find out?"

She stepped into the shower with him to hurry the process along. Becoming the aggressor. Three times she had assumed that role since that man had admired her perfume in the Houston airport. Briefly she worried that Dennis would wonder what was going on with her. But she didn't want to pull back. She wanted to be hot and lusty with her husband. She kissed him under the shower spray and rubbed her body against his. His fingers probed between her legs, both of them groaning with pleasure and desire. Then she slid her mouth down his chest and knelt in front of him, taking him to the very brink.

Suddenly they couldn't get out of the shower fast enough and sank down on the bathroom floor, all mouths and legs and wet flesh, the sound of the shower muffling their groans. She began to come as soon as he entered her. Wave after wave of the most intense pleasure imaginable.

Then they both collapsed against each other, hearts pounding, Dennis whispering that he loved her, over and over again. And she told him the same. Then she began to giggle. And then to laugh. "That, my dear husband, was absolutely glorious."

"We'll have to have your parents fly over more often," he said.

Rhonda almost wished that she could tell her mother about what had happened on the bathroom floor—as proof that she and Dennis were doing *just fine*.

Saturday afternoon they had a successful, three-generational out-
ing aboard the *Texhoma Belle*. The weather was perfect. Her parents greatly enjoyed seeing their friends, and on the way back
across the lake, Jason asked his grandparents what their earliest
memories were, and a wonderfully rich discussion of family history ensued, some of which Rhonda had never heard before.

That night, after they turned out the lights, Rhonda snuggled
against Dennis and suggested they take the boat out again his first
free weekend. Just the two of them. And spend the night on
board. She had reasoned that *just in case* she decided to make the
trip to New York with Holly and Gina Kay, she needed to earn
some good-wife points before she broached the subject with
him. Dennis was so pleased by her suggestion that she felt a bit
guilty.

And so two weeks later, she and Dennis were once again aboard
the *Texhoma Belle*. She had brought along CDs of their favorite
music, baskets of gourmet food and good wine, and a portable
television with a VCR in case they ran out of conversation. She still
hadn't *completely* made up her mind about the New York trip.
When she broached the topic, she had just been sending up a trial
balloon.

"Help me understand," Dennis said, staring at the shoreline.
They were at anchor in a small inlet, the moon reflecting on the
water. The remains of their dinner were on the small fold-down
table. A hurricane lamp cast a soft, flickering light. "Here you are
booked for months in advance at the office yet you have decided
to fly off to New York with some high school friend you haven't
seen in decades and whose name I have never heard you mention
before?"

"Well, I haven't *actually* decided to go," Rhonda hedged.
"Holly's been trying to talk me into it," she added, which wasn't
exactly the truth. Holly had said that she was definitely going but
would understand if Rhonda decided not to, even though Rhonda

must surely be curious about the big explanation Gina had promised. Holly hadn't minded admitting that *she* certainly was.

Rhonda could hear the hurt and frustration in Dennis's voice. And she didn't blame him. She and Dennis hadn't gone on a trip that had nothing to do with family or football in several years. And he had never been to New York.

Rhonda was halfway tempted to tell Dennis the truth or at least a version of it. To explain that Gina Kay had mysteriously eloped with Rhonda's high school boyfriend when to anyone's knowledge the two of them had never been on a date or so much as held hands. And Gina Kay had promised that while they were in New York she would explain how that happened.

But then Dennis would want to know more. Why was what had happened back then so important to her? Had she been thinking about this guy all these years? Had she still been in love with him when Gina Kay married him? Had her heart been broken? Was that why she had never gone to any of those high school reunions that Holly organized? Why had she stayed friends with Holly all these years but not with Gina Kay? Why had she always kept a part of herself walled off from him?

And there were no simple answers to these questions. The reason why she had never probed into Dennis's past was because she didn't want him digging around in hers. And after all this time, she wondered why it still mattered to her.

But it did.

Poor Dennis. She loved him very much but had never been able to convince him of that. "I'm sorry," she told him. "I got caught up in the moment and thought it would be kind of fun to do something young and frivolous with my old high school girl-friends. I'll just tell them that I'm not available."

Dennis said that no, that wasn't necessary. He was teaching this summer, but in the fall maybe they could plan something.

And she plied him with wine and led him down the companionway steps to the tiny forward stateroom and they made love. She sensed that it wasn't lustiness that he wanted but sweetness. Sweet love. And that is what she gave him, reassuring him with her words and her body that he was loved and appreciated.

Which made her feel infinitely sad and more than a little dishonest. She did love Dennis. But maybe she didn't love him enough. Maybe she had indeed reached those restless middle years about which her mother had spoken.

Even after she had purchased her plane ticket, she kept telling herself and Dennis that she wasn't really sure she was going.

❦

The June flight to New York was the first time she'd been on a plane since the perfume incident in the Houston airport. She thought about that while she got dressed that morning, dabbing just a suggestion of the same perfume behind her ears, having a bit of a fantasy about seeing the man once again.

The fantasy rode with her to the airport and hovered around her as she walked down the concourse. When she actually saw him in the waiting area she thought her eyes were playing tricks on her. Then she had felt so juvenile, like a silly teenager, that she had harbored thoughts of seeing him again.

Chapter nine

The ride from La Guardia Airport into Manhattan seemed endless. Delays caused by road construction put them in the middle
of the rush-hour traffic. Their driver and numerous other drivers
in the vehicles surrounding them had resorted to continuous
horn honking. The din made conversation difficult, and the three
passengers crowded in the backseat sat quietly, purses on laps.

How weird, Rhonda thought, that all these years after their
three-way friendship ended, she was trapped with Gina Kay and
Holly in a New York traffic jam. Three little maids from school
who left girlish glee behind and went their separate ways. Rhonda
wondered if they would have stayed close over the years if Gina
Kay had not married Terry. Gina Kay might have ended up here in
New York if she had become an actress or fashion model. Or in
California. She had been that beautiful. She still was beautiful;
when the driver took a pause from his honking, he stared at Gina
Kay in the rearview mirror. Maybe if she had stayed at UT, she and
Holly could have encouraged one another and given each other
the strength to follow their dreams. Maybe they would have gone
to Hollywood together, become fabulously successful, and arrived
in chauffeured limousines when they came back to Lamberton for
high school reunions.

And she herself could have been the one who married Terry
and stayed on in Lamberton, Rhonda thought. She might even
have been the classmate who organized the reunions and sent out
the annual newsletter.

After years of saying she wanted to finish college first, she had already promised Terry they could get married at the end of her second year. He said that he didn't believe her. And besides, two years wasn't good enough. If she was serious about marrying him, it would have to be sooner than that.

"Why in the hell do you keep stringing me along?" he had demanded the last time they were together. "You're just waiting for the right frat boy to come along, then you'll drop me like a hot poker. Sometimes I think I might as well find myself someone else now instead of waiting around for you dump me."

His words had scared her—a lot.

Did he already have his eye on some other girl? The thought threw her into a panic.

Back in the dorm, she had written two letters—one to Terry, the other to her parents—explaining that she had decided to marry Terry at the end of her freshman year at UT. And even hinted at a Christmas wedding, before her parents moved to Arizona. She would not allow herself to think about her parents' disappointment, concentrating instead on how happy Terry would be. Her beloved Terry. She was put on this earth to make him happy. Even as she was writing the letters, though, she wondered if she had the courage to mail them. Or the courage *not* to mail them.

She had gone downstairs to the front vestibule where the mail slot was located and dropped the two letters inside. Just like that. It was done. The rest of her life decided.

She wondered if the letters would arrive before the weekend. Terry had told her he was going to a weekend cattle auction with his father. Probably his letter would be waiting for him when they returned.

In bed, with the lights out, she imagined Terry reading the letter, imagined his joy. He would have rushed to the phone to call her, to tell her how much he loved her, how happy she had made him, that he would love her forever and ever. And wasn't Terry's happiness all she needed to be happy herself?

Rhonda had always wondered if Terry had ever read that letter. Had the housekeeper dropped it on the way from the mailbox to the house and a brisk Texas wind whisked it away? Had Terry already made his decision to marry Gina Kay and torn the letter into tiny pieces?

When her parents arrived in Austin to give Rhonda the news in person, she actually thought they were playing some sort of hideous joke on her. How could Terry be the love of her life one day and married to Gina Kay the next?

Eventually, Rhonda stopped missing Terry and Gina Kay's presence in her life, but the pain of their betrayal had never completely gone away. She just thought about it less and less over the years. But she had thought about it a lot in the months since Terry's death.

And now, if Gina Kay were true to her promise, she would explain how it was that she came to be married to Terry Lee Robertson. Not until the last day of their trip, she had said. Otherwise Rhonda might bolt and go home.

Their luggage had not all fit in the trunk, and the driver had put one of the larger suitcases on the front seat, which meant she had to share the backseat with both Holly and Gina Kay. Fortunately, Holly was sitting in the middle, and Rhonda was spared rubbing shoulders with Gina Kay. Even so, she pressed herself more firmly into her corner of the backseat and clasped her arms more tightly around her purse. Once physical contact among the three of them had been natural and comforting—holding hands or linking arms as they cut across fields to one another's houses or walked from the high school to the Shack for an after-school Coke. As they painted one another's toenails or fixed one another's hair. Backrubs were a given whenever they spent the night together, the three of them in a double bed.

She thought of the man on the airplane. Michael Forester. They had touched—mostly a brushing of elbows and hands. But it had been deliberate. And exciting.

What would it be like to have clandestine sex with a strange man for no other reason but the thrill of it? With no commitment? No future? Just wanton screwing? She had the feeling that Michael Forester knew well how to pleasure a woman and that part of the thrill for him would be making a woman tremble with desire, begging him to take her over the edge. Rhonda sucked in her breath at such thoughts. And felt a warm rush of arousal infiltrate her body.

She had planned to recount for Holly and Gina Kay her experience with the forward young man on the airplane and even rehearsed its telling in her mind as she exited the plane and walked toward baggage claim. An amusing anecdote to break the ice. But after Michael Forester came rushing up with her glasses case, she decided not to say anything about her in-flight flirtation. Was that in case she decided to slip off to meet him? Not to have sex, of course. Just for a cocktail or a cup of coffee. And experiencing a bit more titillation to make her feel sexy and young.

If Gina Kay had been sitting next to a forward young man on her flight, she could have arranged an assignation. Gina Kay was two months and one week a widow. And she hadn't exactly seemed prostrate with grief after the funeral. But then, one would hardly expect her to be tearing out her hair or beating on her chest. She had become much too refined for that.

So why had this refined lady agreed to appear at a second-rate beauty pageant, Rhonda wondered as the driver attempted to maneuver the car through the bottleneck of vehicles approaching the Queensboro Bridge. If Gina Kay were a former Miss America, it might be okay. But a former *Miss American Teenager*? Rhonda hadn't heard of the pageant in years, but then, she didn't keep up with such things. In fact, she hadn't been to a beauty pageant or watched one on television in all the years since that incredible summer when the three of them had pulled off a miracle of sorts.

Attending this year's pageant was just an excuse, of course, a way to get the three of them back to that time when their friendship was still a precious thing. And it had been precious, Rhonda acknowledged. Whenever she came across *Days of Our Lives* or *Guiding Light* on her television screen, she would pause a moment to remember how truly satisfying it had been to watch soap operas and eat potato chips with Mama Matthews and her two best friends in the whole world. Gina Kay had spoiled those memories. She had never been able to hate Terry, however, or to stop imagining a time in the indefinite future when she might see him again.

Surely, now that Terry was dead, Gina Kay didn't think the three of them were going to take up where they left off. *No way,* Rhonda told herself as the car finally reached the bridge She had agreed to come on this trip for one reason and one reason only: She wanted to fill in the missing pieces of a very old puzzle.

Of course, knowing how it was that Terry and Gina Kay came to be married wasn't going to change anything, but perhaps it would allow her finally to close the book, something she should have done years ago. Right now, though, what she needed most was for this long ride to end. She clutched her purse more closely to her chest. She was sorry she had agreed to the trip—*very sorry.* If she wanted to revisit New York, she should have come on her own.

But suddenly she realized that a magnificent view of the towers of midtown Manhattan was visible from the bridge. "Look!" she said.

She couldn't control the excitement in her voice as she pointed out the United Nations Building along the East River, the Chrysler Building with its stainless-steel pinnacle reflecting the sunlight, and the grand Empire State Building.

Holly began to sing, "New York, New York, what a wonderful town." Gina Kay joined in. Then Rhonda, too. And the driver.

Holly grabbed Rhonda and Gina Kay's hands, physically connecting the three them once again, which Rhonda endured for several heartbeats before discreetly pulling her hand away.

❦

"You look very nice," Gina Kay said.

Holly made a pirouette for Gina Kay's benefit, showing off the outfit she had created for her first evening in New York. The black, silk-faille pantsuit featured a fitted peplum that had a definite slimming effect. She had searched all over Waco for a pair of high-heeled sandals in which she could actually walk and the perfect scarf to add a dash of color.

Gina Kay was wearing the same tan pantsuit she had worn on the plane but had changed her black pullover for a silk animal-print blouse and her loafers for high-heeled mules. She was holding a cup of steaming coffee. Her cell phone was on the coffee table.

"Did you call Ann Marie?" Holly asked.

"Yes, I already miss her," Gina Kay said, then gestured toward a tiny kitchenette. "I made coffee. And there's beer, wine, and soft drinks in the refrigerator."

They were staying in a charming two-bedroom suite on the third floor of a small mansion-turned-hotel a block and a half east of Central Park. Gina Kay and Holly were sharing the larger bedroom, and Rhonda had the smaller bedroom and bath to herself. Between the bedrooms was a cozy sitting room, which, like the bedrooms, was furnished with period pieces and suitably worn Oriental rugs. A small fireplace with a brick hearth occupied one end of the sitting room and the kitchenette with folding louvered doors the other end. A spacious window seat was tucked under a panel of windows that wrapped around one corner of the room, with smaller window seats in both bedrooms. The windows were composed of small panes of wavy, vintage glass that made the street scene below look like a painting. Holly could only guess at how much their five-night stay was costing Gina Kay. If Holly had been paying her own way, she definitely would have found something less pricey.

She cranked open one of the windows and looked down through the treetops at the people and traffic below. Even on what was a quiet side street by New York standards, there were dozens of people on the sidewalks, some rushing, others strolling. A boy on a skateboard whizzed by. A clown on a bicycle wound his way through the cars waiting at the intersection. To her left, Holly could see the treetops of Central Park. To her right, according to the desk clerk, was Madison Avenue with its exclusive shops.

"I can't believe I'm really here," Holly said as she poured herself a cup of coffee. Before sitting down, she couldn't resist checking her appearance in the mirror over the sofa. Not bad, she decided.

She had other new outfits created just for this trip. And she'd had her lashes and brows dyed and treated herself to a manicure and pedicure. She wanted to look nice, not so much for Gina Kay and Rhonda, but for herself and the confidence it would bring her. A fashion editor at the *Dallas Morning News,* an old friend from her college days, had arranged for Holly to attend a couple of fashion shows—nothing major, just showings by a couple of the smaller houses specializing in evening wear—and given her the names of possible contacts at a couple of other establishments in the garment district. Holly hoped to glean some insights that would help her branch out a bit and not depend altogether on brides and beauty queens for her clients. She had even brought a portfolio of her designs with her on the outside chance someone in the know might be willing to take a look and offer a helpful critique.

Using the upcoming trip as an incentive, Holly had spent the last two months dieting. This time she had gone to a nutritionist. Of course, she already knew everything the woman told her about calories and fat content and portion size. She knew about eating slowly and being aware of every bite she put in her mouth. "You need to enjoy your meals and eat enough food that you don't feel hungry," the woman told her. "The key is not to eat food that makes you fat." She had made it seem so simple that Holly wanted to punch her.

Back in high school Holly sometimes wondered what in the hell she was doing hanging out with two girls who were sleek and slim. Rhonda and Gina Kay looked good in whatever they put on. They never knew what a sacrifice it was for Holly to always be compared to them.

Rhonda was also wearing the same pantsuit in which she had arrived but with a dressier blouse and shoes. Her silky brown hair was shorter than usual with a soft curl and bangs brushed to one side. The style made her looker younger and more carefree and accentuated her hazel eyes. And thanks to her dedication to running, Rhonda looked tan and quite fit. "You look like a fashion model," Holly told her.

If Rhonda thought Holly looked nice, she didn't say so. Rhonda had seemed preoccupied on the ride into town. She still seemed that way. Holly hoped a couple of drinks would loosen her up. Otherwise, it was going to be a long evening. A long five days.

When the driver dropped them off at the hotel, he had introduced himself as "G. W. Andropov," and informed them in heavily accented English that he was the most honest and reliable driver in New York City and had never had a ticket or been in an accident. Apparently Rhonda had engaged a car service for their entire stay, and the service was operated by a relative of Mr. Andropov's, who seemed to have appointed himself their designated driver. He had given each of them a business card and asked what time he should return.

And sure enough, when they walked out the entrance of the hotel, G. W. Andropov came driving up. Instead of the nondescript white vehicle he had been driving earlier, he was behind the wheel of a shiny black vintage Buick. Andropov jumped out of the car and opened the door for them. He was wearing a coat and tie with a pair of neatly pressed jeans. "The car of my uncle," he explained when Holly complimented him on the Buick.

Gina Kay got in the front seat, and Holly got in back with Rhonda. As they rolled away from the curb, Holly leaned forward and asked, "Hey, G.W., where are you from?"

The driver answered that he was from Krasnoyarsk, Siberia.

"I thought Siberia was a vast, uninhabited wasteland," Holly said.

"*Vasteland?* What is 'Vasteland'?" the driver demanded.

"Well, it's a place with not much of anything," Holly said. "You know, just snow and ice and political prisoners."

"No. My city is beautiful place. Tomorrow I bring pictures."

Suddenly Holly noticed a woman sitting on the sidewalk. She was wearing military camouflage clothing and a huge red picture hat decorated with vividly blue flowers and was surrounded by numerous bulging shopping bags. "Oh, my God," Holly excitedly. "It's a bag lady. A real live bag lady! The kids won't believe it."

Aware that G.W. was staring at her in his rearview mirror, Holly explained, "We don't have bag ladies in Waco."

"Where is this Vaco?" G.W. asked.

"Texas, honey. Deep in the heart of Texas. Tomorrow I bring pictures."

The second-floor bar Gina Kay had selected overlooked Times Square, a location that should help break the ice, Holly thought hopefully. They'd all seen the newsreel footage showing the square packed with people celebrating the end of World War II and had watched New Year's Eve celebrations there on television since they were little girls. And they'd all read how the area around the Times Square was once known for sex shops and prostitutes but was now respectable.

Holly looked out at the famous square with its huge billboards—one featured a frontal view of a hunk in designer briefs, with the bulge in his crotch as big as a car. The hunk was staring at an equally gigantic billboard across the square that showed the rump of a nubile young female wearing the same brand of briefs. "Remember the picture of that sailor kissing the nurse after World War Two?" Holly asked. "Can you imagine what it must have been like to be down there on that day? Such unbounded joy that they had all lived to see that hideous war end. I don't think there's a time in our own lives that would even begin to compare."

"No, nothing like that," Gina Kay agreed. "Perhaps the most glorious historic moment for our generation would be Neil Armstrong walking on the moon. We were just little kids, but I remember seeing him on television and then going outside and looking up at the real moon. It was mind-boggling to think that there were people walking around up there."

Holly waited for Rhonda to contribute to the conversation, but she simply took another sip of her drink.

"Or the Berlin Wall coming down," Holly added. "There was jubilation then but nothing like the end of World War Two."

"What about tomorrow?" Rhonda abruptly asked Gina Kay. "I guess you'll be tied up most of the day with rehearsal for tomorrow evening."

"Yes. You can spend the day shopping or sightseeing. Holly is going with me in the morning to check on my gown, then she has her own plans for the afternoon. I thought you both could join me backstage around five thirty to help me get ready. I was wondering if you would put my hair up, Rhonda. You were always so good at that. I think it's long enough for an upsweep."

Rhonda hesitated half a beat before saying "Sure," while continuing to stare down at Times Square. "There's probably no one moment or place to define it—unless it's Billy Jean King beating Bobby Riggs—but I'd like to think that the most historic thing our generation has lived through is the Women's Movement."

"But you have reservations?" Gina Kay asked.

"Well, I absolutely believe in equality, but it's never going to happen. I sometimes wonder if equality for women is counter to the survival of the species."

"How's that?" Holly asked.

"Well, you can't have a next generation without kids, and most of the mothering is still done by women, which means they are limited in the time and energy they can devote to their careers," Rhonda said with a shrug. "Maybe the demands placed on mothers is not a plot to keep women in their place, but the end result is still the same."

Holly nodded her agreement. "Sandy is good at teaching the kids how to throw a ball and carting them around, but I do all the rest. If I don't, I get punished. When I get home from this trip, there will be dirty clothes and dirty dishes everywhere."

"Do you still love Sandy?" Rhonda asked.

"Sure," Holly said. "He's a very lovable guy. But that doesn't mean he's perfect or that my marriage is perfect. Do you still love Dennis?"

"Sure," Rhonda said. "He's lovable, too. And he's wonderfully helpful around the house the little time he's at home. The thing about being married to a physician is how can you complain if they're off healing people. I know two young female physicians whose husbands stay at home and look after the kids. People make jokes about these men behind their backs, and their wives probably harbor deep-seated feelings of guilt. That's what does us women in, you know. The guilt. Our mothers sacrificed for us. Womanhood and self-sacrifice are supposed to be synonymous."

There was a pause while Holly and Rhonda waited for Gina Kay to say that Terry, too, had been lovable. When she didn't, Rhonda asked. "What about Terry? Of course, your marriage was different. You weren't pursuing a career. But did you find your marriage to him repressive or liberating?"

"Let's wait to talk about Terry," Gina Kay said.

"I'd rather do it now and clear the air," Rhonda said.

"And I would rather wait," Gina Kay told Rhonda, her tone pleasant but quite firm. "If we took care of that on the front end and it didn't go well, you'd pack up and leave. By waiting, I'm guaranteed time with both of you, which is very important to me."

Rhonda looked startled, and Holly had to suppress a smile. The Gina Kay Rhonda remembered had been more pliable, but over the years Gina Kay's backbone had turned to steel. Actually, Holly, too, would prefer they get the Terry business over with up front. Five days of this tension was not going to be pleasant.

Holly listened while Gina Kay asked Rhonda how she and Dennis had met and how old their children were. And she was relieved when Rhonda's answers were reasonably pleasant. Her motherly pride showed through as she talked about her twin sons.

Holly was curious as hell about what Gina Kay would say about Terry. Rhonda had always assumed that she knew how it was that Gina Kay came to be married to Terry, but Holly didn't have a clue. She had been as shocked as Rhonda when she learned that Gina Kay had packed up and gone home to Lamberton claiming she had mono when she hadn't been sick at all. Two days later, Holly had been at the library when Rhonda's folks drove over to give her the news. When Holly got back to the dorm, there was a note to her from Mrs. Hayes saying that Gina Kay and Terry had gotten married and Rhonda was very upset. They were taking her home for a few days while she got used to the idea. Holly read the note again and again. It made no sense. She was fairly certain that Rhonda had been sneaking off to see Terry on a regular basis. Why would he have up and married Gina Kay?

Later that same evening, Gina Kay called her. "Do you hate me?" she asked.

"No, but I imagine Rhonda does," Holly said. "Are you and Terry really married?"

"Yes."

"But why, Gina Kay? *Why?*"

"Because it was what we both needed to do. And that's all I'm ever going to say about it."

Gina Kay had been true to her word.

Holly had promised to stay in touch with Gina Kay, and she truly wanted them to stay friends. But Gina Kay was now a married woman. At night, she slept in the same bed as Terry. Holly hadn't a clue as to how to conduct a friendship with this reincarnated Gina Kay and kept putting off a visit. Finally, in February, when she drove home for her mother's birthday, she spent more than an hour in Mrs. Iverson's Gift Emporium trying to select a suitable wedding gift. At Mrs. Iverson's suggestion she finally decided on a pewter tray and watched while the shop owner wrapped the tray in white paper and tied it with a satin bow. Holly drove out to the ranch to make a call on Mrs. Terry Robertson. "I brought you a belated wedding present," she said when Gina opened the door. Then they sat in the stiff, formal living room that was exactly the same as it had been when Terry's mother died, and Gina Kay opened the present. A fire was burning in the massive stone fireplace, but the room had a chilly, unused feel about it.

"It's beautiful," Gina Kay said.

"I guess you don't do much entertaining yet," Holly said. Then she burst into tears.

Gina Kay knelt in front of her, and they hugged and cried together. "I've missed you so," Gina Kay said.

With the ice broken, Holly dropped by to see Gina Kay whenever she was in town. But for a long time, Holly didn't tell Rhonda that she and Gina Kay had reconnected. Then one day, Rhonda asked if she ever saw Gina Kay, and Holly confessed. "It must be hard for you, caught in the middle like that," Rhonda had said.

Now here the three of them were together once again, sitting in a New York bar and struggling to carry on a conversation when once they had been like three magpies.

Holly took a sip of her margarita and was surprised when the waiter put a second one beside her almost full glass. "From the gentleman at the bar," he explained. Holly glanced over at the bar where a nice-looking man with graying hair was looking her way. Surely the waiter had put the glass in front of the wrong woman. But Gina Kay was drinking wine, Rhonda a gin and tonic. "Well, what do you know!" Holly said. "That's a first. What do I do now?"

"Just smile and nod," Rhonda said, "then don't look his way again or he'll want to come sit with us."

Holly did as she was told. "I'm blushing all the way to my toes," she said, staring at the second margarita.

"I told you that you looked nice," Gina Kay said with a smile.

"Yes, you do," Rhonda agreed. "You've lost weight, haven't you. And I like your hair a bit longer. You look positively glamorous."

Holly felt prettier than she had in years. Maybe ever. She almost wished she could go sit with the admiring man at the bar instead of enduring the unease at their table.

*C*hapter ten

Traffic sounds from the street were becoming more demanding, and daylight was finally peeking around edges of the window shades, which were the old-fashioned parchment kind like the ones that had been on her bedroom windows back in Lamberton. There had been two windows with a dresser in between. A picture of Terry was on the dresser, a purple and white LHS pendant over the mirror.

Rhonda stretched in her bed and inhaled the aroma of coffee. *Good* coffee. Gina Kay had brought her own. Rhonda recalled how Gina Kay had been a coffee drinker even back in high school, when most of the kids got their caffeine fix from Cokes. She hadn't thought of that in years, of Gina Kay ordering a cup of coffee at the Shack. She drank it black.

An image flashed into Rhonda's mind of Gina Kay sitting in a booth right next to the big plate-glass window with the sunlight making a halo of her amazing golden hair. She wondered if Gina Kay drank coffee because at the Shack it was only a dime. The price was painted on the window in red letters: "Coffee 10¢." In her mental picture, Rhonda could see it written backward, right over Gina Kay's head. Holly would be sitting next to Gina Kay with Rhonda alone on the other side of the booth so there would be a place for Terry in case he came. Although most likely Terry would have been at ball practice, and someone else probably would have joined them in the booth or pulled chairs over to their table. Sometimes they squeezed three to a side. She imagined who else might have been with them. She had so many friends because of Gina Kay and Holly. Rhonda knew that she would have been feeling very happy sitting there. Completely happy. Those were wonderful times. Maybe her young life would have been just as good if her parents had retired in some other town, but she didn't think so. She'd been a weird bookworm of a kid before Lamberton. Every couple of years, her father would be stationed someplace else, which meant that she had to start over in a new school, and she was shy about making new friends. So books became her friends. Novels mostly. She read everything, going from Nancy Drew to Dickens as easily as she changed her shoes, but she'd never been any good at making flesh-and-blood friends.

Gina Kay and Holly had made it easy for her. They took her home with them like they would an abandoned puppy. She'd never had a best friend before. Now she had two. With Gina Kay and Holly as her best friends, she felt like she belonged. Or maybe because they were her friends, the other kids forgave her for always having the correct answer in class and being obsessive about her grades.

She had assumed that her friendship with Gina Kay and Holly would endure. BFF. *Best Friends Forever*. It took three to have a friendship like that. *A threefold cord is not quickly broken*. Where was that from? The Bible, Rhonda decided. Or maybe Shakespeare.

Holly was up now, too. Rhonda could hear the two of them out in the sitting room, talking softly so as not to wake her, having a cup of good coffee before dressing and heading out for their busy day. Holly was going with Gina Kay to the convention center this morning to unpack her evening gown and do any steaming that was necessary on it and the gown of the Texas contestant. Then she was going to a fashion show in Chelsea, and Gina Kay would spend the rest of the day with the contestants, attending their luncheon and press conference and rehearsing her part in the telecast.

Which left Rhonda on her own until the evening, a fact that had made sleep difficult. If she were a character in a novel, she would be an unsympathetic one. A sympathetic female character would not even consider a clandestine meeting with a man who wanted to have an affair with her, not when said female character had a husband who by all indications was a really good guy.

In the night, Rhonda had tried to convince herself that Dennis might have been unfaithful to her at some point in their marriage. He wasn't a hunk, but he was a pleasant-looking man with a flat stomach and an endearing grin. Everyone liked him—from the hospital custodians to the dean of medicine. How many times over the years had a patient, resident, student, colleague, friend, or acquaintance sought her out to tell her how much they admired her husband. Many of those admirers were female. Did Dennis ever step down off the pedestal that came with his profession for a roll in the hay with one of those admiring females? Opportunity abounded in his life. He had a built-in excuse for being gone at all hours of the day or night.

Around two AM, Rhonda had finally given up on falling asleep on her own and taken a sleeping pill. While she waited for it to take hold, she went through a list of possible candidates for Dennis's hypothetical infidelity. Which was insane. No wife in her right mind wanted her husband to stray. But if she could convince herself that Dennis had screwed around on her, she might then be able to find some justification in making a tit-for-tat decision to screw around on him.

Why did she even want to do such a thing? No matter how skillful Michael Forester might or might not be between the sheets, she would not go forth from such an encounter any younger or richer or more fulfilled, and she would probably like herself a hell of a lot less.

So why was her body on fire at the thought?

Holly had had an affair. Rhonda didn't know with whom. That

was the only time Holly had ever come to Rhonda's office in Dallas, when she came to ask for help. Rhonda hadn't asked why she needed an abortion, but apparently Holly thought she deserved some sort of explanation. Sandy had had a vasectomy, she said. The clinic insisted that someone had to accompany her when she had the "procedure," someone who would drive her home afterward and check on her throughout the next twenty-four hours. Rhonda wondered why Holly hadn't gone to Gina Kay for help but had actually been flattered that Holly had chosen her. The next day they had faced a gauntlet of antiabortion protesters singing hymns and waving posters with blown-up images of aborted fetuses. It had been ghastly. *Really* ghastly. By the time they got inside, Rhonda was shaking, and Holly was hysterical. She had clung to Rhonda like a terrified child, saying over and over again that she was so sorry. Rhonda couldn't decide if Holly was apologizing for the inconvenience she had caused or for having an affair and getting herself pregnant.

Rhonda believed in a woman's right to choose but had been eternally grateful that she herself had never had to go through with an abortion, eternally grateful to Dennis for giving her an out. Did she really want to be unfaithful to such a man?

Last night, over dinner at a swank restaurant, they had talked about their children. Rhonda was making a concerted effort to be less standoffish than she had been in the Times Square bar, but the pride and adoration in her voice came naturally as she talked about Scott and Jason and acknowledged that her twin sons had been the best part of her life.

She owed the best part of her life to Dennis.

The Terry fantasy had come less and less over the years, and when it came, it usually had them bumping into each other in Houston or Austin or San Antonio. They both would be away from home. Staying in hotels. It would just sort of happen. A one-time thing. Bittersweet because it would be that one last time for a lifetime. She had never wanted to divorce Dennis and marry Terry. She just wanted to have Terry in her arms one last time. And to know that she had been the great love of his life and whatever his reason was for marrying Gina Kay, it had been a mistake and he had never stopped loving her. Was that what she wanted from Gina Kay, to learn that Terry had lived out his life filled with regret? No, not *filled* with regret. She wouldn't have wanted him to be miserable. She hoped he loved his children and took plea-sure in being a father. She would have liked to know, however, that he thought about her from time to time and had *some* regret and had dreamed of seeing her once again. But would Gina Kay have a clue about how Terry felt?

Gina Kay was Rhonda's only link to Terry, however, her only chance to glimpse into his mind and understand the past.

Last night at the restaurant, when it came Gina Kay's turn to talk about her children, she had spoken of them lovingly. "Mitch and Kelly both have a scholarly bent—like you, Rhonda. I think about you when they come up with some obscure piece of knowl-edge to make their point. And they love horses and the outdoors. And they both loved the rodeo. Mitch participated in calf roping and saddle-bronc riding. When Kelly won a state championship in barrel racing, I thought Terry was going explode with pride. Now Kelly and Mitch are both serious young adults determined to make the world a better place. After she graduates from UT, Kelly plans to spend a couple of years in the Peace Corps as sort of a payback for being raised rich and privileged. Mitch wants to help farmers and ranchers hang on to their land and learn how to take better care of it." Then Gina Kay paused, and the expression on her face softened. "As for Ann Marie, she came along at a time of great need in my life. She is probably not as precocious as her brother and sister, and she is afraid of horses. But she is a precious little soul and has filled my heart."

Rhonda wanted to hear more about Ann Marie—Terry's little

Sunshine—and the "time of great need" in Gina Kay's life, but Gina Kay was already asking Holly when Melissa was going to come to stay with them again. Apparently the girls got along well, and Melissa was in love with the Shetland pony that Ann Marie refused to ride.

From children, the conversation turned to the restaurant's decor.

All around the room, huge beveled mirrors in massive frames were mounted high on the walls, tilting outward so that they reflected a bird's-eye view of the diners below. And they reflected candlelight. Every surface in the room was covered with lighted candles—the tables, the bar, the tops of cabinets. Hundreds of candles, with the mirrors reflecting all that flickering candlelight, as well as the other mirrors as they all reflected flickering candlelight into infinity. The effect was dazzling. While Gina Kay and Holly discussed how they might strive for such an effect on a smaller scale in their own dining rooms, Rhonda found herself imagining what it would be like to dine with Michael Forester in this fantastic, mirrored room, at one of the smaller, more intimate tables so that their knees would touch. They would order this same marvelous wine with the candlelight reflecting in the crystal goblets. Would he call her "lovely" again?

Holly interrupted her fantasy with a snap of her fingers. "Hey, Rhonda," she had said, "come on back and join the party."

Rhonda had mumbled something about being tired then excused herself and headed for the ladies' room. She could almost imagine Gina Kay and Holly discussing how distracted she seemed. She patted her flushed face with a damp paper towel and made her decision. She would call Michael Forester in the morning to invite him to breakfast. Just for the fun of it. It would be no different from the innocent flirtations she sometimes indulged in at cocktail parties, when her husband was probably on the other side of the room doing exactly the same thing. She understood how Holly had felt earlier at the Times Square bar, when the man bought her a drink and thereby had given her that absolutely delicious moment of realizing that a man other than her own husband found her attractive and desirable.

When they walked out of the restaurant, G. W. Andropov pulled up in the Buick and jumped out to open the door for them. Holly got in the front seat with G.W. Rhonda watched out the window as he gave them a dazzling nighttime tour of midtown and lower Manhattan but only half listened to his commentary. It had been a long day, and she was ready to be alone with her thoughts.

Holly and Gina Kay lingered in the sitting room, turning on CNN to catch up on the news of the day. Rhonda had said good night and gratefully closed the door behind her.

Now it was morning. Day two of their five-day trip. Rhonda stretched and looked at the clock on the bedside table. It was twenty minutes after eight, and G. W. Andropov was supposed to pick up Holly and Gina Kay at eight thirty. Surely they were about to leave. She wanted them gone. Wanted to make her phone call.

She wondered if Holly had ever had another affair or if it was just that one time. She had realized later that the reason Holly had not asked Gina Kay to accompany her to the abortion clinic was because Gina Kay's mother was dying. Grotesque, beloved Mama Matthews. Holly said she had weighed less than a hundred pounds when she died after a long battle with diabetes. Rhonda had sent an expensive floral tribute and received a proper, handwritten thank-you note from Gina Kay's daughter Kelly.

Rhonda swung her feet out of the bed and sat looking at her reflection in the bureau mirror. Her hair was tousled, the strap of her nightgown hanging from one shoulder. In the dim light, she looked pretty damned good. Like a woman who had just been laid.

I just want to experience that same high again that I felt on the airplane, she told herself. *I don't have to go to bed with him for that.*

As soon as she was certain that Gina Kay and Holly had left, she called the hotel where Michael Forester was staying and asked to be connected to his room. He answered on the first ring. "Is this who I think it is?" he asked.

Startled, she asked, "Just who do you think it is?"

"Rhonda from the plane. I was just lying here hoping you would call. Tell me, lovely Rhonda, what is your pleasure?"

Her heart was pounding. *Really* pounding. She tried to sound casual as she said, "Breakfast. I was thinking about bagels and coffee in a park. Actually, I am not too far from Central Park."

As soon as she put down the receiver, she heard her cell phone ringing in her purse. Her home phone number appeared on the phone's tiny screen. *Dennis.* She felt as though she'd been caught in the act.

She let it ring and headed for the bathroom. Later, wrapped in a towel, she played back Dennis's message: "I kept hoping you would call last night. The house is empty without you. I love you. Take care."

She sighed and planted a light kiss on the phone. "I love you, too, my darling. Really I do."

Then she looked at her watch and considered calling her parents. It was two hours earlier in Arizona, but they were early risers. She didn't want to talk to her parents either, however. If they needed to get in touch with her, they knew her cell phone number and where she was staying in New York.

Since she'd learned of her mother's stroke, whenever she saw their phone number on the caller-ID screen, fear would grip her heart like a vice. She hated that.

And there were those other thoughts that had crept into her

mind. Sands-through-the-hour-glass kind of feelings. She'd thought of the line from the Robert Herrick poem: *Gather ye rosebuds while ye may.*

Was that what this Michael Forester thing was all about? Her growing awareness of the finiteness of passion and possibilities?

She took great pains with her makeup and slipped into gray slacks and a hot pink blouse with a matching sweater draped over her shoulders. After leaving the hotel, she walked west to Fifth Avenue, then south on the broad, shaded sidewalk that skirted the park. She could see the park's lushness over a stone wall. A forest, lakes, and rolling meadow in the middle of the city. A magnificent city. A glorious day. And she liked herself in pink.

Michael Forester was waiting for her by the statue of General Sherman in the plaza just outside the park, as he said he would be.

⟨⟩

That evening, G. W. Andropov pulled up in front of the hotel promptly at five fifteen. A handsome coffee-table book entitled *Spectacular Siberia* awaited Holly and Gina Kay in the backseat.

"Where is other lady?" he demanded.

"She can look at the book later," Holly assured him.

"Open page twenty," he commanded. "What do you see? *Tomatoes*. Beautiful tomatoes. You think tomatoes grow in vasteland. Now look page twenty-seven, twenty-eight, twenty-nine. That is my city. Real city, yes. Not vasteland."

Holly had to work hard not to giggle.

"It's a very nice city," Gina Kay said, taking charge of turning the pages.

"Hey, G.W., what about page fifty-two?" Holly asked. "You've got to admit that there is a lot of snow and ice in Siberia."

"Not important," he said. "Look at other pages."

"Do you still have family there?" Holly asked.

"Yes. Some family there. More family here. My wife and daughter are here. And my brother and his family. My brother has Russian restaurant. Best Russian food in New York City."

"Really?" Gina Kay said. "You'll have to take us there."

"Here's the only picture I have with me of Waco," Holly said, handing G.W. a picture of her three children standing in front of the Baylor University football stadium. "You'll just have to trust me that there are no bag ladies. Those are my kids."

At the convention center, Gina Kay and Holly were shown to a tiny dressing room. At least she had a space of her own, Holly thought. She remembered how contestants had to make do in a huge dressing area filled with fifty mirrored dressing tables and chaos. "You get settled in," Holly said. "I need to go check in with Miss Texas and make sure her gown arrived okay."

Holly found the Texas contestant and her mother both in tears. The girl's name, incredibly, was Tamara Truehart. She came from Beaumont, which was located in the southeastern-most corner of Texas where the culture and drawl were more reflective of the Old South than the Old West. Tamara had blond hair and blue eyes and was just pleasingly plump enough to remind one of a delectably ripe peach. Except this ripe peach of a girl was now sporting on her right shoulder one of the most impressive hickeys Holly had ever seen.

"You should have left your boyfriend back in Beaumont," Holly said.

"What are we going to do?" her mother wailed. Mrs. Truehart was an older version of Tamara. She was wearing a celery-colored Armani pantsuit. Her shoes and bag were equally impressive.

"I've got industrial-strength cover-up here in my bag of tricks," Holly said, patting the canvas bag she always carried with her to pageants and weddings. Along with the makeup, it contained sewing supplies, mending tape, a glue gun, aspirin, Midol, fake fingernails, nail file, scissors, antiseptic ointment, Band-Aids, Kotex, hand-held steamer, and spot remover.

"She has to have her picture taken in her bathing suit this afternoon," Mrs. Truehart said, blowing her nose.

"I'll show you how to apply the cover-up," Holly promised, then explained that no, she could not hang around to apply it herself. No way was she going to miss the fashion show in Chelsea to work on Tamara's hickey. She did, however, spend almost an hour steaming Tamara's gown, which looked like it was straight out of *Gone With the Wind*, complete with hoopskirt and endless ruffles. A first for Holly, but spoiled, pouty Tamara Truehart was a blond Scarlett. No question about it.

The dress she'd designed for Gina Kay was simple and elegant. Made of heavy Venetian needlepoint lace, it had long fitted sleeves, with a V-neck in front and a V in back that plunged almost to Gina Kay's waist. It had traveled much better than Tamara's dress. Holly touched it lovingly. If she lost ten more pounds, she might be able to pull off a dress like this, but she'd settle for getting her butt into a pair of size ten jeans.

With everything under control at the arena, Holly called G.W. on his cell phone and went to wait for him at the front entrance to the arena. When he arrived, she got in the front seat. "Tell me about your daughter's wedding," she said.

Chapter eleven

A uniformed security guard scanned a list of people who were approved to go backstage and carefully studied Rhonda's driver's license to assure that she was really the person she claimed to be. After he had scrutinized the contents of her purse, the young man gave her directions to Gina Kay's dressing room. "Is your daughter in the pageant?" he asked.

"No," she answered, "but a friend of mine is on the program." Then she felt a wave of irritation that she had said such a thing. Gina Kay wasn't a friend. She was a *former* friend.

As she hurried down the tunnel-like hallway, Rhonda glanced at her watch. She had let the time get away from her and raced back to the hotel to change clothes for this evening. She was only a few minutes late, though. There was still plenty of time to fix Gina Kay's hair.

Which she did not want to do.

Rhonda had gotten quite proficient at fixing Gina Kay's hair during their pageant days. Gina Kay usually wore it down for the bathing suit competition and in a loose ponytail when she did her dramatic reading, but the three of them were in agreement that a graceful upsweep was more appropriate for the evening gown competition. An upsweep showed off Gina Kay's slender neck and made her look regal, like a beautiful queen awaiting her crown. Rhonda remembered how it felt to bury her hands in all that luxuriant, silky hair. She had put it up loosely with a soft, slightly puffy look and used a curling iron to finish it off with a few spiraling tendrils for softness. Often when she was done, she would hug Gina Kay from behind and smile at their two young faces in the mirror. A moment of friendship. And love.

Now Rhonda was put off by the thought of touching Gina Kay's hair, of physical contact with a woman she had hated for almost twenty-five years. Other than a perfunctory hug after Terry's funeral and a quick brushing of cheeks yesterday at the airport, Rhonda hadn't touched her since the day Gina Kay packed up her belongings and left Austin. Holly and Rhonda both had labs scheduled that Friday afternoon. Apparently Gina Kay had planned to pack up and sneak away without good-byes. But Rhonda had come back earlier, in case Terry called. When she opened the door, Gina Kay was standing in the middle of the dorm room holding a large box, an open door revealing the empty interior of her closet, her bed stripped.

"What's going on?" Rhonda demanded.

"I'm leaving."

"Leaving? I don't understand. Why are you leaving? Where are you going?"

"I left a note," Gina Kay said, nodding at an envelope on Rhonda's desk. "It's to you and Holly. I've got to go. My daddy is waiting for me."

"Aren't you coming back?" Rhonda asked incredulously.

"No, I can't," she said, looking away. Not meeting Rhonda's gaze.

Gina Kay started for the door. "I don't understand," Rhonda protested. Then realizing that Gina Kay really was leaving, reached out to her, and with Gina Kay still holding the box, managed a clumsy embrace.

"When will we see you again?" Rhonda asked.

"I don't know," Gina Kay said and hurried out the door.

Rhonda watched out the second-floor window as Gina Kay climbed into her father's ancient pickup truck and rode away, her possessions piled in the back.

The note had said she was going home to recuperate from mono and would not be coming back to school. She wasn't cut out to be a college student after all.

Gina Kay really didn't have mono. The note had been written to buy time. If she had said she planned to marry Terry, Rhonda might have tried to stop her.

Rhonda had tried to call Terry that night to make sure he had really gone to San Antonio. The Mexican housekeeper said that he had. Which was true. Only he had gone with Gina Kay and not his father, and it was his honeymoon.

The door to the dressing room was ajar. When Rhonda pushed it open, she immediately noticed three things. The tiny room was full of flowers. Holly wasn't there yet. And Gina Kay's hair was already in a soft upsweep.

"I could tell you really didn't want to deal with my hair," Gina Kay said, looking at Rhonda's reflection in her dressing table mirror.

"Where's Holly?" Rhonda asked, almost in a panic. She didn't want to be alone with Gina Kay.

Gina Kay turned around, her arm over the back of her chair. "She is helping the Texas contestant get ready. Wait until you see the girl's dress. It is really incredible. A number of the contestants have asked Holly for her business card."

"What's with all the flowers?" Rhonda asked, still standing in the doorway.

Gina Kay explained that the huge mixed bouquet in the corner was from the pageant board of directors. The large arrangement of gladiola was from the Miss American Teenager–Texas pageant directors. Holly had sent the tulips. The nosegay of violets on the dressing table was from their driver, G. W. Andropov. And the red roses came from her son, Mitch, the yellow roses from her daughter Kelly.

"Probably you should have brought your children with you

instead of Holly and me," Rhonda said, moving a three-legged stool to the corner of the room before she sat down.

"Oh, Mitch and Kelly are slightly embarrassed that their mother was once a beauty queen. Kelly especially, who correctly believes that beauty pageants only serve to objectify women. Of course, Ann Marie thinks it's wonderful, but she's only eight. I just talked to Ann Marie," Gina Kay said with a soft smile. "Several of her friends are spending the night with her. They're going to have a pageant watch party."

Then Gina Kay turned her head from side to side. "Does my hair look okay? I decided that tendrils were too youthful."

"Probably so," Rhonda agreed, wishing Holly would return.

Gina Kay stood and removed the protective makeup cape from her shoulders. "What do you think of the dress Holly designed for me?"

"It's stunning," Rhonda acknowledged.

"You're sorry you came, aren't you?"

Rhonda was spared an answer when Holly came through the door. "Hey, none of that, you guys. Let's play this thing out then see how we feel. I'm kind of excited about it actually. It's like a board game. If we play by the rules, Gina Kay will solve the mystery at the end of the game."

Then Holly tugged on Rhonda's sleeve. "Come on, there's sandwiches and beverages down in the big room. Let's go get some food and bring it back here. Then we can go out for a real dinner after the pageant. I'm actually kind of excited about the competition. Tamara won the swimsuit competition this afternoon. Maybe buxom is coming back in vogue. Wouldn't it be something if she made the finals? Of course, if she does, she'll have to answer one of those awful questions."

Then Holly, affecting a broad, toothy grin and holding an imaginary microphone, launched into an imitation of Danny Boyd, the television game show host who was serving as the pageant's master of ceremonies. "Miss Texas, what do you believe is the solution for hunger worldwide?"

Then, using a youthful, slightly breathless voice, Holly answered, "Why, I think the world needs more grocery stores. If we build grocery stores close to where hungry people live, they will have a place to buy food and won't need to go hungry anymore."

Gina Kay laughed. Rhonda stood and headed for the door.

"Gina Kay's hair looks nice," Holly said as they walked down the hall.

"She fixed it herself," Rhonda said.

"You okay?"

"Sure."

"No you're not," Holly said, taking her arm. "What did you do today?"

"Wandered around. Shopped."

"I thought maybe you were going off to meet the hunk from the airplane."

Rhonda's heart took a lurch. "What in the world made you think a thing like that?" she demanded.

"Just the way you looked when he came rushing up to you at the airport yesterday. I thought to myself, now there's a lady in heat."

"I am a happily married woman," Rhonda said firmly.

"Me, too," Holly said. "But even the happiest of marriages has its rocky places. That's when we get ourselves into trouble, when we're crawling across those damned rocks."

While they were gathering up snacks in the big room, several contestants approached Holly wanting to know if she was really the person who made Miss Texas's gown and how could they get in touch with her. Holly would point out that she was the person who *designed* the dress and her seamstresses actually *made* it. She seemed almost reluctant about giving them her business cards. "I'm probably doomed to spend the rest of my life dealing with beauty queens and brides," she told Rhonda as she piled finger sandwiches onto a Styrofoam plate.

"How was the style show?" Rhonda asked.

"Weird!" Holly said gleefully. "Weird location—in a creepy old church. Weird food. Weird models. Weird fashions. Weird spectators." Then she turned to face Rhonda. "And it was *wonderful*. Absolutely *wonderful*! Can you image having the freedom to push the envelope? To experience the joy of designing clothes for grown-up women who leave their mothers at home?"

"Sounds like you need a change," Rhonda said.

"Only if I can accomplish it without financial risk," Holly said.

Back in the dressing room, Holly produced a bottle of wine and corkscrew from her canvas bag. "Have you talked to Dennis?" Holly asked Rhonda as she removed the cork.

Rhonda shook her head. "We've been playing telephone tag," she said, which was sort of the truth. She had returned Dennis's phone call but had deliberately done so during clinic hours when she knew he wouldn't be taking calls. "What about you?" she asked. "Have you talked to Sandy?"

"Yes. Nothing but chaos on the home front, which is normal."

After they'd finished their snack, the three of them made their way to the pressroom, where Gina Kay and Miss Texas were to be interviewed by a stringer for the Texas News Network. When the young woman realized that the same person had created both Gina Kay and Tamara's gowns, she turned her attention to Holly and, at the end of the interview, insisted that Holly be photographed with them. Rhonda watched as the reporter and photographer decided how to pose their subjects. They asked Holly to sit on a tall stool and positioned Gina Kay to her right and Tamara to her left. Tamara was a bit disgruntled over having to share the spotlight, but she managed a brilliant smile when the photographer raised her camera. Gina Kay put her arm around Holly's shoulders.

As Holly and Rhonda made their way to the auditorium, Holly called home to make sure her daughter hadn't forgotten about tonight's telecast and knew which channel to watch. The show opened with all fifty contestants being introduced and parading up and back on the runway. Then the young women arranged themselves onstage and sang a jazzed up version of "Danny Boy" by way of introducing the master of ceremonies. Danny Boyd came bounding onto the stage to welcome the national television audience and gush about the beautiful, talented teens grouped behind him, any one of whom would be a worthy Miss American Teenager. Then, after a drum role, Danny proceeded to announce in alphabetical order by states the names of the ten semifinalists. Holly and Rhonda both applauded loudly when the ninth name he called was "Tamara Truehart, Miss American Teenager–Texas."

After Danny Boyd gushed a bit over the ten excited semifinalists, they were hurried offstage to change for the talent competition, and it was time for him to introduce Gina Kay.

"In honor of the twenty-fifth anniversary of her reign as Miss American Teenager," he began, "we have invited as our special guest, Gina Kay Matthews Robertson, of Lamberton, Texas, who will in turn introduce our current Miss American Teenager on the last night of her reign."

Then switching to an almost reverent tone, Boyd announced, "The Miss American Teenager Pageant board of directors has voted to honor Mrs. Robertson tonight for the exemplary job she has done of living up to the Miss American Teenager ideal of service, education, and family."

Rhonda looked at Holly, who shook her head. She hadn't realized either that Gina Kay was being given an award.

After explaining that Gina Kay had been recently widowed after almost twenty-five years of marriage and was the mother of three children, Boyd enumerated her accomplishments. Rhonda was surprised to learn that Gina Kay had earned a degree in social work from a small college about a hundred miles from Lamberton and was currently a member of the college's board of regents. That she served on the boards of numerous civic and cultural organizations, including the Waco Symphony and a state program that promoted adult literacy, and was a founding board member of another state program designed to keep teenage mothers in school. That she also served on the national board of an organization that advocated the humane treatment of agricultural animals and was cochair of a national task force dedicated to saving family farms. And she was spearheading efforts in her hometown to add on to the library, restore the county courthouse, and plant one hundred trees in the courthouse square and along the town's main street.

Then Danny Boyd stood very straight and said in his most formal voice, "Ladies and Gentlemen, it is with great pleasure that I present Gina Kay Matthews Robertson, the winner of the first annual Miss American Teenager Exemplary Achievement Award." One of the nonfinalist contestants stepped forward to hand him a handsome plaque.

"You didn't tell me that she had done all those things," Rhonda whispered.

"I didn't know about most of them myself," Holly whispered back. "And besides, I don't tell Gina Kay stuff about you, and I don't tell you stuff about her. I'm the one walking the tightrope, remember."

Rhonda joined in the applause as Gina Kay walked to center stage. She did look lovely, Rhonda had to acknowledge, like Grace Kelly before she became matronly. She smiled graciously as Boyd handed her the plaque. Then she stepped to the microphone and formally thanked the board of directors for the award. Boyd carried the plaque offstage, as she continued her remarks.

"I'm delighted to return to the Miss American Teenager pageant, which opened up possibilities in my own life and those of so many other young women. Even though I waited several years to use the scholarship money that came with my title, I did eventually earn a college education and fulfill a promise I had made to my mother. I have visited with many of this year's contestants, who look forward to the educational opportunities provided by the Miss American Teenager Pageant. Miss Colorado plans to go to medical school. Miss New Jersey wants to earn a degree in archaeology. Miss California already has completed a year of college and is on her way to a degree in occupational therapy. Other contestants plan to be teachers, health care workers, and pursue a variety of other fulfilling careers. And the young woman who has carried the Miss American Teenager title over the past year will begin her studies at the University of Oklahoma next fall, launching an academic journey that will lead to a degree in Native American studies and a life of service to her tribe and community. Over the last year, she has visited with young people in over one hundred Native American communities all over the country and told them they can best honor their families and tribes by staying in school. It is with great pleasure that I present Miss American Teenager Phyllis Running Bear of Deer Creek, Montana. Please help me congratulate her on the final night of her outstanding reign."

Rhonda was stunned by what had just taken place. More than stunned. Almost angry. She found herself only half watching as the first semifinalist tap-danced to a medley of show tunes. Gina Kay was not an uneducated nobody from no place. Rhonda had always assumed that any woman who opted for life in a town like Lamberton would be burying herself alive. Did that mean that she herself should have married Terry after high school? But just because Gina Kay made the most of what she was given didn't mean that Rhonda herself would have done likewise. Damn, it was all so confusing. She didn't want to admire Gina Kay. Hating her had become so ingrained.

Finally, with a headache threatening, she forced the tumultuous thoughts away from Gina Kay and tuned into what was happening on the stage. The contestant from West Virginia was yodeling. Then Miss Wisconsin performed a gymnastics routine, and Miss Georgia and Miss Utah each sang an operatic aria. Several semifinalists sang pop tunes. And finally Tamara—wearing a red, white, and blue dress—accompanied herself on the piano as she sang a rousing rendition of Woody Guthrie's "This Land Is Your Land." What Tamara lacked in talent, she made up for with enthusiasm.

And low and behold, Tamara was selected as one of the six finalists. Holly and Rhonda both clapped enthusiastically. The six young women reappeared in a surprisingly short time in their evening gowns to nervously await the all-important question— their last chance to make an impression on the judges.

When Tamara's turn came, Danny Boyd said, "That is a very beautiful dress. You look like a Southern belle."

"Well, sir," Tamara answered in a decidedly Southern drawl, "I come from Beaumont, Texas, which is just twenty miles from the Louisiana line. But even though our accents are Southern and our trees have Spanish moss and our ladies pour tea from sterling-silver teapots, deep in our hearts, we are true, blue Texans."

Danny smiled his toothy smile, then said, "Miss Texas, are you ready for your question?"

"Yes, sir, I am ready."

"If you had to choose between winning a million-dollar lottery and being named Miss American Teenager, which would you choose?"

Tamara took a deep breath, and with her hands folded demurely at her waist, said, "Well, Mister Boyd, I would choose the Miss American Teenager title because it would give me the opportunity to speak with other young people all over our great land and enlist their help in the war against drug and alcohol abuse. I have seen firsthand in my own high school and even among my own circle of friends the devastation that drugs and alcohol can bring, and I promised myself that if I were so fortunate as to win the Miss American Teenager title, I would select preventing drug and alcohol abuse as my national platform."

"Not bad," Holly whispered admiringly.

"I think she's going to win," Rhonda said.

Rhonda was right. When her name was called, Gina Kay and Phyllis Running Bear came forward to set the glittering tiara on Tamara's head and place the bouquet of long-stemmed roses in her arms. And even if her heart was Texan, in her magnificent gown she did look every inch a Southern belle as she took her victory walk down the runway, throwing kisses, shedding the obligatory tears of joy.

"How does it feel to have designed the victory gown?" Rhonda asked as they made their way backstage.

"Like I need to hire a couple more seamstresses," Holly said. "But Sandy and I will probably be able to send our kids to any college that accepts them."

"Then what?" Rhonda asked.

"What do you mean?"

"After the kids have left home, then what?"

"Melissa is only ten. It's going to be a while. Any words of advice from a woman who is already there?"

But they arrived at Gina Kay's dressing room, and Rhonda was spared an answer. Holly packed Gina Kay's gown while she changed into a simple red silk dress with a matching fringed stole. "I just talked to G.W.," Gina Kay said. "He's waiting out front. We have reservations at Tavern on the Green."

Rhonda was a bit surprised when Holly insisted they take the flowers with them and asked two of the stagehands to help carry them. "They'll just be thrown away, and that would a shame," Gina Kay said from behind the bouquet of yellow roses. "I hope we can fit them all in G.W.'s car.

"He said his wife and her sister were going to watch the pageant tonight," Gina Kay continued. "They live in Brighton Beach, in south Brooklyn. It's a whole community of Russian immigrants with Russian stores, beauty shops, restaurants, and nightclubs. New Yorkers refer to it as Little Odessa. I want him to take us there after we eat. In fact, I asked him to invite his wife to join us at her cousin's nightclub."

"Sounds like you're now lifelong friends with the guy," Rhonda observed.

"I invited him to Texas," Gina Kay said. "He thinks he might want to live there someday. He would like to grow things. I told him I could spare a few acres."

"You are kidding, aren't you?" Rhonda said.

"Not really. I doubt if he'll ever leave New York and the extensive Russian community here, but if he wants to try Texas, I'd be willing to help him."

"What would your family think about that?" Rhonda wanted to know.

"Well, since my husband is dead and my two older children no longer live in Lamberton, I pretty much answer to myself. Actually, I have been in charge at the ranch for years."

Rhonda wanted to ask what Terry's position had been if Gina Kay was the one in charge, but she shied away from mentioning his name. "What about Mr. Robertson?"

"Ward is my friend and staunchest ally."

All these years Rhonda had assumed that Gina Kay was living the life of a homebound, docile housewife as she saw to the needs of her husband, put up with a grumpy father-in-law, and raised countrified children. Apparently she had been incorrect in those assumptions. What if she now discovered that Terry and Gina Kay had been deeply in love and gloriously happy? How would that make her feel?

Chapter twelve

G.W. was waiting by the Buick. He helped them load the flowers then headed for the hotel, where Gina Kay asked the doorman to see that the floral arrangements, the suitcase with her pageant attire, and Holly's canvas tote were taken up to their suite. Gina Kay got into the front seat next to G.W., and he headed for the restaurant.

Looking out the window of the fine old automobile, Holly thought of all those movies and television programs she'd seen over the years that were set in New York. None of them had even come close to capturing the feel of actually being here. No Texas city, not even Dallas or Houston, could even begin to duplicate the stream of humanity flowing through man-made canyons illuminated by endless light displays and serenaded by such a jumble of sounds. Even at this hour, the traffic was as congested as at midday and the sidewalks just as full.

Last night after dinner, G.W.'s introductory tour of Manhattan had included Chinatown and other ethnic neighborhoods—Ukrainian, West Indian, East Indian, Greek, and Jewish Orthodox. Store signs often were written in languages other than English. Voices were speaking these languages. Tonight, at Gina Kay's request, they were going to visit Little Odessa. An incredible city, Holly acknowledged with awe. She could see why Rhonda had been tempted to finish law school here all those years ago.

Holly leaned forward and tapped G.W. on the shoulder. "You know, in Waco, people are usually in bed at this hour, and we're just now going out to dinner. So are lots of other folks apparently.

Or maybe they're going drinking and dancing. Wherever they're going, they're going there later than we do in Waco, Texas. What about your town in Siberia, G.W.?" she asked. "Is there much nightlife there?"

"*Nightlife*? I like that word," he said. "In Siberia not so much nightlife. In my city, friends come together in homes to eat and drink. Most people have no money for restaurants and bars. Here in America, Russian people have more money. In Brighton Beach, Russian people like nightlife."

"Tell us about your daughter," Holly requested. "Do she and her boyfriend go out at night?"

G.W. explained that Tatiana and her boyfriend often spent time with friends and family in the back room of her uncle's restaurant but also went to concerts and movies and nightclubs when they had the time. There was pride in his voice as G.W. told them about his daughter, who waited tables and cleaned apartments during the day and went to college at night. In two more years, she would have a degree in chemical engineering and work for an important American company and make enough money to buy a house with a yard in Brooklyn. Her fiancé also worked two jobs and went to school at night. To art school. He was going to be a great artist and have his paintings in the Metropolitan Museum of Art, and someday there would be a grand exhibition in a museum in Moscow or St. Petersburg honoring him.

It was Rhonda who asked about Tatiana's wedding plans. Holly was pleased to be spared from bringing up the topic herself. She had already quizzed G.W. a bit about the wedding but wanted Rhonda and Gina Kay to think that what she had in mind was at least partly their idea. Holly knew that G.W.'s wife wanted their daughter to get married in a very beautiful dress and have a wedding with flowers and candles. But, as G.W. explained, Tatiana was twenty-eight years old and had a "hard head." She had decided it was more important to have a nice party for the wedding guests than to have a very beautiful dress and flowers.

Throughout her busy day, Holly had found herself thinking about Tatiana's wedding. Even though she was burned out on wedding dresses, Holly had a love-hate relationship with weddings in general. They were too expensive and in no way assured happily ever after, but they always made her sentimental. Females, it seemed, were born with a genetic predisposition to wanting all the traditional trappings when they said "I do." Even twenty-eight-year-old women with a hard head. In response to Rhonda's question, G.W. explained that his daughter's wedding would be day after tomorrow, in the evening, but he would arrange to have a substitute driver for them.

"No, that's not what I meant," Rhonda said. "I was curious about the wedding itself."

Tatiana and her fiancé would say their vows at city hall, G.W. told her, followed by a meal for family members and friends at the restaurant of his brother.

"Tatiana is such a pretty name," Rhonda commented.

"Yeah," Holly agreed. "I love the way it kind of rolls off the tongue. What does Tatiana look like? Is she tall or short? Is she slender like Gina Kay and Rhonda or not so slender like me?"

"Skinny girl. Not tall, not short," G.W. replied.

"What will she wear when she gets married?" Holly asked.

G.W. shrugged. "Her most good dress, I think."

"You know, G.W.," Holly said, trying to sound as though an idea just popped into her head, "Gina Kay wore a very beautiful dress tonight at the pageant. I designed it for her. That's what I do, design beautiful dresses for brides and for girls who compete in beauty pageants. Gina Kay's dress is floor-length and made of ivory lace and would make a perfect wedding dress. All I would have to do is come up with some sort of veil. And you saw all those flowers we left at the hotel. They'll still be fresh and pretty day after tomorrow. I think that Gina Kay and Rhonda and I should make a beautiful wedding for your daughter that she will remember all of her life."

"In her heart, every girl wants a beautiful wedding," Gina Kay said, glancing over her shoulder to give Holly a nod of support.

"No," G.W. said firmly. "I cannot pay for this dress."

"But you can *borrow* it," Holly said. "Just for one night. No need to pay. Gina Kay is going to take it back to Texas and probably will never wear it again. This beautiful dress will just hang in her closet, and it really should be worn. My mother always said that it was bad luck for a dress to be worn only once," she improvised. "And it would be a shame for those flowers to die up there in our hotel room when they could be used for a wedding. How big is the back room at her uncle's restaurant? Maybe they could get married there instead of city hall."

"Is room for many people," G.W. said. "But Tatiana and Ivan must go to city hall for marriage. Ivan says a judge must marry them. No religion. No church person."

"I'll bet we could scare up a judge to perform the ceremony," Holly said, "and we can put up some decorations to make it look more festive."

At this point in her argument, Holly scooted over a bit and stuck her elbow in Rhonda's side to warn her that something a bit preposterous was about to be said and she must keep her mouth shut. "In fact, Rhonda here is an important lawyer in Dallas, and I bet someone in her law office knows a New York judge who would marry your daughter just so he or she could have a nice Russian meal. All we would need to buy is some baby's breath to use with the roses to make centerpieces for the tables, and we'll need some ribbon and candles, but those things would cost next to nothing. Very little money. Of course, your daughter would have to try on the dress to make sure it fits. Not that it has to fit perfectly. I can take some tucks if she's skinny. Your Tatiana will look like a Russian princess."

Holly paused to take a breath. And realized the car was filled with stunned silence. *Oh, dear,* Holly thought. Probably she really should have talked this over with Rhonda first. Gina Kay already had an inkling of what she had in mind, but she was hitting Rhonda from out in left field.

What if Rhonda didn't want to spend part of her time in New York putting on a makeshift wedding for a girl she had never laid eyes on? But the three of them *needed* to do something together, something that would re-create at least for a time the camaraderie they shared during that summer they traipsed around the state of Texas so Gina Kay could compete in all those pageants and become a national beauty queen and make her dear mother proud. Those were the days when their friendship was the sweetest. If they could just get back a tiny bit of that feeling, even if they weren't best friends for the rest of their lives, they could at least go home with lighter hearts.

"Well, will somebody please say something?" she demanded.

"You speak very fast," G.W. said as he turned into Central Park, where Tavern on the Green was located. "I do not understand. *Baby's breath?* There is no baby at wedding."

Rhonda began to giggle. Then to laugh out loud. "Oh, my God," she snorted, bending forward and holding her sides.

Gina Kay was laughing, too. "I wish I had a recording of that," she said turning sideways and stretching over the seat to reach for Holly's hand. "Oh, Holly, what would we do without you?"

"Does this mean it's okay with you guys?" Holly asked.

Rhonda dug in her purse for a tissue to dab her eyes. "I am ruining my makeup," she said, sniffling and dabbing. "You better repeat all that at a slower tempo so poor G.W. can understand."

But they were pulling up to the restaurant. A doorman stepped forward to open the door for them. "G.W., you have to trust us," Holly implored, putting her hand on his shoulder. "We want your daughter to have a wedding, and it will not be charity. Do you understand the word 'charity'?"

"Charity is no pay," he said.

"No, charity is when someone else pays. We are not paying for anything. The money has already been spent. This is just our way of thanking you for making our trip to New York special. You have become more than our driver. You are our host. Our friend. We want to do this for your daughter because it will be the most fun we have had together in a long, long time. And because Gina Kay and Rhonda never had beautiful weddings of their own. They know that someday your daughter will have to tell her daughter that no, she did not get married in a nice place wearing a princess dress, and her daughter will be sad. Just think, G.W., you and Tatiana's mother will have a picture of your daughter in a white lace dress on her wedding day to look at for the rest of your life. Now, unless you tell us not to, we would like to talk to your wife about this when we meet her tonight. I want you to help us make your wife understand that we have a princess dress that really needs to be worn and that Texas ladies just love to put on weddings, and it will make our trip to New York much happier if you please let us do this."

Holly was very aware of the looming presence of the doorman at the open car door. A limousine had pulled up behind them.

"Go," G.W. said in a firm voice, but there was a suggestion of a smile at the corners of his mouth.

The three of them stood on the sidewalk and watched the black Buick drive away. Then the laughter returned. Holly joined them this time, the sweet nectar of success infusing her veins. *She had done it.* Whatever happened now, there had been at least this one joyous moment that hearkened back to the way they were.

"So when did your mother tell you it was bad luck to wear a

dress only one time?" Rhonda said, still laughing. "I missed out on that piece of wisdom."

"Well, it sounds like something my mother might have said," Holly said.

"And what about 'Texas ladies just love to put on weddings'?" Gina Kay asked.

"Well, lots of them do," Holly said defensively. "And I ought to know. I deal with weddings practically every day of my life."

The laughter continued as they made their way into the restaurant and were led down a corridor filled with Tiffany chandeliers and Tiffany windows into the glass-enclosed Crystal Room. When they were seated, Rhonda said, "I need to set the record straight. I really never wanted a big wedding."

"Sure you did," Holly said blithely. "You have chosen to forget it. We all wanted a big wedding."

"But I grew up," Rhonda protested. "It didn't bother me that Dennis and I got married at city hall. It was the sensible thing to do at the time."

Holly shrugged. "Whatever," she said with a dismissive wave of her hand. She started to ask Gina Kay if she regretted not getting married in a church, but realized she didn't want to go down that road, which went directly through a minefield. She knew that Gina Kay and Terry had gotten married in the Matthewses' living room so Gina Kay's mother could be there. Gina Kay's father was there, too, and Terry's father. The entire Matthews clan. And over in Austin, Rhonda had been waiting in her dorm room for Terry to call.

At least her performance in the car had lightened the mood for a while, Holly thought with satisfaction. She planned to have three glasses of wine and enjoy her exorbitantly expensive meal. And tonight she would pay for it herself. No Gina Kay picking up the tab. No charity.

❦

Rhonda stared unseeing at the menu, pondering what had just happened. She had allowed herself to be manipulated. Holly had dreamed up this whole wedding thing to lighten the mood and give them a shared goal rather than have them all go their separate ways and get together on the last day of their trip for the big denouement. Maybe she and Gina Kay had planned it this way all along, with G.W. and his daughter and all the wedding guests hired from central casting.

But Holly didn't have it in her to be *that* devious, Rhonda decided. Gina Kay yes, but not Holly.

The menu was overwhelming. She didn't have the patience to read it or the inclination for artful food and decided to request grilled salmon and steamed vegetables. She closed the menu and scanned the room, which was still full though many of the diners were lingering over coffee or brandy.

Rhonda recalled Michael Forester mentioning that the restaurant was one of his favorites, especially if he could charge the meal to his expense account.

Abruptly she stopped looking around the room and, on the off chance that Michael Forester might be among the lingering patrons, sank a little lower in her chair. If he was here, she didn't want to see him. Didn't want him to see her.

Rhonda had been taken by surprise when Holly asked if she had seen "the man from the airplane" today. Was she that transparent?

She had been thrilled to see him waiting for her by the statue. Such a good-looking guy. Which made her worry how her skin looked in the sunlight and if he would notice the gray hairs that were starting to assert their presence. But mostly she felt alive. And younger than she had in a long time. They found an empty park bench, and he handed her a tall latte and spread her bagel with cream cheese. The foliage in the park was luxuriant. Flowers were blooming in the beds. Birds sang happily overhead. People were jogging, skateboarding, strolling, walking dogs, lounging in the grass, flying kites. She was glad to be alive and sitting in this beautiful place with this beautiful man.

They talked about the city, what they liked and didn't, what they would miss about Texas if they lived here. He would miss the mild climate with year-round golf days. She would miss the wide-open spaces and big sky. Then, their coffee and bagels finished, they strolled past the Gothic-looking building that housed the park headquarters and down a stately, shaded promenade, past statues of Shakespeare and Columbus. Their conversation was of the harmless variety. Had she seen the view from the Empire State Building? What were his favorite New York restaurants? Finally they sat on another bench not too far from the Alice in Wonderland sculpture. Children were climbing on top of the huge toadstool where Alice basked in the sunlight. After a time, he glanced at his watch.

"I need to talk frankly," Michael said, taking her hand. "I am very attracted to you, but I don't have time in my life for a relationship with frills. Mostly I like to fuck. I'd like to fuck you. A lot. All the time. But it will have to be in motel rooms. Or sometimes a hotel with dinner in the room, but not often. This may be the only walk in the sunlight we ever take. What I want is to open the door and see you naked in bed. And already turned on. I promise to make it good for you. *Really* good, so that you can hardly wait until the next time. So that you will have a hard time thinking about much else. I want to be on your mind wherever you are and whatever you're doing, even when you are making love to your husband. And I'd like for our first time to be right now."

He took her hand and pulled her to her feet. "I have a luncheon meeting," he said. "We have just enough time to get acquainted."

She walked beside him toward the nearest park entrance. They did not hold hands. Did not touch. Her heart was pounding. Her armpits and crotch were moist. More than moist. She wanted to do this, but she wasn't sure why. Was it an act against Dennis or a statement to herself that she still had an appetite for sex, that she was still desirable?

She felt like a robot as she walked along. Or a puppet. Yes, a puppet. Her strings were being pulled. She was doing exactly what he wanted her to do. No negotiating of terms, just an acceptance of his. She would be "the other woman." She would be an adulteress. An unfaithful wife to a man who deserved better. Unless Dennis had been unfaithful to her. Maybe she should call him up and ask him. *Hi, Honey. I am about to screw this guy I met on the airplane but didn't think it would be cricket unless you have screwed around on me.* Maybe she and Dennis could negotiate an open marriage. She had heard of such things. Two people wanted to stay married but wanted to fool around on the side. *Fool around.* Where had that expression come from? Only fools could fool around.

She wondered if Michael Forester charged the rooms he used for assignations to his expense account.

She imagined a future spent waiting for his calls. Such a relationship could not endure. It could ruin her marriage. Destroy her family. No way could it be worth such a price.

But still, she walked along beside him, wishing he would take her hand. *Desperately* wishing he would take her hand.

Chapter thirteen

In anticipation of a headache, Holly cautiously moved her head back and forth on her pillow. Sunlight was edging its way around the window shades. Across the room, Gina Kay was curled on her side, her face to the wall.

Holly was trying a cautious full-body stretch when the phone rang. Without lifting her head from the pillow, she reached for the receiver, but Rhonda had already picked up the extension in her bedroom. Holly heard Melissa's excited voice. "Is my mother there?"

Holly's heart lurched in her chest. "Honey, I'm right here. Is something wrong?"

Gina Kay sat up in bed, a worried look on her face. Rhonda, in her bathrobe, pushed open the bedroom door and stood there waiting to find out what warranted the early-morning phone call from Waco.

"You're in the newspaper!" Melissa said.

"I'm what?" Holly said.

"Your picture is in the newspaper. On the front page! You're sitting on a stool between Gina Kay and Tamara. Daddy let me call you. Someone just called to tell him you're in the Dallas paper, too. You're famous now, aren't you?"

Holly waved and smiled at Rhonda and Gina Kay to let them know there wasn't an emergency back home. Rhonda went back to her room and Gina Kay headed for the bathroom. Holly cautiously put her head back onto the pillow. A headache definitely was lurking.

Holly glanced at the clock. Not so early. Seven thirty in Waco. And eight thirty here, but it had been three in the morning when G.W. delivered them back to the hotel after their visit to Brighton Beach. "A little bit famous," she told Melissa. "What does it say under the picture?"

"It says, 'Waco fashion designer Holly Warner, center, created the gown worn by Beaumont resident Tamara Truehart, right, who was named Miss American Teenager last night in New York City. Warner also designed the gown worn by Lamberton resident Gina Kay Robertson, left, who also wore a Warner-designed gown when she won the national Miss American Teenager title twenty-five years ago. The pageant board gave Robertson an award for living up to the Miss American Teenager ideal. See page D-eighteen for details.'"

"That's great," Holly said. "They didn't call me a 'Waco dressmaker.' But 'Waco fashion designer' does seem like an intentional oxymoron."

"A what?" Melissa asked.

"Never mind. I'm thrilled. I'm going to send flowers to the reporter."

"Is it okay if I take the newspaper to camp and show everyone?"

"Fine by me. Tell your daddy to buy a couple of extra copies. Did you watch the pageant last night?"

"Yeah. It was cool. Gina Kay looked pretty, and I was real glad Miss Texas won. I remember when Tamara came for her fitting. You said she was a spoiled brat."

Holly winced. "I was probably having a bad day. I would appreciate it if you wouldn't tell anyone that I said that."

"Sure," Melissa said. "Mom?"

"Yes."

"Can I go to softball camp in Austin? It starts in two weeks. Kendra Carter is going and asked me to room with her. We get to stay in a dormitory and eat in the cafeteria just like college kids. It'll be really cool."

Holly started to say no. Melissa was attending a softball camp at Baylor this week, and if they let her go to two sports camps, they'd have to let Joey do likewise. Then she thought of how much she spent for dinner last night and felt guilty. "Well, after all this publicity, probably the phone is going to start ringing off the wall with calls from all those girls who need pageant gowns. I think we can probably manage another camp, but your father and I have to talk it over."

"Daddy said to ask you."

"In that case, the answer is yes. Is your brother around?"

"He's still upstairs and is going to make us late. Daddy says he's going to have to ride his bike to baseball practice if he doesn't get his butt down here in the next five minutes. Daddy's here. He wants to talk to you."

"Thanks, sweetie. I miss you. I bought you a really cute T-shirt with the Statue of Liberty on the front."

"Cool. I miss you, too. Here's Daddy."

"The picture's in color and above the fold," Sandy's voice said. "And it made the *Dallas Morning News,* also above the fold and in color. One of your Dallas mothers-of-the-bride called before seven to tell you. Millicent something. I have it written down upstairs. You look great. So does Gina Kay. The story in the Waco paper tells all about how other winners of a lot of other pageants were also wearing dresses you made. I guess you'll be busier than ever now."

He didn't sound particularly excited about the prospect. "Are you proud of me?" Holly asked, putting a hand over her eyes to protect them from the offensive daylight that was peeking around the window shades.

"Sure. But I would be even if you were just a normal housewife. The article didn't say anything about your family."

"The reporter didn't ask anything about my family. When reporters write about your football teams, they don't mention the wife and kids. So, how are things on the home front?" she asked, deliberately changing the subject.

"Disorganized. I can't find Joey's mitt or Melissa's left sneaker."

"Where did you find the right sneaker?" Holly asked.

"Under the coffee table in the family room."

"Then the other one is probably under the sofa. Joey's mitt is probably in the Explorer or the truck, depending on which vehicle he rode in last. Don't forget his orthodontist appointment this afternoon. Any word from our collegiate underachiever?"

"Hey, Carter was a standout in spring practice," Sandy said indignantly.

"Yeah, but they'll kick his butt off the team if he doesn't make his grades. Summer school is his last chance."

"He knows that."

"I hope so. Maybe you better call him and give him a pep talk. And please make sure that the dog and bird have food and water. You have been taking care of them, haven't you?"

"I thought that was Melissa's job."

"Hey, she's a kid. You're supposed to make sure she really does what she's supposed to do." Holly closed her eyes. Her head was beginning to throb, and she was saying all the wrong things.

There was a second or two of silence before Sandy's voice said, "I wish you were coming home sooner. Things don't go so well when you're not here."

"Hey, if I never went away, you and the kids would never learn to appreciate all that I do. Happy hunting, and thanks for calling. It was sweet of you to let me know about the picture in the newspaper. Maybe we can find a *Dallas Morning News* on a newsstand up here. If you have a chance, send a clipping from the Waco paper to my mom."

"I'll take care of it. I am proud of you, Holly. Really I am."

"Thanks, honey. I'm proud of you, too. You were born to be a football coach and teach kids to be good sports for life."

"Hey, I thought I was a born lover."

"That, too. I'll be needing some of that when I get home for sure! Love you, darlin'."

With as little movement of her head as possible, she replaced the receiver and smiled as she allowed herself to imagine her first night back home. Maybe they could farm out Joey and Melissa and have the house to themselves. With her new, skinnier body, she was feeling pretty damned sexy. She'd light some candles and open a bottle of wine. They could drink wine naked in bed and fool around by candlelight until they got really hot. Such thoughts brought about a nice little wave of sexual turn-on. She considered calling Sandy back and telling him so, but he would be frantically trying to get the kids fed and in a vehicle so he could drop them off on his way to the high school, where he was teaching driver's ed in summer school.

She hoped Sandy remembered to check on the pets. Whose fault would it be if they died of thirst or starvation, Melissa for forgetting to care for them, Sandy for not reminding her, or the errant mother who went off and left them all?

Yesterday, sitting at that funky fashion show, surrounded by an incredible array of people who dressed to suit themselves, unlike back home where some unwritten dress code said that ladies must wear proper little outfits to fashion shows, Holly found herself wishing Melissa had been there with her to people watch. Melissa would have gotten a kick out of it all—the music, the models, the clothes. Her sons would have been uncomfortable and would want to know if any of the men were gay.

Holly speculated about what her children would be like if they were being raised in New York. She had always assumed that a nice family-values type of city like Waco was the best place to raise a family, even if it wasn't necessarily the best place for the mother of said children to be living and conducting her career. But Waco kids grew up thinking that football was more important than art and that the Bible was to be taken literally. Of course, she herself had grown up in Lamberton where "cosmopolitan" was the name of a magazine, yet she had dared to dream of becoming a citizen of the broader world.

She had gotten no farther than Waco, however, which in many ways was just a big Lamberton. Not that there weren't sophisticated people who lived in Waco, but they had to swim upstream. And Holly was so busy raising her children and running her business that she had never rubbed shoulders with any of them. She had considered taking some art history and drawing classes at Baylor, but the only times she ever visited the campus was to attend athletic events—which she loved, especially when she took Melissa to an occasional women's basketball or softball game. But why had she never taken her to the city's art museum? To the symphony? To campus theatrical productions?

And why was she thinking just about her daughter? Did that mean she had given up on her sons? Sandy tended to divide boys into two groups—those who did sports and those who were sissies—and she had never once contradicted that assessment. As a result, her sons felt the same way as their father, who really was a good guy. A good husband and father. Sandy was limited, though, unwilling to try anything new, be it Thai food or live theater.

It would have been better if she could have married Sandy at age thirty instead of age twenty. By then she would have known if she had it in her to be a successful designer or was ready to come back home to Texas and raise kids. And Sandy would have known exactly what he was getting—a career woman or a dedicated homemaker.

Maybe if Gina Kay's marriage to Terry hadn't been such a sensitive issue, she might have asked Gina Kay if she was sorry that she had married so young, if she ever wished she had waited. But she had not done that. In spite of her best intentions and the pewter serving tray wedding gift, she and Gina Kay had drifted apart, seeing each other only every so often, conducting proper little visits that in no way resembled the intense friendship they used to share—until Mitch was born. Then, any questions Holly had about why Gina Kay had given up on college and moved back to Lamberton, when that was the one thing the three of them said they were never going to do, seemed irrelevant. More than being a married woman, more than being a former beauty queen, more than being someone who had given up without really trying to follow her dreams, more than the girl who stole Terry Robertson from Rhonda, Gina Kay had become the mother of a beautiful baby boy, thus achieving Madonna-like status in Holly's eyes. When Gina Kay asked Holly to be the baby's godmother, Holly felt as though she had been anointed. She would have a sanctioned place in the life of that precious child. Because of baby Mitch, the bonds of friendship between her and Gina Kay were strengthened. Holly felt perfectly comfortable picking up the phone and calling Gina Kay if for no other reason than to ask how she was getting along and, of course, to hear about the latest cute thing that little Mitch had done.

Were it not for the continuing presence of Rhonda in her life, Holly probably would have abandoned any further consideration of how it was that Gina Kay Matthews came to be married to Terry Robertson. But over the years, she realized through words said and unsaid that Rhonda continued to grieve for Terry. Even long for him. Which wasn't good for her marriage.

Even after Holly became a mother herself and realized the job did not come with a halo or a pedestal or a 401(k), she still thought of Gina Kay as having achieved a higher state. Gina Kay was a full-time mother. Gina Kay never lost her temper. Her children were well behaved and never ate junk food. Her home was serene and well run. Holly never thought of Gina Kay as having a life outside of Lamberton. She had been as surprised as Rhonda had at Danny Boyd's introduction of Gina Kay last night. Holly had known that Gina Kay supported several worthy causes, but she had no idea how broadly she had cast her net.

Holly was interrupted in her musings by the sound of a door opening and closing. Rhonda had said last night that she planned to jog in the park this morning. Apparently she really meant it. Which seemed amazing. Holly was dreading the movement it would take to get her body out of bed. And into the bathroom. She tried to remember how much vodka she had consumed at the Russian nightclub.

She had to smile, though, when she thought of their midnight journey to Brighton Beach. It was like a trip to another country—a country in south Brooklyn where people spoke Russian and stayed up very late. The sidewalks along Brighton Beach Avenue were packed with people, including young lovers, elderly couples, parents pushing strollers with sleeping babies, brazen teenagers. Occasionally a train thundered overhead on an elevated track that, G.W. explained, was really part of the subway. Many of the signs on the stores were in Russian—the Cyrillic alphabet, Rhonda had explained. And there were more nightclubs in the four- or five-block strip than in the entire city of Waco. Many of the nightclubs had promised "table dancing" on their marquees.

The club where G.W. took them was run by his wife's cousin and featured the "Brighton Beach Folies Bergère." G.W.'s wife was waiting out front. Marta was a tall handsome woman with dark hair and a tentative smile. She shook hands with the three women her husband had been taxiing around.

"My sister and I watched the beauty pageant on television," she told Gina Kay. "You spoke very well."

"Why, thank you," Gina Kay responded.

"And you looked like a Hollywood movie star in that beautiful gown," Marta added.

"Holly designed the gown," Gina Kay said, nodding in Holly's direction. "She also designed the winner's gown."

Marta's eyes grew wide. "With so much talent, you must be very famous," she told Holly.

Holly decided that now was not the time for modesty. "Yes, I am well known, especially for my wedding gowns," she said. She wanted to jump up and down. *The bride's mother liked the dress!* That surely meant the battle was half over.

Marta's cousin led them to a table in front of the small stage. Almost immediately they were served drinks and a platter of smoked fish. Holly had requested wine but ended up with chilled vodka, as did Rhonda and Gina Kay. G.W. insisted that drinking vodka chilled prevented a hangover.

Holly decided that their table was the only one in the entire establishment at which English was being spoken, and she, Rhonda, and Gina Kay seemed to be the only women with unexposed cleavage. Marta's dress was more modest than some but still revealed a substantial portion of her impressive bosom, and even sagging old women with hair dyed lollipop red wore low-cut garments.

Shortly the house lights dimmed and conversation ceased. The stage show featured showgirls in feathers and fur and a man billed as the "Russian Tony Bennett," who actually sang "I Left My Heart in San Francisco" in Russian.

When the show was over, the band played high-decibel dance music, and the patrons rushed onto the dance floor. Inhibition obviously was not a Russian trait, or maybe it was the vodka at work. If women had no partner, they danced with each other. Apparently no move on the dance floor was too outrageous. Everyone did their own thing, from Elvis Presley hip gyrations to Fred and Ginger suave. When G.W. insisted they join the dancers, Holly pulled Rhonda and Gina Kay to their feet and G.W. grabbed his wife's hand. And they had had fun. Riotous, unforgettable fun. Even Rhonda.

When the band took a break, Holly learned that Marta worked as a bookkeeper in a dentist's office and took English lessons two evenings a week. Then Holly steered the conversation to weddings. And *the* dress. Which would probably never be worn again what with Gina Kay living on a cattle ranch and having little use for evening gowns. And it would make *such* a beautiful wedding dress.

Gina Kay joined in, mentioning that she had received a roomful of flowers for which she had absolutely no use. G.W. nodded. "Yes, many very nice flowers."

"Holly is not only a famous designer of wedding gowns," Gina Kay continued, "she is an expert on weddings—from the tastefully simple to the lavishly ostentatious—and really should write a book on the subject."

After they had danced their way through the band's next set, G.W. went to get the car. As he pulled up in front of the apartment building where he and Marta lived, Holly reached for Marta's hand. "I want Tatiana to at least try on the dress," she said. "Why don't you and she come by our hotel in the morning? Your husband is making our visit to New York City so much more memorable than it would have been if we were on our own. Tell Tatiana that we would love to be able to show our appreciation by helping make her wedding more memorable."

"I must work tomorrow, but I will speak with my daughter," Marta said. Then she added with a smile, "My husband is correct when he says that you are nice ladies."

Holly suggested that Tatiana come before ten and had written her cell phone number on one of G.W.'s business cards so that Tatiana could let her know if another time would be better.

Holly knew exactly where her cell phone was. It was in the

smart little handbag she had carried last night, where a tin of aspirin also resided. Trouble was, she didn't know where the smart little handbag now resided.

The time had come for her to get out of this bed.

As "the most honest and reliable driver in New York City," G.W. had changed to Coca-Cola after only one glass of vodka. That's what she should have done, Holly realized as she tentatively lifted her head from the pillow. Chilled vodka may have prevented hangovers in Russians, but the damned stuff seemed to have pickled her poor American brain, which was beginning to throb. Gina Kay seldom drank anything but a glass or two of wine and probably had allowed herself only an occasional dainty sip of vodka for the sake of politeness. And if Rhonda was up to taking a run, she must have just sipped, too. Which irritated Holly. She didn't want to be the only one who was hungover.

She moaned as she crawled out of bed and went searching for her purse. She found it in the sitting room, which looked a bit like a funeral parlor with all those flowers. She downed two aspirin with a glass of water and made a pot of strong coffee. As soon as Gina Kay was finished in the bathroom, she would take a long, therapeutic shower.

Or maybe she'd use Rhonda's bathroom to speed the process along. She wanted to be presentable if G.W.'s daughter did come to try on Gina Kay's dress. And later this morning, if Tatiana liked the dress and was amenable to having a real wedding instead of simply reciting vows at city hall, G.W. was going to show them his brother-in-law's restaurant, which would then be the site for both the ceremony and the dinner. Gina Kay originally had planned for them to spend the entire afternoon sightseeing, but they would have to find time to shop for the things they needed for the wedding. And tomorrow morning, they would need to decorate the restaurant. Maybe G.W. could take them sightseeing later today. And tomorrow afternoon.

She wondered how much Gina Kay was paying G.W. for his services. And for five nights in a suite at a hotel just east of Central Park. Gina Kay was now a rich widow with no restraints whatsoever on how she spent money. Holly remembered when Gina Kay made fifty cents an hour plus tips at the drive-in. One night a man left a five-dollar tip, and she ran after him thinking he had made a mistake. When he insisted that she keep it, Gina Kay had been so excited she had to call her mother.

When Holly emerged from the bathroom, Rhonda was waiting for her in the sitting room with a big smile on her face as she held up a copy of the New York *Daily News*. On the front page was the picture of Holly, Gina Kay, and Tamara. "Oh, my God!" Holly said. "A New York paper, too! Sandy and Melissa called to say the picture was in the *Waco Herald Tribune* and the *Dallas Morning News*."

"I couldn't believe it when I saw it on the newsstand," Rhonda said excitedly. "I didn't have any money with me, so I tried to convince the man at the newsstand that I'd come back later to pay him, but even though I resorted to my very best Texas drawl, he wouldn't even discuss it. So a nice woman bought me a newspaper. She said she was a former Miss Albany and had watched the pageant last night. The story is all about you, Holly. It's a bit condescending, saying that Texas is the beauty pageant capital of the world and Waco has become a mecca for contestants whose parents were willing to foot the bill for a custom-designed gown, but overall it's good press. We need to buy some other copies. We have to send clippings to our mothers, and I'd like to send one to Jason and Scott in Colorado. They'll get such a kick out of it. My God, Holly, you'll probably be having contestants flying down to Waco from New York. From all over."

Holly grinned. "I guess I'm going to have to invest in a tulle factory." When Rhonda frowned, she said, "T-u-l-l-e."

Tatiana had seen the morning paper and was impressed with Holly's credentials but not bowled over by them. Not convinced she wanted to have anything to do with the women from Texas her father had been driving around.

Holly had been expecting a shy little peasant girl, but Tatiana was poised and even a bit leery and standoffish. She had lustrous black hair and large dark eyes that stood out against her fair skin. Beautiful skin. Not a freckle to be seen. She obviously hadn't grown up in Texas with its unrelenting sunshine.

The lace gown was hanging on the bedroom door. Tatiana crossed the room and stood regarding it for a long moment before asking, "Why do you want to do this? Are you so bored with New York that you need to put on a wedding for a woman you have never met?"

Holly was surprised when it was Rhonda who volunteered an answer. "Holly is a professional fairy godmother. Like in Cinderella. Do you know the story of Cinderella?"

Tatiana nodded.

"Good," Rhonda said. "The issue is if you and your parents are okay with it. We don't want to intrude. It's *your* wedding. *Your* party. *Your* call."

Holly could feel herself grinning. *Fairy godmother*. She stood on her tiptoes, swung an imaginary wand in an arch and began singing "Bibbidi-Bobbidi-Boo" in her best fairy-godmother voice. Then she stopped abruptly and put her hands to her aching head. "Remind me never to go drinking with your father again," Holly told Tatiana.

A small suggestion of a smile had crept onto Tatiana's face. "It is a very beautiful dress," she said touching the tip of one sleeve.

"The lace was made in France," Holly said. "Gina Kay is rich so cost was no object."

"Do you think it will fit me?" Tatiana asked.

"Let's find out," Holly said eagerly.

While Tatiana was changing, Holly took two more aspirin, drank another cup of coffee, and ate toast from the breakfast Gina Kay had ordered. "Give me another hour, and I will be as good as new," she promised Gina Kay and Rhonda. Then she nodded toward the bedroom and whispered, "All she has to do is see herself in that dress, and the battle is won."

When Tatiana shyly opened the door to the bedroom, the three of them burst into applause. "You look beautiful!" Gina Kay exclaimed. "Absolutely beautiful!"

Tatiana dark eyes were sparkling. She had seen herself in the mirror and was ready to buy into the dream of a fairy-tale wedding.

Holly was relieved. All she would have to do was turn up the hem an inch or so and take in the waist a bit. Already her mind was dealing with a veil. Something quite simple. Fingertip length.

Gina Kay brought out the ivory satin sandals she had worn with the gown. They were just a bit too long but not bad. It was all going to work, Holly decided.

"What about her hair?" she asked Rhonda. "Do you think she should wear it up or down?"

"I'm sure that you and Gina Kay can make that decision on your own," Rhonda said. Then she shook Tatiana's hand, said that she enjoyed meeting her, and disappeared into her room. Tatiana headed for the other bedroom to change back into her street clothes.

Gina Kay and Holly exchanged woeful glances. "For a moment, I thought Rhonda was on board," Gina Kay said.

Chapter fourteen

Rhonda was sitting on the side of the bed, waiting for Holly's tap at the door. When it came, it was accompanied by Holly's voice saying, "Hey, Rhonda, it's me."

The door opened. Holly stepped inside and closed it behind her. "What's going on?" she asked.

"I'm just trying to decide what to do next," Rhonda said. "I could change hotels. I could call the airline and book the earliest available flight out of here. I could have a torrid affair with a stranger. I could get drunk. I could take a long nap. I could go on a shopping binge. Or take a slow boat to China. All sorts of possibilities."

Holly sat on the window seat. "What's going on?" she asked.

Rhonda sighed. "This whole wedding thing . . . I suddenly felt as though I had stumbled onto the set of one of those old Judy Garland–Mickey Rooney movies. You know, where everyone gets all excited and says, 'Let's put on a fabulous musical production in the garage and make everyone feel so very good and solve everyone's problems and we can all be friends forever.' It made me nauseous."

"For a minute, I thought you were buying into it."

"For a minute, I almost was," Rhonda admitted. "Then I realized I was being manipulated. Well, in spite of last night's silliness at the Russian nightclub, which I did enjoy, I am too old and tough and cynical to pick up where we left off. You and Gina Kay go ahead and play fairy godmother. I want no part of it."

Rhonda paused, considering her next words before plunging

on. "In fact, I want no further part in this entire trip. It was all a stupid idea from the get-go. What difference does it make why Gina Kay and Terry got married? He's dead now. It is all irrelevant. I am never going to see him again, and it just took me a while to realize how liberating that is. I don't have to think about him anymore. I should be turning cartwheels."

"And you don't have to hate Gina Kay anymore," Holly added.

"Don't hold your breath on that one," Rhonda said.

Suddenly feeling very weary, she pulled off her running shoes, swung her legs onto the bed, and leaned against the headboard. Maybe she should take a nap. Even with the sounds of the street drifting up from below, the room itself seemed unnaturally silent. Like a padded cell. Or a womb. It would be nice to just curl up and sleep for a long time. And wake up at home in her own bed with this whole stupid trip behind her.

"And you no longer give a damn how it was that one of your two best girlfriends came to be your boyfriend's wife?" Holly asked.

"What difference does it make now how or why it happened?" Rhonda demanded, picking up a pillow and clutching it against her middle. "The end result is still the same. Gina Kay and Terry stabbed me in the back, and it took me a long time to get over it. I lost count of how many men I screwed trying to get over it. I went on a real quest. At first I was looking for a man who could make me forget Terry. Then it took years to find a man who could make me *feel* without having to get myself stoned or drunk first. One night in bed with my husband with our twin babies in the next room, poor Dennis somehow pulled it off. I cried so hard, he was sure he had broken my ribs or something, and I couldn't tell him why I was crying. I couldn't tell him it was the first time in years I'd had a climax without the help of half a bottle of booze or a joint or two."

"Did you really love Terry that much that it took years to get over him, or was it your wounded pride just doing a number on you?" Holly asked.

Rhonda considered whether she should be merely annoyed or downright angry by Holly's question. But either response was too much of a bother. "Both maybe," she said with a shrug. Then she added, "I really did love Terry, and I also resented the hold he had over me. Then he tried to kill me. To kill the two of us, actually."

Rhonda found the look of horror her admission had brought to Holly's face oddly satisfying. "I never told anyone about that," she admitted. "It was the night of my birthday. I told Terry that I still wanted to marry him but for now I didn't want to go steady anymore. Suddenly he was driving a hundred miles an hour down a country road and then deliberately crashed the car into a tree. I had nightmares for years about that night. But then I had been the one who started things up again."

Rhonda clutched the pillow more tightly to her middle. "Maybe it was just the intensity that I couldn't put behind me," she continued. "After Terry, college boys seemed like so many rodents looking for cheese. None of them was willing to die for love, that's for sure. Terry was crazy, but he loved me. *Really* loved me. I know that for a fact. I guess that I still think he was somehow coerced into marrying Gina Kay. I made myself crazy trying to figure out how she managed to seduce him. I was sure she had deliberately gotten herself pregnant."

Rhonda paused, remembering how she had calculated when such a baby might be born, how she had waited for Holly to say that she'd heard that Gina Kay was pregnant, then, when that time arrived, she waited for Holly to say Gina Kay had had a baby. But there was no baby. Not for a couple of years.

Of course, Gina Kay could have miscarried.

But how could a boy who was willing to die for love be subject to coercion? Wouldn't Terry have just paid for Gina Kay to have an abortion and had his daddy give her a bundle of money for her trouble? He wouldn't have had to *marry* her.

Rhonda reached for a bottle of water on the bedside table and took a swig. "As you and my mother both have pointed out on numerous occasions," she continued, "maybe if I'd married Terry it wouldn't have lasted. But I had earned the right to give it a try. And if our love had died of its own accord, I could have walked away sadder but wiser."

"Maybe so, honey, but that's not the way it went down," Holly said. "So what now? Which of all those options you rattled off are you going to choose? Take a nap? Have an affair? Go home?"

She got up and came to sit on the side of the bed. Rhonda started to roll away from her, but Holly grabbed her arm. "Why not let Gina Kay just play things out to the finish? Maybe you'll find out that Terry was your long-lost brother, and by marrying him, Gina Kay saved you from an incestuous marriage. Or maybe Terry had been two-timing you all along. Come on, Rhonda, inquiring minds need to know. *I* need to know, and I think you do, too. You need to banish the Ghosts of Lamberton Past once and for all."

Rhonda pulled her arm away, and Holly moved back to the window seat. "Just don't have an affair," she told Rhonda, "at least not while you're in this frame of mind."

"Don't worry. At least *I* won't end up pregnant."

"Hey, isn't that hitting a little below the belt?" Holly demanded.

"Yeah, I guess it is," Rhonda admitted with a sigh. "Do you ever see that man—the one who made you pregnant?"

"No, he moved away."

"Do you ever think about him?"

"Not really, at least not in the way you mean," Holly said. "Screwing him didn't solve a damned thing and caused me a great deal of grief. After I put on my clothes and sneaked down the back stairs of the motel, I was still married to the same man. I still had to go home and cook dinner. I didn't even have time for a shower. There I was slinging hash for my kids and husband with some guy's cum on my panties. Then we all rushed off to a game. And you know what? I didn't even have an orgasm," she said with a rueful laugh. "He just stuffed it in and started saying, 'Oh, baby, baby, baby.' Then it was all over, and I was lying there thinking, 'For *that* I was unfaithful to my husband?' It was not my finest hour. No, not even an hour. More like twenty minutes, from the time I walked in that door until I walked out."

"And what was it you were trying to solve?" Rhonda asked.

Holly shrugged. "Restlessness, I guess. I could hear Peggy Lee singing 'Is That All There Is?' "

"Is she still singing it?"

"I wear earplugs now. Don't do it, Rhonda. If you do, then on top of everything else, you'll have to deal with guilt. And believe me, it's pretty daunting."

"I got pregnant with Scott and Jason because my IUD had fallen out," Rhonda said. "How come you got pregnant in the motel room?"

"Since Sandy had had a vasectomy, I was no longer taking birth control pills. I bought some of that foam stuff. Obviously, it didn't work."

Rhonda stared across the room at her own reflection in the dresser mirror. Sweat from her run had made her hair go flat. She looked older when her hair was flat, but she resisted the urge to fluff it a bit. "But before the sex, when you were on your way to meet this guy, didn't you feel like you'd come to life after years of being in limbo?"

"I suppose," Holly said, staring at her fingernails. "But mostly I think I was feeling unappreciated. The night before, at the annual football awards banquet, Sandy's team gave him a special award, and since Carter was one of the team captains, he got to make the

presentation. The speech Carter gave about Sandy was all about
how he was the best dad and the best coach ever, how much
Sandy cared, how hard he worked, the sacrifices he had made.
Mine were the only dry eyes in the house. I just sat there thinking,
'Yeah, but the world's greatest coach doesn't ever close a drawer or
hang up a towel. He never enters the checks he writes in the
checkbook or puts his dirty clothes in the hamper. And his kids
are growing up just like him.'"

She paused and chewed on her lower lip a minute before continuing. "I guess I was jealous. No one was ever going to give a
speech saying what a great mom I was. In fact, my kids resent me
because I bitch at them to eat their vegetables and clean up their
room. And no one seems to realize that the money I make working *damned* hard creating all those gowns for an endless succes-
sion of brides and beauty queens has anything to do with paying
bills and keeping them in name-brand sneakers. I know it all
sounds petty, but that's how I was feeling. Carter's little speech
just put me over the edge. So the next day I called this guy who
had been claiming for years that he had a thing for me. I guess I
thought I was going to pay Sandy and the kids back for being
unappreciative slobs, which is totally irrational, since they were
never going to know about it. Oddly enough, though, it did make
me reassess. I put down a few ultimatums and hired a woman to
come in once a week and clean up after them so at least I wasn't
always the one doing it."

"And what about you and Sandy?" Rhonda asked.

"Well, after having an abortion to save my marriage, I damned
sure wasn't going to give up on it. So I made some rules. For
example, Sandy can't just roll over in the middle of the night and
announce that he's horny. The idea of sex must be introduced earlier in the day, and we have to spend a bit of quality time together
before going to bed. He has to court me. Nothing spectacular. Just
watching a television program with me that isn't a sporting event

will suffice. Pouring me a glass of wine. Anything that even remotely resembles a romantic gesture. And it has been better. Sometimes he is positively adorable in the things he comes up with. He bought himself some sexy underwear and me a red teddy. Boy, would I have liked to have been a fly on the wall when he was making those purchases," she said with a sweet little smile. "That took real courage, you know. I do love him, Rhonda. Really I do. It's not his fault that I was too insecure to go for the big time and married him instead. We are two imperfect people who love our imperfect kids to distraction, and when I'm on my deathbed, it is his face and those of my kids I want to see and not those of clients and employees. I forgive him his faults, and he forgives me mine."

"Then your indiscretion did have some positive outcomes?" Rhonda inquired. She sounded like she was in a courtroom cross-examining a witness, trying to get him or her to respond in the way that she wanted.

"Only because it scared me shitless," Holly answered, her voice wavering as she remembered. "Surely there's a more sane way to reassess one's life. Politically I believe in abortion, but still, some-times . . ."

Holly's voice trailed off and Rhonda rolled off the bed, knelt in front of her, and put her arms around her. "I'm sorry you had to go through that, but I'm glad you turned to me for help," she said. "It was a privilege. A real privilege."

Holly began to sniffle. Then to cry. Really cry. Tears that had been a long time in coming, Rhonda suspected. God, why did life have to be so damned complicated? She stroked Holly's back and planted kisses on her hair, like she had done for her children when they fell down and hurt themselves. She loved the woman in her arms. And needed her.

Rhonda got Holly some tissues and sat by her on the win-dow seat while she regained control. "Please don't leave," Holly implored. "I know being here with Gina Kay is difficult for you, but she is a good person. You've got to trust me on that. I know that she must have a good reason for planning this trip and for marrying Terry. Let's enjoy Tatiana's wedding and doing some more New York things together. It might turn out better than you think. Can't you just enjoy being here, and allow yourself to feel some sense of relief that, after all this time, you are finally going to find out what happened back then? I'm as curious as hell, and I think that deep down, you are, too."

"What if I decide to go off with the hunk from the plane?" Rhonda asked.

Holly shrugged. "It's your choice, I guess."

"How do you know I wasn't with him yesterday?"

"I don't. Were you?"

Before Rhonda could answer, her cell phone rang. Holly kissed her cheek. "Tell Dennis I said hello and don't forget that you need to find a judge to marry our bride and groom," she said and left her alone.

Rhonda glanced at the number on the tiny screen. It was indeed a call from Dennis. "Hi, honey," she said. "We keep missing each other."

"Yeah, they told me at the clinic you tried to call. Everything all right on your end?"

"Sure. Holly says hello. We got the beauty pageant over with. Now Holly's got us involved in putting on an instant wedding for the daughter of our Russian driver." Rhonda took a few minutes to explain about G.W. and Tatiana.

"Sounds like a worthy cause," Dennis said, but his voice was flat.

"I hear traffic. You're in your car, aren't you?" she asked.

"Yes, I'm on my way home from the hospital to shower and catch a little sleep before my afternoon appointments. We spent most of the night trying to save a three-year-old girl who was

medevaced in from some little town east of here. Her father acci-
dentally backed over her in the driveway. God, how I wanted to
make it all right for him. And for her. For her mother. For a while
I thought I was going to win, but I lost her. It was so late that I
went ahead and made rounds."

Rhonda sighed. Medicine could exact such a horrible emo-
tional toll on its practitioners. This was one of those moments
when she couldn't even begin to imagine what her husband was
going through, when she wished he had chosen dentistry for his
profession. Or art. That would have been the best. He could have
painted at home and looked after the boys while she had a fabulous legal career. But it was silly to think such things. There was
no going back.

"I can't do this too many more years," Dennis said.

"I know," Rhonda responded. "I love you, Dennis."

"That's nice to hear. I love you, too."

Rhonda peeled off her jogging clothes and headed for the
shower. The water wasn't as hot as she would have liked, but it
did feel good. She stood there letting the water cascade over her
from head to toe, remembering how yesterday morning she had
been standing here alive with anticipation, her meeting with
Michael Forester little more than an hour away. Showering itself
had become a sexual act as she lathered her body, touching every
inch of herself. She imagined how it would be if it were Michael
Forester's hands touching her, his hands enjoying the smoothness
of her skin and exploring the contours of her breasts and waist
and rump. And she allowed her fingers to probe between her legs.
God, she was so turned on. So open. So hot.

And dressing herself, fixing her hair, putting on her makeup
had all been done with an elevated sense of her own skin, her own
body. Yet she made no promises to herself. She was *not* planning
on an assignation, just open to possibilities. And she was having

fun anticipating how it would be to see him once again. She felt invigorated and young and alive. She still felt that way when she met Michael Forester in Central Park and while she was walking at his side up the avenue and through the lobby of his hotel and in the elevator with three other people all staring in silence at the door. Surely they could hear her heart pounding.

His room was on the eighth floor at the end of an empty corridor. They walked side by side. She still wished he would take her hand.

He unlocked his door and stood aside so she could enter. The room was generic. The bed was already made.

He came up behind her, put his arms around her waist, and nibbled on her ear. "I thought about you all night. Had to jack off twice. I knew you were going to call."

"It could have been your wife calling."

"Yeah, she called, too," he said, still behind her, taking her breasts in his hands and rubbing his crotch against her buttocks. "Nice boobs. Oh, baby, are we going to have ourselves a time."

Then he began unbuttoning her blouse. Soon it was on the chair, and he quite proficiently undid her bra. Then he spun her around, sat on the bed in front of her, and began sucking with great gusto on her right breast. Too hard. She winced.

Then quite suddenly, he flopped back on the bed, his arms spread-eagled over his head. "Unzip me, baby," he demanded, in what apparently was intended to be a sexy growl.

Rhonda stood looking down at him. And started to laugh.

He looked ridiculous. She felt ridiculous standing there bare to the waist. She could smell the Chanel body cream with which she had anointed herself. She hadn't spent that much time getting ready for a date since she prepared herself for sexual encounters with Terry. For even though she had not quite admitted it to herself, she had been a lady on her way to get laid.

"What's so funny?" he asked.

"You," she said backing away. "Us." She reached for her blouse. "Sorry."

"You're kidding," he said sitting up and unzipping his own pants. He took out his engorged penis and started waving it around like a wand. Rhonda wondered if the sight of it was supposed to make her fall on her knees.

Rhonda picked up her purse and stuffed her bra inside. "I'm sorry," she repeated. "I should have known better."

"You bitch," he yelled, his face an angry red mask. "You goddamned, cock-teasing bitch." She heard the lamp crashing to the floor as she pulled the door closed.

She hurried toward the elevator. Two other women were standing there, waiting. They glanced at Rhonda then quickly looked away.

She looked down. Her blouse was open. She quickly buttoned it and stuffed the tail inside her slacks. And realized she had left her sweater back in the room.

On the first floor she found her way to the ladies' room and put on her bra and put herself back in order. She debated about trying to get her sweater back but decided she didn't want to risk further contact with Michael Forester. What she needed was a drink, but not here. Not in *his* hotel. Someplace else.

She left the hotel and wandered around for a time, trying to decide what to do with the rest of her day. Instead of something alcoholic, she settled for a bottle of water from a curbside vendor and walked back in the direction of the park. Then she turned up Fifth Avenue, walking along the park on the broad shaded sidewalk toward the city's great art museums: the Metropolitan, Guggenheim, Frick, and others—places she had visited during her idyllic, long-ago summer in New York. The Frick came first, so she crossed the street and went inside.

The museum was housed in a building that dated back to the days when millionaires built mansions along Fifth Avenue and filled them with art treasures. The works of art and the furnishings were arranged as though the Frick family still lived there, with no regard to chronology or period. She wandered about a bit unable to focus then seated herself on a bench in the library where a Stuart portrait of George Washington hung. She took comfort in the lone American presence among all the European masterpieces.

George and Martha Washington probably never fooled around on each other. Surely Martha never went to a hotel with a stranger.

Gradually, with quiet all around her, Rhonda had felt herself relaxing. And trying to decide if she had just gone through a life-altering event. Would she return to Dallas and never think impure thoughts again? She thought about packing up and leaving. Of calling Dennis and telling him she was on her way home.

But she hadn't done that. She had a solitary lunch in a little French place on Madison Avenue then wandered around looking in the shop windows, sometimes going inside. Suddenly she realized how late it was. She needed to change clothes and get herself to the convention center.

And now, the following morning, she was still unsure as to whether she should go home or stay for the grand finale. She was curious as to what Gina Kay would say. *Very* curious. Probably she had been rehearsing for her big moment over the last two months, making sure she would put just the right spin on her words.

Rhonda stepped out of the shower and wrapped herself in one of the hotel's wonderfully thick towels. She wrapped a smaller towel turban style around her wet hair.

Rhonda wiped the water vapor off the mirror and stared at her image. She looked youthful but not young. Her youth was gone. It was time for her to figure out what to do with the rest of her life.

Gina Kay got to start all over again. Widowhood offered a clean slate of sorts. Rhonda knew women who claimed they already had decided what they would wear to their husband's funeral should the heart attack ever come or the plane go down. But she could not bring herself to have such thoughts. She would always wish Dennis well whether or not their marriage endured.

Chapter fifteen

Once she was dressed, Rhonda called the NYU law school and asked to speak with Mary Jimerson, who had been one of her favorite professors at SMU until she left after Rhonda's second year to accept a faculty position at NYU.

"Of course, I remember you," Professor Jimerson said. "Not only were you a good student, you were the only pregnant student in the entire law school. What did you have?"

"Twin sons," Rhonda said. "They just finished their freshman year at UT."

"And your practice?" the professor asked. "I remember that your interest was in family law. In fact, I still have the paper in my files that you wrote on shared custody for the *SMU Law Review*. It was brilliant."

Rhonda found herself explaining somewhat apologetically that her husband was a chest surgeon and had seldom been available for kissing ouchies and car pooling, so she ended up working part time while their sons were growing up and only made partner six years ago.

"Yes, we see that a lot," Professor Jimerson said. "It's such a problem for young women attorneys. How can they climb the ladder when they are unable to put in sixty-hour weeks? And then, of course, if they make it up the ladder, there's the glass ceiling. But at least you're still in practice. And you have a family, which is more than I can say. So, tell me, what is this 'strange request' you are calling about."

Rhonda felt a bit foolish explaining that she was looking for a judge to marry the daughter of the Russian driver who had been taxiing her and her companions around the city.

"What fun!" Professor Jimerson said. "Actually, I know just the person, a dear friend who was born in Russia. He's a brilliant scholar of constitutional law and taught on faculty until he was appointed to the federal district court."

"Oh, my," Rhonda said, "we really don't need someone prominent. A traffic court judge would do just fine."

"Alex might enjoy it," Mary said. "His wife died last year, and he's become somewhat of a recluse. You tell him I said it's either an evening with the Russians or I'm going to make him serve on my Moot Court Committee again."

Even after Rhonda repeated the professor's warning, Justice Alexander Resnick was reluctant, explaining that his Russian mother had died when he was a boy, and he had been raised by an American stepmother and lost most of his childhood Russian.

Rhonda assured him that he wasn't expected to conduct the ceremony in Russian. English would be fine.

"Well then, I suppose I could help you out," he said. "My children and friends keep telling me it's time for me to start getting out more. If I do this, though, I'll need to meet the bride and groom beforehand and find out what their wishes are."

Rhonda agreed to arrange such a meeting or at least have Tatiana and her fiancé give him a call. Then she told him the name and address of the restaurant. The ceremony was scheduled for eight o'clock tomorrow evening with a dinner to follow.

After she hung up, there was a tap on the door. "Are you ready?" Holly called out. "G.W. is waiting."

Rhonda grabbed the judge's phone number.

As soon as she got in the car, she handed the number to G.W. and explained that either Tatiana or her fiancé needed to give the judge a call.

Rhonda listened while he made a call on his cell phone and

read the number—in Russian, of course. How different the language was from English and Spanish, which normally were the only languages Rhonda heard day in and day out, languages that were closely related on the linguistic family tree. How difficult it must be to come to America as an adult and learn a language that had almost no similarity to one's own.

If she had been in New York on her own she probably wouldn't have struck up a conversation with a Russian driver, and she certainly wouldn't have found herself dancing with him in a nightclub and getting involved with his family. Yet here she was once again on her way to Brighton Beach, this time with a carload of flowers. She didn't know if she should feel pleased or irritated.

Leon's Russian Food was on Neptune Avenue, not far from Coney Island. There was a Mermaid Avenue, too. The amusement park was still in operation but a faded vestige of its heyday when it had been the most famous such establishment in the world.

Leon, an older, larger, and stockier version of G.W., came rushing out to meet the "Texas ladies" and helped G.W. carry the flowers inside and place them in a walk-in refrigerator. Before they went inside, Holly snapped a couple of pictures of neighborhood storefronts with their signs written in Russian. "To show my kids," she explained. "Hey, Rhonda, tell me again, what do you call those kind of letters?"

"Cyrillic," Rhonda said and heard herself automatically adding, "They're based on the Greek alphabet." And winced, realizing what a know-it-all she sounded like.

"Spoken like the class valedictorian," Holly said with a grin. "You always did know stuff that no one else did, like when you were the only person in Miss McCrory's world history class who knew that the capital of Luxembourg was the City of Luxembourg. I have remembered that bit of information ever since, but this is the first time I've ever been able to work it into a conversation."

"Do you still know all the verses to the 'Star-Spangled Banner' and the name of every bone in the body?" Gina Kay asked.

"I suppose I remember the verses," Rhonda said reluctantly, "but I doubt if I could name all the bones. That was just a phase I went through in grade school. I didn't have any friends so I sat around memorizing things. Poetry especially. *Long* poems. To my parents' relief, most of that stopped when I moved to Lamberton and met you guys. My life sort of began the day you two adopted me." Then, to avoid any further reminiscing, Rhonda abruptly reached for Holly's camera and offered to take a picture of her and Gina Kay in front of a beauty shop next door to the restaurant. The shop's indecipherable name was painted on a plate-glass window along with a colorful rendering of an ornate onion-domed spire.

Holly and Gina Kay stood with their arms around each other's waist, and Rhonda was reminded of all the other times she had taken pictures with the two of them standing like that. Shining hair. Easy camaraderie. Happy smiles. And she thought of the twenty-five years of friendship the three of them could have shared.

When G.W. was finished carrying in the flowers, Holly took his picture with Gina Kay in front of his brother's restaurant. Rhonda had hung back, unwilling to be in a photograph with Gina Kay. Holly made a face at her then tucked the camera in her purse, and they all went inside.

The front part of the restaurant was configured like an old-fashioned diner with stools lined up in front of a long counter and ten or so booths that looked out on the street. The walls were covered with Oriental rugs and travel posters featuring Moscow's Red Square, an outdoor market, and a frozen lake covered with ice skaters. Leon led them down a narrow hallway, past the kitchen and restroom, to the back room where wedding receptions and other gatherings were held.

The walls of the large unembellished room had recently been painted a high-gloss hospital white. Even the room's four windows were painted over. Bare lightbulbs in the light fixtures illuminated numerous folded tables leaning against the walls and a jumble of mismatched chairs. The two windowless walls each had a long shelf mounted about eighteen inches from the ceiling that held an assortment of objects—trophies, books, a collection of Russian stacking dolls, and a soccer ball covered with autographs.

With Leon and G.W. waiting expectantly for some comment, Holly said a bit too brightly, "This will be just fine."

After the two men left the women to their planning, Holly said, "Just think of it as a bare slate."

"A very white bare slate," Rhonda observed drily and sat down on a chair with a fraying cane seat.

Ignoring the sarcasm, Holly said, "We'll need to buy shades for the light fixtures."

"We have to be clever about this," Gina Kay pointed out. "G.W. expects to reimburse us for whatever we spend."

"We can use butcher paper to cover the tables," Holly suggested, "and divide up the roses into smaller arrangements for table centerpieces. We'll need to make a Wal-Mart run to buy some cheap glass vases and maybe something to use for bunting to drape around the room and brighten it a bit. Crepe paper in pastel colors might work, and it wouldn't cost much."

"The closest Wal-Mart is probably in New Jersey," Rhonda pointed out, "and given the weekday traffic, it would take half a day to drive over and get back. Any shopping needs to be conducted here in the neighborhood."

"No Wal-Mart!" Holly said with genuine surprise. "Oh my gosh. How do New Yorkers survive? Even Lamberton has a Wal-Mart."

"Which has put half of the stores on Main Street out of business," Gina Kay observed. "There must be some sort of mom-and-pop variety store in the neighborhood where we can buy whatever we need."

"Leon is making the wedding cake," Gina Kay said, "and we have permission to use our hotel's silver punch bowl—and the candelabra. All it will take is a security deposit for twice as much as they are worth. But our main problem is some sort of backdrop for the actually ceremony. What do you think, Rhonda?"

Rhonda shrugged, unwilling to be drawn into the planning. She had already fulfilled her assignment. There would be a judge to perform the ceremony.

While she half listened to Gina Kay and Holly discussing how to proceed, she considered leaving the rest of the planning to them and spending the remainder of the day on her own. They were fretting about where in the room the judge could actually perform the ceremony and where they might borrow a trellis under which the bride and groom could stand. Then they would have to find some ivy—real or artificial—to twine through the trellis, and they probably should cover up the blank wall behind the trellis. Maybe they could use one of the Oriental rugs displayed in the front part of the restaurant. Or rent some artificial trees and strings of little white lights.

Rhonda felt herself growing increasingly impatient. Finally she stood up and said, "You are making this far too complicated."

"So, what do *you* think we should do?" Holly asked. "We can't have them getting married in front of a blank wall."

"Remember, the bride and groom were going to settle for city hall," Rhonda reminded them. "Anything we come up with will be a step up from that."

Rhonda paused, regretting her use of the word "we." But someone needed to take charge here. "I noticed a scarred-up old sideboard in the kitchen where they stack the clean plates," she said.

"We can bring it in here, cover it with a tablecloth and set the large bouquet of mixed flowers on it along with the candelabra and hang a big mirror behind it to reflect the candlelight. Remember that restaurant the night before last with all the mirrors and candles, which made an ordinary room look positively magical. We need to buy candles—lots of candles—and borrow some mirrors to hang around the room. Actually, now that I think about it, I saw an antique mirror in a shop window on Madison Avenue. I was thinking about going back and buying it. We could use it over the sideboard before I ship it home."

Gina Kay actually clapped her hands. "Oh my gosh, mirrors and candlelight. That's perfect. That's absolutely perfect."

Holly hugged Rhonda and teased, "Let's put on a play in the garage and make everybody happy."

"Let's do *what*?" Gina Kay asked with puzzled frown.

"Private joke," Holly told her.

They decided that G.W. could borrow mirrors from family members and friends, and they would talk to Marta about adding some Russian touches to the decor. Holly fished around in her purse for a scrap of paper and a pen. They needed to buy a roll of butcher paper, dozens of candles in all sizes, ribbon, masking tape, picture hangers for the mirrors, and baby's breath. "No Wal-Mart," Holly lamented again. "I just can't believe it."

"What about music?" Rhonda asked.

"A relative is going to play the violin for the ceremony," Holly said. "And there will be a trio of musicians, also relatives, who will provide dance music afterward."

"Dance? Like at the Russian nightclub?" Rhonda asked.

"I hope so," Holly said. "I don't know about you guys, but I'm having fun," she added giving Gina Kay a hug.

Not wanting to be a part of any hugging, Rhonda headed for the bathroom. But she was pleased to have come up with the mirror idea. It would make the stark room come alive. She imagined the look on Tatiana's face when she saw the transformation.

They left to do the shopping with Leon expecting them back at the restaurant for a late lunch.

G.W. took them to a neighborhood variety store, a small establishment just a couple of blocks away with an incredible amount of merchandise piled on and under tables and stacked on floor-to-ceiling shelves. The proprietors were indeed a mom and pop, and Russian, of course. G.W. handled the introductions then stepped to one side, and Rhonda watched in amazed admiration as Holly took over, explaining that she and her two friends—they were all from Texas—wanted to create a beautiful wedding for G.W.'s daughter. She asked the couple if they had had a beautiful wedding. And where they had gotten married. And soon the woman had produced a picture of her and her husband in their traditional wedding finery. "Forty-five years ago," the woman said, pointing at the picture. "In our village."

The couple then took Holly's list and scurried about the store, reaching under piles and behind stacks, climbing up ladders to pull things from top shelves, coming up with every listed item plus a few extra, except the butcher paper, which they would have to buy from a butcher.

G.W. then drove them to a nearby butcher store for a roll of butcher paper and to a florist for baby's breath. Then they headed back to Manhattan—to upper Madison Avenue so Rhonda could purchase the mirror. The salesperson, an elegant Frenchwoman with silver hair, agreed that, for an additional fee, the mirror would be delivered to Leon's Russian Food on Neptune Avenue in the morning and picked up the following morning for shipment to Dallas.

While Rhonda was making her purchase, Gina Kay found a mirror leaning against a wall that she decided to buy. A *very* large mirror. Too big and grand to use for the wedding. "It will look nice in my entry hall, don't you think?" Gina Kay asked Holly as she handed the woman a credit card and explained that she would like the mirror shipped to Lamberton, Texas.

"Is that near Dallas?" the woman asked in her elegantly accented English.

"No," Gina Kay said. "Lamberton is closer to San Antonio than to Dallas, but it's really not close to either one. It's kind of off by itself."

The woman put her reading glasses on her nose and looked down at the address Gina Kay had written. "What is the remainder of this address?" she asked.

"That's all you need: Robertson Ranch, Lamberton, Texas, and the ZIP code," Gina Kay said.

"No, no, no," the saleswoman chastised. "There *must* be a street address."

Gina Kay shrugged. "The ranch is located on a private road, and there is no house number," she explained. "All it says on the mailbox is Robertson Ranch."

"But I must have a street address," the woman insisted. "I am quite sure the postal service will demand it."

Holly stepped up to the counter. "You see, ma'am, the postal people will drop the mirror off at the Pony Express Station outside of Dallas where the paved road ends," she explained. "And then the Pony Express folks will take it cross-country by stagecoach to Lamberton where the sheriff will direct them out to the ranch, unless the creek is too high, in which case they will leave the mirror with him, and when the water goes down, Gina Kay will come to get it in her buckboard."

"*En vérité!*" the woman exclaimed. "Like in the films. How *very* interesting."

They held their mirth until they had gotten back into the

Buick. Then the dam burst. Out-of-control laughter filled the inside of the vehicle. Rhonda laughed so hard she had to hold her sides. *The Pony Express!* And the woman had believed her!

"I can't believe you told her all that," Gina Kay told Holly, fishing a tissue out of her purse to wipe away the tears streaming down her face.

"I'm can't believe she believed me," Holly said, grabbing one of Gina Kay's tissues. "How *very* interesting," she mimicked in a stilted French accent.

"She's going to tell all her customers that she shipped a mirror to a town in Texas via Pony Express," Rhonda said, gasping for air.

When G.W. asked what was funny, they burst out laughing all over again. Rhonda couldn't remember the last time she had laughed so hard. It was wonderful. She reached over and squeezed Holly's hand. "Remember when we were on the way to a pageant in Houston and stopped for gas at a truck stop out in the middle of no place? And in the women's restroom, right next to the Tampax dispenser, there was a dispenser for 'pecker pleasers'?"

This brought another round of laughter. "Yeah," Holly said, clutching her sides. "We just had to know what in the hell a 'pecker pleaser' was, so we put four quarters into that machine and nothing came out. Then we really lost it trying to decide which one of us was going to go out there and tell the man at the cash register that his pecker-pleaser machine was not working and ask for our money to be refunded. I laughed so hard I wet my pants."

"I still don't know what was in that machine," Gina Kay said.

"They probably made a fortune from all the curious females who wanted to find out and were too embarrassed to ask for their money back," Rhonda added.

"Hey, remember when that uppity pageant director in Galveston wouldn't let Gina Kay wear red shoes because 'only women of ill repute wore red shoes'?" Holly asked. "And Gina Kay asked her in all innocence what made their reputes ill."

Rhonda didn't want to laugh anymore but she couldn't help it. Her mirth was tinged with such sadness, though. And anger. True friendship was a rare and beautiful thing, and Gina Kay had spoiled theirs.

Chapter sixteen

When they arrived at the restaurant, Marta, Leon, and a distinguished-looking man in a suit and tie were sitting at a table in the back room with Tatiana and a large young man with a mane of curly blond hair whom Rhonda assumed was the bridegroom. An opened bottle of vodka was sitting in the middle of the table along with a platter of bread and cheese.

"Here is father of the bride and the Texas wedding ladies," Leon announced.

The three men stood, and Leon made the introductions.

Rhonda was surprised to learn that the man in the suit was Justice Alexander Resnick. "Justice Resnick, you are so gracious to help us out," she said, shaking his hand.

"Please call me Alex," he said. "I'm glad to be of assistance, but I must admit that when Leon called and insisted I come right down for lunch, I almost said no. I haven't been getting out much since my wife died, but I am glad Leon wouldn't take no for an answer. We've been having a good visit. And I predict great things for Tatiana and Ivan. If hard work and perseverance are any indication, they should have a wonderful life together."

A distinctive-looking man in his mid-fifties with silvery hair and a kindly expression, Alex Resnick reminded Rhonda of Robert Young during his Marcus Welby years, except his expensive gray suit hung a bit loosely on his frame and his eyes had a sad look about them. Apparently Mrs. Resnick had been greatly loved.

Ivan had a boyish face and massive body and looked more like a football player than an artist. But there were paint stains on his jeans and his chambray work shirt.

Once they were all seated, a pitcher of iced water, at Holly's request, was brought from the kitchen. Alex picked up a small notebook from the table and slipped it into his breast pocket. "I've been taking notes about the ceremony," he explained to the newcomers. "Tatiana and Ivan were telling me what they want included in their vows."

"Just 'love and honor,' " Tatiana said with a smile. "No 'obey.' "

"Here, here," Holly said lifting her water glass. "I'll drink to that. *No 'obey.'* "

Marta joined them with a grin in G.W.'s direction.

Alex smiled at Holly and lifted his glass along with her. But he was looking at Gina Kay when he took a sip.

"Alex remembers prayer his grandmother teach him," Leon said, patting Alex's arm and beaming at him proudly. "He will use prayer in wedding."

"When Leon asked if I knew any Russian," Alex explained, "that old prayer was all I could come up with, although I do recognize some Russian words and phases when I hear them. I knew the prayer by rote and really wasn't even sure what the words meant, but Leon translated it, and as it turns out it's a blessing and actually will be an appropriate touch with which to end the ceremony." He paused, once again glancing in Gina Kay's direction. "I can't believe that I am actually going to be saying something in Russian in front of a gathering of native speakers, but Leon helped me straighten out my pronunciation."

"If Alex go to Russia, in three months he speak like he never leave," Leon proclaimed as he pushed back his chair. "Now, we eat," he announced, and he and Tatiana headed for the kitchen.

Leon carried out a large tureen of borscht and began filling bowls and passing them around the table. Tatiana placed loaves of dark bread on the table along with a bowl of mayonnaise and two platters filled with cheeses, sliced tomatoes and onions, and lumps of tuna. Leon added a platter of pickled vegetables.

As she enjoyed her soup, Rhonda listened to Holly, Marta, and Tatiana discuss veils and tucks. And Gina Kay asked Marta and Tatiana if they had "something Russian" they could add to the wedding decor.

Then Alex responded to a question from Gina Kay asking if he had any memories of his early years in Russia. "Just a few," he said. "I remember riding in a horse-drawn sleigh and watching my grandfather chop wood. And I remember my mother being sick in bed, but I don't remember her death. I don't remember anything about leaving. I've been told it was a harrowing journey. An escape, really. The Soviet government didn't allow emigration."

"Have you ever returned?" Rhonda asked.

"Just as a tourist to Moscow and what was then Leningrad. That was back when the Soviet government carefully controlled all travel by foreign visitors. The town where I was born is near Sverdlovsk, where Czar Nicholas and his family were thought to have been executed, and tourists were not allowed in that area. I used to think about going back someday to visit my mother's grave and see if I could locate any long-lost relatives, but my wife's health began to fail."

"You should make that trip," Gina Kay said. "It would be a good way to connect with the past and begin a new life for yourself." That said, Gina Kay turned her attention to Tatiana and Ivan, asking where they lived and how long before they finished their studies. And she wanted to know if Ivan's art reflected his Russian roots.

"I think artists should not run away from who they are," he explained. "I am a Russian American. I draw from both traditions."

The judge wanted to know which Russian artist had influenced Ivan the most. His answer was Marc Chagall, which seemed to please Alex. "He is a particular favorite of mine," Alex said.

"Mine, too," Gina Kay said. "One of my most prized possessions is a Chagall lithograph. His work is so fanciful. And joyous. So much art is not."

"Hear that, Ivan," Alex said, turning to the young artist. "Don't forget joy." Then he asked Gina Kay if she had seen the Chagall tapestry at the Metropolitan Opera House or the Chagall holdings at the Museum of Modern Art. When she said no, he moved to the other end of the table apparently to discuss the Russian artist. And probably to offer to take her to see the New York Chagalls, Rhonda decided.

Gina Kay had not been flirting with the judge. At least not overtly. She had been paying no more attention to him than she had the other people sitting around the table. But she was having a marked effect on the man. In a very short period of time, the grieving widower had unknowingly switched gears and seemed younger than Rhonda had at first thought. He was sitting up straighter and even seemed to have expanded, with his suit appearing less slack across his shoulders. His expression was more animated, his voice deeper.

Or maybe it was just the vodka.

Rhonda took only tiny sips of vodka and washed them down with generous swallows of water, as had Marta, who had already excused herself and headed back to work promising that she and Leon's wife would be here in the morning to help prepare the room for the wedding. Holly and Gina Kay were drinking only water, as was G.W. Leon, on the other hand, got more and more talkative as he opened a second bottle of vodka and brought additional platters and bowls of food, most of which seemed to be either pickled or served with mayonnaise or both. He and G.W. talked about their growing up years in Siberia with both nostalgia and bitterness and spoke enthusiastically about America and the opportunities their families had found here. "Now," G.W. said proudly, "we are red, white, and blue Russian Americans."

Tatiana turned to her father. "Have you told them what the G.W. stands for?" she asked.

"My Russian name is hard for American people to speak," G.W. explained. "So I change to American name. Now I am George Washington Andropov."

"Here, here," Holly said, raising her glass once again. "Here's to George Washington Andropov, the most honest and reliable driver in the city of New York."

Then Alex asked Gina Kay to tell them about her ranch. "I've never known a rancher before," he said.

Gina Kay spoke about cattle production. And sheep. She had several hundred acres currently dedicated to sheep, which was becoming ever more important to the ranch's profit line. The ranch also grew its own alfalfa, oats, and hay to feed their animals. And they maintained an extensive kitchen garden, which had to have a ten-foot-tall fence to keep out the deer. "The deer can have all the oats and alfalfa they want but not my tomatoes and green beans," Gina Kay said.

"It sounds like you are the ruler of a small kingdom," Alex observed with admiration in his voice.

Gina Kay smiled. "Yes, you might say that. My late husband wasn't interested in the business side of ranching. He liked growing things, and he enjoyed working with the animals. My father-in-law is still alive, but he mostly serves as my adviser. The days when he could mount a horse and ride the range are long over."

"And you do that?" Alex asked. "You 'ride the range'?"

Gina Kay smiled. "Almost every day, usually at daybreak. And I usually see something that needs changing or fixing. Actually, it's the best time of the day to collect my thoughts and commune with nature. There's one place especially, on the highest point of the ranch, where it seems like you can see forever. Over the river, across the rolling countryside, all the way to the horizon. The sunrises are so beautiful. And the sunsets, too. They are inspiring and humbling."

The highest place on the ranch. Rhonda knew exactly where that was. It was where she and Terry made love. Under a giant live oak tree. Their special place. She wondered if Terry showed it to Gina Kay or if she found it on her own.

Her late husband. Gina Kay had managed to work that into her comments, Rhonda thought with irritation. But then the judge had made a reference to being a widower.

She watched the judge lean closer to Gina Kay and say something for her ear only. Amazing. His period of mourning had just ended. And Rhonda could understand why. Gina Kay was beautiful, ruled over a small kingdom, and owned a Chagall lithograph.

When had Terry first realized that he was attracted to Gina Kay, a girl he had known his whole life? Rhonda found herself wondering if he had sometimes been thinking of Gina Kay during that last summer when they were making love at every opportunity. Had his first sexual conquest only whetted his appetite for someone else? Then Rhonda discarded that notion. The love she and Terry had experienced that summer had been genuine. His disillusionment had come later. After the wreck. After it seemed as though he had lost her forever. Maybe his trips to Austin started earlier in the semester—to see Gina Kay, only to drop her when Rhonda wrote him that first letter.

Rhonda shook her head with irritation and took another sip of vodka. How many times over the years had she gone down this road, trying to figure out why *it* happened and how? It had long since ceased to be a daily agony, more an annoying curiosity. A puzzle that went unsolved. A puzzle she thought about less and less and seemingly had little relevance to her present-day life. Since Terry's death, however, she once again was preoccupied with it. And she didn't want to be. It was stupid. She was a stronger person than that. But no matter how much she told herself that what happened back then no longer mattered, she wanted to know about it. She wanted very much to have the puzzle solved and fervently hoped that Gina Kay would have an explanation that she could believe, an explanation that allowed her to bury her thoughts of Terry once and for all.

At the end of the meal, Leon taught them the chorus to a Russian folk song that would be sung tomorrow evening. A song about true love lasting forever, Leon explained.

Although Rhonda did not understand the words, Leon's rich baritone, combined with the song's haunting melody, brought tears to her eyes even though she wasn't sure she knew what true love was.

※

With a glance at her watch, Gina Kay announced it was time for the Texas ladies and G.W. to be on their way. They thanked Leon for lunch and promised they would return in the morning to prepare for the wedding.

From the restaurant, Gina Kay instructed G.W. to take them to the Empire State Building. On the way, they agreed that they would get themselves back to the hotel and decided on the time that G.W. should pick them up. Plans for the evening included a play with dinner afterward.

After they emerged from the car, the three of them stood on the sidewalk staring up at the towering structure. It seemed impossibly tall and looking up at it made Rhonda dizzy. One hundred and two stories—she had known that statistic since she was a little girl and the building had been the tallest in the world.

She had never forgotten how wowed she had been by the view from the top of the building. Even the view from the top of the doomed World Trade Center, spectacular as it had been, could not compare to the matchless experience that awaited one atop the

Empire State Building, which was surrounded on all sides by the sheer grandeur and concentrated mass of the countless other towering buildings that made up midtown Manhattan. For Rhonda, it was the quintessential New York experience, one that no photograph or painting or movie could even remotely capture. It ranked right up there with her first glimpse of the Grand Canyon and the redwood forests of northern California.

And now, two decades later, she was once again riding the elevator to the building's observation deck, this time anticipating the pleasure she would glean from watching Holly witness the spectacular view for the first time. With the sky dazzlingly clear, it was the perfect day for it.

Rhonda would have preferred to take Holly up alone. But Gina Kay said that going to the top of the Empire State Building had been her most memorable New York experience during her pageant trip twenty-five years ago, and she, too, was looking forward to being with Holly when she first experienced the view.

Holly didn't disappoint them. She wrapped her arms around her body and said, "Oh, my God" several times. Then she announced, "This settles it. I have to come back here. I am going to bring my kids to New York City. It is my moral responsibility as their mother."

Rhonda and Gina Kay followed Holly as she walked slowly around the deck, taking in the view from all directions. "I'm not going to take pictures," she said. "They could not possibly begin to capture all this."

Rhonda and Gina Kay exchanged glances much like two proud parents taking a shared satisfaction in their charming offspring. "It was worth coming to New York just for this," Gina Kay said.

"Yes," Rhonda agreed, as they followed Holly on her second turn around the deck. "Thank God Holly never became blasé."

"What would we do without her?" Gina Kay said. "It's been hard on her, you know, maintaining friendships with both of us."

"I'm sure it has," Rhonda said, feeling a wave of discomfort. "I thought the three of us would be friends for life. It never crossed my mind that it would be otherwise. Even if we moved to opposite sides of the globe, I knew we would always be there for each other. But then, the primary ingredient of true friendship is trust." That said, Rhonda went to stand beside Holly.

Back down on the street, the three of them parted for the rest of the afternoon with Holly heading south toward the Fashion Institute in the Garment District where she was going to attend a showing of evening gowns by a designer who was becoming popular with a number of celebrities. Gina Kay was going to spend the rest of the afternoon at the Metropolitan Museum of Art. And Rhonda was going to wander around her old stomping grounds in Greenwich Village.

After studying a subway map, Rhonda headed underground. At this time of day, there were seats for everyone. Rhonda sat in the back of the car and regarded her fellow passengers, recalling how some of the best people watching in New York was found on the subway. No one talked much. Mostly passengers either dozed or stared blankly. Or read a newspaper. As much as their faces, the newspapers attested to the diversity of the city. From her vantage point, Rhonda could see several people reading newspapers written in vertical Asian scripts. A Hasidic man with his traditional black hat and long black coat was reading a Hebrew newspaper. A pretty young woman with a baby asleep in her arms was reading a Spanish-language newspaper. And an elderly woman with a string shopping bag was enjoying a newspaper written in Russian. Or maybe it was Greek.

Rhonda got off at the West 4th Street station and climbed several flights of stairs before reaching the street.

And there she was once again, in the familiar environs of her long-ago summer in New York. She crossed the street to Washington Square Park where she had come to read or doze or enjoy the sunshine. Most of the benches in the vast square were occupied, many by young men and women who, with their backpacks and scruffy appearance, Rhonda judged to be NYU students. Many of the NYU buildings were scattered throughout the city, but the library, student center, law school, and administrative buildings lined the park, which had been the center of Rhonda's existence that summer. The building where she had lived was just a block away. If she leaned out the window of her one-room apartment, she could see a corner of the imposing arch that dominated Washington Square.

She strolled around a bit, noting the changes. Some of the old buildings were gone, replaced by atrocious excuses for modern architecture. Some of the elegant row houses on the north side of the square were still intact, but she had read they were in danger of encroachment as the university grew. She recalled the names of famous writers who had lived around the square—Willa Cather, Edith Wharton, and Mark Twain, among them.

She had to smile at the sight of an elderly black man wearing a tattered wedding dress, flowing veil, and combat boots. She watched as he marched around the square placing stacks of pennies on the ends of benches and on the retaining walls around trees. No one was giving the man a second glance.

Rhonda found an empty bench by the square's amphitheater and watched a bare-chested young man with flowing black hair pantomime a bullfight. While he stomped his booted feet and swished a red velvet cape, the man called out an endless litany of social injustices, none of which seemed to have anything to do with bullfighting. Those scattered around the amphitheater studiously ignored him, choosing instead to sun themselves or read.

Rhonda sat for a while enjoying the only-in-New York feel of her surroundings while she reminisced. She had sworn off men that summer, not so much because she felt committed to Dennis—no words of commitment had been spoken between them—

but because she was weary of dating, weary of knowing a relationship was going no place but still sleeping with the guy anyway. She had deliberately left her birth control pills back in Dallas. She hated the damned things anyway. The standard dose was higher back then, and they made her feel bloated and her breasts so tender that during her period she couldn't bear to take her bra off. She wasn't sure she even liked sex anymore, yet she had taken the hated pills. And entered into one relationship after another—in search of another Terry, she supposed. Except Terry had dumped her. Why would she want another man like him? In fact, they all dumped her, except for the guys she managed to leave before they had a chance to walk away. Whichever scenario, however, each time a relationship ended, instead of being devastated, she had been relieved.

Rhonda lifted her face to the sun and recalled how she had truly enjoyed her chaste summer in New York. She had stopped wearing makeup, stopped polishing her nails, and only washed her hair when her scalp itched. Her only lover that summer had been New York itself. If she wasn't in class or at the library, she was involved with New York and its museums, libraries, theaters, neighborhoods, shops, foods, smells, voices.

She did think some about Dennis back in Dallas. He was what her mother would have called "a good man," meaning a man that a woman should grab hold of and never let go. But all summer she hadn't called him or even sent him a postcard. Then at the airport, she did call him, planning to tell him she was on her way to visit her parents in Phoenix and would be back in Dallas the following week. But he wasn't in, of course. That was during his residency, when he was putting in one-hundred-hour weeks at the hospital.

She spent a week in Phoenix, allowing her parents to spoil her a bit before she returned to Dallas and law school. While she was in Phoenix, she went to see her mother's gynecologist. That was when she had an IUD inserted. No more birth control pills.

She tried calling Dennis again. This time she called during the day and had him paged at the hospital. He was surprised to hear from her. And cool. "After three months without so much as a postcard, I assumed I was history," he said. She could hear sirens and loud voices in the background. He was in the ER and really couldn't talk, he explained. Hurriedly she told him that she was in Phoenix but heading back to Dallas tomorrow afternoon. If he happened to be free tomorrow evening, maybe they could see each other.

Dennis was waiting for her at the Dallas airport. An unexpected surprise, as was the undeserved warmth of his embrace.

She wanted to love him, but what if he left her?

She must have gotten pregnant the second week she was back. It took her a while to realize that she wasn't just late with her period. Pregnancy was the farthest thing from her mind. After all, there was the IUD. She was responsible about sex and birth control.

But her body had rejected the IUD.

She hadn't wanted an abortion, but what else could she do?

Dennis was more than the father of her children. He was the savior of her children.

She assumed throughout her pregnancy that he would leave after the babies were born. Then she assumed that he would leave after she had established a law practice and was on her own.

She kept waiting for Dennis to leave, but he never did.

And sitting there in Washington Square Park, with its stately arch designed by Stanford White, the infamous architect who had courted then dumped the most beautiful woman of his time, Rhonda realized that she was still waiting for Dennis to leave, maybe even assuring that he would leave by never quite opening her heart to him. After all this time, she was still doing that when he had proven himself over and over again.

A young couple on a shaded bench were smooching a bit. Just

touching and nibbling. Nothing over the top. She felt old watching them. She didn't want to be old. Not yet. She felt as though she had never been young.

She wanted to walk through the law school library for old time's sake, but a security guard turned her away. Instead, she wound her way over to the Strand Bookstore, which had been one of her favorite haunts. It was exactly the same as she remembered, a creaky old building with an endless maze of narrow aisles between towering stacks of used books.

Then she wandered over to Bleecker Street and poked around in some of the tiny specialty shops. She bought tooled leather belts for Dennis and the boys, and a hair ornament for Jason's girlfriend—for Sarah, whom Rhonda had never met but who made her son blush with delight from just saying her name.

She tried to call Dennis, but his office manager said he had actually gotten away early and was heading for the lake. He didn't answer his cell phone, and she didn't leave a message. But she thought of him out on the lake in his sailboat. Alone, she hoped. *Please let him be sailing alone.*

Soon, Rhonda promised herself, she would spend another evening with him on the lake with no hidden agenda to discuss but just because she wanted to be with him. Maybe they could spend the night, letting the movement of the water rock them to sleep after sex.

Chapter seventeen

Even though Gina Kay had told G.W. that they would find their own transportation after the play, there he was in front of the theater waiting to drive them to the China Grill for their after-theater meal. Once again, Holly thought of Waco, where at this hour restaurants would be winding down for the evening, but in New York City, restaurants stayed open to accommodate the after-theater crowd.

The decor of the stylish China Grill included elegant floral displays and quotations from Marco Polo inscribed on the floors. Gina Kay ordered a bottle of champagne, which was served in traditional champagne glasses rather than the more usual flutes.

Holly felt like a star from an old black-and-white movie—Marlene Dietrich or Greta Garbo—as she sipped from the elegant glass. She thought of the smart little cocktail hats Marlene and Greta wore with a bit of veil for mystery. And they would have been smoking a cigarette in a long holder. She doubted if cigarette holders would ever be back in style, but maybe it was time to bring back cocktail hats.

While she sipped, Holly half listened over the background din to the short discourse Rhonda offered on the importance of Marco Polo in world history and surreptitiously glanced about the room. Gina Kay had read that the restaurant was a good place for catching glimpses of the rich and famous, and sure enough, Holly spotted a couple of semicelebrities among the diners. She didn't know their names, but she was certain a broad-shouldered, well-dressed man at the next table was a professional football player, and across the room she recognized a model whose face appeared in television and print ads for a prominent cosmetic line.

"Gee whiz," Holly said when Rhonda finished her little history lesson. "I didn't know old Marco was so important. He sort of created wanderlust, didn't he? I guess Mrs. Polo would have been stuck back home raising the kids while he was hobnobbing with emperors and khans. Which allows me to segue into a discussion of tonight's play. Marco and all the discovery guys did pretty much what they wanted with their lives, unlike the men in the play, who started out in charge but ended up henpecked. It was all very funny, but on hindsight I have decided that it irritated me."

Holly had seen something of herself in the first act of *I Love You, You're Perfect, Now Change*, which portrayed young women being sweet and accommodating in order to attract a mate. The second half of the play showed the same couples after years of marriage with the power pendulum having swung the other way and the men in charge only when they were behind the steering wheel of a vehicle.

"Of course, the play was written by a man," Holly pointed out. "And it's true that some women start realizing that 'accommodating' is just another word for 'doormat.' But it seems to me that a lot of women just seethe in silence and a lot of others never allow themselves to acknowledge any sort of discontent."

"Sometimes it's a case of selecting your issues," Rhonda said. "I didn't think it was a good idea for Dennis to buy a sailboat when both of us were so busy and neither one of us knew a thing about sailing, but since I hadn't sought Dennis's input when I redecorated the downstairs, I didn't offer any opposition." Then she asked Holly, "Do you ever ask Sandy to hold your purse?"

Holly recalled the scene in the play when, after twenty or so years of marriage, the once ultra-cool, in-charge kind of guy was meekly standing on the sidewalk holding his wife's purse and packages while she ran back into a store. "No," she answered, "but I can remember my father doing that. He would hold Mom's purse while she took me to the bathroom or ran into a store to check prices or whatever. I always thought he looked pretty silly. When I got older, I made sure I was the one holding her purse. But I can't ever remember my mother driving a car in which my father was riding. They had a good marriage, though, a real partnership.

"I stopped scooting over and letting Sandy drive if I'm picking him up at the high school or wherever," Holly continued. "It took fifteen years of marriage for me to cure myself of that. Then suddenly both of our vehicles had bucket seats with the gear box and drink holders sticking up in the middle, and for Sandy to drive, I either had to climb over all that stuff or get out and walk around to the passenger side. I remember thinking how stupid that was. Then one day, I just sat there. He opened the driver's side door and waited for me to get out so he could get in. And I didn't move. We had a big argument about it. He claimed it was emasculating for a man to ride in a car with a woman driving. What about Dennis?" she asked Rhonda. "Does he always drive when the two of you are in the car?"

"Actually, he prefers that I drive in town," Rhonda said. "As many years as he's lived in Dallas, Dennis still gets turned around if he gets off his beaten path. When we go out of town, he usually drives, and I navigate, but it's never been an issue."

There was a pause, and then Rhonda turned to Gina Kay. "What about you and Terry?"

"It was an issue," Gina Kay said, picking up the menu. "Terry was not a safe driver. So, what shall we order? The food here is supposed to be a 'fusion of American, European, and Asian cuisine.' "

Oh, dear, Holly thought, realizing how thoughtless it had been for her to bring up anything having to do with a husband behind the wheel of a vehicle. "I'm so sorry," she mouthed to Gina Kay.

Gina Kay offered her a nod followed by a small but forgiving smile.

Holly picked up her menu and tried to concentrate on the words. After having pickled stuff for lunch and committing a really stupid faux pas, she was ready for some comfort food. What she really wanted, Holly realized, was chicken-fried steak and mashed potatoes and gravy, but since such a meal wasn't on the menu, she ordered a steak. Gina Kay went with the pork tenderloin, and Rhonda ordered an exotic chicken dish.

Their orders taken, Gina Kay lifted her glass. "Here's to 'the Texas ladies.' I hope the wedding is a great success."

Holly touched glasses with Gina Kay and Rhonda. She was both excited and apprehensive about tomorrow. So many things could go wrong at a wedding.

And then the day after would be the big climax when Gina Kay told them how it was that she came to be Terry's wife. After that, they were either going out on the town for their last night together in the Big Apple, or Rhonda would go into her bedroom and close the door. Their flights left the following morning. One way or the other, Gina Kay's experiment would be over. Probably it was too much to hope that the three of them could suddenly be best friends again, or even just plain friends, but Holly hoped that Gina Kay and Rhonda could at least wish each other well.

After dinner, G.W. drove them along the East River to the marvelous Brooklyn Bridge, which connected the Lower East Side to Brooklyn. They crossed to the Brooklyn side, and G.W. accompanied them on a leisurely stroll along the riverfront promenade, which offered a spectacular nighttime view of lower Manhattan and the incomparable bridge itself.

"It's the Emerald City," Holly said, gazing across the river. Then she found herself attempting to explain to G.W. about *The Wizard of Oz* and Dorothy and Toto. Finally, she gave up and told him to rent the video. "It's required viewing for all red, white, and blue

Russian Americans," she said, giving his arm an affectionate squeeze. "Then when tourists stare up at the skyscrapers and say they are not in Kansas, you will understand why."

Then she asked, "Have you ever brought Marta here to walk along this promenade and look at Manhattan mirrored in the water?"

G.W. shook his head.

"You should do that," Rhonda said. "Tomorrow night after the wedding. Tell her she is beautiful in the moonlight and you love her just as much now as you did on the day you got married."

"Does your husband tell you nice words?" he asked Rhonda.

"Yes," she said, "as a matter of fact, he does."

The next morning, Rhonda rose early and went jogging in Central Park along with a small army of joggers who ranged from the truly athletic who ran as though they were competing in the Olympics to folks who barely picked up their feet and just shuffled along. Rhonda was someplace in the middle. Someday, before she was too old even to consider such a thing, she would like to step up the running a notch or two, maybe even join a running club and compete with other women in her age group. She loved feeling fit, loved having muscular calves and being able to dash up multiple flights of stairs without being winded. Of course, she dashed up stairs because she was too impatient to wait for elevators, so she also would like to become less impatient.

It was a wonderful morning, crisp and clear. The squirrels dashed about, and the birds were happy. Only two more days of this difficult trip, then she would be flying home. As difficult and tension-filled as the trip had been so far, she was glad to be reacquainted with New York. She had stayed away too long.

She was actually looking forward to the day. To Tatiana and Ivan's wedding day. She and Holly and Gina Kay would work their magic on Leon's back room and probably get a bit maudlin this evening during the wedding itself. Back in Lamberton, they had daydreamed about their someday weddings, each secure in the knowledge that her two best friends would be participants. But that hadn't been the case for any of them, thanks to Gina Kay.

She and Dennis would have their twentieth anniversary in November. Dennis had suggested they repeat their wedding vows in front of their children, parents, siblings, and special friends to make up for their hurry-up, city hall marriage. Rhonda had been cool on the idea, although she wasn't sure why. Perhaps it was because a restating of vows would indicate permanence, a way of saying this marriage truly was about till death us do part. In the beginning, their marriage, at least in Rhonda's mind, had nothing to do with permanence. Marriage was just a way to get through a difficult situation. As discontented as Holly had sometimes seemed in her marriage, Rhonda realized that Holly now considered it to be a lifetime contract. Her one infidelity and subsequent abortion had only served to reinforce her commitment.

Holly considered her marriage a work in progress. She changed what she could and accepted the things that she could not.

As for Gina Kay and Terry's marriage, Rhonda's only clue came last night when Gina Kay indicated that Terry hadn't been romantic. Rhonda had felt smug satisfaction when she heard those words. *It served Gina Kay right.*

Remembering her reaction, Rhonda stopped in her tracks. A male jogger cursed when he had to swerve to miss her. Hands on her hips and chest heaving, Rhonda walked over to a bench and dropped down on it, elbows on knees, leaning forward to catch her breath. Sweat dripped to the grass below.

It served Gina Kay right.

Rhonda contemplated this decidedly vindictive thought. She was deeply curious about what Gina Kay would say tomorrow when she finally got around to the trip's main event. But did she really want to learn that Gina Kay and Terry had found nothing but unhappiness in their marriage?

Did she really hope to learn that Gina Kay and Terry's three children had been raised by unhappy parents?

After all the pain they had caused her, Gina Kay and Terry damned well better have had at least a marginally good marriage. She'd hate to think that it had been all for naught.

Rhonda sat on the bench contemplating this realization, trying it on for size, as her breathing and heart rate slowed.

Then she put the thought aside.

She would decide what she should or should not think about their marriage tomorrow. After all, wasn't that why they came to New York?

Chapter eighteen

Marta greeted them with a broad smile when they arrived at Leon's restaurant the next morning. Rhonda watched while Holly gave her the garment bag that held what was now referred to as "the wedding dress" and a box with the veil she had created. Marta unzipped the garment bag just enough to allow her to touch the lace. "I can hardly wait to see my daughter in this dress," she said.

Marta introduced them to Leon's wife, Anna. Rhonda was surprised to learn that Leon and G.W.'s wives were sisters. While Tatiana was G.W. and Marta's only child, Anna and Leon had two sons who, like their cousin Tatiana, worked eight-hour days and were also college students. Both sons would be at the wedding tonight.

Marta and Anna had already scrubbed the back room and cleared away the assorted paraphernalia from the two long shelves. And Leon proudly showed off the four-tiered wedding cake. The cake was decorated with brightly colored folk designs seen on traditional Russian costumes. "I've never seen anything like it," Rhonda said quite sincerely. "It is a masterpiece."

Leon and G.W. moved the heavy sideboard in from the kitchen, which was a beehive of activity with preparations for the wedding feast. At the women's direction, the two men placed tables against the wall at opposite ends of the room, one for the wedding cake and the other for the punch bowl. Both tables were covered with white tablecloths, as was the sideboard. They covered the other tables with butcher paper then folded and stacked them in a corner for use after the ceremony. The chairs were arranged in rows facing the sideboard, where the actual ceremony would be conducted. Rhonda wished they could think of some sort of camouflage for the mismatched assortment of chairs, but the best they could do was to group the chairs in rows according the height of their backs.

Then it was time to hang the mirrors. Since the mirrors had been Rhonda's idea, Gina Kay and Holly deferred to her on their placement. G.W. and Leon had actually gathered up more than were needed so Rhonda was able to pick and choose. She had the men hang the smaller mirrors above the two long shelves and the larger ones throughout the room. After each was hung, pieces of Styrofoam were placed behind the top of the mirrors to make them tilt out from the wall and better reflect the candlelight.

The mirror Rhonda had purchased at the Madison Avenue antiques store was delivered midmorning, and the men hung it over the sideboard with oohs and aahs of approval from the women.

Holly placed the large candelabra from the hotel and the large bouquet of mixed blossoms on the sideboard. Marta added three ornate icons that had been in her family for generations. The five women stepped back to access the overall effect, which met with their enthusiastic approval.

After they had put the tapers in holders and the larger candles on small plates, Rhonda placed them around the room—along the shelves, on the windowsills, on the punch and cake tables. She looked forward to this evening when the candles would all be lit and the room was transformed into a magical place. She felt an almost childlike sense of excitement for the evening to come. They had pulled off a minor miracle. And it was her idea that had made it all come together.

Rhonda looked around for her purse, which she located under a table. She pulled her cell phone out of the side pocket and punched in her mother's number. "Mom," she said, "you're not going to believe what I'm doing!"

She described in great detail how she had spent the morning. Yes, Gina Kay and Holly were here with her. The bride was going to wear the dress that Holly designed for Gina Kay to wear during her pageant appearance. Then, of course, she had to explain who in the world all these people were and how it was that she and Holly and Gina Kay became involved in their wedding preparations.

"From Siberia!" Cathy exclaimed. "I didn't know anyone actually lived in Siberia." Then Rhonda heard her call out, "Frank, the girls are putting on a wedding for a girl from Siberia." Then into the phone, Cathy said, "We saw Gina Kay on television the other night. Wasn't she just wonderful! You tell her that we said she is still as beautiful as ever, and that we're proud of what she's done with her life. Her parents must have been so proud of her. What a shame they weren't still alive to see her get that award on national television."

Holly walked over and held out her hand for the phone. "Yes, they would have been proud," Rhonda acknowledged. "Here's Holly, Mom. She wants to say 'hello.' "

Rhonda listened while Holly explained that the mirrors and candles had all been Rhonda's idea. "It is going to be fabulous!" Holly said. "I can hardly wait to see all that candlelight in all those mirrors and the look in our bride's eyes when she sees it. She's a lovely girl and will make a beautiful bride. Her father has been our driver." Holly paused a minute, listening, then said, "Yes, Siberia. He showed us pictures. Tomatoes grow there."

Then without first checking with Rhonda, Holly handed the phone to Gina Kay, who had just come into the room carrying the final bouquet of flowers from the refrigerator. "It's Cathy Hayes," Holly explained.

"Oh, my God," Gina Kay said putting down the flowers and grabbing the tiny phone. "Mrs. Hayes, it's Gina Kay," she said.

Rhonda glared at Holly. She didn't want Gina Kay talking to her mother.

"Oh, I've missed you, too," Gina Kay was saying. "And Colonel Hayes. I never drive by your old house without thinking of all the wonderful times I had there and how good you and Colonel Hayes were to me. I'd never heard of a thank-you note until you taught me how to write one—with black ink and plain white notepaper. Like Mama said, you were a lady with class." Gina Kay paused and wiped away tears with the back of her hand. "I was so lucky. I had three sets of parents—my mama and daddy, you and Colonel Hayes, and Mr. and Mrs. Burgess. I appreciated so much the lovely letter you wrote after Terry died."

Then with genuine affection in her voice Gina Kay spoke for a few minutes with Rhonda's father. "I still remember the name of every one of your horses," she said. "Blondie was the one I always rode."

Rhonda had never really considered the loss to her parents when her three-way friendship ended. She and Holly and Gina Kay had shared each other's parents and learned different things from each. It had been a wonderful time in all their lives. In Rhonda's mind those memories had ugly X's marked across them, but obviously her parents still felt affection for Gina Kay in spite of what she had done to their daughter. Her mother had even written Gina Kay a sympathy letter! And that made Rhonda angry.

But then her parents never wanted her to marry Terry in the first place.

God, it was all so confusing. She didn't want to be angry with her parents. Or with anyone else. Anger was so exhausting. It kept one from feeling other emotions.

Her mother must be back on the phone again. Gina Kay was

asking for her stollen bread recipe and recalling all the Christmas baking she had done. The conversation ended with Gina Kay saying that she would like to see them again, too. Soon she hoped. Then Gina Kay handed Rhonda the phone. "Your mother wants to talk to you again." Then she lowered her voice. "I'm sorry if my speaking to your parents upset you."

Rhonda shrugged and turned away. She put the phone to her ear and said, "Mom, I want you and Daddy to celebrate your birthday in Dallas with Dennis and me. And hopefully Jason and Scott will be back from Colorado by then. We'll do the mirror and candle thing in the dining room. Seventy-six candles for my mother. It will look glorious."

"My goodness, Rhonda, you'd have to have the fire department standing by! How about one candle for every decade or something like that? Thank you for calling, dear. I'm so glad you girls are enjoying yourselves. I'd like you to invite Holly and Gina Kay to my birthday party."

"Don't hold your breath on that one, Mom. This trip has been . . . *difficult*."

Rhonda had planned to call Dennis and tell him about the wedding preparations, but she had lost her enthusiasm and returned the phone to her purse.

❦

Holly had an appointment later in the afternoon and had brought a change of clothes with her. After eating one of the sandwiches Leon had prepared, she got ready while the others put the final touches on the room. Then G.W. drove them to the site of the World Trade Center.

The three of them had agreed shortly after they arrived that they wanted to visit the site. If Gina Kay and Holly hadn't wanted to come, Rhonda would have come alone. She felt that it was her duty.

Rhonda closed her eyes imaging how it had looked when the two elegantly simple columns were still dominating the lower Manhattan skyline. The three women stood for a time, each silently remembering that horrible day when they, along with the rest of the world, had watched their television screens in horror as the towers collapsed and carried so many people to their death. Then another plane flew into the Pentagon. And a fourth was diverted from its target by heroes who sacrificed themselves to save others.

Rhonda had been ready to walk out the door that morning when Dennis called her from the hospital. "Turn on the television," he said. "Something terrible is happening in New York." She turned on the kitchen TV just in time to see the jet plane flying into the second tower. Her knees had gone weak as realization dawned that this was not an accident, that another plane had already flown into the first tower. And people were dying a horrible death. Hundreds of people. Some jumping to their death rather than enduring the inferno. Then came the ultimate disaster when first one and then the other building collapsed, killing not hundreds of people, but thousands. No response seemed adequate for all that horror.

She wished that Dennis were there with her. She didn't want to endure this nightmare alone.

And quite miraculously, there he was.

Never had his arms felt so strong and reassuring. He had wept with her. And reassured her. This was not the end of the world. They and the nation would get through this. Their sons were safe. They had each other.

From lower Manhattan, G.W. drove to the Garment District where Holly, armed with her portfolio, and Rhonda got out of the car. As Rhonda watched the Buick pull away from the curb with Gina Kay still inside, she wondered how Gina Kay was going to spend the afternoon. All she had said was that she would see them back at the hotel. Tonight G.W. would be driving Tatiana and her mother in the Buick. He had offered to find other transportation for them, but they insisted he had enough to think about.

Rhonda's plan for the afternoon was to check out the Chelsea Antiques Building then head uptown to browse in the shops along Fifth Avenue.

"I feel guilty going off in search of frivolous pleasures after seeing where all those people died," Rhonda admitted.

"You know what our wise mothers would say?" Holly asked. "They would say life is for the living. Let's take a deep breath and feel grateful."

Rhonda did just that. *Grateful*. She did need to practice gratefulness.

"Do I look okay?" Holly asked.

Holly was wearing a cream-colored linen jacket over dark brown slacks and a matching shell that were the exact shade of her eyes and hair. On her head was a roll-brim raffia boater, and her shoes were brown mules with three-inch heels. A handsome leather bag hung from her shoulder. "You look super," Rhonda said. "Who are you trying to wow?"

"Well, I was supposed to go to another style show, but the head designer with a company who makes evening gowns saw my picture in the *Daily News*. Fortunately I have a business listing in the Waco telephone directory under 'Holly Warner' or he never would have been able to track me down. He left a message with Sandy who called to pass along the guy's phone number. Jerry Winston is his name. He asked me to bring my portfolio. Do you know how many years I've been waiting for someone to do that?"

Holly wasn't the only one in view carrying a large portfolio. Rhonda wondered if sketches of next season's fashion were lurking in the portfolios being carried by the men and women rushing up and down the sidewalks and winding their way in and out of the slow-moving traffic. Many of them were talking on cell phones. All of them were young. Too young. What the fashion world needed was more designers like Holly, who understood how few women really wore a size four.

"You just march right in there and wow him," Rhonda told her. "You're the best! Remember that. I'll see you back at the hotel and have a bottle of wine waiting. What about Gina Kay? What was she going to do for the rest of the afternoon?"

Holly shrugged. "I don't know, but I can guess."

"Did the judge call her?"

"First thing this morning while you were in the shower," Holly said as she glanced at her watch.

"She isn't *interested* in him, is she?"

"I don't know. Do you have a problem with that?"

"My God, Holly, Terry's been dead for only two and a half months."

"Rhonda, you know next to nothing about Gina Kay's life and marriage. And in spite of what you may think, there're lots of things *I* don't know. Let's just give her the benefit of the doubt— at least until tomorrow. Okay?"

Then Holly gave Rhonda a one-armed hug. "Got to go, sweetie," she said and ducked around a rack of clothes being pushed along the sidewalk by a lanky young man with dreadlocks.

Rhonda watched Holly cross the street. She looked quite smart and slim enough. She wouldn't be Holly if she were skinny.

And she wouldn't be Holly if she didn't speak her mind.

Chapter nineteen

When Holly opened the door to their hotel suite, Rhonda was already there, shoes off, curled up on one end of the sofa with a glass of iced tea in her hand and CNN on the television screen. She picked up the remote and turned off the television. "I decided to forgo wine since I'm sure we'll be indulging in a bit of libation at the wedding."

"Are you mad at me?" Holly asked over her shoulder as she carried her portfolio, handbag, and hat into the bedroom.

"Because you told me to withhold judgment on Gina Kay's behavior?" Rhonda called after her.

"Yeah. I was afraid I made you mad," Holly said as she came back into the room and poured herself a glass of tea.

"I was peeved," Rhonda acknowledged, "but I had an epiphany of sorts this morning while I was jogging in the park. All these years I've been hoping that Gina Kay and Terry had a rotten marriage. But after all the pain they caused me, I realized that they damned well better have had a reasonably good one. I'd hate to think I went through all that for nothing. But if Gina Kay is willing to get involved with a man so soon after Terry's death, that would lead me to believe that she's not exactly overwhelmed with grief."

Holly stepped out of her shoes, and settled in at the opposite end of the sofa. "So, Gina Kay and Terry should have had a happy marriage because they owed it to *you*? And Gina Kay should not get involved with the judge because it would offend *you*?"

"Now you *are* making me mad," Rhonda said, her spine stiffening as she carefully placed her glass in the precise center of a coaster.

"Well then, I'll take a different tack. How would you feel if Dennis died?"

Rhonda's eyes widened. "Jesus, Holly, what a terrible thing to say! I would be devastated, of course."

"Good, I'm glad to hear it. But you really can't absolutely say that you would turn away a really nice man if he came along a few months later, can you? After all, as a woman with a still very alive husband, you apparently came perilously close to getting involved with another man. Or maybe you *did* get involved with another man." When Rhonda tried to interrupt, Holly held up a hand. "And given my own history," she continued, "I think that neither one of us has the right to judge Gina Kay if she spent the afternoon screwing the judge."

Rhonda took a sip of tea, then swirled the ice cubes around in the glass for what seemed like a very long time before she responded. "You're right. Judging Gina Kay is a knee-jerk thing for me." She drank the remainder of the tea, once again taking great pains to place her glass in the exact middle of the coaster, then met Holly's gaze.

"I know you think I haven't been a good wife to Dennis because I've never quite gotten over what happened in my life long before he came onto the scene," Rhonda said. "But that is not true. And in spite of my *almost* indiscretion, of which I am deeply ashamed, I do love and respect Dennis. He is a fine man—as good as they come. We have a solid marriage. And two wonderful sons. A beautiful house. We both have successful careers. A good life. A *very* good life." Then she sighed again and offered a helpless little shrug. "But after Terry, I've never been able to give my heart completely to a man. No matter that I tell myself Terry was just an adolescent love affair and that he wasn't half the man that Dennis is, I can't erase his memory. The kind of intense love or passion or obsession or whatever it was that I felt for him is not based on an intellectual decision. You can't just tell your heart how it should or should not behave."

"Oh, I'm not so sure about that," Holly said when what she really wanted to say was "Bullshit." "Just because poison tastes good doesn't mean you have to drink it. Sometimes you have to intellectually give love a chance. Or intellectually withdraw from a destructive relationship. After all, we aren't gnats flying into the porch light."

Holly put down her glass and scooted over to take Rhonda's hand. "My darling Rhonda, tonight we are going to celebrate love and marriage. I don't know about you, but I plan to cry real tears into a wad of Kleenex while I listen to two young people full of love for each other recite their wedding vows. I want you to go to this wedding with an open heart and a willingness to reaffirm your belief in true love. Maybe you and Terry had a semblance of that for a time, but it had turned into something else by the time he married Gina Kay. Your parents have hung on to love all these years. And my parents did, too. My father's last words were for my mother, telling her she had made his life beautiful. Even Gina Kay's parents loved each other in that special way. It was a wondrous thing the way that spindly little man and that enormously fat woman looked at each other with love. And Sandy and I, in spite of our imperfections, have managed to cling to our version of true love. Wouldn't you rather be genuinely in love with your husband than still carrying a torch for the boy you loved in high school? It's been *twenty-five years,* Rhonda. You need to turn loose of the Terry thing and give Dennis a chance."

"You make it sound like I've been pining away for Terry all these years," Rhonda said, pulling her hand from Holly's grasp, her chin beginning to quiver. "That is *not* so. I do love Dennis. You've seen us together. We never fight, never raise our voices. We're affectionate with one another. And respectful."

Holly grabbed both of Rhonda's hands this time and held them tightly in her own. "But you've never trusted Dennis with your heart. By your own admission, you've still got it locked away. What are you waiting for, Rhonda? The years are flying by, honey. You figured out that having an affair isn't going to cure what's missing in your life. If your anger over what happened back then is what's holding you back, then it's time for you to let it go. You need to let it go no matter how justified that anger may or may not be. And if you're going to put a damper on tonight's celebration by glowering at Gina Kay and the judge, who may or may not be attracted to one another, then I wish you'd just stay here and have a pity party with yourself."

Rhonda reclaimed her hands and buried them between her knees. Then she just sat there, still as a statue, staring at nothing.

Holly held her breath. There was such a thing as being too honest. And probably she had just crossed over the line. No, most certainly, she *had* just crossed the line.

And suddenly there was a key turning in the lock. Gina Kay came rushing in, carrying a large shopping bag bearing the logo of the Museum of Modern Art.

"Great place," she said breathlessly, holding up the bag. Her hair was windblown, her checks flushed. "Wonderful collection. Great museum store. And after we finished there, we took the ferry over to Staten Island. I wish you guys had been with us. Such a view—both ways, on the way over to the island and of Manhattan on the way back."

While Gina Kay carried her handbag and shopping bag into the bedroom, Holly and Rhonda sat wordlessly at their respective ends of the sofa. When Gina Kay returned, she said to Holly, "I want to hear how your interview went." Then she looked at Rhonda. "Did I miss hearing about it? Have you already told Rhonda?"

"Not yet," Holly said glancing at Rhonda, half expecting her to head for her bedroom and close the door.

Gina Kay poured herself a glass of tea, sat in the wingback chair, and looked at Holly expectantly. "So, what was Jerry Winston like?"

Holly needed to go to the bathroom, but she didn't dare leave Rhonda and Gina Kay alone in the same room. God, she was tired of being in the middle, of being good old Holly while Gina Kay held herself above the fray and Rhonda seethed. She was ready to go home. Even at its chaotic worst, home was better than this.

She took a deep breath and mentally shifted gears. But not altogether. Her little lecture about true love had not been for Rhonda's benefit alone. She had needed to hear herself saying those words, to test them and see if they rang true. Because this afternoon, she herself had been sorely tempted by a charming man who had the power to change her life completely.

❦

"You look real," Jerry Winston had said when the receptionist showed her into his impossibly cluttered office. Winston was a tall, slender man in his late forties dressed in neatly pressed jeans and a white dress shirt with the sleeves rolled up.

"Real in what way?" Holly asked as she moved aside a stack of *Women's Wear Daily*s and sat on the sofa facing his desk. She took off her hat and ran her fingers through her hair.

"Well, the only visible part of your body that is pierced is your ears," he explained. "Your lipstick is a soft coral rather than brown or black or purple. You are not anorexic. And your hair—it's your natural color, isn't it? And I'll bet it's never been permed. It is the most beautiful hair I have seen in years. Maybe ever."

"So, is 'real' good, or should I leave?" Holly asked.

"It can be good," he said, coming around his desk and making a place for himself on the sofa. "Let's have a look at your portfolio." He put the portfolio on top of the clutter on the small coffee table and began leafing through.

"But I think I hate 'real,'" Holly protested. "I want to be inno-vative. I want to go a little crazy."

"And you should. Real doesn't have to be boring. What the fashion world needs is designers who create exciting clothes that a woman who has never worn exciting clothes looks at and thinks, 'Hey, I could wear that.'"

Holly's heart was pounding as she watched Jerry Winston look at her designs. He lingered over a sketch for an evening suit with a close-fitting Eisenhower jacket and a narrow skirt with a thigh-high split.

"What fabric did you have in mind?" he asked.

"Heavy silk faille in either bright red or white. The little draw-ing there in the corner is of one of the buttons. I want them to be copies of small Napoleon-era military medals done in white and blue enamel with semiprecious stones."

The next design was a strapless evening gown styled like a sarong. "I thought it would be nice in some unlikely fabric such as velvet or even military khaki with a bold Hawaiian floral print," Holly explained. "Hibiscus maybe. Or large white gardenias would be good."

Another strapless gown was made of fabric with a bold harle-quin design. "It could be silk taffeta, but I actually had red and black leather in mind," she told him.

Other pages showed slinky pants outfits reminiscent of Kath-arine Hepburn. And there was a 1940s-style cocktail suit with prominent shoulder pads. Just this morning, Holly had added a small hat with a bit of a veil to the drawing. "Looks like something Joan Crawford would have worn," Winston commented.

"Exactly. Again, I'd use important buttons—rhinestone pavé, perhaps, or mother-of-pearl. I'd love to bring back shoulder pads," she added. "They make a woman look smart and self-assured. Hats do, too."

After Winston had finished with her portfolio, he showed her through the design studio, and then they crossed the street to the workrooms, which occupied a three-story brick building that had once been a warehouse. They rode a freight elevator to the top floor, where spreaders laid out multiple layers of cloth on large tables and markers outlined each piece of the pattern with chalk. They stopped and talked with the spreaders, who all were immigrants, but Holly quickly realized this was no sweatshop. The men and women laughed and joked with Winston in their broken English.

On the second floor, sorters numbered the pieces and placed all the pieces for one garment in a bundle along with necessary buttons and trimmings. These were taken to the sewing room on the first floor, where each sewer worked on only one or two parts of a garment in assembly-line fashion. Finishers did all the outside stitching, and pressers ironed the completed garments. On the way back to his office, he explained that they contracted out the hand-sewing that was required for the most expensive garments.

In his office, Winston had poured them each a finger of Crown Royal and asked when she could move to New York.

"For a minute or so," Holly admitted to Rhonda and Gina Kay, "I imagined myself living the life of a New York fashion designer. An apartment with a balcony and spectacular view. Dressing the part."

"So what did you tell him?" Gina Kay wanted to know.

"That I couldn't do that to my family. Of course, he wanted to know why they couldn't move up here with me. He's never been to Texas, and I had a hard time explaining to him about our life and how even if I wanted them to live up here, it would never work. Jerry even asked me if my husband would turn down a wonderful coaching job in New York City out of consideration for me and the kids."

"Good for Jerry," Rhonda said, speaking for the first time since Gina Kay's arrival. "How did you answer him?"

"I didn't even try. His point was valid, I suppose, but I have to do what I feel is right for my family. Maybe if the kids were younger and Sandy more adaptable, I might be able to pull it off. But they are who they are, and I love them that way."

"Couldn't you work in Waco and send him the designs?" Gina Kay asked.

"Not really," Holly said. "What he was offering was total immersion—working with a team and being involved from design to finishing. And designers for mass market need to know trends, to be a part of the fashion world and to know what is going on at other houses and go to all those fashion shows. And so much of what makes a successful design is selecting the right fabrics and trims. That means working with importers here and sometimes even going to South America and Europe and Asia in search of the new and exotic."

Rhonda was shaking her head in disbelief. "I can't believe that you finally have the chance to achieve your lifelong dream and are turning your back on it."

"Yeah, I couldn't quite believe that I had found the pot of gold at the end of the rainbow and was going to turn around and head back to Texas," Holly admitted. "But Jerry Winston wasn't all for naught. I know now that I'm good enough to move up to the next level. And even higher. I will raise my prices and hire a publicist and cast a wider net. If I'm staying in Texas, I will make the most of it. Holly Warner Inc. will become the best place in the Southwest to come for custom-designed gowns—wedding and otherwise. I thought I might try a marketing campaign pitched to the society gals in Dallas and Houston. And I'd like to try my hand at mass producing a line of great-looking but inexpensive prom dresses. I still remember all those sleazy dresses Gina Kay tried on when we were trying to find her a prom dress she could buy on a carhop's salary. With an expanded clientele, I can justify coming up here a couple of times a year to shop for fabrics and trims and to attend fashion shows. I can bring Melissa with me. And the male members of my family, too, provided there is a major sporting event for them to attend."

"You go, girl!" Gina Kay said with a thumbs-up. "I think you're going to be a huge success."

"But you could travel back and forth from Waco to New York," Rhonda protested. "You could work up here and head home on weekends, or be here one week and in Waco the next. There has to be a way to make it work. You can't come this close to fulfilling your dream and just turn your back on it."

"Yes, I can," Holly said. "As much as I've been wowed by this city, I really don't belong here. I want to bring my kids here for a visit and maybe help them branch out a bit, but I'm going to finish raising them in Texas. This city is not a part of who we are. If Carter gets himself off academic probation, he'll play football for the University of Texas Longhorns, and I plan to be in the stands watching every single play."

Then she paused, thinking of what she was going to say next. And felt her eyes go misty. "You know, about forty miles or so after you leave I-thirty-five and head out west to Lamberton, you crest this rise and suddenly you can see forever. The last time I drove that road, there were these magnificent huge thunderheads in one part of the sky and a double rainbow in another. I pulled off the road and got out of the car to just stand there and be glad I was alive and lived someplace where I got to see something that inspiring."

She took her napkin and dabbed her eyes before concluding. "Everything I need is down home in Texas. My children. My husband. My home. My business. I just need to do a better job of making sure that we enjoy the richness that is all around us. Every so often, I will make them all dress up and go to something other than a sporting event—to a symphony or a theatrical production. Melissa will be easy, but my guys will come around. And we're going on some trips that have nothing to do with sports. We're going to start with exploring Texas. We've lived there all our lives and never been to Big Bend National Park. Or to Tyler when the roses are in bloom. Or floated the Guadalupe River. Then we're all going to pile on an airplane and come up here and go to museums and the theater and visit the Statue of Liberty and Ellis Island. We're going to do all those things and more no matter how much they grumble. Sandy will probably grumble the loudest, but I know how to sweeten him up." She paused and smiled. "So, I'm fine," she said. "Really truly fine. My hope is that my two best friends go home feeling the same way."

Then Holly took a breath. "Now, I need to ask a *very* important question." She paused and regarded the expectant faces of her two best friends. "What are you guys wearing to the wedding?"

It was as though a heavy cloud lifted from the room. "Oh God, I am so glad you asked," Rhonda exclaimed.

An intensive conversation ensued. Should they dress up or down? True, the wedding was in a back room at an inelegant restaurant, but it was going to look quite elegant when they got all those candles lit. And the bride was wearing a floor-length gown.

Rhonda pointed out that they must not be more dressed up than the mother of the bride, and none of them had a clue as to what Marta was planning to wear.

"Well then, we've got to dress down," Holly pointed out.

Gina Kay worried that black might not be appropriate for a wedding, which put her in a quandary since her traveling wardrobe was heavy on black.

They scurried off to the bedrooms, returning with articles of clothing. "How about this?" Gina Kay said, holding up the pants outfit she'd worn the first evening.

Holly had a long black skirt that she could wear with a red silk sweater. "Would pearls or a scarf be better?" she asked.

Rhonda held up a street-length burgundy-colored dress and a

navy pantsuit. "I really don't have the right shoes for the pantsuit," she said. "I was hoping to find some up here."

Suddenly Holly began to giggle. "We sound like we're seventeen years old and back in Lamberton trying to figure out what to wear to a Saturday-night dance."

"But we would have started much earlier," Rhonda said with a grin. "Days before—over Cokes at the Shack. And we would have passed notes in class."

"I remember the homecoming dance our sophomore year," Gina Kay said. "I was going to have to wear the same dress I wore to the back-to-school mixer because I really didn't have anything else. And you both did the same thing so I wouldn't be the only girl there without a new frock."

Chapter twenty

The first drink of the evening was served in the diner part of Leon's establishment, with his son and daughter pouring shots of vodka, glasses of wine, and an occasional soft drink. The bar was lined with trays of hot appetizers, including stuffed grape leaves, stuffed cabbage, and tiny crepes filled with preserves and sour cream.

The men wore suits or sports jackets with bright ties and colorful shirts. The women all seemed to manage to have some sort of animal print as part of their outfit, and there were a number of leather dresses and suits, many trimmed in fur. Rhonda remembered the shop windows along Brighton Beach Avenue; the Russians had obviously brought their love of fur and leather garments with them from the old country. She was relieved to see that she was neither over- nor underdressed for the occasion, but still she could not relax. She was nervous with anticipation. And worry.

What if the mirrors and candles made the back room look like a fancy brothel? Of course, the decor at the mirrored restaurant had not affected her and Holly and Gina Kay that way, but maybe Russians had different sensibilities.

She worried that maybe Tatiana hadn't taken the time to eat anything. Rhonda had been to two weddings where the bride fainted because she had been too excited or too busy and had not taken the time to eat.

And she worried that the guests and family members would think the three Texas women were intruding on a very private

event and searched the faces of the gathering guests for disap-
proval, but she saw nothing but graciousness.

Rhonda patted her handbag to make sure the box of wooden
matches still resided there. And realized she had forgotten to take
out the guest book she had bought. She placed the guest book on
the bar and appointed herself attendant. As she asked people to
sign the book, she watched Alex Resnick hovering at Gina Kay's
side as they visited with the groom's family. Gina Kay smiled and
nodded pleasantly, but her body language seemed neutral. *Why do
I care so much whether or not Gina Kay is getting into a relationship
with the judge?* Rhonda asked herself. It seemed incomprehen-
sible, though, that Gina Kay could seem so ready to get on with
the rest of her life. It was as if she were erasing Terry, something
Rhonda had never been able to do.

She smiled at an elderly man in a beige corduroy suit and
invited him to sign the guest book. Soon, she had people waiting
in line, eager to sign the book. Everyone knew that she was one of
the "Texas ladies."

When Leon came to tell them that the bridal party had arrived
and was waiting in the kitchen, Rhonda hurried with Holly and
Gina Kay down the hall to the back room to light the candles.
When the task was completed they allowed themselves a minute
to admire their handiwork. The mirrors reflected the flickering
flames of dozens of candles, and it looked splendid. *Magical.*
More like a heavenly chapel than a brothel.

Holly stepped between Gina Kay and Rhonda and put her arms
around their waists, drawing them close. "We did good, ladies,"
she said. Then she presented them each with a small package of
tissues, just in case. Holly went to tell Leon the guests could be
seated, and Rhonda tapped on the kitchen door then opened it
just a crack. "We're ready," she said without looking inside. She
wanted her first look at the bride to be by candlelight.

The guests filed into the room and soon had filled the chairs.

Then Alex and Ivan took their place in front of the sideboard with
its flowers and candles and icons. A small elderly man with a violin took his place in the corner of the room and began playing the
traditional wedding march.

Rhonda's eyes misted over as she watched Marta and G.W.
escort their daughter to the front of the room. Together, they
placed her hand in Ivan's. Rhonda pulled the package of tissues
from her purse and gave Holly a grateful pat. Holly was right.
Weddings did indeed make her teary-eyed. It was the hope that
got to her. The odds were against a bride and groom having a successful, enduring marriage, yet they always presented themselves
to each other with such high hopes. The only wedding Rhonda
had ever been to where hope was missing was her own.

Tatiana looked every inch the princess bride in the elegant lace
dress and the simple fingertip veil Holly had attached to a band of
fresh flowers. When Marta and G.W. turned to take their seats in
the first row, Rhonda could see the tears rolling down G.W.'s
cheeks. A proud father's tears broke down whatever was left of
Rhonda's reserve, and the mist in her eyes turned to full-fledged
tears. *George Washington Andropov.* Such a quirk of fate. Because
he just happened to be up next for an airport run, they were experiencing the sweetest part of their trip to New York.

Rhonda had anticipated that the bride and groom's faces would
be reflected along with candlelight in her magnificent mirror, but
she had not realized how intimate that would make the ceremony,
how the guests would be able to see the love glowing on two
young faces as they made their promises to each other. It was a
good thing to do that, she decided, to recite wedding vows in full
view of family and friends. Certainly it was better than a hurry-up
ceremony in front of an anonymous judge in a dusty room at a
courthouse. With no flowers. No candles. No well-wishers. No
wedding feast. Rhonda couldn't even remember any of the judge's
words or the vows she and Dennis had taken. All she remembered

was feeling nauseous and being so thankful when she was finally able to say "I do" and sit down.

Alex Resnick was doing a fine job. He spoke of his own marriage as being the greatest event of his life. Not that marriage is without stress and sadness, "But where there is love, there is strength," he said. "To give yourself to another human being in marriage is both the greatest of all gifts and the most selfish because out of this act you reap joy and family and comfort and a place in this world where you most belong."

Alex read their vows in English, but the bride and groom recited them in Russian. The word "obey" was absent. But something Rhonda had never heard before was included. Ivan and Tatiana promised to respect and support each other in their chosen life's work.

There was such conviction in Alex's voice as he pronounced them husband and wife that Rhonda's chest swelled, and tears threatened once again. They overflowed as Marta came forward to lift the veil from her daughter's face and lead the applause while Ivan enveloped Tatiana in his arms and gave her a perfectly splendid kiss.

After Alex offered the Russian blessing, the violinist began playing a triumphant march, but the bride and groom stayed where they were, greeting their guests, receiving their congratulations and hugs.

And while that was going on, Leon and several other men, with great dispatch, set up the tables and put chairs around them. Rhonda, Holly, and Gina Kay helped set the tables and place the centerpieces. And over Leon's protestations, the three of them helped carry out plates of food—beet salad, eggplant stew with mushrooms, spinach with walnuts, jellied beef feet, broiled duck, gefilte fish, marinated fish, herring with onions, skewers of grilled lamb. And there were pickled items—tomatoes, cucumbers, carrots, watermelon, red cabbage. So much food. And with the food, came vodka. Glasses and plates were filled and refilled.

At the end of the meal, everyone gathered around the wedding cake. Cameras flashed as Tatiana and Ivan fed each other the first bites. So radiant they were. So in love. *I can never be young again but I want to feel love like that again,* Rhonda thought.

After the cake was cut, people took their seats for an endless round of toasts—in Russian, of course. Every male in the room took a turn. Marta sat with her American-born guests for a time and gave them the gist of what was being said. Two themes recurred. These people valued family and expected Tatiana and Ivan to create a family and make it the center of their existence. And while they believed that Tatiana and Ivan had a better chance for happiness because they lived in America, they didn't want them to forget where they came from and who they were. Undaunted by the all-male toasting, Holly got into the act. Speaking on behalf of the "Texas ladies," Holly wished Tatiana and Ivan a lifetime of "happy trails," which meant they would encounter no gully washers, rattlesnakes, or bandits along the way and have a lifetime of beautiful sunsets and gentle breezes.

Then Tatiana rose and asked Holly, Gina Kay, and Rhonda to stand because she had a special toast in English just for them. "I tried to convince myself that I was too modern and too intellectual for a traditional wedding," Tatiana admitted, "but when I saw this wonderful dress, I knew I wanted to wear it when I married Ivan, and that I wanted flowers in my hair and candlelight all around. And did these ladies ever come through! Especially on the candlelight. I can't thank the three of you enough, but please know that you will always have Russian friends in New York City, and we expect to see you here again and again."

Rhonda had to reach for her tissue once more. She truly would not have missed this evening for the world. Of course, the evening was not yet over. Under Leon's direction, the men were folding some of the tables to make room for the dancing, and the musicians plugged in their instruments and amplifiers.

The trio of musicians had an amazing repertoire. Tatiana and Ivan danced the first dance to a traditional waltz. Midway, Tatiana pulled her father onto the floor, and Ivan his mother. Then the serious dancing began. There was wild, riotous dancing with napkins and neckties waved in the air. And there was jitterbugging. Rock and roll. Polkas. Slow dancing. Rhonda danced every dance, first with Holly, then with the judge, who danced like a man who had just discovered his own body and his ability to move with music, to express joy through movement. It was something to see. But then Alex was probably thinking the same thing about her. She felt joyous as she danced with G.W., Leon, Ivan, and other Russian men with their bad haircuts, their jackets long since shed, their gaudy neckties loosened or gone altogether. Tatiana changed into a black sheath so she could dance more freely and was obviously endeavoring to dance with every male guest. Rhonda imitated the movements of the Russians with their lack of restraint. If there wasn't an available partner, she danced alone. Her clothes became damp. Her underwear clung to her skin. But still she danced, going wherever the music took her. Even when the musicians played melancholy Russian folk songs, she allowed the music to fill her body and thought with sadness of missed opportunities, of the ways she could have been a better mother, a better daughter, a better wife, a better person. She should have gone to the funeral of Holly's father. She should do more pro bono work at the law office. When the music was joyous, she celebrated life and health and possibilities. She could learn from her mistakes. She would work on happiness.

And finally, well after midnight, the violinist stepped forward and, playing spirited Tchaikovsky, led a procession out to the sidewalk in front of the restaurant, where the Buick was waiting to whisk away the bride and groom. Everyone threw flower petals as the couple drove off to honeymoon on the New Jersey shore. Then there were hugs all around. It had been a good night. A *very* good night. A night to remember always.

In a borrowed car, G.W. and Marta took Holly, Rhonda, and Gina Kay back to their hotel, thanking them for a beautiful wedding and crying because their little girl was all grown up and married.

Once they were back in their hotel suite, there was an awkward moment. The night had been triumphant, but tomorrow lay ahead. Rhonda was grateful when Gina Kay simply said good night and headed into the bedroom she shared with Holly.

"We did a fine thing," Holly told Rhonda and gave her a hug.

"Yes, we did," Rhonda agreed.

"Are you apprehensive about tomorrow?" Holly asked.

Rhonda nodded. "Yeah, I am. Big time."

"Me, too. Do you have something to help you sleep?"

Rhonda nodded again.

"Well then, sleep tight, my dear friend," Holly said. "Remember, no matter how things turn out tomorrow, I will always be your friend."

"Thank you. I needed to hear that."

*C*hapter twenty-one

"So tell me, whose idea was it that you and Terry run off and get married?" Rhonda asked.

Gina Kay put her coffee cup on the small table beside the wing chair and rested her head against its high back. Rhonda and Holly had already claimed the sofa by the time she had poured her coffee and spread a bagel with cream cheese. She should have settled in on the window seat, she realized. The wing chair was too regal—a bit like a throne.

Rhonda's tone had been flippant, as though the question had just popped into her head, the invisible wall with which she surrounded herself already firmly in place. Last night and other times over the last four days there had been moments when Gina Kay had a seen a softening in Rhonda's reserve, when she dared hope that they could come together this morning with a bit of the old intimacy restored.

But apparently that was not to be. Poor Rhonda. How great her pain must have been that she had carried it with her all these years.

Gina Kay felt her courage slipping away from her. Could she do this? Was it an exercise in futility?

She had thought of Rhonda as she knelt beside Terry's body crushed to death under a tractor, her son at her side screaming denial at the heavens. *Holly would have to tell Rhonda.* She would have to tell Rhonda that Terry the man was dead. But Rhonda had loved Terry the boy. For her he would remain forever young.

And in the midst of all that horror and despair, Gina Kay had wondered if Rhonda could now let go of her hatred.

They were waiting to hear what she had to say—Holly and Rhonda, the two girls who had changed her life. Without them, she would never have had the courage to enter all those pageants, to change the way she spoke, dressed, and conducted herself. "Putting on airs," her sisters had called it. But because of Rhonda and Holly, she had learned to hold her head up. Learned to believe in herself. Whatever she had accomplished in this life was because of them. And her mama.

But her mama was dead, and Rhonda hated her. Even after all these years, whenever she and Holly were together, Gina Kay thought of Rhonda and missed her presence. Two friends were not the same as three.

Whose idea was it that you and Terry run off and get married? For twenty-five years, Rhonda had been puzzling over that question. Holly, too.

Gina Kay closed her eyes for a minute, collecting her thoughts before she began. She should be ready for this. In her mind, she had gone over it dozens of times as she imagined telling Rhonda just how it had all happened and trying to make her understand.

Now that the time to say those words out loud had finally arrived, Gina Kay couldn't remember what she had planned to say first, so she focused on Rhonda's question.

"It was his father's idea that we get married, but I need to back up before I get into that," she said, then took a deep breath. "It all started the night of your birthday, Rhonda, the night Terry wrecked the convertible."

❦

Holly had given Gina Kay a ride home that night. As Holly turned her parents' Pontiac sedan into the rutted lane that led to the Matthewses' house, she and Gina Kay made plans for tomorrow.

The JCPenney in Killeen was having a big sale, and they still needed some things for their dorm rooms. Holly would come by for her early, since she still had a lot of packing to do. Rhonda already had made plans to go shopping with her mother.

"It's hard to believe we're actually going off to college after years of dreaming about it," Holly said.

"Yeah," Gina Kay said. "It's exciting, but scary, too. In fact, I'm scared to death."

"We're going to have the time of our lives," Holly promised with great confidence in her voice.

But then Holly had never had any trouble making good grades. She wasn't a brain like Rhonda, but she was good at figuring things out. Gina Kay had always worked, though, and looked after her mother. What little free time she had, she liked to spend with her friends. It had been hard to find the time to study, and she wasn't very good at it anyway.

"'Night," Gina Kay said as she got out of the car, picking up the container with the two slices of birthday cake Rhonda's mother had sent to her parents. "I'll see you in the morning. I hope that's some kind of sale over in Killeen. It will have to be if I can afford to buy anything."

The Miss American Teenager scholarship would cover her tuition, room and board, and books, and the wardrobe the pageant had provided for the year of her reign meant she was heading to Austin with more suits and gowns than she'd ever possibly need, but she was short on casual clothes. She had to provide whatever else she needed and earn her own spending money. She had some money saved but would have to find a part-time job. She already had filled out forms with the university's student employment service and hoped she could find a job either on campus or close by. Otherwise, she was going to have to ride the bus to work. And they only came every so often, which would tie up even more of her time.

Gina Kay watched as Holly backed down the rutted drive then started across the yard. There was no walk. No yard really. Just weeds.

Even moonlight could not soften the stark reality of the dwelling where Gina Kay had lived her entire life. The front porch had a noticeable list. The exterior of the house needed paint, and shutters were missing from the windows.

As soon as she opened the door, her mother's voice called out, "That you, honey?" The only light in the room came from the television screen, where an old black-and-white movie flickered. Bing Crosby, wearing a clerical collar, was kneeling at an altar rail.

Her mother was alone. Her father would have nodded off and retired hours ago to his cot in the back bedroom. Her mother seldom slept. Sometimes she didn't even bother to make the arduous journey down the hall to her bedroom, going only as far as the bathroom then returning to the sofa. Gina Kay's father had taken down the narrow door to the bathroom and enlarged the opening to accommodate her mother's enormous body, then covered the resulting opening with a folding door. And he had removed the bathtub and turned the space into an extra large shower.

"Hi, Mama, how ya doin'?" Gina Kay asked, bending over to kiss her mother's cheek.

"Jus' fine, baby. Get me a Coke will you, and then tell me all about your evening. Did you have a nice time?"

"Sure did," Gina Kay said, heading for the kitchen.

It was part of the ritual of her life, telling Mama in great detail everything that had happened that day. Her sisters had never done that, and Gina Kay knew how that had hurt Mama. Kara Lynn and Ruth Ann didn't seem to care that Mama was a prisoner in this house and needed for them to bring the outside world to her. Even now, when Mama telephoned her two older daughters to ask about their day, they usually would answer "fine" or "terrible." They never just started talking and shared their lives with Mama.

And they didn't bring their children by to see her often enough. Kara Lynn especially. Her two children always regarded Mama with big, frightened eyes and wouldn't go near the sofa. If Kara Lynn would bring them more often, her children would come to know that the immense woman on the sofa was a loving grand-mother who would give anything if they would talk to her and let her touch their faces and stroke their hair.

Usually, the only time either of Gina Kay's sisters came to see their parents was after their respective husbands had gambled away or drunk up their paychecks and the utilities were about to be turned off and all there was to feed the kids was stale bread or popcorn. Kara Lynn frequently pointed out that she could get a job and kick her worthless husband out on his ass if her mother wasn't so damned fat that she couldn't look after her own grand-kids. Then she would take whatever wadded-up bills Daddy had dug out of his pocket, grab her kids, and leave without so much as a thank-you.

Gina Kay, however, took pleasure in the time she spent with her mother and enjoyed sharing every detail of her life with her. Throughout the day, she would remind herself to be sure and tell Mama this or that. One of the reasons why she loved Rhonda and Holly so much was that they were willing to talk to her mother and tell her about school and club meetings and their families. No detail was too small. Mama wanted to know how many tomatoes and cucumbers Rhonda's daddy had picked from his garden that week or what Holly's mother had served for Sunday dinner. She loved hearing about school dances and shopping trips. She wanted to know what they had studied that day in school and who was going with whom. Gina Kay knew that when Rhonda and Holly looked at her mother, they didn't see just a hugely obese woman who made the floor sag when she propelled her walker to and from the bathroom. They saw her for the caring human being that she was.

Gina Kay handed Mama a Coke then pulled the ottoman over beside the sofa and began telling her about Rhonda's birthday party. After she'd named who all was at the party, Mama asked, "My goodness, did Rhonda's daddy grill steaks for all those people?"

"Actually, he grilled shish kebabs," Gina Kay explained. "Mrs. Hayes had put pieces of steak on these long metal things, along with shrimp, green peppers, onions, potatoes, squash, and mushrooms," Gina Kay said. "They really tasted good."

"My goodness. Shish kebabs in Lamberton!" Mama exclaimed. "Isn't that something. Now, what else did they serve? Was there a salad?"

"Mrs. Hayes made a real pretty salad with fresh spinach and strawberries and walnuts." Gina Kay paused while her mother marveled over a salad that contained berries and nuts. "She got the recipe out of a magazine," Gina Kay explained. "And there was French bread with garlic butter. Rhonda's birthday cake was German sweet chocolate. Mrs. Hayes had to make two of them since there were so many people. Mrs. Hayes sent you and daddy each a big slice."

"Isn't that nice of her to think of us!" Mama said. "You tell her that I really appreciate her kindness. Now, tell me all about Rhonda's birthday presents."

"Well, she got a lot of books. And she got perfume and stationery and some cute socks. Holly made her a darling summer bathrobe, and Rhonda loved the picture that I gave her. That was a great idea, Mama, to put that picture in a frame. I think it was the first one that was ever taken of her and Holly and me."

"What about Terry? What did he give Rhonda?"

"I'd been saving that for last," Gina Kay said.

Mama smiled in anticipation. "It must have been something real nice."

"Oh, it was," Gina Kay said, pausing for effect. "Terry gave

Rhonda a fourteen-karat-gold friendship ring with a *real* pearl and two *real* diamonds. It is *really* beautiful. I don't think Colonel and Mrs. Hayes were too happy about it, though. And I'm not sure Rhonda was either. I guess a friendship ring is just one step away from an engagement ring."

"Poor Rhonda," Mama said with genuine sympathy. "She can't decide if she wants to marry Terry or be a brain surgeon. Where did Terry buy the ring?"

"At a fancy jewelry store in Temple. No telling how much it cost. But now that he's graduated, Terry is working full time for his daddy at the ranch and gets a salary."

Then Gina Kay told how, after the party had ended, most of the kids went to park behind the high school gymnasium and drink beer. "I promise that I didn't drink any beer, Mama," Gina Kay said. "I don't want the Miss American Teenager folks taking back my scholarship money because I haven't been behaving myself."

"I bet Terry and Rhonda didn't stay there long," Mama said.

"No, they went off in Terry's new convertible."

"I hope she and Terry aren't having sex," Mama said. "If she turns up pregnant, she's probably not going to go off to college, and that would be a shame, smart girl like that. It would break her parents' hearts. Just like your sisters broke my heart. Your sisters are going to end up poor and fat, just like their mother. And their children will never amount to a hill of beans. At least if Rhonda has Terry's baby, that child will live in a big house and have all the opportunities that money can buy."

Gina Kay helped her mother make the slow and laborious journey to the bathroom. Then on to the bedroom. Gina Kay could hear her father snoring in the tiny back bedroom. Mama Matthews's bed had broken under her years ago, and the mattress now resided on a sturdy wooden platform that her father had built. Mama thought she might be able to do more than doze tonight if Gina Kay would bring the sofa cushions in here to prop her up a bit. Her breathing was better if she wasn't flat on her back.

Gina Kay knew the day was coming when her mother would no longer be able to leave her bedroom. She just hoped that by then she had married a rich man and would be able to see that her mama was looked after properly and that her nieces and nephews were sent to school in decent clothes with lunch money in their pockets. Not that she wanted to live next door to her parents. Or even down the road. What she wanted was to live close enough to Lamberton that she could pop in often and make sure her mother got good care but far enough away that she had a separate life. And she would call her mother daily and send lots of Hallmark cards. She would still be a good daughter. Always.

Gina Kay hoped and prayed that she would be in love with the rich man she married, but whether she was in love with him or not, she would be able to provide for her family and live a gracious life. Holly had asked her once if she was sure such a man was out there, adding that she was sure any number of men would want to marry Gina Kay but was worried that none of them would be rich. "That's why I have to go to college," Gina Kay had reminded her. "The only rich man around here is Terry's father. And I'm sure not going to marry him. I don't want to marry an old man, or a mean one, and Mr. Robertson is both. Even his own son is afraid of him."

After she had gotten her mother settled in for the night, Gina Kay went back to the living room to tidy up and turn off the television set. When the room went quiet, she heard something out on the front porch. A scratching sound.

Something was scratching on the front door.

She opened the door a crack expecting to see a stray dog or cat. But there was a man lying there. Not moving at all.

"Gina Kay," the man whispered. "Help me."

Gina Kay turned on the porch light. It took her several heartbeats to realize that the man was Terry. And there was no vehicle in the driveway. He had come here on foot.

She knelt beside him. "What happened?" she asked. "Where's Rhonda? Where's your car?"

"Wrecked," he said.

"Where's Rhonda?" she repeated.

"She left me," he said with a groan.

"Is she okay?"

"I think so," he said.

"Where are you hurt?"

"My ribs. I can't walk anymore. Please help me."

"You want me to call your father?"

He grabbed her wrist. "No, please don't."

She pulled her father's pickup up to the porch and helped Terry inside. He cried out with each movement.

Officially, old Doc Templeton had retired more than a decade ago, but he still looked in on Mama Matthews and a few other longtime patients who wouldn't get the same level of care and concern from the two younger doctors in town.

She rang the doorbell and waited. "Who's there?" Doc Templeton's voice called down from an upstairs window.

She stepped out in the yard. "It's Gina Kay Matthews," she called up to him. "I've got Terry Robertson in the truck. He's wrecked his car and is hurting pretty bad."

Wearing a bathrobe over his pajamas, Doc Templeton helped Gina Kay get Terry from the truck. Terry cried out with each step as they helped him up the front steps and into the doctor's office, which had its own door off the front porch.

Doc Templeton poked around a bit and listened to Terry's chest. "Lungs okay," he observed. "What we've got here is cracked ribs and a dislocated collarbone. You'll live, son, unless your father kills you."

Terry screamed when the doctor put his collarbone back in place. Gina Kay helped Doc Templeton tape Terry's ribs. It was strange to be touching his bare flesh.

When the doctor was finished, he said, "I'm going to call your father now and explain to him what happened."

When Terry tried to rise up on his elbow and protest, Doc Templeton added, "I'll make him promise not to lay a hand on you, son, and tell him that if he does, I'll call the sheriff. I'm also going to tell him that he needs to take you into the clinic for X-rays tomorrow to make sure I haven't missed anything. If he doesn't do that, you call me."

When Gina Kay pulled up in front of the Robertson Ranch, Mr. Robertson was waiting on the porch. He had dressed but was shoeless, and his shirt was untucked. He looked as though he hadn't shaved in days.

"Afraid to face me alone, boy?" he snarled as he watched Gina Kay help Terry out of the truck.

"Yes, sir," Terry mumbled.

"What happened?"

"A tree got in the way."

"Anyone else hurt?"

"No sir."

"I'll deal with you in the morning," Mr. Robertson said, turning to go back into the house. "And the car," he added over his shoulder.

"I need you to help me get him in the house," Gina Kay called after him.

Mr. Robertson hesitated, then went to Terry's other side. He was larger than Terry. But not strong. And he smelled of whiskey. Gina Kay found herself bearing most of Terry's weight. She could feel Terry fight back groans as they half carried him into the house, up the broad staircase, and down a long, musty-smelling hallway.

Such a big house, she thought, for just the two of them. What would it be like to live in a house with so many rooms? She thought of how clearly she could hear her daddy's snores and farts on the other side of the paper-thin walls of her bedroom.

Terry's spacious bedroom had a desk, bookcase, sofa, easy chair and ottoman, and a large cabinet filled with a television, stereo, and stacks of tapes. His bed was a massive four-poster.

With great care, she helped Terry sit on the bed, then lie back. He grabbed a pillow to stifle his groans.

"How come he's with you and not that Hayes girl?" Mr. Robertson asked.

"I think he and Rhonda broke up," Gina Kay said. "Then I guess he must have gone a little crazy and ended up wrecking his car—probably out west of town—and started walking home but couldn't make it. My house must have been the first one he came to."

"I suppose he totaled the damned car," Mr. Robertson growled.

"I don't know about that," Gina Kay said. She felt the man's eyes on her as she pulled off Terry's shoes and covered him with a quilt. Then she turned to face him. "Terry is going to need to be looked after for a few days. I doubt if he can even get to the bathroom on his own."

"Are you volunteering for the job?" Mr. Robertson asked with a leer on his face and innuendo in his tone.

"No, sir. He is your responsibility, not mine."

"You're that Matthews girl that won the big beauty pageant."

"Yes, sir."

"You're the *good* Matthews girl, the one who looks after her mother."

Gina Kay didn't respond.

"Your sisters are whores," he said.

"And you are a nasty man," she told him.

Then she had leaned over the bed, returning her attention to Terry. "I'm going now. Do you want me to tell Rhonda anything?"

Gina Kay paused in her tale, remembering how Terry answered her question, telling her in no uncertain terms that he didn't want her to tell Rhonda anything. "I hope she goes to hell," he had said.

"No, you don't," Gina Kay told him. "You love Rhonda and always will."

She had been wrong in that assessment.

Terry needed someone to keep him from screwing up his life. When he realized that person was not going to be Rhonda, he went through a range of emotions, from hate to anger to indifference. For the last decade of his life, Gina Kay was quite certain he thought of Rhonda only in passing.

Chapter twenty-two

Gina Kay got up from her chair and walked over to the window. It had rained during the night, and the street was dotted with puddles. A police car drove by. Then a garbage truck. People were hurrying along the wet sidewalks. A dog walker was barely managing seven dogs.

Behind her Holly asked Rhonda, "Whatever happened to that friendship ring?"

"I lost it during or after the wreck," Rhonda said. Then raising her voice a bit, she addressed Gina Kay at the window. "Why didn't you tell me that Terry had come to your house that night?"

Gina Kay turned. "Because he asked me not to. He said what he did was no longer any of your concern."

"Help me understand," Rhonda demanded. "You took him home injured the night of my birthday party. Two days later, Holly and I were on our way to Austin for rush week. Is that when you started seeing Terry? Is that when you started sleeping with him?"

"I called to ask if he was feeling better, but I didn't see Terry again until the day we got married," Gina Kay said. "I had never so much as kissed him until our wedding night. I knew everyone assumed I must be pregnant. Why else would Terry Robertson marry me? I avoided going to town because people kept glancing at my belly to see if I was showing yet. I almost felt sorry to have to disappoint them so."

"I find all this damned hard to believe," Rhonda said, with a decided edge to her voice. "You never went out with him, never had sex with him, never even kissed him, then you up and marry him?" She threw her hands in the air in a gesture of exasperation, then turned away from Gina Kay and folded her arms across her chest.

Gina Kay walked over to the bar, poured herself a glass of water, and drank it down. Then she took her seat once again and leaned her head against the chair's high back. Poor Rhonda, she thought. She had been dragging all that hurt around with her for so many years that it had become a part of who she was. *Rhonda the Betrayed.* And she had been betrayed. She was entitled.

"You and Holly and I went to Austin with such high hope," Gina Kay told Rhonda. "You were depressed about breaking up with Terry but eager to find out if there was life after him. I remember the first boy you went out with. His name was Robert, and he was from Burkburnett. You had a terrible time deciding what to wear. Holly and I sat on the bed, trying to help you make up your mind."

"Yeah," Rhonda recalled, her tone softening a bit. "Terry was the only boy I'd ever dated. I was so nervous my stomach hurt. But Robert wasn't so bad. We went to the movies and shared a pizza. He was shy and sweet. But it was so strange being with a boy who wasn't Terry, and I never returned Robert's phone calls."

"And you started seeing Terry again, didn't you?" Holly asked.

Rhonda nodded. "I wrote to him that I wanted to see him again, and he started driving over every four or five days—in the evenings when I was supposedly at the library. I told him I didn't want you and Gina Kay to know, or my parents, until I figured things out."

Then Rhonda directed her next words to Gina Kay. "The reason I came back to the dorm early that day and caught you in the act of moving out was because I was anxious to be there in case Terry called. I had written him a letter telling him that I would marry him the end of my freshman year. Or maybe even Christmastime. I wrote a letter to my parents telling them the same thing. Terry had mentioned that he and his father were planning to go to a cattle auction in San Antonio, and I wanted the letter to be waiting for him when he got back." Rhonda paused and took a deep breath. "When I dropped those letters in the mail chute, I knew there was no backing out. Then two days later in the middle of my chemistry lab, I started wondering if Terry had said that he and his dad were definitely going to San Antonio or *might* be going to San Antonio. Maybe he was trying to call me that very minute. I told the lab instructor I had a sick headache and went racing back to the dorm, and there you were, all packed up and ready to leave. I knew you didn't have mono."

Rhonda stared at the windows for a second or two. "Holly and I knew that something was very wrong. All evening we tried to figure out what the hell had happened. Had we hurt your feelings? Did you not have enough money? Were you flunking your classes? Then I called your house, and Kara Lynn answered. She said it was none of my business where you were. On Saturday, I pretended that I was sick and had Holly bring me food from the cafeteria. I jumped out of my skin every time the phone rang. By Sunday afternoon, I didn't have to pretend to be sick. I had made myself physically ill with needing to hear Terry's voice, needing to hear the happiness I knew would be there after he read that letter. But the phone call from him never came," she said. "My parents drove over to tell me that you had married Terry. It would have been easier if they'd told me he was dead."

"We got married on Friday evening then drove to San Antonio for a few days," Gina Kay said softly. "When we got back, I was the one who found the letter on the table by the door. I recognized your handwriting right away."

"Did you read it?" Rhonda demanded, her eyes narrowing.

"No, I gave it to Terry, and he tore it up without opening it. He said he never wanted to hear or see your name again."

Rhonda rose from the sofa and walked over to the window seat, perching on the edge like a bird about to take flight. There were tears in her eyes. Gina Kay wanted to put her arms around her and tell her to be glad. But Rhonda needed to hear the rest of the story and come to her own conclusion.

Holly cleared her voice. "Okay, Gina Kay, how come you and Terry got married?" she asked, repeating Rhonda's original question. "And what did his father have to do with it?"

Gina Kay looked at Rhonda and Holly's expectant faces. They were waiting. She leaned her head against the chair back and closed her eyes.

🙛🙙

Gina Kay never told her parents about Terry's wreck and her late-night trip to the Robertson Ranch. She had been tired to the bone the next morning as she and Holly drove to Killeen for the JCPenney sale. Gina Kay thought about Terry during the day, wondering how he felt and if his father was taking care of him and had taken him for an X-ray, if his wrecked car had been towed from the scene. At dusk, Holly came by for her and Rhonda, and they cruised Main Street for a while then pulled in at the Dairy Dream. Rhonda was quiet and said nothing about the wreck, nothing about Terry. Other Main Street cruisers pulled in beside them to wish them well and say good-bye. Holly and Rhonda were leaving in the morning for rush week. Since Gina Kay wasn't going through rush, she would leave the following Saturday. The three of them promised their friends that they would come home for Homecoming Weekend, but already Gina Kay could feel a gulf between them and the kids they were leaving behind. Some of their classmates were already married, no longer among the Main Street cruisers. Two were expecting. The ones who planned to stay on in Lamberton already had jobs either in town or were making the commute across the vast Fort Hood reservation and working at the military base. Only those who were college-bound were allowed to avoid adulthood for four more years.

The following Friday, Gina Kay finished packing her clothes and loaded her possessions in the truck, which her papa had scrubbed and polished as best he could in preparation for the drive to Austin. He had even borrowed a second spare tire, just in case. He didn't want anything to go wrong on such a special journey.

Saturday morning, he put on his Sunday best to drive Gina Kay to Austin. Her sisters and their children even came by to tell her good-bye and say they were proud of her. "And jealous," Ruth Ann admitted. "I should have kept my legs together like you've done, but at least you've learned from Kara Lynn's and my mistakes."

When it came time for Gina Kay to say good-bye to Mama, she knelt beside the sofa and buried her face against the mountain of flesh that was her mother's bosom. Who was going to wash between all these folds of flesh and make sure she didn't get a fungus infection? Who was going to dry her and sprinkle talcum powder into the creases? The home nurse only came twice a week.

For her entire life her mama had been the center of her existence. Maybe her mama would just cease to exist if she left her.

"Don't you go worrying about me," her mother said as she smoothed Gina Kay's hair. "I thank God for making my dreams come true and making it possible for my little girl to go to college and make something of herself."

"I don't have to go all four years," Gina Kay said. "If the right rich boy comes along, I'll grab him right away and marry him."

"Just make good and sure that he really is rich and not pulling the wool over your eyes."

"I will, Mama," Gina Kay promised.

"And you have to make sure that he knows that you have family responsibilities."

"I know, Mama. But if I can't find the right rich man, I'll have to finish school and figure out a way to get rich on my own."

Tears were flowing down her mother's face, but she was wearing the most beautiful smile. "God really blessed me the day you were born, honey. I would have just given up and died years ago if it weren't for you."

"I love you, Mama," Gina Kay sobbed. "I love you with all my heart." Which was true, but in her mind she was both anxious and fearful to find what life was going to be like away from this house, away from her mother's smothering love.

Her father gently took her arm. "It's time to go, sister," he said.

Gina Kay sobbed as the truck bumped its way down the rutted drive. But once they were on the road, she settled down and started giving her papa instructions. She had written down everything and put the clipped-together pages on his bureau, but she worried that he would never read them. So she told him that she had thumbtacked the telephone numbers for the home nurse and Doc Templeton to the wall beside the telephone. And that he had to be real careful not to overload the washing machine. The pilot light didn't work on the oven, and he had to use a match. She had bought ahead on canned goods, soap, and toilet paper and stacked it all in the utility room. She wanted to tell him to call if he had questions and to promise that she would call home every day, but long-distance phone calls had to be saved for emergencies. They didn't have the money to pay the regular bill much less one inflated by long-distance charges. Gina Kay was so tired of being poor. She wanted the dignity that money brought. She wanted it so desperately that whenever she thought about it, she got stomach cramps. Sometimes she wanted to be mad at her daddy for not being a better provider. And sometimes she wanted to be mad at God for saddling her with such a family. But being mad at God was surely a sin, and her father did the best he could. And her father had a good heart; she told him that as they drove into the outskirts of Austin. Then she added, "The only reason I'm able to go off to college is that I know you will take care of Mama." When he took out his handkerchief to wipe the tears from his cheeks, Gina Kay took pride in how snowy white it was, how carefully ironed. "Don't forget to wash your handkerchiefs, Papa. They don't have to be ironed, but they do need to be clean. And never mix whites and colors in the same load. And don't forget to buy Mama the *Soap Opera Digest*. It comes out every Saturday."

Then she took a deep breath. The rest of her life was waiting for her.

❧

Rhonda and Holly had pledged the same sorority and immediately began attending weekly pledge meetings and dinner at the sorority house every Monday and Wednesday evening. They also were required to attend study hall at the sorority house for two hours four afternoons a week, and their pledge class had a party with a different fraternity pledge class every Friday night.

Since Gina Kay couldn't afford to join a sorority, she became one of the great pool of students called "independents." Some independents were making a political statement against elitism by not affiliating with a fraternity or sorority, but most were either too poor or too geeky. Most of the girls in their dormitory wore sorority pledge pins on their collars. It was the first thing Gina Kay noticed about a girl.

Word soon got around the dorms that Gina Kay was a former Miss American Teenager, which brought numerous curious stares in the dining hall and at dorm meetings. Mostly, though, she kept a low profile and tried to dedicate herself to her studies. But she was lonely. And the weeks were going by. And not a single rich young man had come acourting.

Her mother had never written letters before, and the ones she sent Gina Kay were written in the form of lists, complete with numbers. She would include any event in her life she deemed worth reporting. Her favorite characters on *Guiding Light* got married. Holly's mother brought over a dozen jars of canned tomatoes. The preacher came to pray with her. Doc Templeton dropped by to take her blood pressure and listen to her chest. Mostly though, she wrote about Terry's visits, which began the day after Gina Kay left for Austin. He came over almost every evening to sit with her parents and watch television with them. He almost always brought a container of Kentucky Fried Chicken or a sack of hamburgers. Once in a while he drove out to the catfish place on the highway and brought a batch of fried catfish and hushpuppies. Sometimes he'd even drop by during the day to help with chores. He helped her father rebuild the motor in his tractor and get his allotment of winter wheat planted.

Gina Kay decided that Terry came to visit her parents because he was a very lonely boy. His daddy was mean and remote. Several of the boys he had hung out with for years had joined the army or headed off to college, some on football scholarships. Others had married and settled down and no longer were available for chug-a-lugging beer and drag racing. Since Rhonda had broken up with Terry, he would no longer be comfortable hanging out with her parents. And Holly's parents were often busy with school activities and traveling around to craft shows to sell the miniature windmill yard ornaments Mr. Burgess made. But Mama Matthews was always there on her sofa. Even if Papa had already gone to bed, Mama would be company for Terry. And he wouldn't have to say a word if he didn't want to. Mama could provide a running commentary about every actor who appeared on the television screen. Whether it was their TV life or their real one, she knew to whom they were married, with whom they were sleeping, and with whom they had made babies.

Gina Kay never mentioned Terry's visits with her parents to

either Holly or Rhonda, although she wasn't sure why. Maybe she just didn't want to upset any apple carts. Maybe Terry would end his nightly visits with her parents if he thought that other people knew about them. And with Gina Kay gone, it was good for them to have company.

When Terry's father called to say that he wanted to drive over to Austin and visit with her about something important, Gina Kay worried that he had found out where Terry was spending all his time and wanted her to put an end to his visits. Although that really didn't make a whole lot of sense. Mr. Robertson never cared where Terry went before. He'd been roaming around on his own since he was five years old. But what else would Mr. Robertson have to say to her?

It was a Wednesday evening. Rhonda and Holly were expected at the sorority house for dinner. Gina Kay waited until after they left to change clothes.

She waited for Mr. Robertson in front of the dormitory. One of the girls asked if she had a hot date.

She'd never seen Terry's father in other than a pickup truck and was surprised when he pulled up in a large, shiny, burgundy-colored Lincoln sedan. Not a late-model Lincoln, she realized, but it looked brand new.

She was glad she dressed up when she saw that he was wearing a suit and tie and his hair was freshly cut, his face freshly shaved. He looked quite different in nice clothes and without the usual stubble on his chin.

"Is this your car?" she asked.

"Yes. I take it out of town sometimes. Not often, though. Had to jump charge the battery to get it started."

He took her to a fine restaurant in a downtown hotel with white tablecloths, potted palms, and tuxedoed waiters. Gina Kay was wearing a dress from her pageant wardrobe—a blue silk sleeveless sheath with matching pumps. The maître d' had stared at the two of them as though trying to decide if Gina Kay was Mr. Robertson's daughter or someone else altogether.

When the wine steward appeared, Mr. Robertson had ordered a bottle of Chablis. "The best goddamned bottle you've got," he instructed.

Unsure as to why she was there with this man and unaccustomed to wine, Gina Kay took only a few tentative sips from her glass while she listened to Ward Robertson tell her how Terry's mother had died, all the time wondering why he was sharing this tragic story with her.

It was all his fault, he told Gina Kay. His wife would still be alive if he'd only let her go home to see her family once in a while. Or hell, he could have brought the whole damned bunch of them to Lamberton. That was probably what he should have done. They were ranchers, too. But the place where his wife had grown up was nothing like Lamberton. It was the most beautiful place he had ever seen. No question about that.

Marie was her name. Ward Robertson had met her on her family's ranch outside of Cochrane in far western Alberta, when his father had sent him up there to purchase a Charolais bull and bring it back to Texas. He had convinced Marie to come back to Texas with him and married her in front of the stone fireplace in the house where she had been born and raised—a log house with a broad front porch for watching the sun set over the Canadian Rockies.

Marie was homesick from the day she arrived in Lamberton, but Ward was afraid she would never come back if he let her return to Cochrane for a visit. He promised her, though, that after their baby was born, she could visit her family. But he kept putting off the trip. She hated the Texas wind and the heat and longed for her mountains. Then, when Terry was four and she was pregnant with their second child, she made Ward swear on a Bible that as soon as that baby was born, they would all go for a long visit. It was a promise he intended to keep. If he went with her, he could make sure that she returned.

The baby was just three weeks old when Marie tumbled down the stairs. Right before the accident, they had had a fight about her visiting her parents. She wanted to go at once, before the summer heat began.

"I had some cotton under cultivation back then," Ward said. "I told her she had to wait until after cotton picking in the fall. But I'd go head and make the reservations and buy the tickets to prove that I planned to be good to my word this time."

Then Ward had to look away for a minute and collect himself before continuing. Their waiter took advantage of the pause in the conversation and stepped forward to fill Ward's wineglass then discreetly melted away.

"But she wanted to go the very next day," Ward continued. "She said her father wasn't well, and she was sick of the heat. She got angry, and Terry started crying. He wanted her to pick him up, but she was holding the baby. She went storming out of the bedroom with Terry running after her. I followed them out into the hall wondering if I should call after her and tell her it was okay, that she could go tomorrow if she wanted to. But I didn't do that. Terry was still crying for her to pick him up. Then he ran at her and gave her a push. She stumbled forward a step or two grabbing for the railing. But she missed and went tumbling down the stairs, the baby with her. Marie died immediately. The baby lived for few days before she died. Her name was Millicent. I don't think I'd ever even held her in my arms. I wish I had done that before I put her in the ground." Ward paused and reached for the wineglass. He downed its contents in one gulp.

Gina Kay was too shocked to speak. Such needless tragedy. Poor Terry had grown up in its shadow.

Ward looked at her face and said, "I guess you'd always heard that I was drunk and the one who pushed her."

Gina Kay nodded. "Yes. And that because you were rich and powerful, the sheriff said it was an accident."

"I let people think what they wanted to protect Terry," he explained. "The boy was barely five, and I always assumed that he didn't remember what happened to his mother and sister. All I ever told him was that they fell down the stairs."

Ward waited while the waiter poured yet another glassful of wine. When the man slipped back into the shadows, Ward said, "I haven't been a good father to my son. I look at him and see his mother. I even thought about sending him off to her people to raise but decided that he needed to grow up on the ranch that would be his someday. Then I thought I'd find another woman to marry and be a mother to him. But such a woman never came along. Or maybe I just never went looking for her. Antonia was good to him, and she looked after my needs in bed and out. Of course, she did all that for money to send back home to her family in Mexico, but I didn't mind. It kept things honest between us. I sure missed her when she went and died, though."

He sighed heavily and stared at some point past Gina Kay's shoulder. "I've always known that I wasn't being a good father to the boy, but I took some solace in the fact that I had protected him from the truth about what happened that awful day. But then last month we got into a shouting match about something or other, and suddenly he's saying that I have every right to hate him, that his mother and sister would still be alive if it weren't for him. That really knocked me for a loop."

Gina Kay found herself wanting to reach out and touch the hand of Terry's father and offer some sort of comfort to him, but she didn't dare.

"Sometimes I wished I was the one who died instead of Marie," Ward admitted, "but then what would have happened to Terry? He's going to inherit all that land, and he doesn't have the sense to come in out of the rain. I thought that Rhonda Hayes would marry him and run things. It eased my mind to think that the smartest student in the whole goddamned high school was going to marry my boy and keep him out of trouble. But she isn't doing right by my boy. She's just stringing him along. Where that girl wants to end up there ain't no place for my son."

Gina Kay took another sip of the Chablis. It didn't seem so strange now. In fact, it tasted dignified. And elegant. Like something a queen would drink. Not a beauty queen. A real queen.

Chapter twenty-three

Gina Kay ordered pecan-crusted red snapper, Mr. Robertson a steak. When the waiter had departed, Mr. Robertson stared across the table at her.

"I want you to marry my son," he said.

Gina Kay was not certain that she had heard him correctly. Sitting very still, with her hands in her lap, she replayed his words in her head to make sure. *Marry his son? Marry Terry Robertson?*

In the corner by an arched window that looked out on an illuminated garden with a fountain, a woman was playing a harp. Gina Kay closed her eyes for a minute, searching for words to go with the haunting melody. *Those were the days, my friend, I thought they'd never end.*

It was such a beautiful restaurant, with rich paneling serving as a backdrop for impressive oil paintings and strategically placed potted palms providing privacy for the diners. The fountain in the garden made her think of their senior prom. No one in Lamberton had a fountain. Someday she'd like to have one in a lovely garden with shade trees and flowers.

Gina Kay had been in many impressive restaurants during her reign as Miss American Teenager but never failed to be awed by elegance—by candlelight, liveried waiters, muted voices, thick carpet, delicate glassware, fine china, artfully prepared food.

Yes, she had tasted the good life and found it pleasing. She enjoyed staying in fine hotels and sleeping on spacious beds with percale sheets and fluffy pillows. She loved bathing in draft-free bathrooms with spacious tubs filled with scented water and breakfasting on freshly ground coffee, freshly squeezed orange juice, and freshly baked croissants. She loved having doors opened for her and chairs pulled back.

But even more than living the good life, she wanted financial security. She couldn't remember a time in her young life when she hadn't worried about money. Almost her entire life she had worked—babysitting, cleaning houses, pulling weeds, picking cotton, washing cars, waiting tables, carhopping. Carhopping had been the most profitable, especially in summer when wearing shorts and a halter-top brought larger tips. Of course, the tips often came with lewd comments and even solicitations for sex. She felt sullied taking such money. Money she earned helped put a new motor in her daddy's truck, replace the pump on the well, and pay the TV repairman when her mother's television went on the blink. Whatever she spent on herself made her feel guilty.

And over the last weeks, she had come to realize just how unlikely it was that she would ever receive an offer of matrimony from a rich man. There were plenty of other girls at the university just as pretty as she was and far more self-assured. Even girls who were less than pretty seemed so confident as they chattered away in the dorm lounge, on their way to class, in the cafeteria. Without Holly and Rhonda at her side, Gina Kay was forced to remember who she really was—a poor girl who grew up in a prefabricated home on a scruffy piece of practically worthless land in a backwater Texas town. And even if she were pretty enough to become an actress or a famous model, it would take years before she had enough income to look after herself *and* her family. And beauty was a fleeting thing. There were pictures at home of her mama when she was young and looked almost exactly as Gina Kay looked now.

Sometimes she found herself wondering what her life would be like if a tornado just up and blew Lamberton away. Her parents didn't have a storm cellar, but even if they did, it wouldn't do her mama any good. If something happened to her mama, she would be sad for the rest of her life, but she would be free.

She loved her mother, though. And it was evil even to think such a thing, *very* evil. She didn't like thinking of herself as an evil person.

Gina Kay was exhausted. Not the sort of exhaustion that went away after a good night's sleep, but exhaustion that she carried with her every minute of the day and night. She had hoped that coming to Austin would be the beginning of a wonderful new chapter in her life.

Gina Kay understood what Ward Robertson wanted from her. He wanted her to save his son.

In return, he would give her the means to look after her family and live well. *Very* well, most likely. Whether or not she now loved Terry or would ever love Terry did not matter. Love was like beauty, not something one could count on for the long haul. She had loved Holly and Rhonda. Truly loved them. Every golden moment of her young life had somehow been connected to them. Her friendship with them had been the fountain from which popularity and success had flowed. Because of them she won a national beauty pageant. But the beauty pageant time of her life was over. The days when Holly and Rhonda would be a part of her day-to-day life also were coming to a close. Already there was a distance between them and her. They were sorority girls, and she was an independent. They had a social life, and she worked. The only person she could count on was herself.

Mr. Robertson's plan was intriguing. If she thought it would succeed, she might at least allow herself to consider it. But it would not work. *Could not* work.

She thought of the whisker burn that appeared on Rhonda's face from time to time when she returned from "studying at the library." She thought of the packet of birth control pills she had glimpsed in the bottom of Rhonda's purse and the distracted way in which she sometimes ran her fingers over her own neck or arm and got a distant, glazed-over look in her eyes. Sometimes Gina Kay had to repeat herself when she asked if Rhonda was ready to turn out the lights or head over to the cafeteria. And Rhonda wrote long letters on creamy white stationery. Not to her parents. She didn't need to write her parents because she called them on the phone several times a week. The letters Rhonda wrote were love letters to the boy she kept dangling back home in Lamberton just in case she lacked the will to wean herself from him.

"Terry is still in love with Rhonda," Gina Kay told Mr. Robertson. "In fact, I think they are seeing each other again." Then she paused, and corrected herself. "Actually, I am quite sure that Rhonda is seeing Terry again."

"You're damned right about that," Mr. Robertson said. "He drives over here to f . . ." He paused, apparently deciding on a different word selection. "He drives over here to have sex with her," he amended, "and then she sends him back home. She won't even be seen in public with a boy whose daddy could buy and sell her folks a hundred times over. I told him if he's gonna be a gigolo, he ought to start charging for his services. After she sends him on his way and goes back to her ivory tower, Terry gets drunk at a roadhouse on Highway one eighty-three. The bartender has called me twice now to tell me to come fetch him. And in the last month, he's run his truck off the road three times—rolled it once. At this rate, it'd probably be cheaper if I bought a goddamned tow truck and pulled his wrecked vehicles out of the ditches myself. So far, Terry has only ended up with cracked ribs and scrapes and bruises, but he's going to get himself killed if I don't do something. I know that I haven't been a good father to my son, but regardless of what you may think, I do love the boy. He is my only connection with his mother and the only flesh and blood I got left on this earth. This may be my last chance to make things right for him."

He paused, reaching again for his wineglass with a meaty, work-worn hand. His eyes seemed misty, but maybe it was just the candlelight. In its kind glow, she could almost see the handsome man he once had been. A more powerfully built man than Terry and with stronger features, Mr. Robertson was an intimidating physical presence. He stared into the candle flame as he said, "I've been thinkin' 'bout you ever since you brought Terry home that night after he wrecked the convertible. You're loyal to your own. And you got balls. I used to think I didn't like that in a woman, but for a boy like Terry, you just might be his salvation."

Gina Kay started to interrupt. She wanted to say that Terry wasn't remotely interested in her, and besides, Rhonda was one of her two best friends in the whole world. And maybe she didn't want to be Terry Robertson's salvation. But Mr. Robertson held up his hand. "Hear me out, girl," he said in a stern voice.

He waited while the waiter stepped forward to drain the wine bottle refilling his glass. Mr. Robertson told the man to bring a second bottle and downed half the glass in one swallow before continuing. "I talked to Doc Templeton about your mother," he said. "He tells me it won't be much longer until she won't be able to get around at all. You're going to need a lift and special bathing facilities and all sorts of stuff to take care of her. *Expensive* stuff. And the doc says it's been real hard for your father to look after her on his own and still try to scrape out a living driving a school bus and selling hay and whatever else he can get to grow on unirrigated land. Your parents need you, girl. And maybe if you lived in Lamberton, you could keep your sisters' brats from becoming as worthless as their mothers."

What was happening to Gina Kay now felt like something from a book. For her entire life, Ward Robertson had been the most notable presence in Lamberton. If she went to town and saw him on the sidewalk or even just driving by in his truck, it was a significant enough occurrence to report back to her mama. Mr.

Robertson never smiled. Never tipped his hat to the ladies. Never said "howdy" to the old men sitting on park benches in the court-house square. He had become their town's dark brooding duke in the castle. The town's citizens treated him with deference and were perhaps just a little bit afraid of him. He owned the land on which many of them lived and eked out a living. And after all, there was the possibility that Wade Robertson had killed his own wife, the beautiful and lonely Marie who was now buried beside her baby in a desolate little cemetery thousands of miles from the home of her childhood. Now, that same powerful man wanted the daughter of the most lowly of commoners to marry his only son.

Gina Kay had loved Terry Robertson in the sixth grade, but the minute she saw Rhonda Hayes, she recognized quality and knew that there was a girl far more worthy of Terry's love and admira-tion than she ever could be. And she put her daydreams of him aside. From that time forward, the starring role in her daydreams alternated between Robert Redford and Omar Sharif. Robert and Omar were safe. They were no more real than Prince Charming in a fairy tale. But she continued to admire Terry. And to live vicari-ously through her beloved Rhonda, who was not only pretty but also smart, the smartest person Gina Kay had ever known. She even daydreamed about Terry and Rhonda's someday wedding with her and Holly as attendants. But sometimes, when she was half-asleep and not doing a very good job of managing her thoughts, she would imagine Terry Robertson kissing her on the lips. And touching her down there. That she had such thoughts was her deepest, darkest secret. She would die if Rhonda ever knew.

The father of Terry Robertson was leaning across the table with its snowy white cloth, the look on his face and the language of his body imploring but his tone commanding, like that of a general in front of his troops. "I want you to listen to me, Gina Kay Matthews, and listen well," he said. "First of all, I know your mother has gotten herself too fat to ever leave that dump of a house, so I'll have the house moved out to the ranch with her in it. I had the house-moving outfit over in Temple drive down and check out the route. I'll have to pay the utilities companies to take down some lines while the house goes by, and I'll have to bulldoze the stone pillars at the entrance to the ranch, but there's nothin' that can't be managed. Your mama can ride her house down the road while she's sittin' on her sofa. Once we get it out there, we can fix it up, get all that handicapped stuff installed, and put in a door big enough to get your mother out in case the place ever catches on fire. Your father can work for me as a handyman or whatever and earn a regular salary and some self-respect. And we can hire someone to help look after your mother."

Gina Kay was stunned by his plan, by the sheer scope of it and the thought that had gone into it. But she didn't want to hear any more. She did not want to assume the mantle of this man's need. She could not rectify the mistakes of his lifetime. She thought of getting up from this table and walking out of the restaurant, leaving him and his impossible scheme behind.

"Your son does not want to marry me," she pointed out.

But he ignored her. "I'll move out back to the house I built for Antonia. You and Terry can have the big house all to yourselves and whatever younguns come along. You can fix up the house however you want. You'll be in charge. Every year for the first ten years you stay married to Terry and live in the same house with him, I will put $50,000 in the bank in your name. No strings attached. You can invest it however you wish. No matter what happens—if I die and Terry loses everything in a poker game or if the whole damned country stops eating beef—you and your kids will be okay."

"All this sounds very wonderful," Gina Kay said, "but even if I were willing to marry Terry, he is still in love with Rhonda." Then she leaned forward and repeated her words, drumming their cadence into the table with her fingertips. "Your son is in love with Rhonda Hayes."

Mr. Robertson dismissed her words with a wave of his hand. "Rhonda Hayes is a stuck-up bitch. I think even Terry is beginning to figure that out. My son is unhappy, Miss Matthews. *Damned* unhappy. 'Bout every time he's with that girl, he ends up almost killing himself. I haven't been a good father to him. I know that. But I'd rather hire someone to kill Rhonda Hayes and risk death row at Huntsville than have my son marry her. I like what I see in you. And I'm not talking about how pretty you are, although a man would have to be crazy not to be affected by that. I like your spunk and the way you care about your own. Doc Templeton tells me that you came up here to the big university to find yourself a rich husband so you'd be able to look after your family. Is that right?"

"Something like that," Gina Kay acknowledged.

"So, how's it goin'? Got any rich college boys sniffin' around?"

Gina Kay winced at his crudeness. "I've only been here two months," she said, then shrugged. "I think the rich boys are all in fraternities, and fraternity boys only date sorority girls. My scholarship money won't pay for me to be in a sorority."

"You tellin' me that a pretty girl like you hasn't gone out with a boy since you got here?"

"I work four evenings a week," she pointed out. "The other nights I need to study. I wouldn't have time even if a nice, rich boy took a notice of me. I guess I'm going to have to finish college and make my own fortune."

"Doin' what?" he demanded.

"I'll probably major in theater and become an actress. I even auditioned for a one-act play just the other day."

"What happened?"

"The drama professor said I was wooden," she admitted. She had hoped that Rhonda and Holly would practice with her, as they had with the dramatic reading she had used for her talent in all those beauty pageants. But they never seemed to have the time.

"If Terry wants to marry you, will you do it?" Mr. Robertson asked.

She said yes just to end the conversation. And maybe she even meant it. If Mr. Robertson was willing to spend all that money to help her look after her mother, how could she say no? Except it meant she would live in Lamberton, Texas, for the rest of her life.

It was not going to happen, though. She had no expectations of that. She was not even going to allow herself to consider the remote possibility that it would happen.

She relaxed a bit when their meal arrived, grateful that the reason for their meeting was over. The food smelled wonderful and was arranged on the plate like a work of art. She didn't say no when the waiter added more wine to her glass.

"So, can we talk about something else now?" she asked.

"Like what?"

"Like your grandfather. Why did he settle in Lamberton? And how did he get all that land?"

His steak grew cold while he talked. He was a man hungry to talk. She found herself almost liking him.

❦

When Gina Kay opened the door to her dorm room, Rhonda was in her pajamas, sitting at her desk studying. Gina Kay regarded the room that had been her home for the last two months. It was far nicer than her room back home but didn't compare with some of the other rooms in the dorm. Some of the girls had painted their rooms and even hung draperies. The mother of one of the girls on their floor had actually hired an interior decorator to make over her daughter's room. Rhonda's mother had offered to pay for matching bedspreads for their twin beds, but Gina Kay had insisted on paying for her own, which meant they had to buy cheap ones. But the spreads they selected were colorful. And they had added throw pillows. Rhonda's mother had provided a braided rug that filled the open space between the two twin beds.

Holly had drawn the short straw and been forced to take potluck on a roommate. She was rooming on the floor above them with Harmony Belknap, a deeply religious young woman from Lufkin. Harmony had a large, framed picture of Christ over her desk, a row of inspirational posters over her bed, and kept her radio turned to a station that played only gospel music. Holly often studied down here in the evenings, especially on the nights when Gina Kay was at work and her desk was free.

"My, you're all dressed up," Rhonda said. "Did you have a date?" she asked hopefully.

Gina Kay had anticipated Rhonda's question and was ready with an answer. "No, I went out to dinner with the director of the state Miss American Teenager pageant. She wanted my thoughts on next year's pageant and took me to a really nice restaurant."

"How come you didn't say anything about your plans earlier? Holly thought you were going to study together for a biology test."

"Miss Johnson called out of the blue. She was in town just for the evening."

Rhonda turned back to her books. "Well, I'm glad you had a night out. Seems like all you do is work, go to class, and study."

"That's pretty much it," Gina Kay said, taking off her dress and slipping on a robe. "Rhonda, do you ever hear from Terry?" she asked as she hung up the dress.

Still staring down at an open textbook, Rhonda took a heartbeat too long to respond. "Why do you ask?" she asked warily.

"Just wondering," Gina Kay said as she put her blue pumps back in their box and stored it under her bed. "You never say anything about him, but sometimes I can tell you're thinking about him."

Rhonda swung her legs around and stared at Gina Kay over the back of her chair. "So, you're a mind reader now," she said, her tone challenging almost to the point of anger.

"No, but you get this sweet, sad look on your face, like you're remembering some nice time with him."

Gina Kay could feel Rhonda's eyes watching her as she turned back her bedspread, propped her pillows into a backrest, and picked up her biology notebook. With no desire at all to memorize the phylum of the animal kingdom, she curled up in bed with the notebook on her lap. And felt so defeated. She not only needed to study for the biology test, she had her weekly vocabulary test in French tomorrow. French was a nightmare. It was difficult for her to find time for the required three hours a week in the language lab, and during every class session, each student was required to read a passage in French out loud. Gina Kay couldn't say two words without the professor correcting her.

"Any regrets about breaking up with Terry?" she asked Rhonda over the top of her notebook.

"Sometimes," Rhonda admitted. "Then I find myself having a really good time with people here on campus. And not just at the sorority house or at parties. I really love my classes. A couple of my professors are so interesting that I'm sorry when the class ends and wish it could just go on and on. I find myself thinking that I never would have experienced anything even remotely like that if I'd stayed in Lamberton." Then she sighed. "But then, there are times when I miss Terry so much it hurts. *Really hurts*. And I get afraid that he'll find someone else."

"But if you aren't going to marry him," Gina Kay said, "I'd think you would be hoping that he find someone else so he can settle down and raise kids and have a normal life."

"You think I'm an evil person, don't you?" Rhonda asked. And suddenly her eyes were glistening with tears.

"I don't think any such thing," Gina Kay said, scooting off her bed and kneeling beside Rhonda, embracing her, stroking her back. "But like my mama always says, fence sitting is really hard on the butt. Eventually it gets to hurting so much that you have to decide on one side of the fence or the other and get down."

"I miss your mama," Rhonda said.

"I do, too. I miss her a lot."

That night, Gina Kay had a dream in which she and her mother were sitting in their house while it rolled down the road to the Robertson Ranch. The look on her mother's face was so joyous, she looked like an angel.

Chapter twenty-four

The next morning, when Gina Kay and Rhonda returned from breakfast in the cafeteria, two girls from their floor were admiring a huge bouquet of long-stemmed red roses sitting on the round table in the dormitory foyer.

The two girls turned and smiled knowingly at Gina Kay.

She realized immediately that the flowers were for her. And that Mr. Robertson had sent them.

"Wow," Rhonda said. "There must three dozen of them. Who's the lucky girl?"

"Gina Kay," the two girls said in unison. One of them removed the small envelope from its plastic holder and handed it to Gina Kay.

Gina Kay slid the envelope into her jacket pocket.

"Well, aren't you going to open it?" Rhonda asked.

"I already know who sent them," Gina Kay said. "They're from Miss Johnson, the woman I had dinner with last night."

"How do you know that?" Rhonda demanded.

"She told me that she planned to send me some sort of surprise," Gina Kay said. "She wants me to take next semester off and work with her on the state Miss American Teenager pageant."

Gina Kay felt her heart race. She hated to lie, and she hated that she was getting so good at it.

"You're not going to do it, are you?" Rhonda asked.

"I don't know," Gina Kay said, heading for the stairs. "I might if she offers me a nice salary. A little money in my pocket would be nice for a change. Maybe instead of hanging around here hoping to meet a rich man, I'll launch a career in pageant management."

"Aren't you going to take the flowers to your room?" one of the girls called after her.

"No, they look nice right there," Gina Kay said over her shoulder.

While Rhonda was in the bathroom, Gina Kay pulled the card out of the envelope and read the five words written on it. *He said yes. Call me.*

Did the message mean what she thought it meant? She tried to consider alternative meanings. Maybe Terry had simply agreed to discuss the remote possibility of their getting married.

But even that would be monumental.

Dear God, what was she going to do?

She sat on her bed and put her head in her hands. How could she choose? She either passed up an opportunity to assure her family's future or she broke Rhonda's heart.

What if Terry was her only chance to marry rich?

If only she had more time to find out before having to make a decision that would affect the rest of her life. She had already promised herself that next semester she would take fewer hours, join some clubs, and get out more. And she would be bolder. Try to flirt a little bit no matter how uncomfortable it made her. And she would ask girls in the dorm to get her blind dates. It was too soon to give up on finding Mr. Right in Austin.

She wished there really were a Miss Johnson and a job opening with the pageant organization. The idea of being on her own and traveling around the state was an appealing one.

She hadn't heard Rhonda come back in the room. Suddenly she was saying, "Hey, are you okay?"

Gina Kay jumped. "I had wine last night," she said, uncovering her face, sitting up straight. "It made me a little shaky."

Another lie, she thought, but at least it was partially true. She had had wine last night, but that wasn't what was making her shaky.

Rhonda glanced at the clock on her desk. "It's time to go," she said, as she picked up her backpack.

"I need to lie down for a while," Gina Kay said, lying back on her bed with a moan.

"You want some aspirin or a drink of water?" Rhonda asked.

"I just need to lie here for a little while with my eyes closed," Gina Kay said. "I'll go to my nine o'clock class."

Nine o'clock was when her biology test was scheduled. If she married Terry, she would drop out of school, and there would be no need to take the test, no need to struggle through her ten o'clock French class.

When Rhonda had been gone a couple of minutes, Gina Kay rolled off her bed and went to the window. She watched until she saw Rhonda crossing the street with several other girls from their dorm. They were talking and laughing, each with a backpack slung over one shoulder. They were wearing just the right style jeans with just the right top and shoes. They looked like they belonged here.

She walked across the small room to Rhonda's desk where the phone sat, which was only fair since Rhonda paid the phone bill. Gina Kay's hand was shaking when she picked up the receiver.

She placed the call collect and listened to Mr. Robertson's voice accepting the charges.

She had to clear her throat before she could speak. "Thank you for the flowers," she said, sinking into Rhonda's desk chair.

"I told the florist I wanted something spectacular."

"They are."

"I'll arrange for the marriage license," he said. "If there's a waiting period, I'll get it waived. How soon can you get down here?"

"Why all the rush?" she asked.

"You got something you need to do first?" he asked.

"I'd like to at least get used to the idea."

"You've got the rest of your life for that, girl. Let's get it done and get your parents taken care of. And my boy. I thought you could get married over at your folks' place this evening, then you and Terry can drive over to San Antonio for a few days. He and I had been planning to go to a cattle auction, so there's already a hotel reservation. I'll see if I can change it to the bridal suite. You'll have to do the driving. After Terry's last accident, the judge finally took away his driver's license for a whole damned year. If you're not comfortable with city driving, I'll take you over."

"You're going too fast," she said, rubbing her forehead. "I need to talk to Terry."

Suddenly there was Terry's voice on the phone. "Gina Kay?"

"This whole thing is just too crazy," she told him. "It has gone too far. You love Rhonda, and I know you don't want to marry me. I only told your father yes so he would stop trying to convince me. I assumed you would have no part of his scheme."

"Well, it isn't what I have been dreaming about for the last five years," he admitted, "but I am willing to give it a try. Anything would be an improvement over the last couple of months."

"I'm afraid you'd just be marrying me to get back at Rhonda."

"Yeah, that's probably right. I don't know up from down these days. I don't know if I love or hate her. I'm sick of it, Gina Kay. Sick of being jacked around. Sick of getting drunk and having my father mad at me all the time. Our lawyer says that I've run out of chits and if I get another DUI, I'll have to go to prison. And he's talkin' state prison, not just a month or two in the county jail. And marrying you is better than putting a dagger in Rhonda's heart, which is what I feel like doing sometimes. She was in the convertible when I wrecked it. I was trying to kill us both just so she couldn't leave me. Which was pretty damned stupid. Rhonda is not worth dying over."

Both father and son had talked about killing Rhonda. And Terry had even tried. He and Rhonda could both be dead right now. A staggering thought. So big that Gina Kay had to put it aside to deal with later.

Gina Kay stared out the window at the river of students hurrying to class. They all seemed so eager. So *prepared*. Rhonda actually enjoyed her classes. She *loved* being a college student. Holly did, too. Gina Kay suffered from sweaty palms, always fearful a professor was going to call on her next and she would embarrass herself.

She decided on a different tack. "Think of how our getting married would hurt Rhonda," she pointed out, "of how awful it would be for her if the boy she loves up and marries one of her two best friends in the whole world. *That* would be worse than a dagger in her heart."

"It would serve her right," Terry said. "Rhonda thinks she can just dangle me on a string until she makes up her mind about what she wants to be when she grows up." He paused then added, "And I do like you, Gina Kay. You are beautiful and kind. And I like your folks. It would be nice for us all to be a family. My dad tells me that he's moving your house with your mother in it and installing it out back in that grove of live oaks so she'll be close by and you can look after her. And he's going to live in the house where our housekeeper used to live."

Terry paused then added, "He's really thought it all through, when I always thought he didn't give a damn. Which makes me wonder. Do you suppose that maybe deep down he really loves me after all?"

"I'm sure that he does," Gina Kay said.

"Maybe I owe it to my dad to make a fresh start. I lost my

mother, and it's time for me to give up on Rhonda. I'd sure hate to lose him, too."

Then he paused and asked, "Hey, are you crying?"

"Yes."

"Who are you crying for? Yourself or me or Rhonda?"

"I'm crying for us all," Gina Kay said, but mostly she was crying for herself, for what she was about to do to Rhonda. Everyone thought she was such a good and loyal person. That was how she thought of herself. No matter that she wasn't a good student like Rhonda or fun to be with like Holly. She was good and loyal Gina Kay. Now that would no longer be true, not if she did something that would break the heart of someone she loved very much.

And did she really want to go back home to Lamberton? *But all that money*. How could a poor girl say no to all that money?

"Will you go talk to my parents and explain everything to them?" she asked. "And tell my daddy to drive up over here and get me this afternoon. Rhonda has a lab this afternoon until about four. I'd like to be gone before she comes back."

"She thinks I'm already in San Antonio with my dad," he said. "She had asked me to drive over to Austin this evening—late, after she got back from some meeting. The only time I ever see her is in my truck or a dumpy motel. The hotel where you and I will be staying is first-rate. Our room will have a balcony overlooking the river, and we'll be served breakfast in bed. We'll eat in the best restaurants and go two-stepping at a western bar. And I'll buy you something pretty. What would you like? A Rolex or a fur coat or a new car? You just tell me, and I'll buy it for your wedding present. My dad said I could."

"But you still love Rhonda," Gina Kay pointed out one last time.

"Yeah, but I hate her, too. A lot."

The living room was filled with flowers—chrysanthemums, roses, daisies, lilies, gladiola. Vases of flowers were sitting on the television, on the coffee and lamp tables, on the kitchen table, on the floor. Her sisters were already there, with their children and husbands in tow. The men and kids were in jeans or shorts, but her sisters were actually wearing skirts. Gina Kay hadn't realized they even owned skirts. They stepped forward with looks of newfound respect on their faces and embraced her. "Way to go," Ruth Ann said.

The look on her mama's face was so joyous it made tears come to Gina Kay's eyes. "I thank the Lord I lived to see this day," Mama Matthews said, tears flowing down her checks. "We're so proud of you, honey. Can you imagine! We're going to live at the Robertson Ranch! And just look at all these flowers Mr. Robertson sent."

Her father was so overwhelmed he could barely speak. He hugged her so tightly she could hardly breathe, and he whispered her name over and over again as he planted kisses in her hair.

Tanya, Kara Lynn's oldest girl, tugged on Gina Kay's hand and said, "Mr. Robertson is going to put this old house on a truck, and Grandma's going to ride in it."

"That's right, honey," Mama Matthews said. "And the newspaper is going to take pictures. Can you imagine, Gina Kay? A picture of our house being moved to the Robertson Ranch is going to be in the newspaper."

Gina Kay stood in the middle of the room, smiling and nodding. The whole scene seemed so unreal. With all the flowers, the room looked like a funeral parlor, a very shabby funeral parlor. She saw holes in the carpet and upholstery that she'd scarcely noticed before, along with the stains on the walls, faded curtains, tattered window shades. The screen door kept banging shut as children ran in and out, their thundering footsteps making the dishes rattle in the kitchen cupboards. Everyone was looking at her, smiling as they waited for her to do or say something. Their faces seemed distorted, their smiles too wide, their teeth too big, their noses too long, their eyes too far apart. She was finding it difficult to breathe, difficult to stand.

She realized her mother was saying something to her. About clothes. She wanted to know what she was going to wear at her "wedding."

Wedding seemed too grand a word. Weddings were something that happened in churches with organ music and bridesmaids. What she was going to do was *get married*. Going to say "I do," and be done with it. And she probably would have to sign her name on something. Which name would she sign? Gina Kay Matthews or Gina Kay Robertson?

What *was* she going to wear?

Her clothes were all piled up in the back of her father's pickup. She'd have to pack a suitcase for San Antonio, too. She didn't own a pretty nightgown. No nightgown at all. Just pajamas.

Tonight she would be Terry Robertson's wife. Tonight she would have sex with him. He would hold her in his arms and kiss her and push his way into her body.

She realized that her knees were about to buckle, but she managed the two steps needed to reach her mother's huge form on the sofa and knelt beside her, put her face on her mama's soft shoulder and felt her massive arms envelop her. Her mother's flesh smelled sour. Not like talcum powder. *Never again*, Gina Kay vowed. She would have a wonderful bathroom built onto the house that had a tub large enough for her mother and a hydraulic lift to put her into it. And she would buy a truckload of the finest talcum powder on the planet. Her mother's skin was never going to smell sour again.

She felt her body relax, felt her breathing come more easily.

"I love you, Mama," she said.

"I know you do, honey," Mama said, smoothing Gina Kay's hair. "I love you, too. You'll never know how much I love you."

"Rhonda is going to hate me," Gina Kay said. "No one has ever hated me before."

"Someday Rhonda is going to realize it was for the best," her mama said in a soothing voice.

"I hope so, Mama. I really hope so."

Chapter twenty-five

For the best. Gina Kay recalled her mother saying those very words. Mama believed that someday Rhonda was going realize she was better off because Gina Kay had married Terry instead of her.

Gina Kay paused in her narration, announcing that she needed a break and was sure Rhonda and Holly did, too. In the bathroom, Gina Kay stared at her tired face and red eyes in the mirror. She'd had a hard time sleeping last night. Why was it that when she needed sleep the most, her mind was the busiest?

Mostly, her middle-of-the-night musings had been precipitated by the apprehension she felt about this morning, when she would have to make good on her promise to explain how it was that she and Terry became man and wife. Her hope was that she and Rhonda would go home if not friends then at least not enemies. Of course, she also hoped that when the time arrived for her to tell her story, Rhonda would be less hostile. While there had been moments during the last four days when Rhonda let down her reserve, Gina Kay realized full well what a formidable task awaited her.

Gina Kay had also found her thoughts turning to Justice Alexander Resnick. She had tried to be friendly without greatly encouraging the man, even though she liked him well enough. Alex was a man hungry for a woman's smile, a woman's touch, and it had been years since she had been physically intimate with a man. It would have been easy to encourage him, maybe even arrange to meet him someplace in a month or two and have an affair with him, perhaps even go with him on a trip to Russia in search of his roots. But ultimately, Alex was the sort of man who wanted a traditional wife to run his household and facilitate his life, and Gina Kay doubted if she would ever marry again. At this point in her life, with Terry and her parents gone and Mitch and Kelly raised, she didn't want to assume responsibility for anyone's happiness except her own and Ann Marie's. And when Ann Marie went off to college, she planned to do something outrageous, like run for Congress or take up flying.

And lastly, as morning approached, with Holly asleep in the other bed and the images of last night's wedding fresh on her mind, Gina Kay had found herself reliving her own marriage—twenty-five years ago this coming October. She remembered it as though it were yesterday.

She had worn a pale green suit with her hair pulled back in a severe chignon. Terry wore a coat and tie, as did his father and hers. Mr. Robertson's expensive-looking western-cut suit looked brand new. Her daddy's suit was old and saggy. The cloying smell of the minister's hair pomade made her stomach queasy. Her mother was sitting upright on the sofa and wearing one of the tent-shaped garments Gina Kay had made for her on Mrs. Burgess's sewing machine.

When Gina Kay said "I do," her family burst into applause. For the first time in Gina Kay's memory, the Matthews family faced a brighter future, and there was more hugging and joy in that room than there had been in years. Maybe ever. And while she smiled and hugged, Gina Kay had pondered her future with Terry. She already knew that he would be yet another person for her to look after, someone else for whom she would feel responsible. And she fully realized that along with responsibility came both love and resentment. She had learned early in life that nothing was ever all one thing or the other.

In the spacious bathroom, with Holly and Rhonda probably

wondering what was taking her so long, Gina Kay soaked a wash-
cloth in hot water and pressed it against her eyes. It felt so good.
She held it there until the cloth began to cool, then repeated the
process.

For the best.

Yes, it certainly had worked out for the best for the entire
Matthews family, she acknowledged. Becoming Robertson in-laws
had definitely made her parents' lives easier. Gina Kay had been
able to send her sisters to beauty college and open a shop for them
on Lamberton's Main Street that had supported them well to this
day. And she had all but raised her nieces and nephews, who realized that behaving themselves and living up to Aunt Gina Kay's
expectations meant they got to have their teeth straightened and
attend school well-clothed and -shod. When they turned sixteen,
they each had a vehicle to drive as long as they stayed sober, and
if they graduated from high school, they had a free ticket to college or trade school.

And in so many ways, her marriage to Terry had provided Gina
Kay with the opportunity to remake herself. Under Wade Robertson's tutelage, she had become a damned good rancher, which
was as much about record keeping as it was overseeing employees
and livestock and growing forage. And it was Wade who encouraged her to earn a college degree and become involved in phil-
anthropic and civic endeavors, and not just in Lamberton but
statewide. He wanted the Robertson name to mean more than just
cattle in the state of Texas. He wanted it to be associated with worthy causes and even the arts. He wanted his grandchildren to be
proud of their name. Even now, Gina Kay still walked across the
backyard to Wade's little house every evening to report on the
day's activity and seek his advice. When she went to tell him that
Terry had died, he took her hand and thanked her for keeping his
boy alive as long as she had and for giving him three fine grandchildren. And she held him while he wept for his son, for the little

boy he had set adrift after Marie died. "I brought you into this family to clean up the mess I made of things," he told Gina Kay, "and I love you like a daughter."

Yes, Gina Kay thought, she was quite sure that Wade Robertson considered himself well served by the bargain he had struck with her. But he gave her too much credit. Along with her successes had been the most painful of failures. Her husband had been a drunkard and came perilously close to killing Ann Marie. She had grieved for Terry long before he died. His death had been a release.

As for Rhonda, had she been harmed for life by the bargain Gina Kay had made with Wade or had her life also turned out "for the best"?

Of course, that was impossible to say. Not even Rhonda herself knew if she really would have put aside her ambition to marry Terry and become a permanent resident of Lamberton. Of course, Rhonda could have finished college as a married student, as Gina Kay herself eventually had done, commuting back and forth to a distant campus, taking a class or two for an endless string of semesters while trying to manage a household and care for children. That sort of student receives little recognition. They are seldom singled out for the honors and accolades that Rhonda so craved. But even if Rhonda had earned a law degree, would she have been satisfied to hang out her shingle above some storefront on Lamberton's Main Street and become a small-town attorney dealing with wills and boundary squabbles?

But then Rhonda could not possibly know how lucky she was to have a sober man for a husband.

Gina Kay looked again at her bare, tired face and applied just a dab of lipstick and a touch of eye shadow and blush before returning to the sitting room. Rhonda and Holly were back in their places at opposite ends of the sofa. Rhonda's foot was tapping impatiently. A fresh pot of coffee was waiting in the kitchenette.

Gina Kay poured herself a cup before resuming her seat. A fat gray pigeon was regarding her from the window ledge. Which made her smile.

She had already decided that she would not say anything about her and Terry's wedding night. But in many ways, it had been a predictor of what was to come. They had gotten married Friday evening, but it wasn't until Sunday afternoon that Rhonda's parents drove to Austin to give their daughter the news in person. So while she and Terry were promising till death do us part, Rhonda would still have been daydreaming about Terry, hoping that he would soon read the letter in which she promised to marry him and come rushing over to Austin to celebrate their love.

Gina Kay thought how she and Terry would have been unlocking the door to the bridal suite of a San Antonio hotel just about the time Rhonda would have given up on hearing from him and gone to bed, with Gina Kay's stripped, empty bed across the room.

Terry had carried their two suitcases inside and, without even looking around, had pulled a bottle of Jack Daniel's from his and carried it out to the small balcony.

Gina Kay headed for the bathroom, where she stood under the shower for a long time. The spray was strong and made her flesh tingle. She deliberately did not think about what awaited her. *About sex.* She wanted it to be nice, but if it wasn't she would still be married to him.

When she came out of the bathroom wearing blue-and-pink shortie pajamas, Terry was still sitting on the balcony taking swigs straight from the bottle. He looked surprised but said nothing when she took the bottle from his hand. She carried it inside to the bathroom and poured its contents down the drain. Then she returned to the balcony and sat with him for a while, watching the last of the day's tourists as they strolled along the river that wound its way between the hotels, restaurants, and shops that comprised the Paseo del Rio area in downtown San Antonio. She commented that it was a pretty night. That San Antonio was a pretty city. Would he like to visit the Alamo tomorrow? She would like to buy some souvenirs for her sisters' kids. Did he like Mexican food? Terry's responses came in the form of grunts. Finally, she took his hand and led him to bed.

He lay there for a time on his side of the bed, then began to cry. She put her arms around him. "We can get it annulled," she told him.

"No, I don't want to do that."

After a time, she realized he had fallen asleep. Eventually, out of sheer exhaustion, she also slept. Toward morning, she awoke when Terry got up to go to the bathroom. When he came back to bed, he had shed his shirt and slacks and was wearing only a pair of undershorts. He lay on his back and stared at the ceiling. She touched his face, then his chest, and finally his penis through the fabric of his shorts. Unsure just what a girl was supposed to do with a penis, she simply patted it like one would a small puppy. She felt it stir then become larger and firmer.

After a time, he wordlessly took off his shorts then took hold of her hand and showed her what she was supposed to do.

She had a sense that this was all that he wanted, for her to continue moving her hand up and down the shaft of his penis. Finally she said, "If we're not going to get an annulment, I would like for you to make love to me."

"Do you want me to kiss you first?" he asked.

"That would be nice," she said.

He took her in his arms and kissed her. Which was indeed nice, but he stopped too soon and crawled on top of her. It hurt when he entered her, but not greatly. Wordlessly, he began to move up and down, slowly at first then faster and faster. She was stunned by the power of his orgasm when it came.

Then he rolled off of her. "I'm sorry," he said.

"Why?"

"Because you weren't ready. I want you to like it. I'll do better next time."

"Do you think you can ever love me?" she asked.

"I hope so."

"I love you already," she had announced, curling her body next to his. "I think I have always loved you."

Almost from the very beginning of their marriage, she was usually the one who initiated sex. If Terry hadn't had too much to drink, he obliged. And there had been times when they experienced true passion and genuine love. She had lived for those times.

In her heart Gina Kay had wanted to believe that Terry would have had a drinking problem no matter who he had married. But she didn't *know* that.

She put her coffee cup on the small side table and directed her attention once again toward Rhonda and Holly. Empty coffee cups and half-eaten bagels were on the coffee table in front of them. Neither Rhonda nor Holly had bothered with makeup. That would come later when they dressed for their last day in New York. Holly was wearing jeans and a T-shirt; Rhonda was in jogging clothes. Gina Kay could see in their faces, as in her own, indications of the older women they would become. All the creams and potions and procedures in the world were not going to bring back the dewy freshness of young flesh. They were three women poised at the crest. No longer young. Ready to begin the descent into old age. It was time for them to deal with the unresolved issues of their youth and strive for a calmer, less-troubled journey on the downhill run.

"Any comments so far?" she asked them.

"Your mother was just placating," Rhonda said immediately, her arms tightly folded, her body tense. "She was telling you exactly what you wanted to hear when she said that I would someday realize that your marrying Terry had been 'for the best.' One would hardly expect her to call you a scheming little bitch, not when you had just made all her dreams come true."

On her end of the sofa, Holly reacted to Rhonda's statement by sitting up straighter, a quizzical look on her face. "Why do you choose to direct all your anger at Gina Kay?" Holly asked. "It wasn't as though Terry's father dragged him kicking and screaming into this marriage."

"Why do you choose to believe *her* version of what happened?" Rhonda demanded.

"If her version isn't true, then Terry was a wimp and not worth all that angst," Holly pointed out.

"I think he was a more troubled boy than you realized," Gina Kay told Rhonda.

"If you're talking about the part of your story where Terry pushed his mother down the stairs, I don't believe a word of it," Rhonda said. "He would have told me if that were true."

"Maybe he was afraid you wouldn't love him anymore if you knew," Gina Kay responded. "Terry thought that his father didn't love him and blamed himself for the death of his mother and sister. Then you came along and became the center of his life. He not only loved you, Rhonda, he was convinced that he needed you. You gave him strength and hope for the future. But you went off to college, and regardless of what your intentions were, Terry believed he was losing you. Then suddenly he was offered a way to please his father and maybe even make amends."

Rhonda shook her head, her eyes wide, anger in her voice. "You don't know what Terry believed, and what you did was a dishonorable thing! Maybe Terry and I would have broken up and never seen each other again. Or maybe we would have beaten the odds and had a damned good life together. But we should have had the chance to let things come to some sort of natural conclusion. There is no way to know what might have been."

"Rhonda, honey," Holly said softly, "I think you are looking back at 'what might have been' through rose-colored glasses. You have chosen to forget Terry's wildness and remember only the good times. And the passion. But believe me, Gina Kay's life with Terry was not a bed of roses."

"Life is *never* a bed of roses," Rhonda said, and still looking at Holly, she pointed an accusing finger in Gina Kay's direction. "And maybe Terry and I would have had a more successful marriage than he and Gina Kay apparently had."

Gina Kay started to respond, to agree with her. But Holly spoke first, her voice gentle. "Maybe if you and Terry had found each other again in middle life," she told Rhonda, "you might have been able to have a successful marriage, but if you two horny kids had gotten married back then, the cards were stacked against you. God, were they stacked against you! Maybe you can look back now and say life with Terry Robertson in a little Texas town wouldn't have been so bad, but that would be because you now know that success is always conditional and that it always comes with a price tag. Back then, though, you had all that potential to realize and a need to live up to your parents' expectations. And to your own expectations. Even if Terry had turned into a different person married to you and had done a better job curtailing his demons, you would have resented the hell out of having to squelch all your ability and ambition and settle for being Mrs. Terry Robertson."

"That is just supposition," Rhonda said. "Let's get back to the facts. I was in love with Terry. Gina Kay *knew* that I loved him. Yet she agreed to marry him."

"And Terry *agreed* to marry her," Holly reminded her. "No one put a gun to his head. He and his father courted her, Rhonda, not the other way around."

"That's because he hadn't read my letter," Rhonda said, her tone mournful. "He didn't know I wanted to marry him."

"Ah, yes, *the letter,*" Holly said. "You wrote it because you were afraid that if you didn't make some sort of concession to him, he was going to tell you to fuck off. You really didn't want to marry him, Rhonda. You just didn't want to lose him. It is not the same thing. You weren't buying bride magazines. You weren't day-dreaming about your bridal gown. I work with brides almost every day of my life, and brides live in a pink haze where select-ing a china pattern is more important than world peace. Brides are *bridal.* They temporarily leave the human race and become their own subspecies. You were still behaving like a sorority girl, looking forward to the Christmas dance and initiation day. Ear-lier *that very same week,* you had been so excited when the rush chairman asked to you to serve on the rush committee. You couldn't wait to call your mother and tell her how you were going to be traveling around the state next summer putting on rush parties."

"Why are you being so ugly to me?" Rhonda said, her voice wavering, tears welling. "I had just made up my mind. I would have gotten to wedding plans later. I don't understand why you are giving me such a hard time, Holly. I was trying to do right by Terry. I *knew* that I had to either marry him or let him go. Can you imagine how much it hurt when I found out what Gina Kay had done?" Rhonda touched her chest, showing the site of her pain. "It still hurts when I think about it."

Then she turned to Gina Kay, her face blotched with anger. "It was wrong what you did! It was a terrible thing to do to someone who loved you. And if you are now planning to tell me that your marriage to Terry was sheer hell and that I should be grateful that you let me off the hook, I don't want to hear it."

Gina Kay took a deep breath before she responded. "Well, there were times of sheer hell, but like any marriage, we had good times and bad. We had passion and anger and joy and sadness."

"Rhonda, honey, after all these years, does it really matter what might have been?" Holly asked, her voice soft. Not accusatory. "Are you sorry that you ended up married to Dennis and still wish that you and Terry had given it a try?"

Rhonda looked away. And said nothing.

Silence hung in the room like a thick fog.

Just because some sort of movement seemed to be called for, Gina Kay got a drink of water and refilled Holly and Rhonda's coffee cups. Then she settled in again.

In the beginning, she told them, Terry really knuckled down and worked hard on the ranch.

It was a busy time, she recalled, getting her parents' house moved out there and fixed up. And then making changes in the big house. The first thing they did was rip out the 1940s-era kitchen. Then they knocked out some walls and created a den.

At first, Terry enjoyed being involved in her projects, but then he got bored with them and spent more time working cattle and cutting hay. His attorney had put the fear of God in him about driving, so he was at home most evenings. Gina Kay would cook dinner, and they would watch television. Sometimes they played gin rummy or took twilight horseback rides. She remembered it as a lovely time and thought that Terry felt the same. They had their courtship after the fact and got to know and understand each other. He wasn't supposed to drive, but since there was no law against riding a horse while drunk, he sometimes went by horseback to the nearest highway tavern and drank himself into a stupor. Someone would put him back on the horse, which would then bring him home. But that didn't happen too often.

"I don't think we ever formally agreed that we would never speak of you," Gina Kay told Rhonda, "but after the phone conversation he and I had the day before we got married, not speaking of you became an unsaid rule. In the twenty-four and a half years that Terry and I were married, neither of us *ever* spoke your name to the other. If he had pictures of you hidden away, I never saw them. If he saved your letters, I never came across them. But I thought about you a lot. All I knew about your life was the bare facts Holly provided—that you finished law school, married, and had twin sons, and lived in an older home near the SMU campus. And I assume she told you the basic facts about my life. I grieved for the loss of our friendship, and I always hoped that somehow the three of us could be friends again someday."

"So, when did the good times with Terry end?" Rhonda asked.

Gina Kay took a sip of water, then began the final chapter of her narration.

After he got his driver's license back, he was gone more often, she explained. His drinking was episodic, though. She would tell herself that he was doing better, then he wouldn't come home for days on end. But he did want children. He believed that he could somehow come to terms with his own rotten childhood by being a good father to his own children. If he were a father, he would have a reason to control his drinking.

Gina Kay told him she wouldn't go off birth control pills until he had been dry for six months. So he went to rehab in San Antonio and did just that. And he stayed sober throughout her pregnancy, but he got drunk the night Mitch was born. Gina Kay had a second baby because she didn't want Mitch to be an only child. After Kelly was born, Terry started having wrecks again. Gina Kay forbade him to ever drive a vehicle in which one of their children was riding. On their ninth anniversary he told her that he wanted to live to see their children grow up and promised that, by their tenth anniversary, he was going to be a new man. He checked himself into a clinic in Houston and stayed for six long months.

Mitch and Kelly decorated the dining room with streamers and balloons for his welcome home dinner.

"I thought we were in the clear," Gina Kay said, "and we did have eight good years. To my knowledge, he didn't touch a drop during that time. It was his idea that we have another baby. Mitch and Kelly were in high school by then, and the idea of another baby to put off an empty nest was an appealing one. While I was pregnant, he fell off the wagon twice. But there were always those promises I wanted so desperately to believe. When the baby was born, we named her Ann Marie after our mothers. She was such a sweet little thing. Such a good baby. Terry was absolutely crazy about her. So were Mitch and Kelly. And she absolutely captivated her grandpa Wade. Then one day, when Ann Marie was eight months old, I realized I had inadvertently scheduled two doctors' appointments on the same day. Ann Marie was due for her DPT booster, and Wade had an appointment with an eye specialist at Scott and White Clinic in Temple. Terry wasn't interested in driving all the way to Temple and probably waiting around for hours, so he offered to take Ann Marie for her shot. Terry hadn't had a drink since before Ann Marie was born, and he would just be driving into town. Less than three miles. I took the infant seat out of my car and put it in the backseat of his truck."

Gina Kay clutched her hands together in her lap then took a deep breath in preparation of the rough going ahead.

"When I got back from Temple," she continued, "Terry and the baby weren't there. The housekeeper hadn't heard from him. I called the doctor's office, but it was already closed. I sent both Mitch and Kelly out to look for them. And the ranch hands. Then I called the sheriff and the Highway Patrol. I knew something was very, very wrong. When Terry came walking in the back door muddy and wet, I could smell the liquor on his breath. I'll never forget the look on his face when I asked him where the baby was.

"He had taken her to the doctor," she said, amazed at how calm her voice sounded, "then carried her over to the barber shop and hung out for a while. Then he put her in the infant seat and got into the truck. In the statement he made to the sheriff, he said that before he even started the motor, he'd reached into the glove compartment for something or other and found a pint left over from his last binge. I'm sure he just planned to take one swig and that, by the time he drained the flask, he had forgotten all about Ann Marie, who apparently had fallen asleep in the infant seat. He stopped at a liquor store and bought a pint to drink on the way to the ranch. Then he missed a curve, and the truck went plummeting down an incline toward the east pond. He jumped free just before it hit the water. And walked home, forgetting all about our baby in the backseat.

"I thought he was going to pass out before he told me where the baby was. He sank to his knees and started screaming and pulling his hair. I beat on him with my fists, demanding that he tell me where she was. But he was incoherent. Finally I understood what he was saying. Ann Marie was still in the truck. And the truck was in the pond.

"I yelled for the housekeeper to tell the sheriff where we were going, and Terry and I headed for the closest vehicle. He started to get in the driver's side, but I pushed him away. I can't remember if Terry said or did anything. Probably he just hung on. I drove like a mad woman, taking off across country, knocking down gates and fences as I went. All I could think of was that my baby was in the water. When we got there, the truck was half-submerged with only part of the cab above the water."

Gina Kay could feel the tears running down her face as she relived the horror of that night. She wiped them away with a napkin and blew her nose. "I plunged into the water. The door on the driver's side was open and I crawled inside. There wasn't a sound in the cab except the water lapping. The top of the infant seat was above water, but Ann Marie was slumped over, her face submerged. I lifted her face out of the water and groped around until I was able to release the catch and pull her out of the seat. She wasn't moving. Wasn't breathing. And she was so cold. Like ice. I started giving her mouth-to-mouth as I was crawling out of that truck. Terry was just standing there on the shore like a statue. I yelled at him to take off his shirt. Which he did, and I wrapped it around her. Over and over, I breathed for her, my mouth over her little face. Then I heard a siren up on the road, and I kept giving her mouth-to-mouth while I climbed up the incline. A patrolman met me halfway and tried to take her out of my arms, but I wouldn't let him. I kept breathing for her while he dragged us the rest of the way up the hill and got us into the patrol car. I didn't know where Terry was at that point and didn't care.

"I breathed for her all the way to the clinic. A doctor and two nurses were waiting for us. Her heart was beating but just barely. There was some water in her lungs, but not a lot. Apparently she had been able to hold her head up until just before we got there but lost consciousness because of hypothermia. I had come within seconds of losing her forever."

Gina Kay had to stop for a minute to compose herself. She put a hand to her chest to quell sobs and reached for the glass of water. Holly blew her nose. Rhonda put her hand over her mouth and closed her eyes. It was hard for them, too, Gina Kay realized. They were mothers. They understood the horror.

"I went with her in the medevac helicopter to Dallas," Gina Kay continued. "It was days before I was sure that she was going to live. More days before I knew if she had brain damage. Then she opened her eyes and smiled. My precious little angel. It was the most joyous moment of my life," she said.

"Terry never came to the hospital. He had disappeared. They dragged the pond. Looked for him everywhere. Finally three days later one of the deputies found him lying unconscious in a field.

He was dehydrated and just barely alive. When he got out of the hospital, they arrested him and charged him with drunk driving and reckless endangerment of a minor. He pled guilty and served six months in Huntsville. Mitch and Kelly drove over to see him every week, but I didn't.

"I never wanted to see him again actually, but he was the father of my children. And Mitch and Kelly still loved him even if I didn't. In my heart, though, I knew that what had happened was my fault. If Ann Marie had died, I would have been responsible. I knew better than to let her ride in a vehicle he was driving. My job was to keep my baby from harm, and I hadn't done that. I think that Mitch and Kelly understood that, because my relationship with them has never been the same.

"When Terry got out of jail, he moved into my parents' old house out in the oak grove. Mitch and Kelly would go out there to see him. Sometimes Mitch would spend the night with him. Gradually, I started letting Terry come up to the house for dinner when his father joined us, and then after a time he pretty much ate most of his meals with us. Mitch and Kelly felt so painfully sorry for him. It hurt me to see the pain in their eyes when they looked at the broken man their father had become. Kelly often would tell me that I was mean. Mitch never accused me in words, just with his eyes. And maybe I was mean, but I was not willing to pretend what I did not feel. What I felt for Terry was pity, and pity is not the same as love. The children knew it, and Terry did, too.

"Mitch had planned to go to Michigan State but went to A&M instead so he could come home weekends and see his father. And Kelly was offered an academic scholarship to Stanford, but she went to UT for the same reason. Their love for their father was boundless. They still loved me at some level, I suppose, but their love for me is more dutiful, and it is almost painful for me to be around them. They will come to the ranch less and less, I am sure, now that Terry is gone. Ann Marie loves me greatly, though, like I loved my mother. She is the light of my life.

"It was almost a relief when Terry died," Gina Kay admitted. "His children didn't have to watch him hating himself anymore. And you know what? Life does go on. I thought it was just an inane expression until I heard Rhonda's voice on the phone after Terry died and realized that I was going to see her again. I felt such hope."

Gina Kay looked at Rhonda. "Wade Robertson offered me the opportunity to help my family in a very significant way, but in doing so I knew I would destroy my friendship with you. I know that I hurt you deeply, and for that I am truly sorry. But if I had it to do all over again, I would make the same choice."

Then she stopped speaking, and silence filled the room. Even the street sounds seemed to have ceased. They were suspended in a soundless vacuum, each woman filled with her own thoughts.

Chapter twenty-six

Rhonda realized she needed to say something. After all, this entire scenario had been played out for her benefit, with Gina Kay seeking her forgiveness or understanding or letting bygones be bygones—anything that stopped short of hatred.

Rhonda's mother used to tell her that it was wrong to hate. Rhonda could dislike people intensely and decide never again to associate with them, but she should never hate them. Hate damaged the person who hated more than the recipient of the hatred. And perhaps her mother was right. But hate wasn't something she could turn off and on like a faucet.

And the only person Rhonda had ever hated was Gina Kay. By putting all the blame on Gina Kay's shoulders, she had been able to remember her relationship with Terry as something special, as a once-in-a-lifetime kind of love. And she could still have those occasional fantasies of what it would be like should she and Terry ever meet again.

Holly had moved to the window seat and was staring down at the street. The sun was shining brightly, the treetops gently moving.

Gina Kay's head was resting against the high back of her chair, her eyes closed. She looked exhausted.

Her stomach told Rhonda it must be approaching lunchtime, but she didn't bother to look at her watch. They had been at this for hours.

"Did your mother really ride in the house while they moved it to the ranch?" Rhonda asked.

Gina Kay opened her eyes—emerald green eyes that were the same color as the prom dress Holly had made for her all those years ago. "It was against the law for anyone to stay in a house while it was being moved," she answered, "but the sheriff wasn't about to arrest her. He wouldn't be able to get her out of the house and take her to jail if he did."

"So that little green house back under those trees was your parents' house?"

Gina Kay nodded.

"I didn't recognize it."

"Well, in addition to the green paint, it has a different front porch, and we added a picture window so Mama's television set wouldn't be her only window on the world," Gina Kay said. "She could watch the comings and goings at the big house and see her grandchildren swimming in the pool and riding their ponies. She was happy there and lived a lot longer than anyone thought she would. And it was an immense comfort for me knowing she was always there ready to ask about my day and listen when I told her."

A soft smile came to Gina Kay's face as she talked about her mother. "I learned a lot from Mama," she continued. "Even after the physical confines of her life had shrunk to one small room, she celebrated life. It was really hard on her when Daddy died, but she kept reminding herself how fortunate she had been to have him all those years."

Then the room became silent again. An awkward silence.

"So what now?" Holly finally asked, still looking out the window.

"I suppose this is where I'm supposed to say that I forgive or understand or am willing to wipe the slate clean," Rhonda said. "But I think I'll take a run instead."

Running was good therapy, Rhonda decided as she fell into a rhythm and headed for the path around the Central Park Reservoir. If she ran full out, all she could think about was her lungs and legs. Sometimes a mind purge was what she required, but right now, she needed to think. She needed to decide who she was going to be when she walked back into that hotel suite.

Was she going to continue in the role of the remote woman so wronged that forgiveness was not an option? That would be the easiest. It was a role she had perfected over the years. She could excuse herself from whatever activities Gina Kay and Holly had in mind for the rest of the day, which thankfully was the last full day of this strange trip, and go to a museum or two on her own, then wander through Bloomingdale's and have a solitary dinner in a nice quiet restaurant. In the morning, she would manage a polite good-bye and never see Gina Kay again. And Holly? Would Holly give up on her? What if the outcome of this trip was that she lost her oldest and best friend?

At midday, there were few joggers on the path. Early-morning rain had left the foliage clean and lush-looking. The birds and squirrels were going about the business of their day. Rhonda ran behind the Metropolitan Museum of Art. Just east of here was the apartment building where Jacqueline Kennedy Onassis had lived. She used to jog here with men from her Secret Service detail. Even after she had cancer, she came here to walk.

Rhonda felt grateful for her own good health, for her strong legs and lungs. She took a deep celebratory breath as she headed up the east side of the reservoir. The sunlight on the water was dazzling. A dozen or so geese were gliding across the surface like a stately flotilla of tiny ships. As she rounded the north end of the reservoir, she lengthened her stride, concentrating solely on her body, and ran full out for a quarter mile or so, then slowed and returned to her thoughts, to her mission. If she was not Rhonda the Remote, then who was she? She was forty-three years old and needed to decide.

She wondered if all women got hung up on the first man they ever made love to. Or was it just overly intense women like herself?

She had thought that the sex had to mean something. That it was something more than just two horny kids finally doing it after driving each other crazy for years. Something *far* more. It was a spiritual thing she and Terry did on the blanket under the stars. A sacrament. She would never have gone all the way with him if she hadn't been convinced they would someday marry. Nowadays, such a notion seemed quaint.

She had clung to the sacrament, though. Clung to the notion that what she and Terry had shared had been more than just sex. And there had to be some dark, ominous reason why he dumped her like a sack of bad potatoes without even a farewell kiss or a last long look.

Did she really believe he and Gina Kay had not so much as kissed each other before they got married in the Matthewses' living room?

True, there was no baby nine months later, but maybe Gina Kay had claimed to be pregnant in order to lure Terry into her trap, then claimed to have had a miscarriage.

Or maybe Terry was so angry with Rhonda for stringing him along and for not being willing to pull the plug on her ambition and cast her lot with him that he simply threw in the towel and went along with his father's proposal.

For so long Rhonda had allowed herself to feel cheated. Of all the words that had been spoken this morning, however, something Holly said had been the most telling: *You really didn't want to marry him, Rhonda. You just didn't want to lose him. It's not the same thing.*

When Holly said that, Rhonda had wanted to scream at her. To tell her that was not so. But there was truth in her words. Rhonda remembered being so confused. She wanted a man to love her the way her father loved her mother, but she did not want to repeat her mother's life.

So what now? Holly had asked.

What indeed? Rhonda thought.

She realized that her life was an unbalanced equation. She loved her children and husband. She was fortunate enough to still have both of her parents alive. And she had managed to have a reasonably successful professional life in spite of the constraints of motherhood. A woman with such a life should be more than *not quite* happy.

But she had never allowed herself more.

She had been overwhelmed with emotion when she heard how close Terry had come to causing the death of his own child. Of Ann Marie, the beautiful little girl she met the day of his funeral. Over the last two months, Rhonda had often thought of the moments she had spent with the child at the top of the stairs. She remembered the clean young smell of Ann Marie's hair, the feel of her healthy little body next to her own. She remembered wishing that the child were hers.

Precious little Ann Marie would have died an infant and been buried in the little hilltop cemetery next to Terry's mother and baby sister if he had collapsed into a drunken stupor on the way home that night. He would have been responsible for the death of his own child if Gina Kay had not been strong enough to take charge of the situation.

Rhonda had to slow her pace. Such thoughts made her feel as though she were wearing lead shoes. A shudder went through her body as she thought of the absolute horror of that night. As she imagined Gina Kay plunging into the lake and retrieving her baby's lifeless body then breathing into her mouth, desperately trying to bring her back from the dead. Any love Gina Kay had in her heart for Terry had died that night, leaving first revulsion and then pity in its wake.

Rhonda thought of the night that Terry had almost killed them both. She remembered other times he had driven drunk with her in the car, thought of the tales she had heard about him. How he would race trains to railroad crossings. And pass cars on curves, playing Russian roulette with the lives of those in his car and any unsuspecting motorists who might be coming around the curve.

Poor tragic Terry. Had it been inevitable that he have an unhappy life? Was it destined to be so after what happened to his mother? She hadn't known that he carried that awful guilt around with him. No wonder he had accepted his father's abuse as though it was his due. If she had known, she would have loved Terry even more tenderly and maybe not have waited so long to make love to him. She could have married him right after high school and dedicated her life to healing him. After all, she had far more resources than he did. She had loving parents and a good mind. She didn't have a weakness when it came to alcohol. The strong should look after the weak. There would have been satisfaction in that. Unless sacrificing herself would not have been enough to save him. Unless she would have ended up feeling nothing but pity for him. As Gina Kay had done.

Rhonda was grateful she had not done that.

She had not answered when Holly had asked if she was sorry that she ended up married to Dennis and still wished that she had given Terry a try. She had been stunned by the question. How could she possibly be sorry to be married to a man like Dennis?

The other day, she had felt almost guilty about still being alive after they visited the site where the World Trade Center once had been. And Holly had reminded her that life is for the living. She told her to take a deep breath and feel grateful.

And Rhonda had done that.

Now, once again, she took a deep breath and felt grateful. Grateful that she had not married Terry.

Grateful.

And she realized her feet were beating out a tattoo on the path. *Grateful. Grateful. Grateful.*

※

Gina Kay and Holly were dressed and waiting when Rhonda got back. "I'll hurry," she promised. "I'm starving," she added. "Let's go someplace decadent for lunch."

"If you can put off decadent until this evening, how about hot dogs and beer on a cruise around Manhattan?" Holly asked.

"Sounds great. Give me twenty minutes. Is G.W. going to pick us up?"

"Yes," Gina Kay said. "He's on his way."

"Good, I need to ask him something."

She could almost feel them exchange looks behind her as she opened the door to her room. And realized she was smiling.

※

Rhonda got into the front seat of the car. "Hey, G.W., did you take Marta to the walk along the river last night after the wedding?" she asked.

He nodded. And blushed. "It was a good thing to do," he acknowledged.

"I'm glad. I'd like to take my husband there sometime for a romantic nighttime stroll. Just because two people are married doesn't mean they can't be romantic. Right?"

G.W. nodded. "Sometimes Marta and me, we work, work, work and forget to be nice."

"I know what you mean. My husband and I are the same way," she said, then abruptly she changed the subject, asking G.W., "Have you ever taken the cruise around Manhattan?"

When he admitted that he had not, Gina Kay and Holly joined her in insisting that he accompany them on the cruise. They waited at the dock while he located a place to park the car. The boatmen were just about ready to take up the gangplank when he came rushing up.

They bought lunch at the snack bar and carried it to the top deck. It was a glorious day. Rhonda felt good. The ice-cold beer tasted incredibly clean and refreshing. She never ate hot dogs, which were caloric, had almost no nutritional value, and were laden with fat and harmful chemicals, but she wolfed this one down and wished for another. The sunshine felt glorious on her skin, and she didn't even care that she wasn't wearing sunscreen. She closed her eyes and lifted her unprotected face to the sun. The feel of its rays on her skin was intoxicating.

As they sailed past the majestic Statue of Liberty, Rhonda got tears in her eyes. And realized her companions were teary-eyed, too, G.W. included. "I know of this statue since I am little boy," he said. "I know someday I see her for real. When my family first arrive in this country, we see her from airplane window and feel very lucky."

They were surrounded by both American and foreign tourists. G.W. found a family of fellow Russians—not immigrants but bona fide tourists, he explained after engaging in a lengthy conversation with them. The family's next stop was Miami, then on to the Grand Canyon and Las Vegas. They owned a small shoe factory in Tula. And they weren't mafia, G.W. said. Not crooks. He seemed quite taken with the idea that regular, hardworking Russians could become rich enough to tour America.

"Do you ever think about returning to Russia and living there again?" Rhonda asked.

G.W. shook his head. "No. America is home. Next year, Marta and me, we take examination to be citizen." Then he paused a minute before adding, "Life is better here, but sometimes I feel a little sad. I cannot go to the graves of my parents and grandparents. Maybe I never again see the place of my family."

Rhonda could not imagine what it would be like to leave the

only world one had ever known and come to a completely new country and culture. What courage that must have taken. She told him so. "You are brave people," she said.

Then, while Gina Kay and Holly went to get another round of hot dogs and beer, Rhonda explained her plan for the evening to G.W. When she was finished, she asked, "Can you arrange that?"

"Is okay with Gina Kay?" he asked. "She is boss. No?"

"Yes, she has been the boss," Rhonda said. "But I want this to be a surprise, so tonight I'm taking over. Tonight I pay, and that makes me the boss. And I want you and Marta to join us for dinner."

"You look happy," G.W. said. "Other days, you are not happy."

"I know. I think the whole reason we came to New York was to get me happy. I guess it worked."

"Happy is good," he said.

"Yes," Rhonda said, planting a kiss on his cheek. "Happy is good. I think I will needlepoint those words on a throw pillow, except that I don't know how to needlepoint."

"What is 'throw pillow'?" G.W. asked.

The cruise was a wonderful idea, Rhonda decided as they enjoyed breathtaking views of Ellis Island, the incomparable Brooklyn Bridge, the Empire State Building, the Chrysler Building, the United Nations complex, and Yankee Stadium. Of *Gotham*. Rhonda could almost see the Superman of her childhood soaring between the towers. She felt wonder that such a city existed, but she also felt homesick for her little corner of the world on a sedate, wooded street in Dallas. Their little family had made lots of nice memories there, but it seemed less a home now with the boys gone. Of course, it was inevitable that Scott and Jason would leave, that it would someday be just her and Dennis left to figure out how they were going to spend the rest of their lives.

After the cruise, they strolled around South Street Seaport, an early-nineteenth-century waterfront that had been restored and even had tall ships anchored along its pier. The complex offered museums, shops, and eateries. Holly loaded up on souvenirs for her family. Gina Kay bought Ann Marie a beautiful doll dressed in colonial attire. And Rhonda bought a book on sailing ships and a captain's hat for Dennis, New York sweatshirts for her father and sons, and a crystal replica of the Statue of Liberty for her mother.

As G.W. pulled up in front of the hotel, Rhonda said, "Tell Marta that casual clothes are fine for this evening. We won't be going to a fancy restaurant."

"I thought we were going to the Boathouse," Holly said.

"There's been a mutiny," Rhonda explained. "G.W. and I have taken over for our last evening on the town."

She knew that Gina Kay and Holly were puzzled. All afternoon they had been trying to figure out what was going on with her. *Was she glad she had come on the trip or not? Did she feel any different now that Gina Kay had bared her soul?*

Well, they would have to wait a bit longer to find out. She was in charge now.

At the appointed hour the three of them were waiting in front of the hotel when G.W. and Marta drove up in a white limousine. Rhonda took great pleasure in the look of surprise on Holly and Gina Kay's faces. "Our coach for the evening, miladies," she said.

Chapter twenty-seven

With G.W. and Marta joining them for dinner at the colorful Chinatown restaurant, the conversation pertained mostly to family and food. Rhonda could sense Holly and Gina Kay's bewilderment as they wondered what might be lurking beneath her calm demeanor. What had her reaction been to this morning's revelations? Had it all been for naught?

Rhonda felt nervous, ebullient, and oddly distant. She knew what Holly and Gina Kay did not. She alone knew the outcome of Gina Kay's attempt to change the future by revealing the secrets of the past.

Rhonda thought of the time her sons dared her to parasail. Always before, she assumed she would never do such a thing. It was too dangerous. She would be afraid. She might throw up or wet her pants. Parasailing was an activity for daredevils, for the young and foolish, and she was a responsible adult. And she had been fearful when she watched her sons and then Dennis taking their turns and sailing hundreds of feet above Padre Island's Laguna Madre. But when she was up there herself, her sons and husband but tiny specks on the barge far below, instead of feeling frightened or insecure, she felt like Wonder Woman with life and power coursing through her veins and such a sense of empowerment. That was how she felt now. And she wanted to keep that feeling to herself for a time and savor it. She mostly listened to the conversation around her, occasionally smiling or nodding. When she did speak, it was some innocuous comment about the food or decor.

"Have you heard from Tatiana and Ivan?" Gina Kay asked Marta.

"Yes, they called this morning from the beach. They sound so happy and in love," Marta said. "They tell me to thank you again for the beautiful wedding. Tatiana says she will remember it always and can hardly wait to see the pictures."

Holly asked about Marta and G.W.'s own courtship and wedding. "G.W. told us that you had been sweethearts since childhood," she said.

"Yes, that is true," Marta said. "Since we were eleven or twelve years old."

Like Terry and me, Rhonda found herself thinking, but she did not go wandering off down the what-if road. She was done with that.

Marta explained that her and G.W.'s wedding had been the usual civil ceremony, but they had a wonderful party afterward. Instead of wedding gifts, the guests brought food and drink. They danced and sang until dawn. "That was before perestroika. Life was very difficult, but still people sang and danced."

"Tatiana looked so beautiful in that dress," Gina Kay said. "I think she should come to Texas and model it when Holly has a gala fashion show to launch her new line of evening wear."

Holly looked at Gina Kay with lifted eyebrows. "I wasn't aware that I was doing that," she said.

"Why, of course you are. Where do think, Rhonda, Dallas or Houston?" Gina Kay asked.

Rhonda obliged. "Definitely Dallas," she said. "At the Dallas Museum of Art. It can be a benefit for the museum. A white tie event with lots of dignitaries."

Marta was more experimental than G.W. about trying traditional Cantonese cuisine. G.W. ordered the closest thing on the menu he could find to meat and potatoes. "Men, they are such babies," Marta said, rolling her eyes, then planted an affectionate kiss on G.W.'s cheek.

After dinner, they took Marta back to Brighton Beach, promising to see her on their next trip to the Big Apple. "And maybe you and G.W. can come with Tatiana and Ivan for the big Dallas gala benefit fashion show," Gina Kay suggested. "You could spend a couple of days with me at the ranch."

"And stay with me when you're in Dallas," Rhonda added.

There were hugs all around as they said good-bye. And they promised Marta that they wouldn't keep G.W. out too late.

"Okay, now on to the purpose of the evening," Rhonda said as G.W. pulled away from the curb. "We are going on a quest," she announced as she removed a bottle of champagne from the limo's refrigerator and quite proficiently removed the cork. She passed glasses to Gina Kay and Holly then lifted her own. "Here's to finding the New York equivalent of Trevi."

"Of what?" Holly asked.

But Gina Kay immediately understood the implication of Rhonda's words and sang "Three Coins in the Fountain" from start to finish, except in her version the fountain wasn't somewhere in the heart of Rome, it was in New York City, which definitely messed with the song's meter.

"I can't believe you know all the words to that sappy song," Rhonda said.

"Ann Marie and I rather like it," Gina Kay said with feigned indignation. "I bought the video last month and showed her pictures from our *Three Coins in the Fountain* senior prom. Since then she and I have watched that old movie at least a half a dozen times and sung along with Frank Sinatra. Ann Marie thought the words to the song sounded selfish, though, so we changed them. Instead of just one wish getting granted and one heart wearing a valentine, our version says, '*All three* wishes will be granted,' and '*Three* hearts will wear a valentine.' And at the end, instead of 'make it mine' three times, we prefer 'make a wish, make a wish, make a wish.'"

"Much better," Rhonda said, taking a sip of champagne. *Good* champagne. She didn't recognize the label, but she had told G.W. the champagne should cost no less than fifty dollars a bottle. "Okay ladies, from the top," she said.

And they sang the revised version of "Three Coins" as the limo headed down Broadway. After the last "make a wish," they burst out laughing. Rhonda loved the feel of her laughter, which seemed to bubble up from inside her like the champagne bubbles in her glass. They sang the song again and improved on the harmony at the end.

"Bravo," G.W. called through the open window in the partition that separated the driver from the spacious passenger compartment.

"What a night that was," Holly said. "Miss Thornton was so proud of that fountain. I still have that picture of her and the three of us standing in front of it."

"I remember the three of us standing *in* it," Rhonda said.

"Yes," Gina Kay said, "that was when we promised that someday we would go to Rome and throw coins in the real Trevi Fountain."

"Well, since that is probably never going to happen, we are going to find a substitute fountain tonight," Rhonda explained. "We are fortunate in that G.W. has seen every nook and cranny of this great city. I asked him to select three fountains as candidates for the New York 'Three Coins' fountain. Nothing modern, preferably ones that are European-looking. After we've viewed all three, we will take a vote as to which one is the blessing fountain and return there for the ritual coin toss. I don't have any smashed pennies, but I do have three Texas quarters."

"You know," Holly said as she accepted a coin that featured an outline of the Lone Star State, "what we were really promising as we stood there dripping wet in that fountain, with Mr. Kingston having a hissy fit over Gina Kay's wet dress with her nipples showing through, was that we were going to stay friends. And that our friendship was not going to end just because our high school days were coming to a close, and we really would be best friends forever."

"Back then I never had a doubt that would be case," Rhonda said, remembering how young and naive they had been. She had been so sure that they were going to fulfill their respective dreams and sail through life on the good ship *Happiness,* staying in touch through frequent phone calls and coming together often to celebrate the triumphs of their lives. They would make other friends along the way, but no other friendship would have the intimacy and complete trust of the one that had begun that long-ago day on a dusty country road in Lamberton, Texas.

"I suppose, at some level," Rhonda continued, "I was more sure that I would be best friends with you guys twenty-five years down the road than that I would still be a part of Terry's life. I loved Terry so very much and felt such an obligation to marry him, but I was never able to imagine him as a grown-up man. And much as I tried, I had a hard time seeing myself living in Lamberton for the rest of my life. I had two dreams: having babies with Terry *and* being a super achiever someplace far away from Lamberton."

"That's quite an admission," Holly said.

"Oh, I don't know," Rhonda said. "When you married Sandy, were you sure that you would be married to him twenty-five years later?"

"No, I suppose not," Holly admitted. "I remember thinking that if it didn't work out, it was better to have a failed marriage under my belt than never to have married at all. But I have no doubt about the *next* twenty-five years. Unless one of us kicks off before then, our poor kids will be obligated to host one of those insipid Golden Wedding things. And you are both invited."

"What about you and Dennis?" Gina Kay asked Rhonda. "Do you think you'll make it to the Golden Wedding Day?"

"I hope so," Rhonda said, "but it's scary to think of a future with just him and me. With the boys gone, the house seems so hollow. We probably won't even have Mildred the dog much longer. She was a present for the boys on their third birthday. They were supposed to take turns sleeping with her, but most of the time, the three of them would pile up in one bed like a litter of puppies."

And suddenly she had an image of her and Dennis burying sweet old Mildred in the backyard and had to fight back tears.

Dennis was a better person than she was. He was kind, hopeful, tender. And loyal. More loyal than she deserved.

Rhonda wanted to feel love as deeply and completely as she had with Terry. It was not the memory of Terry himself that kept getting in the way but the memory of being in love, the memory of how Terry was constantly on her mind no matter where she was or what she was doing. She had lived inside his aura. Her flesh burned under his fingertips. As it had on the airplane under the fingertips of a man she didn't know and certainly didn't love. Her flesh had burned not because of love but because she had needed and wanted it to.

Yesterday, before Tatiana and Ivan's wedding, she had insisted that true love was not an intellectual decision. It was something that just happened, that you couldn't tell your heart how to behave. And Holly had taken exception with her statement, claiming that a person could intellectually remove obstacles from the path of true love.

Obstacles. She had done more than place obstacles in the path, Rhonda realized. She had built a wall around herself, yet she had been willing to open a gate and let a total stranger inside. Thank

God she had not done that. At least in regard to the actual physical act, she had not been unfaithful to her husband. But in her mind she had gone there, with a man she met on the plane and with Terry Robertson—men she had sometimes thought of while she made love to her husband.

Dennis deserved a better marriage and a wife who didn't live behind a wall. All these years, she had been waiting to fall madly in love with him. For it to just happen. Like a bolt out of the blue. With no effort on her part. No intellectually removing of obstacles from the path of true love.

She felt Holly's comforting arm around her shoulders and realized that tears were rolling down her cheeks and onto her blouse. "Are you okay, honey?"

Gina Kay handed her some tissues, her lovely face full of concern.

Rhonda blotted her wet cheeks and dabbed at the corners of her eyes, then blew her nose. "No, I'm not okay," she said with a smile, "but I am working on it."

She realized the limo had stopped. G.W. was looking at her through the open partition, concern on his face, too. "Number one fountain is around the corner," he said. "I park here. You still want to see?"

"I still want to see," Rhonda said. "Let's go, ladies."

The fountain in City Hall Park was located in the middle of a round pool. The actual fountain had a large basin on a pedestal topped by a toadstool-like structure where the water came out. Topping the fountain was a golden two-bar cross with a fleur-de-lis on top that looked like something Crusaders might have carried into battle. The fountain's charm came from the park itself, which was lit with old-fashioned gaslights and surrounded by important-looking buildings, the most impressive of which was a wonderful building that sported a wedding cake tower topped by a golden statue.

"It's very nice," Gina Kay said, regarding the fountain.

"But not special enough," Holly observed.

"I agree," Rhonda said. "On to number two."

They climbed into the limo and G.W. drove them uptown to the famous Plaza Hotel, which stood at the southeast entrance to Central Park. Oh, dear, thought Rhonda as she reluctantly got out of the limo. She had met Michael Forester right across the street. Standing in front of the hotel was a very nice tiered fountain with the water cascading from huge shells, but it was tainted for her, and she didn't want to tell Gina Kay and Holly why.

"I like it," Holly said.

"I want to see number three before we make up our minds," Rhonda insisted.

They got back into the limo, and G.W. drove into the park and made his way north along the East Drive, past horse-drawn carriages taking tourists and couples for moonlit rides through the park. Lit with hundreds of streetlamps, the park was a completely different place at night—romantic and a bit mysterious. G.W. turned left at the 72nd Street transverse and pulled to a stop.

He opened the door for his passengers and escorted them between carved balustrades and down a grand staircase to the formal terrace below. There in the center of a huge round pool was a triple-tiered stone fountain topped by a winged angel. While the fountain itself was not so impressive as Trevi, its pool was much larger. This was unquestionably a fountain worthy of their coins and wishes.

Rhonda kicked off her shoes, handed her purse to G.W., and climbed into the fountain with a cell phone in one hand and her coin in the other.

She punched in her home phone number and prayed for Dennis to be there.

"Dr. Chadwick," his voice said. He sounded tired.

"Hi, there," Rhonda said.

"Hi, darling. I was sitting here thinking how nice it was going to be to have you back home tomorrow evening. Mildred and I are lonely."

"I miss you, too. You want to know where I am?"

"I hear water splashing."

"Yeah. I'm standing in the middle of a New York fountain. And I've had only one glass of champagne."

"Is there some reason why you are doing this?" he asked, a smile in his voice.

"Yes, there is a really good reason." Rhonda motioned for Gina Kay and Holly to join her and smiled as, without hesitation, they handed G.W. their purses, kicked off their shoes, and climbed into the pool. "The reason I am calling you, my darling husband, from the middle of a New York fountain is that I need to make a wish. That's why we're all here—Holly, Gina Kay, and me—with coins in hand, and I am going to make the first wish.

"I am now ready to throw my coin over my shoulder," she told Dennis, "and this is my wish. I wish that my husband, Dennis, would marry me all over again—in front of our kids, my parents, friends, and family during a big party out under the trees in our backyard. And I want Holly and her family to come. And Gina Kay and her daughter Ann Marie. Will you marry me, my darling Dennis? And take me on a honeymoon down on the Gulf Coast so we can start looking for a place to live when we retire? Will you be my husband till death do us part?"

"Wow," Dennis said. "Are you sure about the champagne?"

"I haven't even had a whole glass yet," Rhonda said. "Just a half really. I am stone-cold sober."

Then she waited for his response, but there was only silence.

Rhonda's heart began to pound. Was she too late?

"Dennis, are you still there?" she asked.

"Yeah," he said. "I'm a little choked up, though. I've waited a long time to hear you say words like that."

"I know, darling. Longer than I deserved. *Far* longer. But I want you to know that I have never loved anyone more than I now love you." And her words were true. *Really true.* She realized that, at long last, she had let go of Terry. Like a balloon on a string, she had turned him loose and allowed him to float away. She looked at the night sky. She could almost see the Terry balloon up there. In her mind, she whispered a farewell. A "rest in peace" for the boy she had once loved.

"Rhonda?"

"Yes, darling."

"This is the happiest day of my life."

"Mine, too," she said, and the sobs began forming again. "I love you."

"And I love you, too. I always have, Rhonda, and I always will. I'll be waiting for you tomorrow afternoon at the airport. I made dinner reservations at The Mansion."

"I'd rather drive up to the lake," she said.

"Lady, you've got yourself a deal."

"Goodnight, my darling. Sleep well."

Rhonda pressed the "end" button and handed Holly the phone so she could cover her face and cry full out.

She was loved. Truly loved by a solid, sane man who should have given up on her years ago. Then she took a deep breath and composed herself. She wiped her cheeks with the back of her hand. And looked at Holly and Rhonda. "Well, my wish just came true. You guys can take your turn now."

Holly looked at Gina Kay. "I think ours just came true, too." She looked at Gina Kay and they both tossed their coins over their shoulders. "Best Friends Forever," Holly called out.

Gina Kay repeated her words. "Best Friends Forever."

Gina Kay took a step toward Rhonda. "Do you really want Ann Marie and me to come when you and Dennis renew your vows?"

"More than anything," Rhonda said. And she opened her arms.

To *both* of them. To the two best friends she had ever had. And then, with G.W. holding three purses and watching in amazement, they splashed water on each other like three demented idiots until their clothes were dripping wet. It was glorious, silly, delightful fun.

"Hey, you know what?" Rhonda said. "I'm going to come to that twenty-fifth high school reunion Holly's been planning. I'll even make poor Dennis come."

They linked arms and solemnly sang the Lamberton High School Alma Mater. And then they splashed some more.

Simon & Schuster Paperbacks
Reading Group Guide

A Good Man

"*A Good Man* came about when my nephew Grant complained that there were more jerks in my books than good guys. I did a mental survey and realized this was not true. But in many ways the jerks just seem to stand out more and, in books as in real life, take up a lot of space. But I did take Grant's observation to heart, and a worthy but underappreciated man became the catalyst for this novel." —Judith Henry Wall

Questions for Discussion

1. How did you feel about Rhonda's flirtation on the airplane? Were you shocked when she agreed to see Michael Forester once again? What did she take away from the encounter at the hotel?

2. The women each have vastly different relationships with their husbands. Explore these differences as presented through their actions and thoughts. Do they share any similarities?

3. Rhonda decides to earn some "good-wife points" before broaching the subject of a trip to New York with two high school girlfriends and suggests a romantic excursion aboard the *Texhoma Belle*. Do you believe this is common strategy for wives? Do husbands ever think of marriage in terms of a point system?

4. Describe Rhonda and Terry's relationship as high school sweethearts. What are the main things that motivate each of them? How does Rhonda truly view Terry and vice versa? Do you think they could have had a successful marriage?

5. Do you agree with Gina Kay's decision to marry Terry? Why or why not? How does the relationship between Terry and Gina Kay

compare to that between Rhonda and Terry? What attributes does Gina Kay gain and/or lose throughout her marriage and as a mother?

6. Holly experiences conflict involving her family and her career life. Discuss her situation and choices. Do you think she made the right decision when she married Sandy and later when she decided to decline Jerry Winston's offer to pursue a career as a fashion designer in New York?

7. What do the characters Tatiana and Ivan represent to each of the three women? How do they, along with G.W., help to resolve both internal and external conflict among the three women?

8. Describe the way men are portrayed in the novel. How do the personalities and characteristics of the husbands in the book and the side characters (G.W., Michael Forester, Judge Alexander Resnick) help to shape the lives of the three women? Were you surprised when Gina Kay did not enter into a relationship with the judge? If you had been in her situation, would you have done likewise?

9. Parenthood is one of the main themes explored in the novel. Terry and his father, Gina Kay and her parents and children, Holly and her children, and Rhonda and her parents and children are all different examples. What types of parent-sibling relationships does the book explore? How do these relationships and their accompanying responsibilities affect the characters involved?

10. On page 103, Rhonda ponders how, as a woman married to a physician who spends much of his time "off saving lives," she found herself the "hands-on parent" with her own career on the back burner. She adored her children but never evolved a clear image of what she had expected out of life and always had vague feelings of "missing the mark, of failing." Do you think such feelings are common among career-oriented women?

11. Do you share Rhonda and Holly's comments on page 110 about women's lives in the wake of the Women's Movement?

12. Holly and Rhonda both face unwanted pregnancies. How did you feel about the decisions they each made?

13. What does New York City bring to the story? Discuss each woman's

reaction to the city. Would any other city have worked just as well?

14. Discuss the three women's feelings about Tatiana's wedding and wedding ceremonies in general. How do you remember your own wedding(s) and those of people close to you? Where they wonderful experiences or something you try not to think about?

15. How did your feelings toward Rhonda change as the story progressed? With which parts of her story did you identify?

16. Do you think that most women think about seeing their first love once again? Do you think men also harbor such fantasies?

17. What impact does her mother's stroke have on Rhonda? Is there someone in your own life on whom you rely for praise and support?

18. As teenagers, the three best friends agreed that the one thing they were never going to do was stay in Lamberton, Texas, and repeat their mothers' lives. Gina Kay never leaves the town, however, and Holly admits that in many ways Waco is a larger version of Lamberton. Were their lives limited more by where they lived or by their husbands' career choices? Did you once vow that you would never live your mother's life? Do most women end up repeating their mothers' lives to some extent?

19. If Rhonda had decided to forgive Gina Kay decades earlier, would the two women have been able to resume their friendship, or was the passage of time a necessary part of the healing process?

20. While you were growing up, what sort of things did you vow that you would never do? Were you true to those vows?